Bello:

hidden talent rediscovered

Bello is a digital only imprint of Pan Macmillan,
established to breathe new life into previously published,
classic books.

At Bello we believe in the timeless power of the imagination,
of good story, narrative and entertainment and we want to use
digital technology to ensure that many more readers
can enjoy these books into the future.

We publish in ebook and Print on Demand formats
to bring these wonderful books to new audiences.

www.panmacmillan.co.uk/bello

T0331518

BELL◉

Frances Hodgson Burnett

Frances Hodgson Burnett (1849–1924) was born in Manchester and spent her early years there with her family. Her father died in 1852, and eventually, in 1865, Frances emigrated to the United States with her mother and siblings, settling with family in Knoxville, Tennessee. Frances began to be published at the age of 19, submitting short stories to magazines and using the proceeds to help support the family. In 1872, she married Swan Burnett, a doctor, with whom she had two sons while living in Paris. Her first novel, *That Lass o' Lowrie's*, was published in 1877, while the Burnetts were living in Washington D.C.

Following a separation from her husband, Burnett lived on both sides of the Atlantic, eventually marrying for a second time, however she never truly recovered from the death of her first son, Lionel. Best known during her lifetime for *Little Lord Fauntleroy* (1886), her books for children, including *The Secret Garden* and *The Little Princess*, have endured as classics, but Burnett also wrote many other novels for adults, which were hugely popular and favourably compared to authors such as George Eliot.

Frances Hodgson Burnett

THROUGH ONE
ADMINISTRATION

First published in 1881 by Osgood

This edition published 2014 by Bello
an imprint of Pan Macmillan, a division of Macmillan Publishers Limited
Pan Macmillan, 20 New Wharf Road, London N1 9RR
Basingstoke and Oxford
Associated companies throughout the world

www.panmacmillan.co.uk/bello

ISBN 978-1-4472-6836-9 EPUB
ISBN 978-1-4472-7047-8 HB
ISBN 978-1-4472-6835-2 PB

Visit **www.panmacmillan.com** to read more about all our books
and to buy them. You will also find features, author interviews and
news of any author events, and you can sign up for e-newsletters
so that you're always first to hear about our new releases.

Chapter 1

Eight years before the Administration rendered important by the series of events and incidents which form the present story, there had come to Washington, on a farewell visit to a distant relative with whom he was rather a favorite, a young officer who was on the point of leaving the civilized world fair a far-away Western military station. The name of the young officer was Philip Tredennis. His relative and entertainer was a certain well-known entomologist, whom it will be safe to call Professor Herrick. At the Smithsonian and in all scientific circles, Professor Herrick's name was a familiar one. He was considered an enviable as well as an able man. He had established himself in Washington because he found men there whose tastes and pursuits were congenial with his own, and because the softness of the climate suited him; he was rich enough to be free from all anxiety and to enjoy the delightful liberty of pursuing his scientific labors because they were his pleasure, and not because he was dependent upon their results. He had a quiet and charming home, an excellent matter-of-fact wife, and one daughter, who was being educated in a northern city, and who was said to be as bright and attractive as one could wish a young creature to be.

Of this daughter Tredennis had known very little, except that she enjoyed an existence and came home at long intervals for the holidays, when it did not happen that she was sent to the sea or the mountains with her mother instead.

The professor himself seemed to know but little of her. He was a quiet and intensely studious person, taking small interest in the ordinary world and appearing always slightly surprised when his wife spoke to him; still, his manner toward her was as gentle and painstaking as if she had been the rarest possible beetle, and the only one of her species to be found in any known collection, though perhaps the interest she awakened in him was not so great as it might have been under such exceptionally favorable circumstances. She was not a brilliant or far-seeing woman, and her opinions of entomology and, indeed, of science in general, were vague, and obscured by objections to small boxes, glass cases, long pins, and chloroform, and specimens of all orders.

So, observing this, Tredennis felt it not at all unnatural that he should not hear much of his daughter from the professor. Why his relative liked him the young man was not at all sure, though at times he had felt the only solution of the mystery to be that he liked him because his tendency was toward silence and books and research of all kinds. He thought he was certain that the professor did like him. He had invited him to visit him in Washington, and had taken him to the Smithsonian, and rambled from room to room with him, bestowing upon him tomes of information in the simplest and most natural manner; filled with the quietest interest himself and entirely prepared to find his feeling shared by his charge. He had given into his hands the most treasured volumes in his library, and had even seemed pleased to have him seated near him when he sat at work. At all events, it was an established fact that a friendly feeling existed between them, and that if it had been his habit to refer to his daughter, he would have spoken of her to Tredennis. But Tredennis heard nothing of her until he had been some days in Washington, and then it was Mrs. Herrick who spoke of her.

"Nathan," she said one evening at dinner, "Bertha will be home on Tuesday."

The professor laid his spoon down as if he had rather unexpectedly discovered that he had had enough soup.

"Bertha," he said. "Indeed! Next Tuesday. Well, of course, we must be ready for her. Do you want any money, my dear? But, of course, you will want money when she comes, if she has finished school, as I think you said she had."

"I shall want money to pay her bills," answered Mrs. Herrick. "She will bring them with her. Her aunt has had her things made in New York."

"Yes," said the professor, "I dare say they will be more satisfactory. What kind of things, for instance, Catherine?"

"Dresses," replied Mrs. Herrick, "and things of that sort. You know she is to come out this season."

"To come out," remarked the professor, carefully giving the matter his undivided attention.

"I hope she will enjoy it. What sort of a ceremony is it? And after a young person has 'come out' does she ever go in, and is there any particular pageant attached to such a — a contingency?"

"When she comes out," answered Mrs. Herrick, taking a purely practical view of the affair, "she begins to go to parties, to balls, and receptions, and lunches; which she does not do when she is going to schools. It isn't considered proper, and it wouldn't give her any time for her studies. Bertha hasn't been allowed to go out at all. Her aunt Maria has been very particular about it, and she will enjoy things all the more because they are quite new to her. I dare say she will be very gay this winter. Washington is a very good place for a girl to come out in."

After dinner, when they retired to the library together, it occurred to Tredennis that the professor was bestowing some thought upon his paternal position, and his first observation proved that this was the case.

"It is a most wonderful thing that a few brief years should make such changes," he said. "It seems impossible that so short a time should change a small and exceedingly red infant into a young person returned from school in the most complete condition, and ready to ' come out.' She was not interesting as an infant. I tried to find her so, but failed, though it was insisted that she was an unusually intelligent baby, and I have not seen much of her of late years. When she was growing it was thought that the climate of Washington was not good for her. I am really a little curious about her. My views of girls are extremely undefined. I have always been a bookworm. I have not known girls. They have not come within my radius. I remember one I once knew years ago, but that is all. It was when I was a younger man. I think she was a year or so older than Bertha. She was very interesting — as a study. She used to bewilder me."

He walked over to the table, and began to turn over some papers.

"*She* had gray eyes," he said, in a rather lower voice, — "gray eyes."

He was so quiet for some time that Tredennis thought he had forgotten what he had been talking about; but, after a pause of at least three minutes, he spoke again.

"I would not be at all sorry," he said, "if Bertha was a little like her. I suppose," he added, — referring seriously to Tredennis, — "I suppose they are all more or less alike."

"I think" — faltered Tredennis, "perhaps so."

He did not feel himself an authority. The professor stood still a moment, regarding the fire abstractly.

"She had gray eyes," he said again, — "gray eyes!" and immediately afterward returned to his table, seated himself, and fell to work.

The next week Bertha arrived, and to her distant relative her arrival was a revelation. She descended upon the quiet household — with her trunks, her delight in their contents, her anticipation of her first season, her fresh and rather surprised exultation in her own small powers and charms, which were just revealing themselves to her — like a young whirlwind. Her mother awakened to a most maternal interest in the gayeties into which she was to be drawn; the very servants were absorbed in the all-pervading excitement, which at length penetrated to the professor's study itself, and aroused him from his entomological reveries.

After she had been in the house a week, he began to examine the girl through his spectacles with great care and deliberation, and, having cheerfully submitted to this inspection through several meals, one day at dinner its object expressed herself with charming directness concerning it.

"I do hope you'll like me, papa," she said, "when you have classified me."

"Classified you!" said the professor, in some bewilderment.

"Yes," answered Bertha. "You know I always feel as if you might

4

turn me over gently with your finger at any moment, and watch me carefully while I struggled until you knew all about me, and then chloroform me and stick a pin through me with a label on it. I shouldn't like the chloroform and the pin, but I should take an interest in the label. Couldn't I have the label without the pin, papa?"

"I don't know," said the professor, examining her more carefully than ever. "I am afraid not."

After that it became his custom to encourage her to reveal herself in conversation, which it was very easy to do, as she was a recklessly candid young person, given to the most delightfully illogical partisanship, an endless variety of romantic fancies, and a vivid representation of all facts in which she felt interest. It must be confessed that, for the sake of hearing her talk, the professor somewhat neglected, for the time being, both *Coleoptera* and *Lepidoptera*, and, drifting into the sitting-room upon many sunny mornings, allowed himself to be surrounded by innocent frivolities in the way of personal adornments. And it must also be added that he fell into the habit of talking of the girl to Tredennis, as they sat together by the study fire at night.

"She is an attractive girl," he said once, seriously. "I find myself quite absorbed in her at times. She is chaotic, illogical, unpractical — oftener than not she does not know anything of what she is talking about, but her very absurdities have a kind of cleverness in them. And wit — there is wit in her nonsense, though she is scarcely conscious of it. I cannot help thinking of her future, and what its needs will develop in her. It all depends upon the needs. You never know what will be developed, but you know it depends upon the needs."

"I — hope there will be no painful needs," said Tredennis, looking at the fire. "She is very happy. I never saw any one so happy."

"Yes, she's very happy," admitted the professor. "At present she is not much more than a joyous, perfectly healthy young animal. She sings and laughs because she can't help it, and she adorns herself from instinct. She'll be different in a year or two. She'll be less happy, but more interesting."

"More interesting!" said Tredennis, in a low voice.

"Yes, more interesting," answered the professor, looking at the fire

5

himself, with an air of abstractedly following a train of thought. "She will have made discoveries about herself. It is a pity she can't make them without being less happy — but then, none of us are happy." He paused, rubbed his forehead a second, and then turned suddenly on Tredennis.

"Are *you* happy?" he demanded.

Tredennis started and hesitated.

"Y-yes — n-no," he answered, unsteadily. He would have said yes unreservedly a short time ago; but within the last few days he had been less sure of himself, and now, being confronted with the question unexpectedly, he found that he must answer with a reservation — though he could not at all have given a reason for the feeling that he must do so.

"Perhaps it is not my way to look at life brightly," he added.

"It is her way," said the professor. "She believes in everything in a persistent, childish fashion that is touching to older persons like myself. If you contest her points of belief with her she is simply obstinate. You can't move her."

"Why should any one try?" said Tredennis, warmly.

"There is no need to try," responded the professor. "She will find out for herself."

"Why should she?" said Tredennis, warmer still. "I hope she won't."

The professor took off his spectacles and began to polish them carefully with a corner of his large white handkerchief.

"She is going to be a clever woman," he said. "For her sake I am sorry to see it. She is going to be the kind of clever woman who has nine chances out of ten of being a desperate pain to herself while she is a pleasure to her friends. She hasn't the nature to find safety in cleverness. She has a conscience and emotions, and they will go against her."

"Against her?" cried Tredennis.

"She will make mistakes and suffer for them — instead of letting others suffer. She won't be a saint, but she might be a martyr. It always struck me that it took faults and follies to make a martyr."

He bent forward and poked the fire as carefully as he had rubbed

6

his spectacles; then he turned to Tredennis again — slowly this time, instead of suddenly.

"You resent it all, I suppose," he said. "Of course you do. It makes you angry, I've no doubt. It would have made me angry, I dare say, at your age, to hear an elderly scientist dissect a pretty young creature and take the bloom off her life for her. It's natural."

"I don't like to think of her as — as being anything but happy — and — and good," said Tredennis, with some secret resentment.

"She'll not be bad," said the professor, critically. "It isn't in her. She might be happy, perhaps — if one thing happened to her."

"What one thing?" asked Tredennis.

"*If* she married a fine fellow, whom she was deeply and passionately in love with — which happens to very few women."

In the shadow of his corner Tredennis felt the hot blood mount steadily to his forehead, and was glad of the dim light, for the professor was still regarding him fixedly, though as if in abstraction.

"She will be — likely to marry the man she loves, sir," he said, in a voice neither clear nor steady.

"Yes," said the professor; "unless she makes the mistake of merely marrying the man who loves *her*. She will meet him often enough. And, if he chances some day to be a fascinating fellow, her fate will be sealed. That goes along with the rest of her strengths and weaknesses."

And he gave the fire a vigorous poke, which cast a glow of light upon them both; then, leaving his chair, he stood for a moment polishing his glasses, — staring absently at Tredennis before he put them on, — and wandered back to his table and his specimens.

Tredennis' own acquaintance with his young relative was not a very intimate one. Too many interests presented themselves on every side to allow of her devoting herself specially to any one, and her father's favorite scarcely took the form of an interest. She had not the leisure to discover that he was fully worth the discovering. She regarded him simply as a large and rather serious young man, who, without seeming stupid, listened rather than talked; and yet was not actually a brilliant listener, since he only listened with an air of observing quietly, and keeping the result of his observations to himself.

"I dare say it will suit him to be out among the Indians," she said to her mother upon one occasion. "And I should think it would suit the Indians. He won't find them frivolous and given up to vanity. I believe he thinks I am frivolous. It struck me that he did the other day, when I was talking about that new dress being made. Do you think I talk about my clothes too much, mamma? Well, at all events," with much frankness, "I don't talk about them half as much as I think about them. I am always thinking about them just now. It seems as if I should die if they weren't becoming after they were made. But don't you suppose it's natural, mamma, and that I shall get over it in time?"

She was brushing out her hair before the glass, and turned round, brush in hand, with an expression of rather alarmed interest, and repeated the question.

"Don't you think I shall get over it?" she said. "It seems just now as if everything had *begun* all at once, and anything might happen, and I had rather lost my breath a little in the rush of it. And I *do* so want to have a good time, and I care about everything connected with it, — clothes, and people, and parties, and everything, — but I *don't* want to be any more frivolous than I need be, — I mean I don't want to be a stupid."

She gave the pretty red-brown mane embowering her a little shake back, and fixed her large, clear eyes on her mother's.

"I suppose all girls are frivolous just at first," she said. "Don't you?"

"I don't call it frivolous," said her mother, who was a simple, excellent creature, not troubled with intellectual pangs, and who, while she admired her, frequently found her daughter as far beyond her mild, limited comprehension as her husband was, and she was not at all disposed to complain thereat, either.

The one fact she was best able to grasp at this moment was that the girl looked her best, and that the circumstance might be utilized as a hint for the future.

"That way of wearing your hair is very becoming to you, Bertha," she said. "I wish there was some way of managing it so as to get the same effect."

"But I can't wear it down after I'm 'out,'" said Bertha, reflectively. "I've got beyond that — as I suppose I shall get beyond the frivolity."

And she turned to the glass and looked at herself quite simply, and with a soft little air of seriousness which was very bewitching.

She regarded herself in this manner for several seconds, and then began slowly to dress her hair, plaiting it into soft thick plaits, which she fastened closely and simply at the nape of her pretty neck.

"I believe I'll try not to be *quite* so frivolous," she said.

Perhaps she was making an effort at the accomplishment of this desirable end when she came down to dinner, an hour or so later. Tredennis thought he had never seen her so lovely.

He was standing alone in the fire-light, looking doubtfully at something he held in his hand, and she entered so quietly that he started on becoming conscious of her presence. She wore a dress he had not seen before, — a pale gray, soft in material and very simply made, with a little lace kerchief knotted at her throat.

She came forward, and laid her hand on the back of a chair.

"Papa has not come in — ?" she began, then stopped suddenly, with a quick, graceful little turn of her head.

"Oh, where is the heliotrope?" she exclaimed.

For the room was full of the subtle fragrance of it.

He made a rather headlong step forward.

"It is here," he said. "I have been out, and I saw a lot of it in a florist's window. I don't know whether it's a flower to wear — and that sort of thing — but I always liked the odor of it. So I brought this home."

And he held it out to her.

She took it and buried her face in it delightedly. It was a sumptuous handful, and had been cut with unsparing lavishness. He had, in fact, stood by and seen it done.

"Ah, I like it so!" she cried. "I do like it — it's lovely."

Then she lifted her face, hesitating a second as a new thought occurred to her. She looked up at him with pretty uncertainty, the color rising in her cheeks simply because she was uncertain.

"They — I don't know "— she said. "You didn't— they are not for"—

"For you," Tredennis ended for her, hurriedly. "Yes. I don't know why, but I thought of you when I saw them. It's an idea, I suppose. They are for you, if you'll have them."

"Ah!" she said, "it was so kind of you! I'm so glad to have them. I have always liked them."

She almost hid her bright face in them again, while he stood and watched her, wondering why he felt suddenly tremulous and unreasonably happy.

At last she looked up at him again.

"I wish this was my 'coming-out' night," she said. "I would wear these. You have given me my first bouquet. I am glad of that."

"If I am here on the night of your first party," he answered, "I will give you another, if you will let me."

"If you are here?" she said. "Are you going away?"

And there was an innocent, unconsciously expressed touch of disappointment in her tone, which was a sharp pleasure to him, though he was in too chaotic a mental condition to call it either pleasure or pain.

"I may be ordered away at any moment," he said.

He could never exactly remember afterward bow it came about, that in a few moments more he was sitting in the professor's arm-chair, and she had taken a seat on a hassock near him, with some of his heliotrope in the knot of her hair, some fastened against her pale gray dress, and some loosely clasped in the hand which rested on her lap. He did not know how it happened, but she was there, and the scent of the heliotrope floated about her in the warmth of the fire, and she was talking in the bright, fanciful way which entertained the professor, and he knew that this brief moment he came for the first time within the charmed circle of her girlish life and pleasures, and, though he was conscious that his nearness moved her no more than the professor's would have done, he was content.

There was a softness in her manner which was new to him, and which had the effect of giving him courage. It was a result partly of the pleasure he had given her and partly of the good resolution she had made, of which he knew nothing. He only saw the result, and enjoyed it. She even showed a pretty interest in his future.

"She is what the Italians call *simpatica*," had been one of her father's observations concerning her, and Tredennis thought of it as he listened and watched her.

It was her gift to say well all she had to say. Her simplest speech produced its little effect, because all her heart was with her hearer. Just now she thought only of Tredennis, and that she wished to show her interest in him.

So she sat with her flowers upon her knee and talked, and it was an enchanted hour for Tredennis, who felt like a creature slowly awakening to the light of day.

"I suppose we may not see you again for several years," she said. "I do not like to think of that, and I am sure papa won't, but" — and she turned, smiling into his eyes, her chin resting in the hollow of her palm, her elbow on her knee — "when we *do* see you, of course you will be a most distinguished person, entirely covered with stars and ribbons and — scalps!"

"And you," he said; "I wonder what will have happened to you?"

"Oh, a great many things, of course," she answered; "but only the unimportant things that happen to all girls — though they will be important enough to me. I dare say I shall have had a lovely time, and have been very happy."

And she turned her little smile upon the fire and brooded for a few seconds — still in her pretty attitude.

It was such a pretty attitude and her look was so sweet that both together wrought upon Tredennis strongly, and he felt himself awakening a little more.

"I wish," he said, breaking the brief silence in a low voice, — "I wish that *I* could insure the — happiness for you."

She turned, with a slight start, and some vague trouble in her face.

"Oh!" she said, "don't you think I shall be sure to be happy? There seems to be no reason why I should not. Oh, I hope I shall be happy; I — I don't know what I should do if I wasn't happy! I can't imagine it."

"Everybody is not happy," he said, his voice almost tremulous.

"But," she faltered, "but I — I have always been happy" — She stopped, her eyes appealing to him piteously. "I suppose, after all, that is a poor reason," she added; "but it almost seems like one."

"I wish it were one!" he said. "Don't look like that. It — it hurts me. If any sacrifice of mine — any suffering" —

She stirred a little, moved in some vague way by the intensity of his tone, and as she did so the odor of the heliotrope floated toward him.

"Bertha!" — he said, "Bertha"—

He did not know what he would have said — and the words were never spoken — for at that moment the enchanted hour was ended. It was the professor himself who broke in upon it — the professor who opened the door and entered, hungry and absent-minded, the firelight striking upon his spectacles and seeming to enlarge them tremendously as he turned his head from side to side, inhaling the air of the room with evident delight.

"Flowers, eh?" he said. "What kind of flowers? The air seems full of them."

Bertha rose and went to him, Tredennis watching her girlish pale-gray figure, as it moved across the room, with a pained and bewildered sense of having lost something; which he might never regain.

"They are heliotropes," she said; "Philip brought them to me. It is my first bouquet, so I shall keep it until I am an old woman."

A week later, Tredennis left Washington. It so chanced that he took his departure on the night rendered eventful by the first party. In the excitement attendant upon the preparations for this festivity, and for his own journey, he saw even less of Bertha than usual. When she appeared at the table she was in such bright, high spirits that the professor found her — for some private reason of his own — more absorbing than ever. His spectacles followed her with an air of deep interest, he professed an untrained anxiety concerning the dress she was to wear, appearing to regard it as a scientific object worthy of attention.

"She's very happy!" he would say to Tredennis again and again. "She's very happy!" And having said it he invariably rubbed his forehead abstractedly and pushed his spectacles a trifle awry, without appearing conscious of it.

When the carriage Tredennis had ordered came to the door, at ten o'clock, the coupe which was to convey Bertha to the scene of her first triumphs had just driven up.

A few seconds later Bertha turned from her mirror and took up her bouquet of white rose-buds and heliotrope, as a servant knocked at the door.

"The carriage is here, miss," he said; "and Mr. Tredennis is going away, and says would you come and let him say good-by."

In a few seconds more, Tredennis, who was standing in the hall, looked up from the carpet and saw her coming down the staircase with a little run, her white dress a cloud about her, her eyes shining like stars, the rose and heliotrope bouquet he had sent her in her hand.

"Thank you for it," she said, as soon as she reached him. "I shall keep this, too; and see what I have done." And she pushed a leaf aside and showed him a faded sprig of heliotrope hidden among the fresh flowers. "I thought I would like to have a little piece of it among the rest," she said. And she gave him her hand, with a smile both soft and bright.

"And you really kept it?" he said.

"Oh, yes," she answered, simply. "You know I am going to keep it as long as I live. I wish we could keep you. I wish you were going with us."

"I am going in a different direction," he said; "and" — suddenly, "I have not a minute to spare. Good-by."

A little shadow fell on the brightness of her face.

"I wish there was no such word as "good-by,"' she said.

There was a silence of a few seconds, in which her hand lay in his, and their eyes rested on each other. Then Mrs. Herrick and the professor appeared.

"I believe," said Tredennis, "if you are going now, I will let you set out on your journey first. I should like to see — the last of you."

"But it isn't the last of me," said Bertha, "it is the first of me — the very first. And my heart is beating quite fast."

And she put her hand to the side of her slender white bodice, laughing a gay, sweet laugh, with a thrill of excitement in it. And then they went out to the carriage, and when Mrs. Herrick had been assisted in, Bertha stood for a moment on the pavement, — a bright, pure white figure, her flowers in her hand, the hall light shining upon her.

"Papa!" she called to the professor, who stood on the threshold, "I never asked you if you liked it — the dress, you know."

"Yes, child," said the professor. "Yes, child, I like — I like it.

And his voice shook a little, and he said nothing more. And then Bertha got into the carriage and it drove away into the darkness. And almost immediately after Tredennis found himself in his carriage, which drove away into the darkness, too — only, as he laid his head against the cushions and closed his eyes, he saw, just as he had seen a moment before, a bright, pure white figure standing upon the pavement, the night behind it, the great bouquet of white roses in its hand, and the light from the house streaming upon the radiant girl's face.

Chapter 2

The eight years that followed were full of events for Tredennis. After the first two his name began to be well known in military circles as that of a man bold, cool, and remarkable for a just clear-sightedness which set him somewhat apart from most men of his class and age. Stationed as he was in the midst of a hostile Indian country, full of perilous adventure, a twofold career opened itself before him. His nerve, courage, and physical endurance rendered him invaluable in time of danger, while his tendency to constant study of the problems surrounding him gave him in time of peace the distinction of being a thinking man, whose logically deduced and clearly stated opinions were continually of use to those whose positions were more responsible than his own. He never fell into the ordinary idle routine of a frontier camp life. In his plain, soldierly quarters he worked hard, lived simply, and read much. During the first year he was rather desolate and unhappy. The weeks he had spent with the Herricks had been by no means the best preparation for his frontier experience, since they had revealed to him the possibilities of existence such as he had given no thought to before. His youth had been rather rigorous and lonely, and his misfortune of reserve had prevented his forming any intimate friendships. His boyhood had been spent at boarding-school, his early manhood at West Point, and after that his life had settled itself into the usual wandering, homeless groove which must be the lot of an unmarried military man. The warm atmosphere of a long-established home, its agreeably unobtrusive routine which made the changes of morning, noon, and night all something pleasant to anticipate; the presence of the women who could not be separated in one's mind from the household itself, — all these things were a sort of revelation to him. He had enjoyed them, and would have felt some slight sadness in leaving them, even if he had not left something else also. It was a mere shadow he had left, but it was a shadow whose memory haunted him through many a long and lonely hour, and was all the more a trouble through its very vagueness. He was not the man likely to become the victim of a hopeless passion in three weeks. His was a nature to awaken slowly, but to awaken to such strength of feeling and to such power to surfer, at last, as would leave no alternative between happiness and stolidly borne despair. If fate, decreed that the despair and not the happiness was to be his portion, it would be borne silently and with stern patience, but it would be despair nevertheless. As it was, he had been gradually aroused to a vague tenderness of feeling for the brightness and sweetness which had been before him day after day. Sometimes, during this first year of his loneliness, he wondered why he had not gone farther and reached the point of giving some expression to what he had felt; but he never did so without being convinced by his after reflections that such an effort would only have told against him.

"It wasn't the time," he said aloud to himself, as he sat in his lonely room one night. "It wasn't the time."

He had been thinking of how she looked as she came to him that night, in her simple pale-gray dress, with the little lace kerchief tied round her throat. That, and his memory of the bright figure at the carriage-door, were pictures which had a habit of starting up before him now and again, though chiefly at such times as he was alone and rather feeling his isolation.

He remembered his own feeling at her girlish pleasure in his gift, the tone of her voice, her attitude as she sat afterward on the low seat near him, her chin resting in her hollowed palm, her smiling eyes uplifted to his. Her pretty, unstudied attitudes had often struck him, and this one lingered in his fancy as somehow belonging naturally to a man's dreams of a fireside.

"If the room and fireside were your own," he said, abstractedly, "you'd like"—

He stopped, and, rising to his feet, suddenly began to pace the room.

"But it wasn't the time," he said. "She would not have understood — I scarcely understood myself — and if we should ever meet again, in all probability the time will have gone by."

After such thoughts he always betook himself to his books again with quite a fierce vigor, and in the rebound accomplished a great deal.

He gave a great deal of studious attention to the Indian question, and, in his determination to achieve practical knowledge, undertook more than one dangerous adventure. With those among the tribes whom it was possible to approach openly he made friends, studying their languages and establishing a reputation among them for honor and good faith, which was a useful element in matters of negotiation and treaty.

So it came about that his name was frequently mentioned in "the Department," and drifted into the newspapers, his opinions being quoted as opinions carrying weight, and, in an indirect way, the Herricks heard of him oftener than he heard of them, since there had been no regular exchange of letters between them, the professor being the poorest of correspondents. Occasionally, when he fell upon a newspaper paragraph commenting upon Tredennis' work and explaining some of his theories, he was roused to writing him a letter of approval or argument, and at the close of such epistles he usually mentioned his daughter in a fashion peculiarly his own.

"Bertha is happier than ever," he said, the first winter. "Bertha is well, and is said to dance, in the most astonishingly attractive manner, an astonishing number of times every evening. This I gather not only from her mother, but from certain elaborately ornamented cards they call programmes, which I sometimes find and study in private," — this came the second winter. The third he said: "It dawns upon Bertha that she is certainly cleverer than the majority of her acquaintance. This at once charms and surprises her. She is careful not to obtrude the fact upon public notice, but it has been observed; and I find she has quite a little reputation 'in society' as an unusually bright and ready young creature, with a habit of being delightfully equal to any occasion. I gradually discover her to be full of subtleties, of which she is entirely unconscious."

Tredennis read this a number of times, and found food for reflection in it. He thought it over frequently during the winter, and out of his pondering upon it grew a plan which began to unfold itself in his mind, rather vaguely at first, but afterward more definitely. This plan was his intention to obtain leave of absence, and, having obtained it, to make his way at once to Washington.

He had thought at first of applying for it in the spring, but fate was against him. Difficulties which broke out between the settlers and certain hostile tribes called him into active service, and it was not until the severities of the next winter aided in quelling the disturbance by driving the Indians into shelter that he found himself free again.

It was late on New Year's Eve that he went to his quarters to write his application for furlough. He had been hard at work all day, and came in cold and tired, and pleased to find the room made cheerful by a great fire of logs, whose leaping flames brightened and warmed every corner. The mail had come in during his absence, and two or three letters lay upon the table with the eastern papers, but he pushed them aside without opening them.

"I will look at them afterward," he said. "This shall be done first — before the clock strikes twelve. When the New Year comes in" —

He paused, pen in hand, accidentally catching a glimpse of his face in the by no means flattering shaving-glass which hung on the wall opposite. He saw himself brown with exposure, bearing marks of thought and responsibility his age did not warrant, and wearing even at this moment the rather stern and rigid expression which he had always felt vaguely to be his misfortune. Recognizing it, his face relaxed into a half-smile.

"What a severe-looking fellow!" he said. "*That* must be improved upon. No one could stand that. It is against a man at the outset."

And the smile remained upon his face for at least ten seconds — at all events until he had drawn his paper before him and begun to write. His task was soon completed. The letter written, he folded it, placed it in its envelope and directed it, looking as immovable as ever, and yet conscious of being inwardly more moved than he had ever been before.

"Perhaps," he said, half-aloud, "*this* is the time, and it is well I waited."

And then he turned to the letters and papers awaiting him.

The papers he merely glanced over and laid aside; the letters he opened and read. There were four of them, three of them business epistles, soon disposed of; the sight of the handwriting upon the fourth made his heart bound suddenly, — it was the clear, space-saving caligraphy of Professor Herrick, who labelled his envelopes as economically as if they had been entomological specimens.

"It's curious that it should have come now," Tredennis said, as he tore it open.

It was a characteristic letter, written, it appeared, with the object of convincing Tredennis that he had been guilty of a slight error in one of his statements concerning the sign-language of a certain tribe. It devoted five pages of closely-written paper to proofs and researches into the subject, and scientific reasons for the truth of all assertions made. It was clear, and by no means uninteresting. The professor never was uninteresting, and he was generally correct. Tredennis read his arguments carefully and with respect, even with an occasional thrill, as he remembered how his communications usually terminated.

But this was an exception to the general rule. At the bottom of the fifth page he signed himself, "Your sincere friend, Nathan Herrick." And he had said nothing about Bertha.

"Not a word," said Tredennis. "He never did so before. What does it mean? Not a word!"

And he had scarcely finished speaking before he saw that on the back of the last page a postscript was written, — a brief one, three words, without comment, these: "Bertha is married."

For a few moments Tredennis sat still and stared at them. The glass across the room reflected very little change in his face. The immovable look became a trifle more immovable, if anything. There was scarcely the stirring of a muscle.

At length he moved slowly, folding the letter carefully and returning it to its envelope in exactly the folds it had lain in when he took it out. After that he rose and began to pace the floor with a slow and heavy tread. Once he stopped and spoke, looking down at the boards beneath his feet.

"Bertha is married," he said, in a low, hard voice. And the clock beginning to strike at the moment, he listened until it ended its stroke of twelve, and then spoke again.

"The New Year," he said; "and Bertha is married."

And he walked to the table where his letter of application lay, and, taking it up, tore it in two and tossed it into the fire.

Four years elapsed before he saw Washington, and in the four years he worked harder than before, added to his reputation year by year, and led the unsettled and wandering existence which his profession entailed. At rare intervals he heard from the professor, and once or twice, in the course of his wanderings, he met with Washingtonians who knew the family and gave him news of them. He heard of the death of Mrs. Herrick and something of Bertha's life from the professor, and, on one occasion, while in Chicago, he encountered at the house of an acquaintance a pretty and charming woman who had lived in Washington before her marriage, and, in the course of conversation, the fact that she had known the Herricks revealed itself. She appeared not only to have known but to have liked them, and really brightened and warmed when they were mentioned.

"I was very fond of Bertha," she said, "and we knew each other as well as girls can know each other in the rush of a Washington winter. I was one of her bridesmaids when she was married. Did you know her well?"

And she regarded him with an additional touch of interest in her very lovely eyes.

"Not very well," Tredennis answered. "We are distantly related to each other, and I spent several weeks in her father's house just after her return from school; but I did not know her so well as I knew the professor."

"And you did not meet Mr. Amory?"

"There was no Mr. Amory then," was Tredennis's reply.

"Of course not," said Mrs. Sylvestre. "I might have known that if I had thought for a moment. He only appeared upon the scene the winter before they were married. She met him at a ball at the Mexican minister's, and his fate was sealed."

Tredennis was silent a moment. Then he asked a question.

"Did you know him well?" he said.

She reflected an instant, and then replied, smiling:

"He was too much in love for one's acquaintance with him to progress to any great extent. His condition was something like David Copperfield's when he said that he was 'saturated with Dora.' He was saturated with Bertha."

"They must be very happy," remarked Tredennis, and he did not know that he spoke in a hard and unresponsive tone, and that his face was more stern than was at all necessary.

"Naturally," responded Mrs. Sylvestre, calmly. "They have money, their children are charming, and their social position is unassailable. Bertha is very clever, and Mr. Amory admires her and is very indulgent. But he could scarcely help that. She is that kind of person."

"She?" repeated Tredennis.

Mrs. Sylvestre smiled again.

"Bertha," she replied. "People are always indulgent with her. She is one of those fortunate persons who are born without any tendency to demand, and who consequently have everything given to them without the trouble of having a struggle. She has a pretty, soft sort of way, and people stand aside before it. Before I knew her well I used to think it was simply cleverness."

"Wasn't it?" said Tredennis.

"Not quite. It escapes that by being constitutional amiability and grace; but if it wasn't constitutional amiability and grace it would be cleverness, and you would resent it. As it is, you like her for it. She is pretty and charming, and has her little world at her feet, and yet her manner is such that you find yourself wondering if she even suspects it."

"Does she?" asked Tredennis.

Mrs. Sylvestre turned her attention to the other side of the room.

"There is Mr. Sylvestre," she said, serenely. "He is coming to us. You must know each other."

And then Mr. Sylvestre sauntered up. He was a very handsome

man, with a rather languid air, which remotely suggested that if he took off his manners and folded them away he would reveal the unadorned fact that he was bored. But even he bestirred himself a little when Tredennis' relationship to the Herricks was mentioned.

"What!" he said. "You are Mrs. Amory's cousin?"

"Only third or fourth," responded Tredennis.

"By Jove! You're in luck!" his new acquaintance returned. "Third or fourth is near enough. I wouldn't object to sixth, myself. Do you see her often?"

"I have not seen her for seven years."

Mr. Sylvestre bestowed a critical glance upon him.

"What's the matter with you?" he inquired, languidly. "There's something radically wrong about a man who neglects his opportunities in that way." He paused and smiled, showing his white teeth through his mustache. "Oh, she's a clever little dev" — He pulled himself up with remarkable adroitness. "She's very clever," he said. "She's delightfully clever."

"She must be," commented Tredennis, unenthusiastically. "I never hear her mentioned without its being added that she is very clever."

"You would be likely to find the thing out for yourself when you met her — even if you hadn't heard it," said Mr. Sylvestre.

When Tredennis returned to his room that night he sat down to read, deliberately choosing a complicated work which demanded the undivided attention of the peruser. He sat before it for half an hour, with bent brow and unyielding demeanor; but at the end of that time he pushed it aside, left his seat, and began to pace the floor, and so walked with a gloomy face until it was long past midnight when he put out the light and went to bed.

Chapter 3

Two years later he found himself, one evening in March, driving along Pennsylvania avenue in a musty hack, which might have been the very one which had borne him to the depot the night he had seen the last of Bertha and her white roses. But the streets were gayer now than they had been then. He had arrived only a day or so after the occurrence of an event of no less national importance than the inauguration of a newly elected President, and there still remained traces of the festivities attendant upon this ceremony, in the shape of unremoved decorations fluttering from windows, draping doors, and swaying in lines across the streets. Groups of people, wearing a rather fatigued air of having remained after the feast for the purpose of more extended sight-seeing, gave the sidewalks a well-filled look, and here and there among them was to be seen a belated uniform which had figured effectively in the procession to the Capitol two clays before.

Having taken note of these things, Tredennis leaned back upon his musty cushions with a half sigh of weariness.

"I come in with the Administration," he said. "I wonder if I shall go out with it, and what will have happened in the interval."

He was thinking of his past and what it had paid him. He had set out in his early manhood with the fixed intention of making for himself a place in the world in which he might feel a reasonable amount of pride. He had attained every object he had aimed at, with the knowledge that he had given for every such object its due value in labor, persistent effort, and steadiness of purpose. No man of his age stood higher in his profession than he did — very few as high. He had earned distinction, honor, and not a little applause. He had found himself "a lion" on more than one occasion, and though he had not particularly enjoyed the experience, had not undervalued it as an experience. The world had used him well, and if he had been given to forming intimacies he might have had many friends. His natural tendency to silence and reserve had worked against him in this, but as it was, he had no enemies and many well-wishers. It was not his habit to bemoan even in secret his rather isolated life; there were times when he told himself that no other would suit him so well, but there were also times when he recognized that it *was* isolated, and the recognition was one which at such moments he roused all the force of his nature to shut out of his mind as soon as possible. He had, perhaps, never fully known the influence his one vague dream had had upon his life. When it ended he made a steady effort to adjust himself to the new condition of existing without it, and had learned much of the strength of its power over him by the strength of the endeavor it had cost him. His inward thought was, that if there had been a little more to remember the memory might have been less sad. As it was, the forgetting was a slow, vague pain, which he felt indefinitely long after he thought that it had died away. He put the old drifting fancies out of his mind, and, having no leaning toward self-indulgence, believed at last that they were done with because they returned but seldom; but he never heard of Bertha, either through the professor or through others, without being conscious for days afterward of an unrest he called by no name.

He rested under the influence of this feeling as he was driven through the lighted streets toward his hotel, and his recollection of his last drive through these same streets made it stronger.

"Eight years," he said. "She has been to many parties since then. Let us hope she has enjoyed them all."

He made his first visit to the professor the same evening, after he had established himself in his room and dined. The professor was always at home in the evening, and, irregular as their correspondence had been, Tredennis felt that he was sure of a welcome from him.

He was not mistaken in this. He found his welcome.

The professor was seated in his dressing-gown, before his study-table, as if he had not stirred during the eight years. He had even the appearance of being upon the point of empaling the same corpulent beetle upon the same attenuated pin, and of engaging in the occupation with the same scientific interest Tredennis remembered so well.

On hearing his visitor's name announced, he started slightly, laid his beetle aside with care, and, rising from his seat, came forward with warm pleasure in his face.

"What!" he exclaimed. "What! — *you*, Tredennis! Well, well! I'm very glad, my dear fellow! I'm very glad."

He shook his hand affectionately, at the same time holding him by the shoulder, as if to make more sure of him.

"I am very glad myself," said Tredennis. "It is a great pleasure to see you again."

"And it took you eight years to get round to us," said the professor, looking at him thoughtfully, and turning him round a trifle more to the light. "Eight years! That's a slice out of a man's life, too."

"But you are no older, professor," said Tredennis. "I am older, but not you."

The professor nodded acquiescence.

"Yes, yes, I know all about that," he said. "You're an old fellow, now; I was an old fellow myself forty years ago. There, sit down, and tell me all about it. That is the chair you sat in when you were here last. You sat in it the night — the night we talked about Bertha."

Chapter 4

"How is Bertha?" Tredennis asked.

The professor sat down in his chair and took up the poker quite carefully.

"She is at a party to-night," he said, poking the fire, "though it is late in the season for parties. She generally is at a party — oftener than not she is at two or three parties."

"Then she must be well," suggested Tredennis.

"Oh, she is well," the professor answered. "And she gets a good deal out of life. She will always get a good deal out of it — in one way or another."

"That is a good thing," remarked Tredennis.

"Very," responded the professor, "if it's all in the one way and not in the other."

He changed the subject almost immediately, and began to discuss Tredennis' own affairs. His kindly interest in his career touched the younger man's heart. It seemed that he had taken an interest in him from the first, and, silent as he had been, had never lost sight of him.

"It used to strike me that you would be likely to make something of your life," he said, in his quiet, half-abstracted way. "You looked like it. I used to say to myself that if you were my son I should look forward to being proud of you. I — I wish you *had* been my son, my boy."

"If I had been," answered Tredennis, earnestly, "I should have felt it a reason for aiming high."

The professor smiled faintly.

"Well," he said, "you aimed high without that incentive. And the best of it is that you have not failed. You are a strong fellow. I like — a — strong — fellow," he added, slowly.

He spoke of Bertha occasionally again in the course of their after conversation, but not as it had been his habit to speak of her in her girlhood. His references to her were mostly statements of facts connected with her children, her mode of life, or her household. She lived near him, her home was an attractive one, and her children were handsome, healthy, and bright.

"Amory is a bright fellow, and a handsome fellow," he said. "He is not very robust, but he is an attractive creature — sensitive, poetic temperament, fanciful. He is fanciful about Bertha, and given to admiring her."

When he went away, at the end of the evening, Tredennis carried with him the old vague sense of discomfort. The professor had been interesting and conversational, and had given him the warmest of welcomes, but he had missed something from their talk which he had expected to find. He was not aware of how he had counted upon it until he missed it, and the sense of loss which he experienced was a trouble to him.

He had certainly not been conscious of holding Bertha foremost in his mind when he had turned his steps toward her father's house. He had thought of how his old friend would look, of what he would say, and had wondered if he should find him changed. He had not asked himself if he should see Bertha or hear of her, and yet what he had missed in her father's friendly talk had been the old kindly, interested discussion of her, and once out in the night air and the deserted streets he knew that he was sadder for his visit than he had fancied he should be. The bright, happy, girlish figure seemed to have passed out of the professor's life also — out of the home it had adorned — even out of the world itself. His night's sleep was not a very peaceful one, but the next morning when he rose, the light of day and the stir of life around him seemed to have dispelled the reality of his last night's fancies. His mind had resolved itself into a condition with which he was familiar, and he was aroused to interest and pleasure in his surroundings. His memory was once more the ghost of a memory which he had long accustomed himself to living without. During the morning his time was fully occupied by his preparations for his new duties, but in the afternoon he was at liberty, and remembering a message he was commissioned to deliver to the sister of a brother officer, he found his way to the lady's house.

It was a house in a fashionable street, and its mistress was a fashionable little person, who appeared delighted to see him, and to treat him with great cordiality.

"I am so glad you were so good as to call today," she said. "Mr. Gardner heard that you had arrived; but did not know where you were, or he would have seen you this morning. What a pity that you were not in time for the inauguration! The ball was more than usually successful. I do hope you will let us see you to-night."

"To-night?" repeated Tredennis.

"Yes. We want you so much," she continued. "We give a little party, — only a little one, — and we shall be so glad. There will be several people here who will be delighted to meet you, — the gentleman who is spoken of as likely to be the new Secretary of the Interior, for instance. He will be charmed. Mr. Gardner has told me what interesting things you have been doing, and what adventures you have had. I shall feel quite sure that my party will be a success, if you will consent to be my lion."

"I am afraid my consenting wouldn't establish the fact," said Tredennis. "You would want a mane, and a roar, and claws. But you are very kind to ask me to your party."

The end of the matter was that, after some exchange of civilities, he gave a half-promise to appear, mentally reserving the privilege of sending "regrets" if he did not feel equal to the effort when night arrived. He was not fond of parties. And so, having delivered the message with which he had been commissioned, he made his adieus and retired.

When night came he was rather surprised to find lurking in his mind some slight inclination to abide by his promise. Accordingly, after having taken a deliberate, late dinner, read the papers, and written a letter or so, he dressed himself and issued forth.

On arriving at his destination he found the "little party" a large one. The street was crowded with carriages, the house was brilliantly lighted, an awning extended from the door to the edge of the pavement, and each carriage, depositing its brilliant burden within the protection of the striped tunnel, drove rapidly away to give place to another.

Obeying the injunctions of the servant at the door Tredennis mounted to the second story and divested himself of his overcoat, with the assistance of a smart mulatto, who took it in charge. The room in which he found himself was rather inconveniently crowded with men, — young, middle-aged, elderly, some of them wearing a depressed air of wishing themselves at home, some bearing themselves stolidly, and others either quietly resigned or appearing to enjoy themselves greatly. It was not always the younger ones who formed this last class Tredennis observed. In one corner a brisk gentleman, with well-brushed, gray beard, laughed delightedly over a story just related to him with much sprightliness by a companion a decade older than himself, while near them an unsmiling youth of twenty regarded their ecstasies without the movement of a muscle.

Tredennis' attention was attracted for a moment toward two men who stood near him, evidently awaiting the appearance of some one at the door of the ladies' cloak-room, which they could see from where they stood.

One of them leaned in a nicely managed labor-saving attitude against the door-post. He was a rather tall, blonde young man, with a face eminently calculated to express either a great deal or absolutely nothing at all, as he chose to permit it, and his unobtrusive evening dress had an air of very agreeable fitness and neatness, and quite distinguished itself by seeming to belong to him. It was his laugh which called Tredennis' attention to him. He laughed in response to some remark of his companion's, — a non-committal but naturally sounding baritone laugh, which was not without its attractiveness.

"Yes, I was there," he said.

"And sang?"

"No, thank you."

"And she was there, of course?"

"She?" repeated his friend, his countenance at this moment expressing nothing whatever, and doing it very well.

"Oh, Mrs. Amory," responded the other, who was young enough and in sufficiently high spirits to be led into forgetting to combine good taste with his hilarity.

"You might say Mrs. Amory, — if you don't object," replied his companion, quietly. "It would be more civil."

Then Tredennis passed out and heard no more.

He made his way down the stairs, which were crowded with guests going down and coming up, and presented himself at the door of the first of the double parlors, where he saw his hostess standing with her husband. Here he was received with the greatest warmth, Mrs. Gardner brightening visibly when she caught sight of him.

"Now," she said, "this is really good of you. I was almost afraid to let you go away this afternoon. Mr. Gardner, Colonel Tredennis is really here," she added, with frank cordiality.

After that Tredennis found himself swallowed, as in a maelstrom. He was introduced right and left, hearing a name here and seeing a face there, and always conscious of attaching the wrong names to the faces as he struggled to retain some impression of both in his memory. Mrs. Gardner bore him onward, filled with the most amiable and hospitable delight in the sensation he awakened as she led him toward the prominent official in prospective before referred to, who leaned against a mantel-piece and beguiled his time by making himself quite agreeable to a very pretty young *débutante* who was recounting her experience at the inaugural ball. Here Tredennis was allowed to free himself from the maelstrom and let it whirl past him, as he stood a little aside and conversed with his new acquaintance, who showed deep interest in and much appreciation of all he had to say, and evidently would have been glad to prolong the interview beyond the moment, when some polite exigency called him away in the midst of an animated discussion of the rights of Indian agents and settlers.

When he had gone Tredennis still remained standing where he had left him, enjoying his temporary seclusion and the opportunity of looking on with the cool speculation of an outsider.

He had been looking on thus for some moments, — at the passing to and fro, at the well-bred elbowing through the crush, at the groups gathering themselves here and there to exchange greetings and then breaking apart and drifting away, —when he suddenly became aware of a faint fragrance in the atmosphere about him which impressed itself upon him with a curious insistence. On his first vague recognition of its presence he could not have told what it was, or why it roused in him something nearer pain than pleasure. It awakened in him a queer sense of impatience with the glare of light, the confusion of movement and voices, and the gay measure of the music in the next room. And almost the instant be felt this impatience a flash of recognition broke upon him, and he knew what the perfume was. and that it seemed out of place in the glare and confusion simply because his one distinct memory of it associated itself only with the night when he had sat in the fire-light with Bertha, and she had held the heliotrope in her hand. With this memory in his mind, and with a half smile at his own momentary resentment of the conditions surrounding him, he turned toward the spot near from which he fancied the odor of the flowers came, thinking that it had floated from some floral decoration of the deep window. And so, turning, he saw — surrounded by what seemed to be the gayest group in the room — Bertha herself!

She was exquisitely dressed, and stood in the prettiest possible pose, supporting herself lightly against the side of the window; she had a bouquet in her hand and a brilliant smile on her lips, and Tredennis knew in an instant that she had seen and recognized him.

She did not move; she simply retained her pretty pose, smiling and waiting for him to come to her, and, though she said nothing to her companions, something in her smile evidently revealed the situation to them, for, almost immediately, the circle divided itself, and room was made for him to advance within it.

Often afterward Tredennis tried to remember how he moved toward her, and what he said when he found himself quite near her, holding the gloved band she gave him so lightly; but his recollections were always of the vaguest. There scarcely seemed to have been any first words — he was at her side, she gave him her hand, and then, in the most natural manner, the group about her seemed to melt away, and they were left together, and he, glancing half unconsciously down at her bouquet, saw that it was made of heliotrope and Maréchal Niel roses.

She was so greatly and yet so little changed that he felt, as he looked at her, like a man in a dream. He tried to analyze the change and could not, and the effort to do so was a pain to him. The color in her cheeks was less bright than he remembered it, but her eyes were brighter; he thought also that they looked larger, and soon recognized that this was not only because her face was less girlishly full, but arose from a certain alertness of expression which had established itself in them. And yet, despite their clear brightness, when she lifted them to his own, his sense of loss was for the instant terrible. Her slight, rounded figure was even prettier than ever, — more erect, better borne, and with a delicate consciousness and utilizing of its own graces, — but it was less easy to connect it mentally with the little gray gown and lace kerchief than he could ever have believed possible.

Her very smile and voice had changed. The smile was sometimes a very brilliant one and sometimes soft and slow, as if a hidden meaning lay behind it; the voice was low-pitched, charmingly modulated, and expressed far more than the words it gave to a listener, but Tredennis knew that he must learn to know them both, and that to do so would take time and effort.

He never felt this so strongly as when she sat down on the cushioned window-seat, and made a little gesture toward the place at her side.

"Sit down," she said, with the soft smile this time, — a smile at once sweet and careless. "Sit down, and tell me if you are glad to be stationed in Washington; and let me tell *you* that papa is delighted at the prospect of your being near him again."

"Thank you," answered Tredennis; "and as to the being here, I think I like the idea of the change well enough."

"You will find it a great change, I dare say," she went on; "though, of course, you have not devoted yourself to the Indians entirely during your absence. But Washington is unlike any other American city. I think it is unlike any other city in the universe. It is an absorbingly interesting place when you get used to it."

"You are fortunate in finding it so," said Tredennis.

"I?" she said, lightly. "Oh! I do not think I could resign myself to living anywhere else; though, when you reflect, of course you know that is a national quality. All good Americans adore the city they confer distinction on by living in, and asperse the characters of all other places. Englishmen believe in London, and Frenchmen in Paris; but in America, a New Yorker vaunts himself upon New York, a Bostonian glories in Boston, and a Washingtonian delights in the capital of his country; and so on, until you reach New Orleans."

"That is true enough," said Tredennis, "though I had not thought of it before."

"Oh, it is true," she answered, with an airy laugh. Then she added, with a change of tone, "You have been away for a long time."

"Eight years," he replied.

He thought she gave a slight start, but immediately she turned upon him with one of the brilliant smiles.

"We have had time to grow since then," she said, — "not older, of course, but infinitely wiser — and better."

He did not find it easy to comprehend very clearly either her smile or her manner. He felt that there might be something hidden behind both, though certainly nothing could have been brighter or more inconsequent than her tone. He did not smile, but regarded her for a moment with a look of steady interest, of which he was scarcely conscious. She bore it for an instant, and then turned her eyes carelessly aside, with a laugh.

"I do not think you are changed at all," she said.

"Why?" he asked, still watching her, and trying to adjust himself to her words.

"You looked at me then," she said, "just as you used to when you were with us before, and I said something frivolous. I am afraid I was often frivolous in those days. I confess I suspected myself of it, and one day I even made a resolution" —

She did start then — as if some memory had suddenly returned to

33

her. She lifted her bouquet to her face and let it slowly drop upon her knee again as she turned and looked at him.

"I remember now," she said, "that I made that resolution the day you brought me the heliotrope." And now it seemed for the instant to be her turn to regard him with interest.

"I don't know what the resolution was," he said, rather grimly, "but I hope it was a good one. Did you keep it?"

"No," she answered, undisturbedly; "but I kept the heliotrope. You know I said I would. It is laid away in one of my bureau drawers."

"And the first party?" he asked. "Was it a success?"

"Oh, yes," she replied, "it was a great success. I am happy to say that all my parties are successes, inasmuch as I enjoy them."

"Is this a success?" he inquired. She raised her bouquet to her face again and glanced over it at the crowded room.

"It is an immense success," she said. "Such things always are — in Washington. Do you see that little woman on the sofa? Notice what bright eyes she has, and how quickly they move from one person to another — like a bird's. She is 'our Washington correspondent' for half-a-dozen Western papers, and 'does the social column' in one of our principal dailies, and tomorrow you will read in it that 'one of the most brilliant receptions of the season was held last night at the charming home of Mrs. Winter Gardner, on K street.' You will also learn that 'Mrs. Richard Amory was lovely in white brocade and pearls,' and that 'noticeable among even the stateliest masculine forms was the imposing figure of Colonel Tredennis, the hero of Indian adventure and'"—

She had been speaking in the quietest possible manner, looking at the scene before her and not at him; but here she stopped and bent toward him a little.

"Have you," she said, softly, "such a thing as a scalp about you?"

He was by no means prepared for the inquiry, he sustained himself under it in his usual immovable manner. He put his hand up to his breast and then dropped it.

"I am afraid not," he said. "Not in this suit. I forgot, in dressing, that I might need them. But I might go back to the hotel," he added, suggestively.

"Oh, no, thanks," she said, returning to her former position. "I was only thinking how pleased she would be if you could show her a little one, and tell her the history of it. It would be so useful to her."

"I am very sorry," said Tredennis.

"You would be more sorry," she went on, "if you knew what an industrious little person she is, and with what difficulty she earns her ten dollars a column. She goes to receptions, and literary and art clubs, and to the White House, and the Capitol, and knows everybody and just what adjectives they like, and how many; and is never ill-natured at all, though it really seems to me that such an existence offers a premium to spitefulness. I am convinced that it would make me spiteful. But she never loses control over her temper — or her adjectives. If I weighed two hundred pounds, for instance, she would refer to my avoirdupois as 'matronly *embonpoint*;' and if I were a skeleton, she would say I had a 'slight and reed-like figure,' which is rather clever, you know, as well as being Christian charity."

"And she will inform the world to-morrow that your dress," glancing down at it, "was white" —

"And that my hair was brown, as usual," she ended for him. "And that I carried a bouquet of heliotrope and roses."

"I hope you like it," he said.

"Oh, very much indeed, thank you," was her response. "And if I did not, somebody else would, or it is plain that she would not get her ten dollars a column. It has struck me that she doesn't do it for amusement, or with the deliberate intention of annoying people. For my part, I admire and envy her. There is no collection so valuable as a collection of adjectives. Everything depends on adjectives. You can begin a friendship or end it with one — or an enmity, either."

"Will you tell me," said Tredennis, "what adjective you would apply to the blonde young man on the other side of the room, who has just picked up a lady's handkerchief?"

She looked across the room at the person indicated, and did not reply at once. There was a faintly reflective smile in her eyes, though it could scarcely be said to touch her lips. The man was the one who had attracted Tredennis' attention at the door of the cloakroom, and since coming down-stairs he had regarded him with some interest upon each occasion when he had caught sight of him as he moved from room to room, evidently at once paying unobtrusive but unswerving attention to the social exigencies of his position, and finding a decent amount of quiet entertainment in the results of his efforts.

"I wish you would tell me," said Bertha, after her little pause, "what adjective *you* would apply to him."

"I am afraid," said Tredennis, "that our acquaintance is too limited at present to allow of my grasping the subject. As I don't chance to know him at all" —

Bertha interposed, still watching the object of discussion with the faintly reflective smile.

"I have known him for six years," she said, "and I have not found his adjective yet. He is a cousin of Mr. Amory's. Suppose," she said, turning with perfect seriousness and making a slight movement as if she would rise, — "suppose we go and ask Miss Jessup?"

Tredennis offered her his arm.

"Let us hope that Miss Jessup can tell us," he said.

His imperturbable readiness seemed to please her. Her little laugh had a genuine sound in it. She sat down again.

"l am afraid she could not," she said. "See! he is coming to speak to me, and we might ask him."

But she did not ask him when he presented himself before her, as he did almost immediately. He had come to remind her that dancing was going on in one of the rooms, and that she had promised him the waltz the musicians had just struck into with a flourish.

"Perhaps you will remember that you said the third waltz," he said, "and this is the third waltz."

Bertha rose.

"I remember," she said, "and I think I am ready for it; but before you take me away you must know Colonel Tredennis. Of course you do know Colonel Tredennis, but you must know him better. Colonel Tredennis, this is Mr. Arbuthnot."

The pair bowed, as civility demanded. Of the two, it must be confessed that Tredennis' recognition of the ceremony was the less cordial. Just for the moment he was conscious of feeling secretly repelled by the young man's well-carried, conventional figure and calm, blond countenance, — the figure seemed so correct a copy of a score of others, the blond countenance expressed so little beyond a carefully trained tendency to good manners, entirely unbiassed by any human emotion.

"By the time our waltz is finished," said Bertha, as she took his arm, "I hope that Mr. Amory will be here. He promised me that he would come in toward the end of the evening. He will be very glad to find you here."

And then, with a little bow to Tredennis, she went away.

She did not speak to her companion until they reached the room where the dancers were congregated. Then, as they took their place among the waltzers, she broke the silence.

"If I don't dance well," she said, "take into consideration the fact that I have just been conversing with a man I knew eight years ago."

"You will be sure to dance well," said Arbuthnot, as they began. "But I don't mind acknowledging an objection to persons I knew eight years ago. I never could find any sufficient reason for their turning up. And, as to your friend, it strikes me it shows a great lack of taste in the Indians to have consented to part with him. It appeared to me that he possessed a manner calculated to endear him to aboriginal society beyond measure."

Bertha laughed, — a laugh whose faintness might have arisen from her rapid motion.

"He's rather rigorous-looking," she said; "but he always was. Still, I remember I was beginning to like him quite well when he went West. Papa is very fond of him. He turns out to be a persistent, heroic kind of being — with a purpose in life, and the rest of it."

"His size is heroic enough," said Arbuthnot. "He would look better on a pedestal in a public square than in a parlor."

Bertha made no reply, but, after having made the round of the room twice, she stopped.

"I am not dancing well," she said. "I do not think I am in a dancing mood. I will sit down."

Arbuthnot glanced at her, and then looked away.

"Do you want to be quiet?" he asked.

"I want to be quieter than this," she answered; "for a few minutes. I believe I am tired."

"You have been going out too much," he said, as he led her into a small side-room which had been given up to a large, ornate punch-bowl, to do reverence to which occasional devotees wandered in. and out.

"I have been going out a great deal," she answered.

She leaned back in the luxurious little chair he had given her, and looked across the hall into the room where the waltz was at its height, and, having looked, she laughed.

"Do you see that girl in the white dress, which doesn't fit," she said, — "the plump girl who bags at the waist and is oblivious to it — and everything else but her waltz and her partner?"

"Yes," he responded; "but I hope you are not laughing at her, — there is no need of it. She's having a fascinating time."

"Yes," she returned. "She is having a lively time; but I am not laughing at her, but at what she reminds me of. Do you know, I was just that age when Colonel Tredennis saw me last. I was not that size or that shape, and my dresses used to fit — but I was just that age, and just as oblivious, and danced with just that spirit of enjoyment."

"You dance with just as much enjoyment now," said Arbuthnot, "and you are quite as oblivious at times, though it may suit your fancy just at the present moment to regard yourself as a shattered wreck confronted with the ruins of your lost youth and innocence. I revel in that kind of thing myself at intervals, but it does not last."

"No," she said, opening her fan with a smile, and looking down at the Cupids and butterflies adorning it, "of course it won't last, and I must confess that I am not ordinarily given to it — but that man! Do you know, it was a curious sort of sensation that came over me when I first saw him. I was standing near a window, talking to half-a-dozen people, and really enjoying myself very much, — you know I nearly always enjoy myself, — and suddenly something seemed to make me look up — and there he stood !"

"It would not be a bad idea for him to conceal his pedestal about him and mount it when it became necessary for him to remain stationary," said Arbuthnot, flippantly, and yet with a momentary gravity in his eyes somewhat at variance with his speech.

She went on as if he had not spoken.

"It was certainly a curious feeling," she continued. "Everything came to me in a flash. I suppose I am rather a light and frivolous person, not sufficiently given to reflecting on the passage of time, and suddenly there he stood, and I remembered that eight years had gone by, and that everything was changed."

"A great many things can happen in eight years," commented Arbuthnot.

"A great many things have happened to me," she said. "*Everything* has happened to me!"

"No," said Arbuthnot, in a low, rather reflective tone, and looking as he spoke not at her, but at the girl whose white dress did not fit, and who at that moment whirled rather breathlessly by the door. "No — not everything."

"I have grown from a child to a woman," she said. "I have married, I have arrived at maternal dignity. I don't see that there is anything else that could happen — at least, anything comfortable."

"No," he admitted. "I don't think there is anything comfortable."

"Well, it is very certain I don't want to try anything uncomfortable," she said. "'Happy the people whose annals are tiresome.' Montesquieu says that, and it always struck me as meaning something."

"I hope it does not mean that you consider your annals tiresome," said Arbuthnot. "How that girl does dance! This is the fifth time she has passed the door."

"I hope her partner likes it as much as she does," remarked Bertha. "And as to the annals, I have not found them tiresome at all, thank you. As we happen to have come to retrospect, I think I may say that I have rather enjoyed myself, on the whole. I have had no tremendous emotions."

"On which you may congratulate yourself," Arbuthnot put in.

"I do," she responded. "I know I should not have liked them. I have left such things to — you, for instance."

She said this with a little air of civil mocking which was by no means unbecoming, and to which her companion was well used.

"Thank you," he replied, amiably. "You showed consideration, of course — but that's your way."

"I may not have lived exactly the kind of life I used to think I should live — when I was a school-girl," she went on, smiling; "but who does? — and who would want to when she attained years of discretion? And I may not be exactly the kind of person I — meant to be; but I think I may congratulate you on that — and Richard. You would never have been the radiant creatures you are if I had ripened to that state of perfection. You could not have borne up under it."

She rose from her seat and took his arm.

"No," she said, "I am not the kind of person I meant to be, and Colonel Tredennis has reminded me of the fact and elevated my spirits. Let us go and find him, and invite him to dinner to-morrow. He deserves it."

As they passed the door of the dancing-room she paused a moment to look in, and as she did so caught sight of the girl in the white dress once more.

"She is not tired yet," she said, "but her partner is — and so am I. If Richard has come, I think I shall go home."

Chapter 5

Tredennis dined with them the next day, and many days afterward. On meeting him Richard Amory had taken one of his rather numerous enthusiastic fancies to him, and in pursuit and indulgence of this fancy could not see enough of him. These fanciful friendships were the delights of his life, and he never denied himself one, though occasionally they wore themselves out in time to give place to others.

Tredennis found him as the professor had described him, "a bright fellow, and a handsome fellow." He had thought that when he came forward to introduce himself, as he had done at the Gardners' reception, he had never seen a brighter or more attractive human being. He had a dark, delicate, eager face, soft, waving hair, tossed lightly back from a forehead whose beauty was almost feminine; a slight, lithe figure, and an air of youth and alertness which would have been attraction enough in itself. He was interested in everything: each subject touched upon seeming to awaken him to enthusiasm, — the Indians, the settlers, the agencies, the fort life, — equally interested in each, and equally ready to confront, in the most delightfully sanguine mood, the problems each suggested.

"It is worth a great deal to have an opportunity to judge of these things from the inside," he said. "There are a thousand questions I want to ask; but we shall see you often, of course. We must see you often. It will be the greatest pleasure to us."

His first entrance into their house, the following evening, was something which always set itself apart in Tredennis' memory.

A gay burst of laughter greeted him as the parlor door was thrown open, — laughter so gay that the first announcement of his name was drowned by it, and, as he paused for a moment, he had the opportunity to take in fully the picture before him. The room was a pretty and luxurious one, its prettiness and luxury wearing the air of being the result of natural growth, and suggesting no oppressiveness of upholstery. Its comforts were evidently the outcome of the fancies and desires of those who lounged, or read, or talked in it, and its knick-knacks and follies were all indicative of some charming whim carried out with a delightful freedom from reason, which was their own excuse.

In the open fireplace a bright wood-fire burned, and upon the white wolf-skin before it Richard Amory lay at unconventional full length, with his hands clasped lightly under his head, evidently enjoying to the utmost the ease of his position, the glow of the fire, and the jest of the moment, while near him, in an easy-chair, sat Arbuthnot. Both of them looked at Bertha, who stood with one hand resting on the low mantel.

"I have been waiting for a long time," Tredennis heard her say, and then, as the servant announced his name again, she stopped speaking, and came forward to meet him, while Richard sprang lightly to his feet.

"I will tell you at the outset," she said, "that it is not one of the time-honored customs of Washington for people to receive their guests with this ingenuous and untrammelled freedom, but" —

"But she has been telling us a story," put in Richard, shaking hands with him; "and she told it so well that we forgot the time. And she must tell it again."

"It is not worth telling again," she said, as they returned to the fire; "and, besides, I told it to you in the strictest confidence. And if that is not reason enough, I don't mind confessing that it is a story which doesn't exhibit me in an amiable light. It shows a temper and viciousness that you count among your home comforts, and don't feel it decent to display for the benefit of anyone but your immediate relatives."

Tredennis looked down at her curiously. His first glance at her had shown him that to-night she was even farther removed from his past than she had seemed before. Her rich dress showed flashes of bright color, her eyes were alight with some touch of excitement, and her little wrists were covered with pretty barbarities of bangles and charms which jingled as she moved.

"I should like to hear the story," he said.

"It is a very good story," commented Arbuthnot, laughing; "I think I would tell it over again."

"Oh, yes," said Richard; "Colonel Tredennis must hear it."

Bertha looked across at Tredennis, and as she did so he saw in her eyes what he had seen the night before and had not understood, but which dawned upon him now, — a slight smiling defiance of his thoughts, whatsoever they might be.

"You won't like it," she said; "but you shall hear it, if you wish. It is about a great lady" —

"That will add to the interest," said Tredennis. "You have great ladies in Washington?"

"It is infinitely to our credit that they are only occasional incidents," she answered, "and that they don't often last long. When one considers the number of quiet, domesticated women who find themselves launched suddenly, by some wave of chance, into the whirl of public life, one naturally wonders that we are not afflicted with some very great ladies indeed; but it must be confessed we have far less to complain of in that respect than might be expected."

"But this particular great lady?" said Tredennis.

"Is one of the occasional incidents. Some one said that our society was led by bewildered Europeans and astonished Americans, — Americans astonished to find themselves suddenly bearing the responsibility of the highest positions, and Europeans bewildered by called upon to adjust themselves to startling novelties in manners and customs. This great lady is one of the astonished Americans, and, privately, she is very much astonished, indeed."

Arbuthnot laughed.

"You will observe," he commented, "that Mrs. Amory's remarks are entirely unbiassed by any feminine prejudices."

"You will observe," said Bertha, "that Mr. Arbuthnot's remarks are entirely unbiassed by any prejudice in favor of my reliability of statement." But, she added, with a delusive air of amiable candor, "I am sure you cannot deny that I was very civil to her."

"I have not a doubt of it," responded Arbuthnot. "And I don't mind adding that I should like to have been there to see."

"Colonel Tredennis shall judge," she said, "whether it would have been really worth while. I will make the story brief. Last season the great lady gave me cause to remember her. We had not met, and, to please a friend, I called upon her. We found her in her drawing-room, engaged in entertaining two new newly arrived *attachés*. They seemed to interest her. I regret to say that we did not. She did not hear our names when the servant announced them, and the insignificance of our general bearing was against us. I think it must have been that, for we were comparatively well dressed — at least, Miss Jessup's description of our costumes in the 'Wabash Times' gave that impression the following week. Perhaps we looked timid and unaccustomed to 'the luxurious trophies from many climes' (Miss Jessup again) surrounding us. The ingenuous modesty of extreme youth which you may have observed" —

"Repeatedly," replied Arbuthnot.

"Thank you. But I suppose it told against me on this occasion. Our respectable attire and air of general worthiness availed nothing. The great lady rose, stared at us, gave us her finger-ends, called us by names which did not belong to us, and sat down again, turning her back upon us with much frankness, and resuming her conversation with the *attachés*, not interrupting it to address six words to us during the three minutes we remained. That is the first half of the story."

"It promises well for the second half," said Tredennis.

"The second is *my* half," said Bertha. "Later, she discovered our real names, and the fact that — shall I say that Miss Jessup knew them, and thought them worthy of mention in the 'Wabash Times'? That would, perhaps, be a good way of putting it. Then she called, but did not see me, as I was out. We did not meet again until this afternoon. I was making the Cabinet calls, and had the pleasure of encountering her at the house of the Secretary of War. Perhaps Miss Jessup had sent her a copy of the 'Wabash Times' yesterday, with the society column marked — I don't know. But she was pleased to approach me. I received her advances with the mild consideration of one who sees a mistake made, but is prevented by an amiable delicacy from correcting it, and observing this, she was led into the indiscretion of saying, with graceful leniency, that she feared I did not know her. I think it is really there that my half begins. I smiled with flattering incredulity, and said, 'That would be very strange in a Washingtonian.'

"'When you called' — she began.

"I looked at her with a blush, as of slight embarrassment, which seemed to disturb her.

"'You have not forgotten that you called?' she remarked, chillingly.

"'It would have been impossible for me to forget anything so agreeable,' I said, as though in delicately eager apology. 'I am most unlucky. It was some more fortunate person.'

"'But,' she said, 'I returned the visit.'

"'I received your card,' I replied, smiling ingenuously into her eyes, 'and it reminded me of my delinquency. Of course I knew it was a mistake.'

"And after I had smiled into her eyes for a second or so longer, she began to understand, and I think by this time it is quite clear to her."

"There must be a moral to that," commented Tredennis.

"There is," she responded, with serene readiness. "A useful one. It is this: It is always safe — in Washington — to be civil to the respectably clad. If the exigencies of public position demand that you receive, not the people you wish to see, or the people who wish to see you, but the respectably clad, it is well to deal in glittering generalities of good manners, and even — if you choose to go so far — good feeling. There are numbers of socially besieged women in Washington who actually put the good feeling first; but the Government cannot insist on that, you know, so it remains a matter of taste."

"If you could draw the line" — began Richard. "There is no line," said Bertha, "so you can't draw it. And it was not myself I avenged this afternoon, but — the respectably clad."

"And before she became an astonished American," put in Arbuthnot, "this mistaken person was possibly" —

Bertha interposed, with a pretty gesture which set all the bangles jingling.

"Ah," she said, "but we have so little to do with that, that I have not even the pleasure of using it in my arguments against her. The only thing to be reasonably required of her now is that she should be sufficiently well-mannered during her career. She might assume her deportment with her position, and dispose of it at a sacrifice afterward. Imagine what a field in the way of advertisement, for instance: 'For sale. A neatly fitting suit of good manners. Used through one Administration, Somewhat worn through active service, but still equal to much wear and tear.'"

That which struck Tredennis more forcibly than all else was her habit of treating everything lightly, and he observed that it was a habit Arbuthnot shared with her. The intimacy existing between the two seemed an unusual one, and appeared to have established itself through slow and gradual growth. It had no ephemeral air, and bore somehow the impress of their having shared their experiences in common for some time. Beneath the very derision which marked their treatment of each other was a suggestion of unmistakable good fellowship and quick appreciation of each other's moods. When Bertha made a fanciful speech, Arbuthnot's laugh rang out even before Richard's, which certainly was ready enough in response; and when Arbuthnot vouchsafed a semi-serious remark, Bertha gave him an un- divided attention which expressed her belief that what he said would be worth listening to. Amory's province it seemed to be to delight in both of them, — to admire their readiness, to applaud their jests, and to encourage them to display their powers. That he admired Arbuthnot immensely was no less evident than that no gift or grace of Bertha's was lost upon him.

His light-hearted, inconsequent enjoyment of the pleasure of the moment impressed Tredennis singularly. He was so ready to be moved by any passing zephyr of sentiment or emotion, and so entirely and sweet-temperedly free from any fatiguing effect when the breeze had once swept over him.

"All that I have to complain of in you two people," he said, gayly, in the course of the evening, "is that you have no sentiment — none whatever."

"We are full of it," said Arbuthnot, "both of us, — but we conceal it, and we feel that it makes us interesting. Nothing is more interesting than repressed emotion. The appearance of sardonic coldness and stoicism which has deceived you is but a hollow mockery; beneath it I secrete a maelstrom of impassioned feeling and a mausoleum of blighted hopes."

"There is a fashion in emotions as in everything else," said Bertha. "And sentiment is 'out.' So is stateliness. Who would submit to stateliness in these days? It was the highest aim of our great-grandmothers to be stately; but stateliness went out with ruffles and the minuet, and a certain kind of Roman nose you find in all portraits taken in the reigns of the Georges. Now we are sprightly. It is imperative that we should be sprightly. I hope you are prepared to be sprightly, Colonel Tredennis."

He was very conscious of not looking so. In fact, the idea was growing upon him that upon the whole his grave face and large figure were rather out of place among all this airy *badinage*. His predominant feeling was that his unfortunate tendency to seriousness and silence was not a Washingtonian quality, and augured poorly for his future. Here were people who could treat lightly, not only their subjects, but themselves and each other. The fire-lit room, with its trifles and knick-knacks and oddities; the graceful, easy figure of Richard Amory lounging idly in his chair; Bertha, with her bright dress and fantastic little ornaments flashing and jingling; Arbuthnot smiling faintly, and touching his mustache with a long, fair hand, — each and all suggested to him in some whimsical, vague fashion that he was too large and not pliable enough for his surroundings, and that if he moved he might upset something, or tread upon some sparkling, not too substantial theory.

"I am afraid I am not as well prepared as I might be," he answered. "Do you always find it easy?"

"I!" she returned. "Oh, perfectly! it is only Mr. Arbuthnot who finds it difficult — being a prey to his feelings. In his moments of deep mental anguish the sprightliness which society demands of him is a thing from which his soul recoils."

Shortly after dinner Arbuthnot went away. He had a final call to make upon some friends who were going away, after having taken an active part in the inaugural ceremonies and ball. It appeared that they had come from the West, with the laudable intention of making the most of these festivities, and that he had felt it his duty to do his utmost for their entertainment.

"I hope they enjoyed themselves," said Bertha, as he stood making his adieus.

"Well," was his reply, "it strikes me they did. I took them to the Treasury, and the Patent Office, and the Army and Navy Department, and up into the dome of the Capitol, and into the Senate and the House, and they heard the inaugural address, and danced at the ball, and saw the ex-President and bought photographs of the new one, and tired themselves out, and are going home a party of total wrecks, but without a thing on their consciences; so I think they must have enjoyed themselves. I hope so. I didn't. I don't grudge them anything; but it is the ninetieth time I have been through the Treasury, and the twentieth time I have climbed to the dome, and the exercise has lost its freshness."

After he had left the room he returned, drawing from the pocket of his rather dandyfied light overcoat three small packages, which he laid on a side-table.

"This is for Janey, and this for Jack, and this for Marjorie," he said. "I told them they would find them there in the morning."

"Thank you," answered Bertha, as if the proceeding was one to which she was well accustomed.

When he was fairly gone Richard Amory broke into a half laugh.

"What a queer fellow he is!" he said.

Bertha returned to her place by the fire, taking from the mantel a little screen of peacock feathers and shading her face with it.

"Do you know," she said, "that he rarely leaves the house without one of us making that remark, and yet it always has an illusive air of being entirely new."

"Well," remarked Richard, "he is a queer fellow, and there's no denying it. Imagine a fellow like that coolly rambling about with neat packages of bonbons in his fastidious overcoat pocket, to be bestowed on children without any particular claim on him. Why does he do it?"

"It doesn't exactly arise from enthusiasm awakened by their infant charms," said Bertha, "and he never professed that it did."

"But he must care for them a little," returned Richard.

"The fact is that you don't know what he cares for," said Bertha, "and it is rather one of his fascinations. I suppose that is really what we mean by saying he is a queer fellow."

"At all events," said Richard, amiably, "he is a nice fellow, and one can manage to subsist on that. All I complain of is that he hasn't any object. A man ought to have an object — two or three, if he likes."

"He doesn't like," said Bertha, "for he certainly hasn't an object — though, after all, that belongs to his mode of life."

"I should like," said Tredennis, "to know something of the mode of life of a man who hasn't an object."

"You will gain a good deal of information on the subject if you remain long in Washington," answered Bertha. "We generally have either too many objects or none at all. If it is not your object to get into the White House, or the Cabinet, or somewhere else, it is probably your fate to be installed in a 'department' and, as you cannot hope to retain your position through any particular circumspectness or fitness for it, you have not any object left you."

"The fact is," said Richard, "it would have been a great deal better for Larry if he had stayed where he was and fought it out."

"The fact is," said Bertha, "it would be a great deal better for nine out of ten of the rest if they stayed where they were. And when Larry came he did not come under specially exhilarating circumstances, and just then I suppose it seemed to him that the rest of his life was not worth much to him."

"It has struck me," said Richard, reflectively, "that he had a blow of some sort about that time, — something apart from the loss of his fortune. I am not sure but that I once heard some wandering rumor of there being a young woman somewhere" —

"Oh!" said Bertha, in a low, rather hurried voice, "he had a blow. There is no mistake about that, — he had a blow, and there was a good deal in him that did not survive it."

"And yet he doesn't strike you as being that sort of fellow," said

Richard, still in reflection. "You wouldn't think of him as being a fellow with a grief."

Bertha broke into delighted laughter.

"A grief!" she exclaimed. "That is very good. I wish he had heard it. A grief! I wonder what he would do with it in his moments of recreation, — at receptions, for instance, and *musicales,* and germans. He might conceal it in his opera hat, but I am afraid it would be in the way. Poor Larry! Griefs are as much out of fashion as stateliness, and he not only couldn't indulge in one if he would, but he wouldn't if he could."

"Well, how would you put it," said Richard, "if you did not call it a grief?"

Bertha laughed again.

"If I put it at all," she answered, "I would say that he had once been very uncomfortable, but had discreetly devoted himself to getting over it, and had succeeded decently well; and last, but not least, I would add that it would be decidedly difficult to make him uncomfortable again."

Tredennis found it impossible to avoid watching her with grave interest each time she spoke or moved. He was watching her now with a sort of aside sensibility to her bright drapery, her flashing, tinkling wrists, and her screen of peacock feathers.

"She is very light," he was saying inwardly.

She turned to him with a smile.

"Would he strike *you* as 'a fellow with a grief'?" she inquired.

"No," he answered; "I cannot say he would."

"No," she said, "that is certain enough. If you went away and never saw him again, you would remember just this of him — if you remembered him at all: that his clothes fitted him well, that he had an agreeable laugh, that he had a civil air of giving you his attention when you spoke, and — nothing else."

"And that is not all there is of him?" Tredennis asked.

She looked down at her feather screen, still smiling slightly.

"No," she answered, rather slowly, "not quite all; but even I don't quite know how much more there is, and Richard, who has known him at intervals all his life, lapses into speaking of him as 'a fellow with a grief.'"

Richard rose from his chair.

"Oh," he said, with much cheerfulness, "there is no denying that you two are the outgrowth of an effete civilization. You are always arriving at logical deductions concerning each other, and you have a tendency to the derision of all the softer emotions. You are a couple of worldworn creatures, and it is left to me to represent the youth and ardor of the family."

"That is true," said Bertha, in her soft, mocking voice. "We are battered and worldly wise — and we have no object."

"But I have," said Richard, "and if Colonel Tredennis will come upstairs with me, I will show him what a few of them are, if he takes an interest in, such things."

"What," said Bertha, — "the laboratory, or the library, or" —

"All of them," he answered, "including the new collection." And he turned upon Tredennis the brightest imaginable smile.

Tredennis left his chair in response to it.

"I am interested in all collections, more or less," he said.

"So am I," said Bertha — "more or less." And they went out of the room with this little gibe in their ears.

Before the conclusion of his visit to the domains upstairs Tredennis had learned a great deal of Richard Amory. He had found that he had a taste for mechanics, a taste for science, a taste for literature. He had a geological cabinet, an entomological collection, a collection of coins, of old books, of old engravings, all in different stages of incompleteness. He had, even, in his small workroom, the unfinished models of an invention or two, each of which he was ready to explain with an enthusiasm which flamed up as the demands of the moment required, in the most delightful and inspiring manner.

"I shall finish them all, one of these days," he said, blithely. "I am always interested in one or the other, and they give me an object. And, as I said downstairs, what a man wants is an object. That is what Larry stands in need of. Give him an object, and he would not indulge in that cold-blooded introspection and retrospection. Bertha has told him so herself."

"They are very good friends," said Tredennis.

"Oh, yes! They are fond of each other, in their way. It is their way to jeer a good deal, but they would stand by each other, I fancy, if the time came when it was needful."

He referred, in the course of the conversation, to his profession, and his reference to it caused Tredennis to class it in his mind, in some way or other, with the unfinished models and incomplete collections.

"I can't say I like the law," he said, "but it was a sort of final resource. I tried medicine for a while, — took a course of lectures; but it didn't suit me. And then two or three other things turned up, but I didn't seem to suit them. And so it ended in my choosing law, or letting it choose me. I don't know that I am exactly a success at it. It's well we don't depend on it. Bertha" — He broke off rather suddenly, and began again at once. "I have plans which, if they are as successful as they promise to be, will change the aspect of affairs." And he laughed exultantly.

On their way downstairs they came upon an open door, which had been closed as they went up. It opened into a large, cheerful room, with gay pictures on the walls, and a high brass fender guarding the glowing fire, before which a figure sat in a low rocking-chair, holding a child in its arms.

"That is the nursery," said Richard. "Bertha, what is the matter with Janey?"

It was Bertha who sat in the rocking-chair, and as she turned her face quietly toward them Tredennis felt himself betrayed into a slight start. Neither her eyes nor her color were as bright as they had been downstairs. She had taken off her ornaments, and they lay in a small glittering heap upon the stand at her side. The child's head rested upon her breast, and her bare arm and hand held its body in an easy position with a light, close, accustomed touch. She spoke in a soft, lowered voice.

"Janey is nervous to-night," she answered. "She cannot go to sleep, and I am trying to quiet her. Will you excuse me if I do not come down? She really needs me."

Chapter 6

When Tredennis found himself standing out in the street, half an hour later, it was this picture which remained in his mind, and no other. If an effort had been required to retain the impression upon his mental retina he would have made the effort with the deliberate intention of excluding all else; but no effort was needed.

"I suppose it is sentiment," he said, taking his cigar out of his mouth, and looking up at the starlit sky. "I have no doubt it is sentiment. A man who has lived mooning alone as long as I have, drifts in that direction naturally, I suppose. And I am a rigid, old-fashioned fellow. I don't fit in with the rest of it. But, with her child in her arms and her gewgaws laid on the table, I seemed to see something I knew. I'll think of that, and not of the other."

It was just at this moment that he caught sight of a figure approaching him from a distance of a few yards. It was the figure of a man, wrapped in a cloak, and walking with bent head at a leisurely pace, which argued that he was deep in meditation. As it drew nearer Tredennis recognized something familiar in its outlines, and before it had taken half-a-dozen steps forward the head was raised suddenly, almost as if attracted by something in his gaze, and he recognized the professor, who, seeing him, came toward him at once, and laid a friendly hand on his shoulder.

"You are coming away from the house, are you?" he said. "I might have known I should have the chance of meeting you when I came out to take my ramble before going to bed. I do it every night. I find I sleep better for it. Perhaps Bertha told you."

"No," answered Tredennis; "I had not been told of it."

The professor gave him a little impetus forward with the hand he still kept on his shoulder.

"Walk on with me," he said. "What I like is the deserted look of things, and the silence. There is nothing more silent and deserted than such a street as this at night. There is a quiet and emptiness about it which impress themselves on you more than the stillness of a desert. Perhaps it is the sleep around you in the houses, — the people who have lost their hold on the world and life for the time being. They are far enough away by this time, most of them, and we are no more certain where they are than we shall be after they have lain down for the last time. How did you find Bertha?"

His voice changed as he asked the question, dropping its key somewhat; and, quiet though its tone was, Tredennis thought he recognized a faint suggestion of consciousness in it.

"She looked very well," he answered; "and was very bright."

"She is generally that," said the professor. "Who was there?"

"A Mr. Arbuthnot."

"Arbuthnot! Yes; to be sure. He generally is there. He is a relative of Richard's. They are fond of him. I was to have been there myself, but I had a previous engagement. And I suppose they made light of each other, as usual?"

"You mean"— began Tredennis.

"Arbuthnot and Bertha. They always do it, and Richard looks on and enjoys it. He is a queer fellow."

"Mr. Amory?" Tredennis questioned, uncertainly.

"No, no; Arbuthnot. He is a queer fellow, Arbuthnot."

Tredennis laughed.

"That is what they said in the house," he responded.

"Well, it's true," said the professor, reflectively, "and there is no denying it."

"They said that, too," said Tredennis. "And Mrs. Amory added that it was a habit they had."

"I don't know," said the professor, still keeping his hand on Tredennis' shoulder, and seeming to study the pavement as he walked, — "I don't know what the man has done with his past, and I don't know what he is going to do with his future. I don't think he knows about the future himself."

"It struck me," said Tredennis, — "I don't know why, — that he did not care."

"That's it," said the professor. "He doesn't care."

They walked a few steps in silence, and then he went on:

"He never will care," he said, "unless something happens to rouse him."

"I am obliged to confess," said Tredennis, "that I am afraid I am prepared to underrate him. And it seemed to me that there wasn't much in him to rouse."

"Oh, you'll underrate him," returned the professor, "at first. And you may never get over it; but there are also ten chances to one that you do. I did."

"You began by underrating him?"

"I don't overrate him now," said the professor. "I don't know that I am particularly fond of him, though there have been moments — just moments — when I have been threatened with it. But I have come to the conclusion that there is something in him to rouse, and that it wouldn't be the wisest thing in the world to rouse it."

"Do you mean," said Tredennis, slowly, "that it would take a woman to rouse it?"

"Yes," answered the professor, just as slowly, "it would take a woman. And there are circumstances under which it would be better for the woman if she let what she might rouse lie and sleep."

"For instance?" said Tredennis, with a fierce leap of every pulse in his body.

"If," said the professor, deliberately, — "if she were not free to give what his feeling for her demanded."

He paused to turn Tredennis round.

"Confound him!" he said, with a curiously irritable seriousness. "If he once reached a white heat, — that fellow with his objectless follies, and his dress-coat, and his white necktie, and his opera hat under his arm, — if he once forgot them and himself, it would be her fate to remember him as long as her life should last."

"*Her* fate?" said Tredennis.

"I said it would have to be a woman," said the professor. "I should not like it to be a woman I felt an interest in. We have reached the end of the block. Let us walk back again."

When he spoke again it was of Richard Amory, not of Arbuthnot.

"You went upstairs into the Museum, as Bertha calls it?" he said.

"Yes," answered Tredennis; "and into the workroom."

"And saw the models, and the collections, and the books?"

"Yes."

"He has a good many enthusiasms, Richard," said the professor. "They might form a collection of themselves. He won't tire of life easily. He is a fine contrast to — the other."

They were nearing the house again by this time, and he glanced up at its front.

"There is a light in the nursery window," he said. "It must be one of Janey's restless nights."

"Yes," said Tredennis. "Mrs. Amory was with her when we came downstairs, and she told us that the child was nervous and needed her."

"She has wonderful patience with them," said the professor, "and a sort of genius for understanding their vague young needs and desires. She never does them an injustice for want of thought, and never fails them. I have seen her spend half an hour half-kneeling, half-sitting on the nursery floor, by one of them, with her arm round it, questioning it, and helping it to tell its own story, in a way that was very motherly. There is a great deal of the maternal instinct in her."

Tredennis made no reply, but there rose before his mental vision the picture before the nursery fire, and he saw again the soft, close clasp of the fair hand and arm.

"It's curious how seldom we speak of paternal instinct," the professor went on. "It is always maternal instinct. Well, it is a great thing. And it is a great safeguard where — where life is not satisfactory. And as one grows older one sees a good deal of that. It is pitiful sometimes, when one finds it, as one so often does, in young things who haven't got over their desperate mental insistence on their right to be happy."

He checked himself with a faint laugh.

"I'm prosing, my boy," he said. "I always do it when I take my saunter at night. It is a sort of safeguard against doing it in the day. And I find I am specially given to it when I talk of Bertha. It is the paternal instinct, if there is such a thing. You remember how we talked of her when she came home from school. Do you find her much changed?"

"She has changed from a girl — a child, almost — to a woman," said Tredennis.

"Yes," said the professor, "from a child to a woman. And yet, when you look back upon it, eight years is a very short time. Sometimes it seems only yesterday that she startled me at the dinner-table by saying that she expected me to classify and label her."

"There have been times," said Tredennis, "when it seemed only yesterday to me; but to-night it is something far away."

The professor looked up at him quickly.

"Is it?" he said. "Well, well," rather vaguely, "it is a habit they have fallen into, that of making light of things. It is a kind of fashion nowadays. She did not treat things lightly then, did she? How she believed all that she believed — how frankly she impugned your veracity in argument, without being at all conscious of the incivility! How bright her eyes and lips were when she asked me if she could not have the label without the pin! I wish" —

He stopped suddenly once more.

"We have reached the end of the block again, my boy," he said, "and I have walked long enough, and talked long enough. We must say good-night to each other."

They were standing beneath a street-lamp, and having looked up at Tredennis to say this, he drew back a pace to look again, in whimsically gentle admiration of his stalwart proportions.

"What a soldierly fellow you are!" he said; "and how you stand out among the rest of us!" And then, with an odd change of manner, he drew nearer, and laid his hand on his shoulder once more. "I'll say again," he said, "what I have said before. I wish you had been a son of mine, my boy."

And, as he said it, there fell upon the quiet of the street the sound of approaching footsteps ringing on the pavement, and, turning instinctively toward them, each saw an easily recognized masculine figure, which, reaching the house in which the Amorys lived, paused for a moment beneath the lighted window, and flung forth to the night, airily, and by no means unmusically, a few bars of one of the popular airs from a gay French opera, and then, crossing the street, applied a latch-key to the door of the opposite house, and, entering, closed it.

"The fellow has a pleasant voice," said the professor. "It is a voice you like to hear. And that is one of his whims."

"I thought I recognized the figure," said Tredennis.

"It is"—

"Arbuthnot," said the professor. "Arbuthnot." And then they parted.

Chapter 7

To Tredennis the next three months were full of event. It was mostly quiet event, and yet, as day followed day, he was conscious that, in each twenty-four hours, he lived through some new mental experience which left its mark upon him. The first two weeks seemed to make his old regular, routine-governed life a thing of the far past, from which he was entirely separated by a gulf which it would be impossible to recross. He awakened to a recognition of this at the end of the second week, and told himself that the feeling was due to the complete novelty of his surroundings and their natural influences upon him. He found himself placed among people whose lives, ambitions, and interests were all new to him, and of a kind with which he had never before been thrown into close contact for a length of time sufficient to allow of analysis. In his first visit to Washington he had regarded its peculiarities merely as an amateur and a visitor; now he saw and studied them from a different stand-point. The public buildings were no longer mere edifices in his eyes, but developed into tremendous communities, regulated by a tremendous system for which there could be no medium or indefinite standing, but which must either be a tremendous credit or a tremendous discredit to itself and the power it represented. The human side of the place grew and impressed itself upon him. He began to feel the full significance of the stream of humanity which ebbed and flowed to and from these buildings at stated hours in the day. After a few afternoon walks on the Avenue he could recognize many a face that passed him, and comprehend something of what it typified. He could single out the young woman who supported her family upon her salary, and the young woman who bought her ribbons with it; the widow whose pay fed half-a-dozen children, and the husband whose earnings were appropriated by a wife of fashionable aspirations; the man of broken career, whose wasted ambitions and frustrated purposes were buried in the monotonous routine of a Government clerkship, and who asked and hoped for no greater boon than to be permitted to hold his place through as much of the future as remained to him. It was an orderly and respectably dressed crowd, as a rule; but there was many a sad face to be seen in it, and many an anxious and disappointed one. It never failed to interest Tredennis, and he took his afternoon walk so often at the same hour that the passers-by began to know his tall, soldierly figure and sunbrowned face, and rather expected to encounter them; and when the newspapers had referred to him on a dozen occasions or so, there were not a few who recognized him, and pointed him out to each other as something of a celebrity and a hero, and so worth seeing.

This general knowledge which people seemed to have of one another was one thing which struck him as peculiarly local. It was the rule, and not the exception, that in walking out he met persons he knew or knew of, and he found it at no time difficult to discover the names and positions of those who attracted his attention. Almost all noticeable and numerous unnoticeable persons were to be distinguished in some way from their fellows. The dark, sinewy man he observed standing on the steps of a certain family hotel was a noted New England senator; his companion was the head of an important department; the man who stood near was the private secretary of the President, or the editor of one of the dailies, or a man with a much-discussed claim against the Government; the handsome woman whose carriage drew up before a fashionable millinery establishment was the wife of a foreign diplomat, or of a well-known politician, or of a member of the Cabinet; the woman who crossed her path as she got out was a celebrated female suffragist, or female physician, or lawyer, or perhaps that much-talked of will-o'-the-wisp, a female lobbyist; and eight persons out of every ten passing them knew their names and not a little of their private history. So much was crowded within a comparatively limited radius that it was not easy for any person or thing worthy of note to be lost or hidden from the public eye.

By the most natural gradations Tredennis found the whole tenor of his existence changed in this atmosphere. His fixed habits of life gave way before the influences surrounding him.

One of the most subtle of these influences was that of his intimacy with the members of the Amory household, which grew as he had not at all anticipated that it would. He had thought of the acquaintance in the first place as one not likely to ripen into anything beyond its rather conventional significance. Perhaps, on the whole, he had been content to let it rest as it was, feeling only half-consciously that he should be in a quieter frame of mind and less liable to vague pangs and disappointments.

"It is all different," he had said to himself. "And it is all over. It is better that it should remain as it is."

But after his first visit Richard did not choose to lose sight of him. It was his fancy to seek him out and make much of and take possession of him, with an amiability and frank persistence in the chase which were at once complimentary and engaging.

"Look here!" he would say, having followed him up to reproach him. "You don't suppose we intend to be treated in this manner? We won't hear of it. We want you. Your stalwart solidity is what we have been needing to give us weight and balance. Only yesterday Bertha was holding you up to Arbuthnot as a model of steadfastness of purpose. We thought we were going to see you every other day, at least, and you have not been near us for a week. Bertha wonders what we have been guilty of."

And then he would be carried up to luncheon or dinner, or to spend the evening; and each visit resulted in another and another, until it gradually became the most natural thing in the world that he should drop in at odd hours, because it seemed that he was always expected, and he appeared to have a place among them.

"Do you know what we shall do with you if you remain here a year?" Bertha had said to him at the outset. "We shall domesticate you. We not only domesticated Mr. Arbuthnot, but we appropriated him. We feel that we have invested largely in him, and that he ought to respect our rights and pay interest. Sometimes I wonder how he likes it, and just now it occurs to me to wonder how you would like it."

"The question is," Tredennis answered, "how *you* would like it."

He was always conscious of a silent distaste for being compared to Mr. Arbuthnot, and he was also always conscious of the youthful weakness of the feeling.

"It is the kind of thing which belongs to a younger man," he used to say to himself. "It is arrant folly; and yet I am not fond of the fellow."

But, as Bertha had predicted, he became in a manner domesticated in the household. Perhaps the truth was that his natural tendency was toward the comfort and easy communion of home-life. He was a little surprised to find himself develop a strong fancy for children. He had never been averse to them, but he had known nothing of them, and had never suspected himself of any definite disposition to fondness for them. After he had watched Bertha's during a few visits he began to like them, and to be oddly interested in their sayings and doings. He discovered Jack to be a decidedly sturdy and masculine little fellow, with rather more than his share of physical strength and beauty; and, making amicable advances toward him, was met half-way with a fearless readiness which was very attractive. Then he made friends with Janey, and found himself still more interested. Her childish femininity was even better worth studying than Jack's miniature manhood. She was a small, gentle creature, with clinging hands and much faith, but also with a delightful sense of infantile dignity, and the friendship which established itself between them was a very absorbing sentiment. It was not long before it became an understood thing among the juvenile portion of the establishment that Tredennis was to be counted among the spoils. His incoming was greeted with rapture, his outgoing was regarded as a species of calamity only to be borne because it was unavoidable. He could tell stories of Indians and bears, and on more than one occasion was decoyed into the nursery, and found to be not entirely without resources in the matter of building forts with blocks, and defending them against aboriginal warriors with tin soldiers. His own sense of enjoyment of the discovery of these accomplishments in himself filled him with a whimsical pleasure. He began to carry toys in his pockets, and became a connoisseur of such dainties as were considered harmless to the juvenile constitution; and after having been reproved by Janey, on two or three occasions, for the severity of his air, he began also to have a care that the expression of his countenance should be less serious and more likely to win the approval of innocent small creatures, who considered gravity uncalled for and mysterious. At first he had seemed to learn but little of Bertha herself, notwithstanding that a day seldom passed without their meeting, and there were times when he fancied he had determined that there was but little to learn. The gayeties of the season over, she announced her intention of resting; and her manner of accomplishing this end was to inaugurate a series of small festivities, with a result of occupying each day until midnight. She gave small, informal dinners, suppers, and teas to the favored few who would be most likely to enjoy and find them exhilarating, and, when she did not give a dinner or tea, her evenings were bestowed upon Arbuthnot and half a dozen of the inner circle, whose habit it was to drop in and talk politics, literature, or entertaining nonsense.

At such times it was not at all unusual for the professor to ramble in at about nine o'clock, and profess to partake of the cup of tea Bertha offered him, and which he invariably left more than half full upon the small table by his chair. His old tender interest in her had not lessened in degree, Tredennis noticed, after seeing them together on two or three occasions, but it had altered in kind. Sometimes the look of curious speculation returned to his eyes, but oftener they expressed a patient, kindly watchfulness. It was not long before Tredennis began to observe that this quietly watchful look generally showed itself when Arbuthnot was present. The first time that he felt the full force of the truth of this was one evening when there had been only two or three callers, who had remained but a short time, going away early, and leaving no one in the parlors but himself, the professor, and Arbuthnot.

Arbuthnot had come in later than usual, and had appeared to be in an unusual mood. He was pale when he entered, and had no jesting speech to make. He took his seat by Bertha, and replied to her remarks with but little of his customary animation, now and then lapsing into silence as if he had forgotten his surroundings. Bertha seemed inclined to let his humor pass without notice, as if it was not exactly a new experience; but Richard commented upon it.

"Something has gone wrong," he said. "What is it, Larry?"

"Nothing has gone wrong," Arbuthnot answered, with a short, cheerless laugh. "I have seen a ghost, that is all."

"A ghost!" said Bertha, in a low voice, and then sat silent, guarding her face from the fire with her favorite peacock-feather screen.

The professor began to stir his tea round and round, which exercise was his customary assistance to reflection or debate. He glanced at the peacock-feather screen, and then at Arbuthnot.

"A ghost is always an interesting scientific conundrum," he observed. "What form did it take?"

Arbuthnot laughed his short, cheerless laugh again.

"It took the form of a sanguine young man from the West," he said, "who has just come into a twelve-hundred-dollar clerkship, and feels that unending vistas of fortune lie before him. He was in such good spirits about it that I rather lost my hold on myself, and said things I might as well have left unsaid."

"What did you say?" Richard asked.

"I told him that if he had money enough left to buy a return ticket home he had better buy one; and that, if he had not, I would lend it to him. I told him that at his age it wasn't a bad idea for a man to devote his time to establishing himself in some career he could depend on; and that, in default of having the energy to do that, he might reflect on the alternative of blowing his brains out as a preparation for a peaceful old age. And I told him that I had seen young fellows like himself before, and that the end had been for them what it would be for him."

"Well?" said Richard, as he had stopped.

"It wasn't any use," he answered. "I knew it would not be when I began. I simply made a spectacle of myself in a quiet way to no purpose, and as a result I am uncomfortable. It was all nonsense, but he reminded me" —

"Of what?" said Richard, since he had paused again.

A peculiar expression crossed his face. Tredennis saw him glance at the peacock-feather screen, and as quickly glance away.

"Of — a young fellow of his age I — used to know," he answered.

"What was *his* story?" inquired Richard, with his usual desire for information. "Where is he now?"

"Dead," said Arbuthnot, and, singularly enough, he half laughed again as he tossed his cigar into the grate and went to the piano.

He began to sing in a rather low voice, and while he sang the rest listened. When he referred to his musical efforts it was his habit to treat them as but trivial performances; but he allowed them to lose none of their effectiveness through lack of care and culture. He knew wherein his power lay, and used it well. Tonight, for some reason, this power was at its strongest, and, as he sang song after song, even Tredennis was compelled to acknowledge that, if it was his object to produce an emotional effect, he was in a fair way to succeed.

Richard threw himself upon a sofa and gave himself up to him with characteristic readiness to be moved, the professor stirred his tea slowly and mechanically, and Bertha sat still in the shadow of her screen. But it was she who moved first. In the midst of one of the songs she left her seat, slowly crossed the room to the piano, and stood near it, leaning against the dark wall, her slight white figure thrown into strong relief, her hands — one of them still holding the peacock-feather screen — fallen at her sides, her eyes resting on Arbuthnot's averted face. It seemed to Tredennis that she had moved in obedience to some impulse of whose power she was scarcely conscious. He saw that she also was pale, and looked worn with fatigue, and he was filled, as he had been more than once before, with secret resentment of the fact that no one but himself appeared to notice that she had changed even within the last month.

Arbuthnot continued playing. It was evident that she had not intended to distract his attention when she approached him, and he did not look at or speak to her. As she stood listening, it seemed as if she had forgotten everything but the influence his voice exerted over her for the time being, and that she allowed it to carry her whither it would. Something in the soft, absorbed expression of her face reminded Tredennis vaguely of the look she had worn when she turned to brood over his words on the night when he had felt nearest to her. He was thinking this when a movement from the professor attracted his attention, — a jingling of the teaspoon, a little crash, an exclamation of dismay and confusion, and the little stand had mysteriously been overturned, and the professor was ruefully bending down to pick up the fragments of his small cup and saucer.

"My dear child!" he said to Bertha, who had started forward to his rescue, "what a stupid old Vandal I am, and what an insecure little table to betray me with — and in the midst of Schubert's 'Serenade,' too, which Mr. Arbuthnot was giving us in his most effective manner! Suppose you take me up into the nursery, as an example to the children, while you dry my coat."

He went out of the room with her, his hand upon her shoulder, and Arbuthnot left the piano, and returned to the fire. The spell had been broken with the cup and saucer, and the "Serenade" remained unfinished. He produced a fresh cigar, — which luxury was one of many accorded him in the household, — lighted it, and, rather to Tredennis' surprise, resumed his conversation as if there had been no pause in it.

"The fellow will be an annoyance to me every day of his life," he said, faint lines showing themselves upon his forehead in spite of the half-smile which was meant to deprive them of their significance. "I know that, confound him! He is in my room, and I shall have the benefit of every change in him, and it will be a grind — there's no denying that it will be a grind."

"I should like to know," said Tredennis, "what the changes will be."

"The changes will depend upon the kind of fellow he chances to be," said Arbuthnot. "There are two varieties. If there is a good deal in him he will begin by being hopeful and working hard. He will think that he may make himself of value in his position and create a sort of career for himself. He will do more than is required of him, and neglect nothing. He will keep his eyes open and make friends of the men about him. He will do that for a few months, and then, suddenly, and for no fault whatever, one of these friends will be dropped out. Knowing the man to be as faithful as himself, it will be

66

a shock to him, and he will get anxious, and worry over it. He will see him stranded without resources, struggling to regain his place or get another, treated with amiable tolerance when he is not buffeted, snubbed, and put off. He will see him hanging about day after day, growing shabbier, more care-worn, more desperate, until he disappears and is heard of no more, and everybody is rather relieved than not. He may have been a family man, with a wife and half-a-dozen children all living decently on his salary. Somebody else wanted his place and got it, not because of superior fitness for it, but because the opposing influence was stronger than his. The new man will go through the same experience when his turn comes — that is all. Well, my friend will see this and be anxious, and ask questions and find out that his chances are just the same — no more and no less. He will try not to believe it, being young enough to be betrayed into the folly, and he will work harder than ever, and get over his blow a little until he sees the same thing happen again and again. Then he will begin to lose some of his good spirits; he will be a trifle irritable at times, and lines will show themselves on his face, and he won't be so young. When he writes to the girl he is in love with, — I saw a letter addressed to some young woman out West, lying on his desk to-day, — she will notice a change in him, and the change will reveal itself more in each letter; but he will hang on and grind away, and each election will be a nightmare to him. But he will grind away. And, then, at last" —

He stopped and made a light, rather graceful gesture with his fingers.

"What then?" demanded Tredennis, with manifest impatience.

"There will be a new administration, and, if he struggles through, it will be worse for him than if he were dropped, as in that case he throws away another four years of his life and all the chances for a future they might hold if he were free to avail himself of them."

Tredennis stood up, looking very large under the influence of the feeling which disturbed him. Arbuthnot himself was not entirely unimpressed by his quick movement and the energy it expressed.

"You treat the matter coolly," he exclaimed, as he rose.

Arbuthnot turned his attention to his cigar.

"Yes," he replied. "I treat it coolly. If I treated it warmly or hotly the effect produced would be about the same. My influence upon civil service is just what it might be expected to be, and no more. Its weight is easily carried."

"I beg your pardon," said Tredennis, feeling the justice and adroitness of the speech.

"Not at all," Arbuthnot answered. "It is not necessary. It makes you lose your hold on yourself to be brought face to face with the thing. It is quite natural. It has had the same effect on me, and I am a cold-blooded fellow, and a frivolous fellow into the bargain."

"I have never thought of the matter before," said Tredennis, disturbedly. "I feel as if my indifference is something to be ashamed of."

"If you give your attention as a duty to such subjects," was Arbuthnot's response, "you will be kept actively employed. If you take my advice, you will let them alone."

"The trouble is," said Tredennis, "that every one seems to let them alone."

Richard regarded him, from his place on the sofa-cushions, delightedly.

"Here's an example for you, Larry," he said. "Profit by him. Everything is an object to him, — everything is worth while. He is an example to us all. Let us all profit by him."

"Oh, he began right," laughed Arbuthnot.

"He began where you began," returned Richard.

"I?" was the airy answer; "I never began at all. That is my little difficulty. I am the other one. I told you there was another one. I represent him."

Tredennis regarded him steadily. For the first time in the course of their acquaintance he began to suspect him. His manner was too light altogether, and the odd shade which had fallen upon his eyes before during the evening showed itself again.

"Let us hear about the other one," he said.

"He is easily disposed of," was the answer. "There was nothing of him at the outset. He came to his place without an object. He liked the idea of living in Washington, and of spending his salary. We will say he was a rather well-looking young fellow, and could dance and sing a little, and talk decently well. He had no responsibilities, and never thought of the future. His salary clothed him, and allowed him little luxuries and ordinary pleasures. He spent it when he had it, and made debts when it was gone. Being presentable, he was invited out, and made himself useful and entertaining in a small way. When he thought of the possibilities of his career being brought suddenly to a close, he was uncomfortable, so he preferred not to think of it. It is not a pleasant thing to reflect that a man has about ten years in which to begin life, and that after that he is ending it; but it is true. What he does from twenty to thirty he will be likely to find he must abide by from thirty to seventy, if he lives that long. This man, like the better one, has thrown away the years in which he might have been preparing himself to end decently. When they are gone he has nothing to show for them, and less than nothing. He is the feather upon the current, and when all is over for him he is whirled out of sight and forgotten with the rest. And, perhaps, if he had felt there was anything to be gained by his being a steady, respectable fellow, he might have settled down into one."

He got up suddenly, with a gesture as if he would shake himself free of his mood.

"Here," he said, "I'm going! It is quite time. It's all nonsense talking it over. It is the old story. I have made myself uncomfortable for nothing. Confound you, Dick, why did you let me begin? Say good-night to the professor and Mrs. Amory for me."

"Come back!" called Richard. "Bertha will want to hear the rest of the 'Serenade' when she comes down."

"The 'Serenade'!" he said, derisively. "No, thank you. You have had enough of me, and I have had too much of myself."

He passed into the hall just as the professor descended from the nursery and through the open door. Tredennis heard what they said to each other.

"You did not finish the 'Serenade,'" said the professor.

"No," was the reply; "and I am afraid you were resigned to it, Professor."

"You were singing it very well, and with great effect," the professor responded, amicably.

"You are very kind to say so," Arbuthnot answered. "Good-night, sir."

"Good-night," replied the professor, as he entered the parlor.

As he did so Tredennis heard the sound of feet upon the stairs, and caught a glimpse of Bertha's white figure as she came down.

"You are not going?" he heard her say.

"Yes."

She had reached the last step by this time, and stood with her hand resting upon the balustrade, and she was paler than she had been before.

"I —" she began — "I wanted to talk to you. What is it, Larry?"

Tredennis had never heard her call him by his first name before; and he felt, with a keenness which startled him, the soft naturalness with which it fell from her lips.

Arbuthnot's voice itself had altered when he answered her.

"It is nothing," he said, "but that I am not exactly in a presentable humor, and I want to go and conceal myself. It is the best thing I can do. Good-night."

He held out his hand, touched hers lightly, and then turned away, and the door opened and closed after him, and Bertha came into the parlor, moving slowly, as if she felt tired.

Chapter 8

When Tredennis rose to take his leave, the professor rose also.

"I will go with you," he said. "And if you will, you shall give me a few minutes of your time before going home. I have some new books to show you."

They went out together; but, until they reached the other house and entered the library, very little was said. The catastrophe of the broken teacup, or something of greater moment, seemed to occupy the professor's thoughts. By the time they took their accustomed chairs he appeared to have forgotten the new books. His thoughtful face wore so sadly perplexed a look that he even seemed older than usual.

Tredennis awaited his first words in silence. His quiet fondness for him had become a very warm and tender feeling during the past months. It had been his pleasure to try to be of use to him. He had studied his needs, and endeavored to supply them; he had managed to share hours with him which might otherwise have been lonely; he had brought to him the stir of the outside working world when he seemed to require its stimulant; he had placed his own vigor and endurance at his disposal without seeming to do so, and his efforts at making his rather lonely life a brighter and more attractive thing had not been in vain. It was to him the professor turned in his moments of fatigue and necessity, and it was to him he turned now.

"I am going to do a curious thing," he said. — "I am going to do a curious thing; but I think it is the best thing and the simplest."

"The simplest thing is always the best," said Tredennis, more because there was a pause than because he felt an answer was needed.

"Yes, yes," said the professor, seriously. "I think so. And it is easier to be simple with you, my boy, than with another man. It is your way to be direct and serious. You always had the habit. It never was your way to trifle. It is rather the fashion to trifle nowadays, you know, but you, — I have always liked it in you that you were not a trifler."

"No," answered Tredennis; "I have not trifled much. It may have been against me. Sometimes I have thought it was. I cannot count it among my merits, at any rate. I am a grim fellow by nature."

"No," said the professor. "Not a grim fellow. A silent fellow, and rather unyielding with yourself, but" —

He stopped, and looked up at him with a simple affection which made the young man's heart beat as a woman's glance might have done.

"I think you know I love you," he said. "I have begun to depend on you and count you among my luxuries. I am an old man, and my luxuries are worth a great deal to me. No kindly, thoughtful act of yours has been unregarded, and I have liked your fancy for me almost as a girl likes the attentions of her first lover. Sometimes it has pleased me to be half sentimental over them, and half sentimental over you."

Tredennis flushed with pleasure and warm feeling. He rose impulsively and crossed the hearth.

"I never say things well," he said, "but I should like to try to put into words something of what I feel. You once said you wished I was your son, and I have been glad to remember it. I have no ties. Let your wish be a sort of tie between us. It is a tie I should be proud of, and glad to honor and make an object in my life. Give me what affection you can. I wish for it and need it. If I had been your son you would have counted on me; give me the pleasure and comfort of knowing you count on me now. It has somehow seemed my lot to have no place in the lives of others. Give me this, if I am worth it. I shall be better for it, and happier."

The professor gave him a quiet, half-wistful glance.

"I gave it to you long ago," he said, at length. "The wish has been a tie between us from the first."

And he said it even with a touch of solemnity.

"If it had not been," he added, afterward, "I should not have come to you with my trouble to-night, — feeling so sure that you would understand it."

He made a gesture with his hand.

"Go and walk up and down the room there, as I am used to seeing you," he said. "And I will tell you about it."

Tredennis did as he bade him, — went to the other side of the room and began his measured march.

"We talked of Bertha in this very room years ago," he began. "It seems to be our lot to talk of Bertha. I am going to speak of her again."

Tredennis continued his measured tramp without speaking.

The professor rested his forehead upon his hand and sat so, looking downward. He went on in a quiet voice, and with a quiet, absorbed manner, — the manner of a man who, having the habit of close and careful study, was giving his whole attention simply and carefully to his subject.

"I shall have to go back to that night and repeat something I said then," he went on. "It was that her only hope for happiness would lie in her marriage with a man she loved deeply."

"I remember it," Tredennis answered.

"And I added that the chances were that, instead, she would marry the man who loved her."

"I remember that too."

The professor sighed heavily and wearily.

"The chances were too many," he said. "She married the man who loved her."

Tredennis had marched one length of the room before he continued: —

"He did love her," the professor said, after his pause, "tempestuously — overwhelmingly. Overwhelmingly is a good word to use. He overwhelmed her in the end. At first she liked him; but when the nature of his feeling for her began to express itself, it is my impression that she felt a secret fear of and dislike to it. She tried to avoid him, but he absolutely refused to allow it. He followed her, and was picturesquely wretched before her eyes. There is no denying he was picturesque. That was his strong point. He was picturesque and pathetic

— and poetic. She was only a girl, and she was tremendously at a disadvantage before him. When she treated him badly he bore it with tender patience, and he devoted himself to her with a faithfulness which might have touched a heart harder and more experienced than hers was, poor child! Of course his picturesque unhappiness and his poetic magnanimity told; I knew they would, and they did. Reaction set in, and she began to feel the fascination of making him happy."

He stopped, and suddenly lifted his head.

"My boy," he said, "one of the most damnable things in life is a fascination like that in the mind of a generous, ignorant creature!"

He dropped his head again.

"That is strong language," he said, "and I don't often use strong language. I — don't consider it gentlemanly, but I felt strongly at the moment, and the word is — expressive. Well, the time came when, in a moment when her mood being softer and more sympathetic than usual, and she herself, as a consequence, at a greater disadvantage than ever, — she committed herself; and then it was all over. The trouble is, that the experience of a woman of forty is what a girl needs when she chooses her husband at twenty, and, as the two things are incompatible, the chances are always against her. Bertha had the faults and follies that I told you go to make a martyr. When she had made her mistake, she was strong and weak enough to abide by it. It is mostly imagination in matters of this kind; it was imagination in hers. She was young enough to believe in everything. She believed that if she broke her engagement she would break Amory's heart and ruin his life for him. There was no danger of either catastrophe, but they were realities to her, and they terrified her. Then she had never been touched by any deeper feeling than the anxious tenderness he awakened in her. She had not been given to sentiments, and, Iam afraid, had regarded them rather contemptuously in others. She had no conception of a feeling stronger than herself, and held curiously obstinate and lofty views of the conduct of women who did not hold their emotions neatly in check. Her girlish bigotry was touching to me sometimes, because it was so thorough, and revealed such ignorance. I wish — I wish I could hear something of it now!"

Tredennis had reached the end of the room. He turned sharply, but recovered himself and said nothing.

"Lately," the professor added slowly, "she has been more silent on such subjects than she used to be."

He lifted his head from his hand and looked at Tredennis again.

"Philip," he said, "I — I wish to heaven chance had sent you to us that year."

Tredennis stopped in his walk, a dark and rigid figure in the shadow.

"Had sent me?" he said, in a strained voice. "Me! What — could *I* have done?"

"I — I don't know," answered the professor;" but I solemnly believe, my boy, that *if* you had come, you would have averted an evil."

"Then," said Tredennis, "I wish to God I had!"

"I say it," said the professor, "with all the more certainty, remembering, as I do, one day when she wished for you herself."

"She!" said Tredennis. "Bertha? Bertha?"

"Yes, Bertha herself. It was a few weeks before her marriage, and she had not been exactly herself for a week or more. One evening I came into the parlor and found the room full of the odor of flowers. Amory had been with her and had left her a bouquet of heliotrope. She had some on her knee as she sat on a low seat before the fire. When I seated myself near her, she looked up at me suddenly and said, in a rather unsteady voice, 'Papa, I have been thinking about Philip Tredennis. I have not thought of him for a long time. I should like to see him. I — wish he could come back.' She half laughed at herself as she said it, but her laugh was nervous, and when I said to her, 'Why? Were *you* great friends? I did not know that,' she tried to laugh again, and answered, 'Yes — no — not exactly. But it seems to me that he was a strong sort of person, and sensible, and — and you might rely on his decisions. It is only a fancy, I suppose — but it just came into my mind that I should like to see him again.' There is no doubt, in my mind, that she felt a need of your obstinate strength, which she did not comprehend wholly herself. I wish you had come — I wish from my soul you had!"

"I might have come if I had known," said Tredennis, in a low tone.

"There was nothing — *nothing* to have stood in my way." And he turned and began his walk again.

The professor sighed, as he had sighed before — heavily and drearily.

"But you did not," he said. "And she married Amory."

"I should like to know," asked Tredennis, "if you think she is unhappy now. Do not tell me if you do not wish."

The professor's reply was very simple and direct.

"She has never been given to taking sentimental views of herself," he said, "and she is self-controlled and fond of her children, but she has never been happy for an hour since her marriage. I think the first year was very bitter to her. Amory has always been very fond of her; he is fond of her now, but her illusions concerning his passion for her soon died. She found out in two months that he would not have perished if she had discarded him. She had been his one object at first, but she was only one of a dozen others after they were married. He was amiable and delightful, but he was not always considerate. The picturesqueness of his attitude toward her was lost. He did not require her care and sympathy, and the sacrifices she made for him were very simple and natural matters in his eyes.

"In the beginning she was, perhaps, bewildered and desperate; but, girl as she was, she was too proud and just not to see that her youth and ignorance had led her into a folly, and that the result was its natural punishment. Once she said to me, 'The worse punishments in life are the punishments for ignorance — the worst, the worst!' And I knew what she meant, though she said no more. When her first child was born, she went down to the door of death, and her physicians said there seemed to be a lack of effort. And yet, I tell you she might have been the happiest young mother in the world. When she has been near happiness at all it has been in her quiet moments with her children. If it had not been for her children she might have been a harder and more heartless creature than she can ever be now. If she had been something less and slighter than fate made her she might have been either a dull nurse and house-keeper or a vapid woman of society; in either case she would have been happier than she is to-day. What a long story it is, and I did not think it would be so long when I began."

"I want to hear it all," broke in Tredennis, — "every word. I have not understood the changes I saw in her. I want to understand."

"That brings me to the point of it all," was the reply. "If she had been a laborer's wife she might have been too hard-worked to be restless; but she has had leisure, and social duties, and she has set herself deliberately the desperate task of making them her pleasures. She has found an exhilaration in them which has given her no time for regrets. She is a woman, young, attractive, and spirited. She was too full of spirit to permit herself to be subdued by her disappointment. As she cannot retrieve her mistake, she will make the best of it. She has reasoned herself into a belief that she is satisfied with what fortune has given her, and so long as that belief remains unshaken, she will be as happy as nine women out of ten are. Women are not happy, as a rule, Philip; they are not happy. I have learned that."

"But so long as her belief remains unshaken" — said Tredennis.

The professor interrupted him, gravely, sadly.

"That is the point," he said. "My fear is that it is shaken now."

Tredennis stopped in the middle of the room — stood quite still.

"She has had friends and admirers," said the professor, "scores of them. Perhaps all the more because she has cared less for them than they for her. She has a pretty trick of making the best of people, and it wins the public heart. She has friends, acquaintances, and even harmless devotees; but among them all there is only one man who gauges her, and that man is the one who very naturally presents himself to your mind as a fair dandy, with a ready tongue and good manners."

"Arbuthnot!" exclaimed Tredennis. "Arbuthnot!"

The professor smiled faintly.

"What," he said, "you recognize him at once! Well, my one vanity is my pride in my private knowledge of the thought of others. I am very proud of it, in a senile way. I have been studying and classifying all my life, and "how I sit and look on, and treat human beings as I have treated insects. If it had not been so, I should not have known so much of Bertha. Yes, Arbuthnot. Among all the men she knows and has known — diplomats, literati, politicians, honest men — I have found only one to disturb me, and that one Laurence Arbuthnot."

Tredennis stood still, looking down at the floor, with folded arms.

77

"I" — he began, "I have thought" —

The professor started.

"What!" he exclaimed. "*You* have thought? If you have thought — it must be plainer than I feared."

"No," said Tredennis, hurriedly. "Do not let that trouble you. What I have thought is so trivial and vague that it should not weigh at all. It has only been because I remembered her girlhood, and — and I thought her changed — and did not understand."

"Ah!" said the professor, letting his face fall upon both his hands. "That is not *his* trouble; *he* understands, and that is his strength. He has had his evil hour, that composed, well-dressed fellow, and he did not come out of it without scars. He covers them well, with his light overcoat and the rose in his buttonhole, but they are there, and they have made him wise. He has been silent, but he has looked on too, — as I have, — and he has seen what others were blind to. She has never suspected him, but his knowledge has given him power. When her *mauvais quart d'heure* has come upon her he has known what to say and what to avoid saying, and while she has not comprehended his motives she has been grateful to him. She has liked his songs and his readiness, and his unsentimental air, and she has unconsciously learned to rely on him. Her first sincere liking for him arose from her discovery of his inconsistent and incongruous knack with the children. She had thought of him as a rather clever, selfish, well-mannered creature, and once in a juvenile crisis he surprised her by developing natural gifts — somewhat cold-blooded, but still amazingly effective.

The children began to be fond of him, and his path was smoothed. She began to be fond of him herself, genuinely and simply, and if it had ended there she would have been safer than before. But it did not end there, I suppose. The cup and saucer were not broken too soon this evening, — they were not broken soon enough."

"It was not an accident?" exclaimed Tredennis.

"No, it was not an accident. I have heard his 'Serenade' before. There is the danger. He means no harm; but his 'Serenade,' and the moments when what is past gets the better of him, and the little touches of passion his overcoat won't always cover, and the bits of sincerity he struggles against and she ponders over, are good for neither him nor her. I have heard his 'Serenade' before; but to-night, when she got up and followed him as if he had called her, and — and she had only half heard his voice and yet must obey it; and when she stood there against the wall, with her pale face, and her soft eyes fixed on him, it was time for some common thing to happen to bring her back to life, — and the cup and saucer were offered as the sacrifice."

He said it whimsically, and yet sadly.

"Poor child!" he added. "Poor child! I dare say it was hard enough."

He paused a moment, and then rose, went to Tredennis' side, and laid his hand on his shoulder.

"There," he said, — "there is the confession, and I can make my appeal to you with fewer words."

"Your appeal?" Tredennis repeated.

"I can ask you for your help."

"If there is any help I can give which is worth the asking and giving," said Tredennis, slowly, "you know it will be yours."

"Yes, I know it will be mine, and so I ask it easily. And what I ask is this. Let us walk slowly while we talk, and I will keep my hand on your shoulder, — I like to feel your support. What I would say is this: if you had been my son, you would have watched over her and stood between her and any pain which could threaten her. You know that what I fear for her now is only the desperate, hopeless misery such an experience as this would be sure to bring her if it were allowed to ripen; for her there is nothing else to fear. No, I know I need not have said that to you."

"No," answered Tredennis, "there was no need to say it."

"She does not know herself. I know her, and know what such an experience holds for her. Better that her life should be barren to the end than that she should bear what she must bear if her heart is once awakened."

"Better!" said Tredennis.

He felt the tremulous hand weigh heavily upon him.

"I am an old man," he was answered. "I have lived my life nearly to its close, and I say a *thousand* times better! I married a woman I did not love, and I loved a woman I could not marry."

"And you wished to ask me," said Tredennis, breaking the short silence which followed.

"I ask you to defend her against this pain. If I were a younger and stronger man, I might do for her what I ask of you; but I cannot often be with her. You are with her day after day. She likes you."

"I have fancied," Tredennis said, "that she did *not* like me."

"It is only fancy. She sees in you the strength she vaguely longed for when she was at the turning-point of her life. Let her feel that it is always near her, and that she may rely upon it now. You are fond of her children, — talk to her of them. When you see her inclined to be silent and unlike herself, bring them to her mind; when that fellow is there, manage that she shall think of them. Her tenderness for them is your stronghold and mine. To-night, why did I take her to the nursery? Because they lay asleep there, and when she saw them she stopped to cover them more warmly, and touch them with her hand, and bend to kiss them, and forgot her 'Serenade.' She loves them better than she loves anything else on earth, — better than she could love anything else, perhaps. That's her woman's way. God made it so. That is the one help and safeguard He gave to women out of the whole bitter universe. Bring her back to her children at her saddest and weariest, and when the fight is hardest, and they will beat the rest back. It is Nature. You will do what I ask, I know.

"I shall be more at ease," he said next, "that I have asked this of you. When you are with her I shall feel that she is safe. I trust her in your hands."

"I will try to be worthy of the trust."

"It is rather a strange one to repose in a man of your age, but I give it to you with the rest, — it goes with the tie you wished for. It is a relief to me to share it with a strong fellow who can bear it well."

They talked a little longer, walking across the floor two or three times together, and then Tredennis went away. He was in a strange frame of mind. It was almost as if he had received a blow which had partially stunned him. When he reached the street he stood for a moment looking up at the starlit sky.

"A strong fellow," he said. "*Am* I such a strong fellow? And *I* am to stand between you and your lover, — *I*? That is a strange thing, Bertha — a strange thing."

And, rousing himself suddenly, he strode down the street, and the professor, who had gone to his room, heard his military tread ringing steady and measured upon the pavement, and felt a vague comfort in the sound.

Chapter 9

During the next few weeks Bertha did not appear as well as usual. The changes Tredennis had seen in her became more marked. She lost color and roundness, and now and then was forced to show signs of fatigue which were not habitual with her. She made no alteration in her mode of life, however. When Tredennis called in the evening the parlor was always full, and she was always vivaciously occupied with her guests. Chief among her attractions was counted her pet pretence of being interested in politics. It was not a very serious pretence, but, being managed deftly and with a sense of its dramatic value, animated many an hour which might otherwise have been dull, in view of the social material which occasionally fell into her hands.

"What should I do," Tredennis heard her say once, "if I knew nothing of politics? There are times when they are my only salvation. What should I have done last night with the new member from Arkansas if I had not remembered that he was interested in the passage of the Currency Bill? He is an excellent, solid, sensible creature; we are frivolous, aimless beings compared with him. It is such men as he who do everything worth doing and being done; but he is purely a politician, and he has spent his life in a small provincial town, where he has been a most important person, and he cares as much for the doings of society and discussions of new novels and pictures as I do for the linseed-oil market — if there is a linseed-oil market. When I began to ask him modest questions about his bill, his face brightened at once, and he became a self-respecting and well-informed person, — at ease with himself and with me, and quite forgot his coat and his large boots, which had been slowly and painfully dawning upon him a few moments before when he contrasted them with Mr.

Arbuthnot's silk attire. My very mistakes were a pleasure to him, as they gave him an opportunity to say several things very well worth remembering. He could not have told whether I was well or ill dressed, but he detected my flimsiness in argument in a moment, and gave me more information in half an hour than you scoffers could have given me in a week, and" — with much modesty of demeanor — "he mentioned to Senator Vaughan, in the course of the evening, that I was a most intelligent woman."

Arbuthnot and Richard burst into the laughter which was always her applause upon such occasions.

"You!" commented Arbuthnot. "You are Herodias' daughter, dancing for the head of John the Baptist. You are always dancing in a quiet and effective way for somebody's head. Whose would you like next? How does mine strike you?"

"Thank you," said Bertha. "Would you really give it to me if I danced for you in my ablest manner; and how do you think it would look on a charger?"

There was more than one hard worked politician who, after a day of exciting debate or wearisome battling with windmills, found relief and entertainment in the pretty parlors. Some of those who came had known Bertha in her girlhood and were friends of her father, and with these it was the fashion to encourage her to political argument, and affect the deepest confidence in her statements, with a view to drawing forth all her resources. These resources were varied and numerous, and marked by a charming feminine daring and superiority to ordinary logic which were the delights of the senatorial mind.

"Why should I endeavor to convince you by being logical?" she said. "You have logic — at least we hope so — all day, and sometimes all night, in the Senate and the House, and even then you are not convinced of things. It is not logic which governs you, but a majority. And that is what one should aspire to, after all, — not to be in the right, but to be in the majority. And I am sure one's arguments are much more untrammelled and brilliant for being illogical. And if I convince you without logic, I win a victory worth having. It is like the triumph of an ugly woman who is called a beauty. If I am pretty and you say so, it is simply as if you said, 'white is white, blackness is dark'; but if I am not pretty, and am ingenious enough to persuade you that I am — there is a triumph to be proud of!"

It was nonsense, but it was often sparkling nonsense, whose very lightness was its charm, and the rooms were rarely ever so gay and full of laughter as when there was among the guests a sprinkling of men no longer young, who had come there to forget that they were jaded, or secretly anxious, or bitterly disappointed.

"It pleases me to dance before some of them," Bertha said to Arbuthnot. "I like to think I make them forget things for a little while. If I can do nothing greater and wiser, let me employ my one small accomplishment to the best advantage, and do my harmless best to be both graceful and agile. No one can persuade me that it can be a pleasant thing to engage in a hand-to-hand conflict from three to eight months in the year, and to sit day after day placidly endeavoring to confront men who differ with you on every point, and who count the fact among their virtues, and glory in it, and watch you and listen to you, with the single object of seizing an opportunity to prove in public that you are an imbecile or a falsifier, or a happy combination of both. When I reflect upon my own feelings," she added, with delightful *naïvete*, "when people are stupid and ill-mannered enough to differ with me, I am filled with the deepest sympathy for the entire political body. There is nothing so perfectly exasperating as to know people are differing with you, and I know there is nothing so wearing to the mind."

An exciting debate in the Senate was occupying public attention at this time, and to her other duties and entertainments she added that of following it in its course. She spent an hour or so at the Capitol every day, read the newspapers, and collected evidence and information with an unflagging industry which would have been worthy of admiration if it had been inspired by any serious intention. But she made no pretence of seriousness of intention. She returned home from such visits with derisive little arguments jotted down in her notebook and little sketches of senatorial profiles adorning its pages, and entertained a select audience with them in the evening, — an audience which not infrequently included the political dignitaries themselves. Her manner would have been a mystery to Tredennis if he had not remembered the professor's words of warning, and even with their memory in his mind he was often at a loss. There was a restless eagerness to be amused in all she did, and he felt that, after all, she was privately less successful in her efforts than she seemed. He was, at least, relieved to find that he had but little to do in the role assigned him. When Arbuthnot appeared again, he had entirely recovered his equilibrium, and was unemotional, self-possessed, occasionally flippant, plainly cherishing, at no time, any intention of" regarding himself seriously. He did not sing his "Serenade" again, and, when he sang at all, committed himself to no outreaching warmth of feeling. He rarely spoke to Bertha alone, and the old tendency to airy derision of each other's weaknesses reasserted itself. Only once Tredennis heard him address her with any degree of seriousness, and this was in reference to her visits to the Senate. There had been an all-night session, and it had been her whim to take part in it to the extent of sitting up until after midnight, and she had returned home more tired than she was willing to confess. Arbuthnot— who, with Richard, Tredennis, and a newspaper friend, had been her companions in the dissipation — remonstrated with her after the little supper they had on their arrival at the house.

Bertha had left the table, and was half reclining against a pile of cushions on the sofa, and Arbuthnot followed her, and spoke in a somewhat lowered voice.

"You are making a mistake in doing such things," he said. "Why will you keep it up? It's all nonsense. You don't care for it really. It is only one of your caprices. You have not a particle of serious interest in it."

"I have as much serious interest in it as I have in anything else," she answered. "More, indeed. Do you suppose I was not interested when Senator Ayres got up to-night to be immeasurably superior by the hour? It elevated my mental plane, and gave me food for reflection. It filled me with a burning desire to be immeasurably superior, too. Is he always immeasurably superior? Could he keep it up, do you suppose, in the bosom of his family, — when he is putting salt on his eggs at breakfast, for instance, and thinks no one is looking? When he tries on a new hat, does he do it with a lofty air of scorn, and does he fall asleep and have the nightmare with coldly contemptuous condescension? I don't mind mentioning to you that it is one of my favorite moods to be immeasurably superior. It is such a good way when you cannot get what you want; it disposes of your antagonists so simply and makes you feel so deserving; but I never could keep it up, — but that may be owing to weakness of character, and the fact that I am only an unworthy imitator and lack the vigor to convince myself of my own genuineness. Oh! I assure you, I was very much interested indeed."

"Well," said Arbuthnot, "I might have expected you would say something of this kind. It is your little way of evading matters. You have a knack at it."

Bertha looked down at the footstool on which her small shoe rested, and then up at him with a quiet face.

"Yes, it is my little way," she answered. "I suppose I might count it among my few small accomplishments. But don't you think it is as good a way as any, — particularly if it is the only way you have?"

"It is as good a way as any," replied Arbuthnot, with the calmness of a sensible person addressing an attractive but obstinate child. "But you know it will not prevent my saying again what I said at first. You are very foolish to tire yourself out for nothing, and you will regret it when it is too late."

"Yes," answered Bertha, "if I regret it I shall naturally regret it when it is too late. Did you ever hear of any one's regretting a thing too early, or just in time? That is what regret means — that one is too late."

Arbuthnot sat down near her.

"If you want to talk in that style," he remarked, in the most impartial manner, "I am entirely in the mood to listen, now I have expressed my opinion. It isn't worth much as *my* opinion, but it is worth something as the truth, and I am not afraid you will forget it, but, in the meantime, until Mrs. Dacre is in the mood to be escorted home, you can pander to my lower nature by showing me the sketches you made of Senator Ayres and the Speaker, and the gentleman from Iowa who was afraid to fall asleep."

The next morning, calling with a newspaper she had wanted,

Tredennis, being handed into the room in which Bertha usually spent her mornings at home, found her lying upon a sofa, and, as she did not hear him enter, he had the opportunity to stand for a few seconds and look at her.

While he did so she opened her eyes languidly and saw him, and the thought which held his mind for the moment sprang to his lips and uttered itself.

"I do not think you know," he said, "how pale you are."

"I do not want to know," she answered, with a rather tired little smile, "if it is unbecoming, and I am sure it is. But I will ask you to excuse my getting up."

He entirely passed over the first part of her reply, as she had noticed he had a habit of passing in silence many of her speeches, though she had not been able to decide why he did so.

"You said," he went on, "that when the season was over you intended to rest. Have you been doing it lately?"

"Yes," she answered, with entirely unembarrassed readiness. "I have been very quiet indeed."

At this he was silent for a moment again, and during the pause she lay and looked at him with an expression of curious interest — trying to make up her mind whether he did not reply because he felt himself not sufficiently ready of speech to meet her upon her own ground, or whether his silence was a negative sign of disapprobation.

"I am never tired when anything is going on," she said, at last.

"That is the worst of it," he replied.

"Oh, no — the best of it," she said, and then she looked away from him across the room, and added, in a tone altogether different, "One does not want too much time on one's hands."

Once or twice before he had seen this slight, unconscious change fall upon her, and, without comprehending, had been sharply moved by it, but she always recovered herself quickly, and she did so now.

"I tried it once," she said, "and it did not agree with me, and since then I have occupied myself. As Richard says, 'one must have an object,' and mine is to occupy myself."

"You accomplish your end, at least," he remarked.

"Yes," she answered. "I congratulate myself upon that. Upon the whole I do not know any one who is more fortunate than I am. No other life would suit me half so well as the one I lead. I am fond of gayety, and change, and freedom, and I have all three. Richard is amiable, the children are like him, and there is nothing to interfere with my having my own way, and amusing myself as I please. I should be thoroughly unhappy if I could not have my own way; to have it invariably is one of my laudable ambitions, and as I always get it you see I have reason for being charmed with my lot."

"You are very fortunate," he said.

"I am more than fortunate," she answered. Then she broke into a little laugh. "It is rather odd," she said, "that just before you came in I was lying thinking of the time you were in Washington before, and there came back to me something I said to you the night you gave me the heliotrope."

"Was it," said Tredennis, "what you said to me about being happy?"

"What!" she said. "You remember it? I scarcely thought that you would remember it."

"Yes," said Tredennis, "I remember it."

"I could not bear the thought of not being happy," she went on. "It had never occurred to me that such a thing was a possibility until you said something which suggested it to me. I recollect how it startled me. It was such a new idea."

She stopped and lay for a moment silent.

"And this morning?" suggested Tredennis.

"This morning," she answered, rather slowly, though smiling as she spoke, "this morning, as I said, I decided that I had been very fortunate."

"Then," he said, "you *have* been happy."

"If I had not been," she answered, "it would have been very curious. I have never been interfered with in the least."

"That is happiness, indeed," said Tredennis.

Just now he was reflecting upon the fact that all their conversations took the same turn and ended in the same way. It mattered little how they began; in all cases she showed the same aptitude for making her subject an entirely inconsequent source of amusement. Experience was teaching him that he need expect nothing else. And, even as he was thinking this, he heard her laugh faintly again.

"Shall I tell you what I see in your face," she said, — "what I see oftener than anything else?"

"I should be glad to know," he replied.

"I see that you are thinking that I am very much changed, and that it is not for the better."

He paused a moment before he answered her, and when he did so he spoke with his eyes fixed on the floor, and slowly:

"You are not the Bertha I used to know," he said. "But that I should have allowed myself to expect it shows simply that I am a dull, unprogressive fellow."

"It shows that you are very amiable and sanguine," she said. "I should have been even more fortunate than it has been my fate to be if I had not changed in ten years. Think of the good fortune of having stood still so long, — of having grown no older, no wiser. No," in a lower voice, "I am not the Bertha you used to know."

But the next instant, almost as soon as she had uttered the words, she lifted her eyes with the daring little smile in them.

"But I am very well preserved," she said. "I am really very well preserved. I am scarcely wrinkled at all, and I manage to conceal the ravages of time. And, considering my years, I am quite active. I danced every dance at the Ashworths' ball, with the kindly assistance of Mr. Arbuthnot and his friends. There were *débutantes* in the room who did not dance half as often. The young are not what they were in my generation, — though probably the expiring energies of advanced age are flaming in the socket and" —

She stopped suddenly, letting her hands drop at her sides. "No," she said again, "I — I am not the Bertha you used to know — and this morning I am — tired enough to be obliged to admit it."

Tredennis took a quick step toward her; the hot blood showed itself under his dark skin. What he had repressed in the last months got the better of him so far that he had no time to reflect that his stern, almost denunciatory, air could scarcely be ranked among ordinary conventionalities, and that an ordinarily conventional expression of interest might have been more reasonably expected from him than a display of emotion, denunciatory or otherwise.

"Can you expect anything else?" he said. "Is your life a natural one? Is it a natural and healthy thing that every hour of it should contain its own excitement, and that you should not know what simple, normal rest means? Who could be blind to the change which has taken place in you during the last few weeks? Last night you were so tired and unstrung that your hand trembled when you lifted your glass to your lips. Arbuthnot told you then it was a mistake; I tell you now that it is worse, — it is madness and crime."

He had not thought of what effect he would produce, — his words were his indignant masculine protest against her pallor and weakness, and the pain he had borne in silence for so long. It seemed, however, that he had startled her singularly. She rose from her reclining posture slowly and sat upright, and her hands trembled more than they had done the night before.

"Why," she faltered, "why are you so angry?"

"That," he returned bitterly, "means that I have no right to be angry, of course! Well, I am willing to admit it, — I have no right. I am taking a liberty. I don't even suggest that you are making a mistake, — as Mr. Arbuthnot did; I am rough with you, and say something worse."

"Yes," she admitted, "you are very rough with me." And she sat a few moments, looking down at the floor, her little hands trembling on her lap. But presently she moved again. She pushed one of the cushions up in the sofa-arm and laid her cheek against it, with a half-sigh of weariness relieved and a half-smile.

"Go on!" she said. "After all, — since I have reflected, — I think I don't dislike it. New things always please me, — for a little while, — and this is new. No one ever spoke to me so before. I wonder whether it was because I did not really deserve it or because people were afraid?"

Tredennis stopped in the walk he had begun and wheeled sharply about, fronting her with his disproportionately stern gaze.

"Do you want to know why *I* do it?" he demanded. "I think — since I have reflected — that it is for the sake of — of the other Bertha."

There was a slight pause.

"Of the other Bertha," she said after it, in a low, unsteady tone.

"Of the Bertha who thought it an impossibility that she should be anything but happy."

He had not been prepared for her replies before, but he was startled by what she did now. She left her seat with a sudden, almost impassioned, action; the cushion fell upon the floor. She put her hand upon the mantel, as if to support herself.

"Why did you say that?" she exclaimed. "I do not like it! I do not like to be reminded that it is so long since — since I was worth liking. I suppose that is what it means. Why should you seem to accuse me when you say you speak for the sake of the other Bertha? Am I so bad? You have lived a quiet life because you liked it best; I did not chance to like it best, and so I have been gay. I go out a great deal and am fond of the world, but do I neglect my children and treat my husband badly? Richard is very happy, and Jack and Janey and Meg enjoy themselves and are very fond of me. If I was careless of them, and ill-tempered to Richard, and made my home unhappy, you might accuse me. It is the most mysterious thing to me, but I always feel as if I was defending myself against you, even when you only look at me and do not speak at all. It — it is a curious position! I do not understand it, and I do not like it!"

Her sudden change of mood was a revelation to Tredennis. He began to realize what he had dimly felt from the first, that her mental attitude toward him was one of half-conscious defiance of his very thought of her. He had not known why he had felt at times that his mere presence prompted her to present her worldly, mocking little philosophies in their most incontrovertible and daring form, and that it was her whim to make the worst of herself and her theories for his benefit. He accused himself angrily in secret of overestimating his importance in her eyes, and had reiterated impatiently that there was no reason why she should be at all specially aware of his existence when he was near her, and it had been one of his grievances against himself that, in spite of this, every time they met he had felt the same thing, and had resented and been puzzled by it.

But he had never before seen her look as she looked now. One of his private sources of wonder had been the perfect self-control which restrained her from exhibiting anything approaching a shadow of real feeling upon any subject. He had seen her under circumstances which would have betrayed nine women out of ten into some slight display of irritation, and she had always maintained the airy serenity of demeanor which deprived all persons and incidents of any weight whatever when they assumed the form of obstacles, and her practicable little smile and calm impartiality of manner had never failed her. He had heard her confess that it was her chief weakness to pride herself upon her quiet adroitness in avoiding all things unpleasant or emotional, and upon her faithfulness to her resolve not to permit herself to be disturbed.

"I have seen people who enjoyed their emotions," she had said, "but I never enjoyed mine, even when I was very young. I definitely disliked them. I am too self-conscious to give myself up to them simply. If I had one, I should think about it and analyze it and its effects upon me. I should be saying all the time, 'Now I am hot — now I am cold'; and when it was over I should be tired, not only of the feeling itself, but of taking my own temperature."

And now she stood before him for the instant a new creature, — weaker and stronger than he had dreamed it possible she could be, — her eyes bright with some strange feeling, a spot of color burning on each pale cheek. He was so bewildered and impressed that he was slow to speak, and, when he began, felt himself at so severe a disadvantage that his consciousness of it gave his voice a rigid sound.

"I do not think," he began, "that I know what to say" —

Bertha stopped him.

"There is no need that you should say anything," she interrupted. "You cannot say anything which will disapprove of me more than your expression does. And it is not you who should defend yourself, but I. But you were always severe. I remember I felt that when I was only a child, and knew that you saw all that was frivolous in me. I was frivolous then as I am now. I suppose I have a light nature, — but I do not like to be reminded of it. After all, no one is harmed but myself, and it would be charity in you to let .me go my flippant way and not despise me too much."

"Bertha," he answered, "it is not for me to say that I do not despise you."

He stood with his arms folded and looked down at her steadily. It was very easy for her to place him at a disadvantage. He knew nothing of feminine ways and means, and his very masculine strength and largeness were against him. If she gave him a wound he could not strike back, or would not; and in her last speech she had given him more wounds than one, and they were rankling in his great breast fiercely. And yet despite this it was not she who came off entirely victor. After meeting his gaze with undeniable steadiness for a few seconds, she turned away.

"I told you," she remarked with a persistence which was its own betrayer, "that — it was not necessary for you to say anything." The next moment an impatient laugh broke from her. She held up her unsteady hand that he might see it.

"Look!" she said. "Why should I quarrel with you when you are right, after all? It is certainly time that I should rest when I am so absurdly unstrung as this. And my very mood itself is a proof that something should be done with me. For a minute or so I have actually been out of temper, or something humiliatingly like it. And I pride myself upon my temper, you know, and upon the fact that I never lose it, — or have not any to lose. I must be worn out when a few perfectly truthful speeches will make me bad-tempered. Not that I object to it on moral grounds, but it wounds my vanity to lose control of myself. And now I have reached my vanity I am quite safe. I will leave for Fortress Monroe to-morrow."

"It would be better if you went to a quieter place," he said.

"Thank you," she answered. "I think it will be quiet enough, — if I take the children, and avoid the ballroom, and am very decorous."

There seemed but little more for him to say. She changed the subject by taking from the table the paper he had brought her, and beginning to discuss its contents.

"Richard asked me to read the editorial and the letter from the Washington correspondent," she said. "He is more interested in the matter than I ever knew him to be in anything of the kind before. He is actually making it one of his objects, and flatter me by wanting to know my opinions and wishing me to share his enthusiasm." She sat down to the table, with the paper open before her and her hands lying clasped upon it.

"Have you read it?" she asked. "Is it very clever? Can I understand it? Richard is so amiably sure I can."

"It is well done," replied Tredennis, "and you will certainly understand it."

"I am glad of that," she said, and sat still a moment, with eyes lowered. Then she spoke, rather suddenly. "Richard is very good to me," she said. "I ought to be very grateful to him. It is just like him to feel that what I think of such things is worth hearing. That is his affectionate, generous way. Of what value could my shallow little fancies be? — and yet I think he really believes they should carry weight. It is the most delightful flattery in the world."

"It is your good fortune," said Tredennis, "to be able to say things well and with effect."

"What!" she said, with a half-smile, "are you going to flatter me, too?"

"No," he answered, grimly, "I am not going to flatter you."

"You would find it a very good way," she answered. "We should get along much better, I assure you. Perhaps that is really what I have been resenting so long — that you show no facility for making amiable speeches."

"I am afraid my facility lies in the opposite direction," he returned.

"I have recovered my equilibrium sufficiently not to admit that," she said.

When he went away, as he did shortly after, she followed him to the door of the room.

"Was I very bad-tempered?" she said, softly. "If I was, suppose you forgive me before you go away — for the sake of the other Bertha."

He took the hand she offered him, and looked down at it as it lay upon his big brown palm. It was feverish and still a little unsteady, though her manner was calm enough.

"There is nothing to forgive," he answered. "If there was — this Bertha" — He checked himself, and ended abruptly. "I don't share your gift," he said. "I said my say as bluntly and offensively as possible,

I suppose, and you had a right to be angry. It was all the worse done because I was in earnest."

"So was I — for a moment," she said; "that was the trouble."

And that was the end of it, though even when he dropped her hand and turned away, he was aware of her slender figure standing in the door-way, and of a faint, inexplicable shadow in the eyes that followed him.

He went back to his quarters bitterly out of humor with himself.

"A nice fellow I am to talk to women!" he said. "I have not lived the life to fit me for it. Military command makes a man authoritative. What right had I to seem to assume control over her? She's not used to that kind of thing, even from those who might be supposed to have the right to do it. Some one ought to have the right — though that has gone out of fashion, too, I suppose." Something like a groan burst from him as he laid his forehead upon his hands, resting his elbows on the table before him. "If a man loved her well enough," he said, "he might do it and never hurt her; but if she loved him perhaps there would be no need of it."

He had passed through many such brief spasms of resentful misery of late, and he was beginning to acknowledge to himself that each one was stronger than the last. He had contended his ground with steady persistence and with stubborn condemnation of his own weakness, but he had lost it, inch by inch, until there were times when he felt his foothold more insecure than he could have believed possible a year ago.

"Why should I think of myself as a man who has lost something?" he was wont to say to himself, bitterly and impatiently. "I had won nothing, and might never have won it. I had what would have been opportunity enough for a quicker temperament. It is nothing but sentiment."

And, even as he said it, there would come back to him some tone of Bertha's voice, some pretty natural turn of her head or figure as she sat or stood in the parlor with her small court around her; and, slight as the memory might be, the sudden leap of his pulses had more power than his argument.

It was these trifles and their habit of haunting him which were harder to combat than all the rest. His life had been so little affected by femininity that hers had a peculiarly persistent influence upon him. He noted in her things he might have seen in scores of other women, but half fancied belonged specially to herself. The sweep and fall of her dress, the perfume she used, the soft ruffles of lace she was given to wearing, — each of her little whims of adornment had its distinct effect, and seemed, in some mysterious way, to have been made her own, and to be shared with no other being. Other women wore flowers; but what flowers had ever haunted him as he had been haunted by the knot of heliotrope and violets he had seen her tuck carelessly into the belt of her dress one day? He had remembered them with a start again and again, and each time they had bloomed and breathed their soft scent afresh.

"It is all sentiment," he persisted. "There would be nothing new in it to — to that fellow Arbuthnot, for instance; but it is new to me, and I can't get rid of it, somehow."

He had heard in his past stories of men who cherished as treasures for a lifetime a ribbon or a flower, and had passed them by in undisturbed composure as incidents belonging only to the realms of wild romance; but he had never in the course of his existence felt anything so keen as the inconsequent thrill which was the result of his drawing suddenly from his pocket one night, on his return to his quarters after a romp with the children, a small, soft, long-wristed glove which it had been Master Jack's pleasure to hide there.

He had carried it sternly back the next morning and returned it to Bertha, but the act cost him an effort; it had been like a living presence in his room the night before, and he had slept less well because of it.

He had used his very susceptibility to these influences as an argument against his feeling.

"There is nothing substantial in it," he had said, — "nothing but what a man should find it easy to live down. It is the folly of a boy, intoxicated by the color of a girl's cheek and the curl of her hair. An old fellow, who any day may find a sprinkling of gray in his scalplock, should know better than to ponder over a pretty gown and — a bunch of flowers; and yet how one remembers them!"

And to-day it was the little things, as usual, almost as much as the great ones. The memory of the small, bright room, with its air of belonging to Bertha, and being furnished by Bertha, and strewed with appendages of Bertha; the slight figure, in its white morning dress, lying upon the sofa or standing between the folding-doors; the soft, full knot of her hair as he saw it when she turned her head proudly away from him, — what trifles they were! And yet if the room had been another, and the pretty dress not white, and the soft hair coiled differently, everything might have had another effect, and he might have been in another mood, — or so he fancied.

But he gave himself little leisure for the indulgence of his fancies, and he made his usual effort to crush them down and undervalue them. His groan was followed by a bitter laugh.

"It is the old story," he said. "I please myself by fancying that what would please me would make her happier. Arbuthnot would know better. Control would not suit her, even the gentlest. She has had her own way too long. She is a small, slight creature, but it has been her lot to rule all her life, in a small, slight creature's way. It is the natural sentimentality of an obstinate, big-boned fellow to fancy she would thrive under it. She would know better herself. She would laugh the thought to scorn, and be wise in doing it."

Chapter 10

As he was saying it Bertha had gone back to her sofa, and sat there with the faint, troubled smile still on her face.

"He was angry," she said, "and so was I. It made him look very large; but I was not at all afraid of him, — no, positively, I was not afraid of him, and I am glad of that. It is bad enough to remember that I was emotional, and said things I did not mean to say. It is not like me to say things I don't mean to say. I must be more tired out than I knew. Ah, there is no denying that he was in the right! I will go away and stay some time. It will be better in every way."

For some minutes she sat motionless, her hands clasped lightly upon her knee, her eyes fixed on a patch of sunlight on the carpet. She did not move, indeed, until she heard the sound of her husband's foot upon the steps and his latch-key in the door. He entered the room immediately afterward, looking rather warm and a trifle exhilarated, and all the handsomer in consequence.

"Ah, Bertha, you are here!" he said. "I am glad you are not out! How warm it is! Fancy having such weather early in May! And three days ago we had fires. What a climate! There is something appropriate in it. It is purely Washingtonian, and as uncertain as — as senators. There's a scientific problem for the Signal Service Bureau to settle, — Does the unreliability of the climate affect the senatorial mind, or does the unreliability of the senatorial mind affect the climate?"

"It sounds like a conundrum," said Bertha, "and the Signal Service Bureau would give it up. You have been walking too fast, you foolish boy, and have overheated yourself. Come and lie down on the sofa and rest."

She picked up the cushion, which had fallen, and put it in place for him. There was always a pretty touch of maternal care for him in her manner. He accepted her invitation with delighted readiness, and, when he had thrown himself at luxurious full length upon the sofa, she took a seat upon its edge near him, having first brought from the mantel a large Japanese fan, with which she stirred the air gently.

"Why were you glad that I had not gone out?" she said. "Did you want me?"

"Oh!" he answered, "I always want you. You are the kind of little person one naturally wants, — and it is a sort of relief to find you on the spot. How nice this Grand Pasha business is, — lying on cushions and being fanned, — and how pretty and cool you look in your white frills! White is very becoming to you, Bertha."

Bertha glanced down at the frills.

"Is it?" she said. "Yes, I think it is, and this is a pretty gown. Richard!"

"Well?"

"You said it was a sort of relief to find me on the spot. Did you say it because I am not always here when you want me? Do you think I go out too much? Does it ever seem to you that I neglect you a little, and am not quite as domesticated as I should be? Should you be — happier — if I lived a quieter life and cared less for society?"

There was a touch of unusual earnestness in her voice, and her eyes were almost childishly eager as she turned them upon him.

"Happier!" he exclaimed, gayly. "My dear child! I could not easily be happier than I am. How could I accuse you of neglecting me? You satisfy me exactly in everything. Whose home is more charming, and whose children are better cared for than mine? It is not necessary for you to cook my dinner, but you are the most delightful sauce to it in the world when you sit at the head of the table. What more could a man want?"

"I — I don't know," she said, slowly, "but I could not bear to think that I was not what I should be in my own home. It has always seemed to me that there could be no bad taste and bad breeding so inexcusable as the bad taste and bad breeding of a woman who is disagreeable and negligent in her own house. One has no need to put it on moral grounds even — the bad taste of it is enough. I don't think I could ever be disagreeable, or that you could think me so; but it struck me" —

"Don't let it strike you again," he interrupted, amiably. "It has struck me that there were never two people so well suited to each other as our married life has proved us to be. I don't mind admitting now that once or twice during the first year I thought that you were a little restless or unhappy, but it was when you were not well, and it was quite natural, and it all passed away, and I don't think it would occur to any one in these days to ask whether you are happy or not."

Bertha was playing with his watch-chain, and she separated one charm upon it from another carefully as she answered him in a soft, natural voice:

"There is a legend, you know," she said, "that the first year of one's marriage is always uncomfortable."

"Oh, mine was not uncomfortable," he returned, — "it was delightful, as all the other years have been; but — just occasionally, you know — there was a — well, a vague something — which never troubles me now."

"I must have behaved badly in some way," said Bertha, smiling, "or it would not have troubled you then."

And she stooped and kissed him on the forehead.

"I have a horrible conviction," she said after it, "that I was a vixen. Was I a vixen? Perhaps I was a vixen, and never suspected it, and no one suspected it but you. Poor boy! Why didn't you return me to papa with thanks? Well, as you have kept me so long, you must make the best of me. And it is very nice and polite in you to pretend that I am satisfactory, and don't make you wretched and your hearth a wilderness by being a hollow worldling."

"You are exactly what I want," he responded. "I am a hollow worldling myself. If I were a bricklayer, my idea of domestic bliss might be to spend my evenings at home and watch you mending stockings or knitting, or doing something of that sort; but even then I am afraid I should tire of it, and secretly long for something more frivolous."

"For something as frivolous as I am?" she said, with a nervous little laugh. "Quite as frivolous, Richard — really? But I know you will say so. You are always good to me and spoil me."

"No, I am not," he answered. "It is simply true that you always please me. It is true I am a rather easy-natured fellow, but I know plenty of good-natured fellows whose wives are terribly unsatisfactory. You are clever and pretty, and don't make mistakes, and you are never exacting, nor really out of humor, and it is impossible for me to tire of you" —

"Really?" she said, quickly, "is that last true?"

"Entirely true."

"Well," she commented, the color rising in her cheek, "that is a good deal for one's husband to say! That is a triumph. It amounts to a certificate of character."

"Well," he admitted, after a second's reflection, "upon the whole it is! I know more husbands than one; but no matter. I was going to add that long ago — before I met you, you know — my vague visions of matrimonial venture were always clouded by a secret conviction that when I had really passed the Rubicon, and had time for reflection, things might begin to assume a rather serious aspect."

"And I," said Bertha, a little thoughtfully, "have never assumed a serious aspect."

"Never," he replied, exultingly. "You have been a perfect success. There is but one Bertha" — And her husband is her prophet!" she added. "You are very good to me, Richard, and it is entirely useless for you to deny it, because I shall insist upon it with — with wild horses, if necessary; which figure of speech I hope strikes you as being strong enough."

She was herself again — neither eager nor in earnest, ready to amuse him and to be amused, waving her fan for his benefit, touching up his cushions to make him more comfortable, and seeming to enjoy her seat on the edge of his sofa very much indeed.

"Do you know," she said, at length, "what I have thought of doing? I have thought quite seriously of going in a day or so to Fortress Monroe with the children."

She felt that he started slightly, and wondered why.

"Are you surprised" she asked. "Would you rather I would not go?"

"No," he answered, "if you think it would be better for you. You are tired, and the weather is very warm. But — have you set any particular day?"

"No," she said, "I should not do that without speaking to you first."

"Well," he returned, "then suppose you do not go this week. I have half-invited Senator Planefield, and Macpherson and Ashley to dinner for Thursday."

"Is it because you want them to talk about the bill?" she said. "How interested you are in it, Richard! Why is it? Railroads never struck me as being particularly fascinating material. It seems to me that amateur enthusiasm would be more readily awakened by something more romantic and a little intangible, — a tremendous claim, for instance, which would make some poor, struggling creatures fabulously rich. I am always interested in claims; the wilder they are, the better, and it invariably delights me when the people get them ' through,' to the utter consternation of the Government. It has faintly dawned upon me, on two or three such occasions, that I have no political morality, and I am afraid it is a feminine failing. It is not a masculine one, of course; so it must be feminine. I wish you had chosen a claim, Richard, instead of a railroad. I am sure it would have been far more absorbing."

"The railroad is quite absorbing enough," he answered, "and there is money enough involved in it. Just think of those Westoria lands, and what they will be worth if the road is carried through them, — and as to romance, what could be more romantic than the story attached to them?"

"But I don't know the story," said Bertha. "What is it?"

"It is a very effective story," he replied, "and it was the story which first called my attention to the subject. There was a poor, visionary fellow whose name was Westor, to whom a large tract of this land came suddenly as an inheritance from a distant relative. He was not practical enough to make much use of it, and he lived in the house upon it in a desolate, shiftless way for several years, when he had the ill-fortune to discover coal on the place. I say it was ill-fortune, because the discovery drove him wild. He worked, and starved, and planned, and scraped together all the money he could to buy more land, keeping his secret closely for some time. When he could do no more he came to Washington, and began to work for a railroad which would make his wealth available. His energy was a kind of frenzy, they say. He neither ate, slept, nor rested, and really managed to get the matter into active movement. He managed to awaken a kind of enthusiasm, and, for a short time, was a good deal talked of and noticed. He was a big, raw-boned young Westerner, and created a sensation by his very uncouthness in its connection with the wildly fabulous stories told about his wealth. He had among his acquaintances a man of immense influence, and at this man's house he met the inevitable young woman. She amused herself, and he fell madly in love, and became more frenzied than ever. It was said that she intended to marry him if he was successful, and that she made his poor, helpless life such an anguish to him that he lost his balance entirely. There came a time when he was entirely penniless, and' his prospects were so unpromising, and his despair so great, that he went to his boarding-house one day with the intention of killing himself, and just as he finished loading his pistol a letter was handed in to him, and when he opened it he found it contained the information that another distant relative, affected by the rumors concerning him, had left him twenty thousand dollars. He laid his pistol in a drawer, and left the house to begin again. He had an interview with his lady-love, and one with his man of influence, and at the end of a few weeks had bought more land, and parted in some mysterious way with the rest of his money, and was on the very eve of success. Poor fellow!"

"Poor fellow!" said Bertha. "Oh! don't say that anything went wrong!"

"It would not be half so dramatic a story if everything had gone right," said Richard, with fine artistic appreciation. "You could never guess what happened. Everything he did seemed to work to a miracle; every train was laid and every match applied. On the day that was to decide his fate he did not go near the Capitol, but wandered out and took his place on one of the seats in the park which faced the house at which the young woman was visiting, and sat there, a lank, unshorn, haggard figure, either staring at her window or leaning forward with his head upon his hands. People actually heard of his being there and went to look at him, and came away without having dared to address him. The young woman looked out from behind her blind and was furious, and even sent word to him to go away. But he would not go, and only glared at the man who was sent to him with the message. He sat there until night, and then staggered across and rang at the bell, and inquired for the man of influence, and was told — what do you suppose he was told?"

"Oh!" cried Bertha, desperately. "I don't know."

"He was told that he was occupied."

"Occupied!" echoed Bertha.

Richard clasped his hands comfortably and gracefully behind his head.

"That's the climax of the story," he said. "He was occupied — in being married to the young woman, of whom he had been greatly enamored for some time, and who had discreetly decided to marry him because he had proved to her that the other man's bill could not possibly pass. It could not pass because he had the energy and influence to prevent its doing so, and he prevented its passing because he knew he would lose the young woman otherwise. At least that is the story, and I like the version."

"I don't like it!" said Bertha. "It makes me feel desperate."

"What it made the poor fellow feel," Richard went on, "nobody ever found out, as he said nothing at all about it. On hearing the truth he sat down on the steps for a few minutes, and then got up and went away. He went to his boarding-house and had an interview with his landlady, who was a kind-hearted creature, and when she saw him began to cry because his bill had not passed. But when she spoke of it she found he knew nothing of it; he had never asked about it, and he said to her, 'Oh! that doesn't matter, — it isn't of any consequence particularly; I'm only troubled about your bill. I haven't money enough to pay it. I've only enough to take me home, and you'll have to let me give you the things I have in my room for pay. I only want one thing out of there, — if you'll let me go and get it I won't take anything else. So she let him go, and stood outside his door and cried, while he went in and took something out of a drawer."

"Richard!" cried Bertha.

"Yes," said Richard. "He actually found a use for it, after all — but not in Washington. He went as far as he could by rail, and then he tramped the rest of the way to Westoria; they say it must have taken him several days, and that his shoes were worn to shreds, and his feet cut and bruised by the walk. When he reached the house, it had been shut up so long that the honeysuckle which climbed about it had grown across the door, and he could not have got in without breaking or pushing it aside. People fancied that at first he thought of going in, but that when he saw the vine it stopped him, — slight barrier as it was. They thought he had intended to go in because he had evidently gone to the door, and before he turned away had broken off a spray of the flowers which was just beginning to bloom; he held it crushed in his hand when they found him, two or three days later. He had carried it back to the edge of the porch, and had sat down — and finished everything — with the only thing he had brought back from Washington — the pistol. How does that strike you as the romance of a railroad?"

Bertha clenched her hand, and struck her knee a fierce little blow.

"Richard," she said, "if that had happened in my day I should have turned lobbyist, and every thought, and power, and gift I had would have been brought to bear to secure the passage of that bill."

Richard laughed, — a pleased but slightly nervous laugh.

"Suppose you bring them to bear now," he suggested.

"There would not be any reason for my doing it now," she answered; "but I shall certainly be interested."

Richard laughed again.

"By Jove!" he said, "the poor devils who own it would think there was reason enough!"

"Who owns it?"

"Several people, who speculated in it because the railroad was talked of again, and on a more substantial footing. It fell to Westor's only living relation, who was an ignorant old woman, and sold it without having any idea of its real value. Her impression was that, if she kept it, it would bring her ill-luck. There is no denying that it looks just now like a magnificent speculation."

"And that poor fellow," said Bertha, — "that poor fellow" —

"That poor fellow?" Richard interposed. "Yes — but his little drama is over, you know, and perhaps there are others going on quite as interesting, if we only knew them. It is very like you, Bertha — and it is very adorable," touching her shoulder caressingly with his hand, "to lose sight entirely of the speculation, and care only for the poor fellow. You insist upon having your little drama under all circumstances."

"Yes," she admitted. "I confess that I like my little drama, and I have not a doubt that — as I said before — I could not have lived in the midst of that without turning lobbyist — which is certainly not my vocation."

"Not your vocation?" said Richard. "You would make the most successful little lobbyist in the world!"

Bertha turned upon him an incredulous and rather bewildered smile.

"I!" she exclaimed. "I"

"Yes, you!"

"Well," she replied, after a second's pause given to inspection of him, "*this* is open derision!"

"It is perfectly true," was his response; "and it is true for good reasons. Your strength would lie in the very fact that you would be entirely unlike your co-laborers in the field. You have a finished little air of ingenuousness which would be your fortune."

She shook her head with a pretty gesture.

"No," she said. "I am very clever, and of course you cannot help observing it, but I am not clever enough for that."

He gave her a glance at once curious and admiring.

"By Jove!" he exclaimed, "it is my belief you are clever enough for anything."

"Richard," she said, "shall I tell you a secret?"

"Yes."

"And you will bury it in the innermost recesses of your soul, and *never* divulge it?"

"Certainly."

"And brace yourself for a shock when I reveal it to you?"

"Yes."

"Well, here it is! My cleverness is like what you — and two or three other most charming people — are good enough to call my prettiness. It is a delusion and a snare!"

"Come!" he said. "You are attempting to deceive me."

"No," she answered. "I am attempting to undeceive you. I am not really pretty or clever at all, and it has been the object of my life to prevent its being detected."

She opened her eyes in the most charmingly ingenuous manner and nodded her head.

"I discovered it myself," she said, "long ago, — comparatively early in life, — and resolved to conceal it. And nothing but the confidence I repose in you would have induced me to mention it."

"Well," he replied, "you have concealed it pretty well under the circumstances."

"Ah!" she said, "but you don't know what a burden it is to carry about, and what subterfuges I have to resort to when I seem on the very verge of being found out. There is Larry, for instance, — I am almost sure that Larry suspects me, especially when I am tired, or chance to wear an unbecoming gown. You know how particular I am about my gowns? Well, that is my secret. I haven't an attraction, really, but my gowns and my spirits and my speciousness. The solitary thing I do feel I have reason to pride myself on is that I am bold enough to adapt my gowns in such a way as to persuade you that I am physically responsible for the color and shape of them. You fancy you are pleased with me when you are simply pleased with some color of which I exist on the reflection or glow. In nine cases out of ten it is merely a matter of pale blue or pink, and silk or crepe or cashmere; and in the tenth it is nothing but spirits and speciousness."

"Oh," he said, "there is no denying that you would make a wonderful lobbyist."

"Well," she answered, rising and going to the table to lay her fan down, "when you invest largely in Westoria lands and require my services in that capacity, I will try to distinguish myself. I think I should like to begin with the Westoria lands if I begin at all. But in the meantime I must go upstairs and talk to the seamstress about Janey's new white dresses. You are cool enough now to enjoy your lunch when the bell rings and you shall have some iced tea if you would like it."

"I would like it very well, and, by the by, did Tredennis bring the 'Clarion,' as he said he would?"

"Yes, it is here," and she handed it to him from the table. "You can read it while I am upstairs."

"Have you read it?" he said, opening it and turning to the editorial.

"Not yet. I shall read it this afternoon."

"Yes, do. The facts are put very forcibly. And — you will decide not to go to Fortress Monroe just yet?"

She hesitated a moment, but he did not observe it.

"I must be here when your friends dine with you, of course," she said. "And a week or even a little more does not make so much difference, after all. It may be quite cool again to-morrow."

And she went out of the room and left him to his paper.

Chapter 11

It was two weeks after this that Arbuthnot, sauntering down the avenue in a leisurely manner, on his way from his office, and having a fancy to stroll through Lafayette Park, which was looking its best in its spring bravery and bloom, on entering the iron gateway found his attention attracted by the large figure of Colonel Tredennis, who was approaching him from the opposite direction, walking slowly and appearing deeply abstracted. It cannot be said that Mr. Arbuthnot felt any special delight in the prospective encounter. He had not felt that he had advanced greatly in Colonel Tredennis' good opinion, and had, it must be confessed, resigned himself to that unfortunate condition of affairs without making any particular effort to remedy it, — his private impression being that the result would scarcely be likely to pay for the exertion, taking into consideration the fact that he was constitutionally averse to exertion.

"Why," he had said to Bertha, "should I waste my vital energies in endeavoring to persuade a man that I am what he wants, when perhaps I am not? There are scores of people who will naturally please him better than I do, and there are people enough who please me better than he does. Let him take his choice, — and it is easy enough to see that I am not his choice."

"What is he thinking of now, I wonder?" he said, a vague plan for turning into another walk flitting through his mind. "Are his friends, the Pi-utes, on the war-path and actively engaged in dissecting agents, or is he simply out of humor? He is not thinking of where he is going. He will walk over that nursemaid and obliterate the twins — yes, I thought so."

The colonel had verified his prophecy, and, aroused from his reverie by the devastation he had caused, he came to a stand-still with a perplexed and distressed countenance.

"I beg your pardon," Arbuthnot heard him say, in his great, deep voice. "I hope I did not hurt you. I had forgotten where I was." And he stooped and set the nearest twin on its feet on the grass and then did the same thing for the other, upon which both stood and stared at him, and, not being hurt at all, having merely rolled over on the sod, were in sufficiently good spirits to regard with interest the fact that he was fumbling in his coat-pocket for something.

The article in question was a package of bonbons, which he produced and gave to the nearest toddler.

"Here!" he said. "I bought these for another little girl, but I can get some more. They are all right," he added, turning to the mulatto girl, whose admiration of his martial bearing revealed itself in a most lenient grin, — "they won't hurt them. They can eat them all without being harmed."

And then he turned away, and in doing so caught sight of Arbuthnot, and, somewhat to the surprise of the latter, advanced toward him at once with the evident intention of joining him.

"It is rather a curious thing that I should meet you here," he said. "I was thinking of you when I met with the catastrophe you saw just now. Do you often go home this way?"

"Not very often," Arbuthnot replied. "Sometimes, when things look as they do now," with a gesture indicating the brilliant verdure.

"Everything looks very fresh and luxuriant," said Tredennis. "The season is unusually far advanced, I suppose. It is sometimes a great deal too warm to be pleasant."

"It will be decidedly warmer every day," said Arbuthnot. "We shall have a trying summer. The President is going out to the Soldiers' Home next week — which is earlier than usual. There are only two or three of the senators' families left in the city. The exodus began weeks ago."

"Such weather as we have had the last few days," said the colonel, with his slight frown, "must be very exhausting to those who are not strong, and who have gone through a gay winter."

"The best thing such people can do," responded Arbuthnot, dryly, "is to make their way to the mountains or the sea as soon as possible. Most of them do." Tredennis' reply was characteristically abrupt. "Mrs. Ampry does not," he said. "No," answered Arbuthnot, and he looked at the end of his cigar as if he saw nothing else. "Why doesn't she?" demanded Tredennis. "She ought to," said Arbuthnot, with calm adroitness. "Ought to!" Tredennis repeated. "She should have gone months ago. She — she is actually ill. Why in heaven's name does she stay? She told me two weeks since that she was going to Fortress Monroe, or some such place."

"She had better go to a New England farm-house, and wear a muslin gown and swing in a hammock," said Arbuthnot.

"You see that as well, do you?" said the colonel. "Why don't you tell her so?" and having said it, seemed to pull himself up suddenly, as if he felt he had been unconsciously impetuous. Arbuthnot laughed.

His smile had died completely away, however, when he gave his side glance at his companion's face a moment later.

"She was quite serious in her intention of going away two weeks ago," he said. "She told me so; nothing but Richard's dinner-party prevented her departure in the first place."

He spoke in an entirely non-committal tone, but there was a touch of interest in his quiet glance at Tredennis.

"You dined there with Planefield and the rest, didn't you?" he added.

"Yes."

"I didn't. Richard was kind enough to invite me, but I should only have been in the way." He paused an instant, and then added, without any change of tone or manner, "I know nothing of the Westoria lands."

"Was it necessary that you should?" said Tredennis. "I did not."

"Oh," Arbuthnot answered, "I knew they would discuss them, and the bill, as it pleases Amory to be interested in them just now."

"I remember that the matter was referred to several times," said Tredennis; "even Mrs. Amory seemed to know a good deal of it."

"A good deal!" said Arbuthnot. "In favor of the bill?"

"Yes," Tredennis answered. "She had been reading up, it appeared. She said some very good things about it — in a laughing way. Why does she waste her time and strength on such folly?" he added, hotly. "Why — why is she allowed to do it?"

"The New England farm would be better for her just now," said Arbuthnot — again adroitly.

"Why should Amory waste his time upon it?" the colonel went on; "though that is his affair, of course, and not mine!"

They had reached the gate by this time, but they did not pass through it. Finding themselves near it, they turned — as if by mutual consent, and yet without speaking of doing so — into the walk nearest them.

It was after taking a few steps in silence down this path, that Colonel Tredennis spoke again, abruptly:

"When I was thinking of you just before we met," he said, "I was thinking of you in connection with — with the Amorys."

He knew the statement had a blunt enough sound, and his recognition of it irritated him, but he was beginning to be accustomed to his own bluntness of statement, and, at any rate, this led him to the point he meant to reach.

Arbuthnot's reply was characteristic. It was not blunt at all, and had an air of simple directness, which was the result not only of a most creditable tact and far-sightedness, but of more private good feeling and sincerity than he was usually credited with.

"I am always glad to be thought of in connection with the Amorys," he said. "And I am glad that it is perfectly natural that I should be connected with them in the minds of their friends. There has been a very close connection between us for several years, and I hope they have found as much pleasure in it as I have."

Tredennis recognized the tact even if he was not aware of the good feeling and far-sightedness. The obstacles had been removed from his path, and the conversation had received an air of unconstrained naturalness, which would make it easier for him to go on.

"Then," he said, "there will be no need to explain what I mean by saying that I was thinking specially of your interest in Mrs. Amory herself — and your influence over her."

"I wish my influence over her was as strong as my interest in her," was his companion's reply. "My interest in her is a sincere enough feeling, and a deep one. There is every reason why it should be."

"I," — began the colonel, — "I" — And then he stopped.

"Your interest in her," Arbuthnot went on, seeming to enjoy his cigar very much, "is even a more natural feeling than mine — though I scarcely think it can be stronger. It is not a matter of relationship so much, — as a rule, relationship does not amount to a great deal, — but the fact that you knew her as a girl, and feel toward the professor as you do, must give her a distinct place in your mind."

"It is a feeling," said Tredennis, "which disturbs me when I see that she is in actual danger through her own want of care for herself. Are women always so reckless? Is it a Washington fashion? Why should she forget that her children need her care, if she does not choose to think of herself? Is that a Washington fashion, too?"

"You were thinking," said Arbuthnot, "and flattering me in doing it, that what I might say to her on the necessity of leaving the city might have some little effect?"

"Yes," Tredennis answered. "And if not upon herself, upon Amory. He is always ready to listen to you."

Arbuthnot was silent for some moments. He was following a certain train of thought closely and rapidly, but his expression did not betray him at all.

"She would have gone two weeks ago," he said quietly next, "if it had not been for Richard's engagements with Planefield and the rest. He has had them at his house two or three times since then, and they have made little parties to Mount Vernon and Arlington and Great Falls. Planefield is a lady's man, and he finds Mrs. Amory very charming."

"What!" exclaimed Tredennis, with intolerant haughtiness, — "that coarse fellow?"

"He isn't a nice fellow," said Arbuthnot, "but he won't show his worst side to her — any more than he can help. He is a very powerful fellow, they say."

Here he stopped. They had reached their gate-way again.

"I'll do what I can," he said. "It won't be much, perhaps; but I will do what I can. I fully appreciate the confidence you showed in speaking to me."

"I fully appreciate the manner in which you listened to what I had to say," said Tredennis.

And, somewhat to Arbuthnot's surprise, he held out his hand to him.

Chapter 12

Instead of making his way home at once Arbuthnot turned up the side of the street on which the Amorys' house stood. As he reached the house the door was opened, and a man came out and walked down the steps. He was a man with a large frame, a darkly florid complexion, and heavily handsome features. As he passed Arbuthnot he gave him a glance and a rather grudging bow, which expressed candidly exactly the amount of pleasure he derived from encountering him.

Bertha was in the parlor alone. When Arbuthnot entered he found her standing in the middle of the room, looking down at the roses on her gayly painted fan, and evidently not seeing them.

"Well," he began, by way of greeting, "I hope you have been enjoying yourself — with your senator's."

She looked up, and made a quick, eager little movement toward him, as if she was more glad to see him than usual.

"Ah!" she exclaimed. "I believe I was wishing you would come."

"Thank you," he said; "but the compliment would be greater if you were sure of it."

"I think I am sure of it, now you are here," she answered, "though I don't know at all why I wanted you — unless it was to tell you that I have not been enjoying myself in the least — with my senators."

"I am delighted to hear it," he replied. "Nothing could please me better. They are always too numerous, and lately one is continually meeting them on the steps and being scowled at."

She shut her fan quickly, with a slight frown.

"Why scowled at?" she said. "That would be absurd enough."

"Absurd or not," he laughed, "it is true."

But, notwithstanding his laugh, there was no change in her face he did not see.

They had seated themselves by this time, and Bertha was looking at her fan again, and opening and shutting it slowly.

"They are not my senators," she said. "They are Richard's, and — I am getting a little tired of them, though I should not like to tell him so. When it is warm, as it is to-day, I am very tired of them."

"I should not think it at all improbable," remarked Arbuthnot, dryly. "It has struck me that it would be necessary for the mercury to be several degrees below zero before you would find the one who went out just now, for instance, especially exhilarating."

"He is not exhilarating at all," she said. "Richard likes him," she added, a moment afterward. "I don't know exactly why, but he really seems to admire him. They are quite intimate. I think the acquaintance began through some law business he gave him in connection with the Westoria lands. I have tried to like him on Richard's account. You must remember," she said, with a smile, "I first tried to like you on Richard's account."

"I hope you succeeded better than you will with Planefield," he said.

"I might succeed with him if I persevered long enough," she answered. "The difficulty lies in the perseverance. Richard says I would make a good lobbyist, but I am sure I should not. I could not be persistently amiable and entertaining to people who tired me."

"Don't deplore your deficiencies until it becomes necessary for you to enter the profession," said Arbuthnot. "I don't like to hear you speak of it," he added, with a touch of sharpness.

"I don't deplore them," said Bertha. "And it is only one of my little jokes. But, if the fortunes of the Westoria lands depended on me, I am afraid they would be a dismal failure."

"As they don't depend on you," he remarked, "doesn't it occur to you that you might as well leave them to Senator Planefield? I must confess it has presented itself to me in that light."

"It is rather odd," she said, in a tone of reflection, "that though I have nothing whatever to do with them, they actually seem to have detained me in town for the last two weeks."

"It is quite time you went away," said Arbuthnot.

"I know that," she answered. "And I feel it more every day."

She raised her eyes suddenly to his.

"Laurence," she said, "I am not well. Don't tell Richard, but I think I am not well at all. I — I am restless and nervous — and — and morbid. I am actually morbid. Things trouble me which never troubled me before. Sometimes I lose all respect for myself. You know I always was rather proud of my self-control. I am not quite as proud of it as I used to be. About two weeks ago I — I positively lost my temper."

He did not laugh, as she had been half-afraid he would. His manner was rather quiet; on the contrary — it was as if what she said struck him as being worth listening to with some degree of serious attention, though his reply was not exactly serious.

"I hope you had sufficient reason," he said.

"No," she answered. "I had no reason at all, which makes it all the more humiliating. I think I have been rather irritable for a month or two. I have allowed myself to — to be disturbed by things which were really of no consequence, and I have taken offence at things and — and — resented trifles, and it was the merest trifle which made me lose my temper — yes, actually lose my temper, and say what I did not intend to gay, in the most open and abject manner. What could be more abject than to say things you did not intend to say? You know I never was given to that kind of thing."

"No," he responded, "it cannot be said that you were."

"It was so — so revolting to me after it was over," she went on, "that it seemed to make me more weak-minded than ever. When you once give way to your emotions it is all going downhill — you do it again and again. I never did it before, but I have been on the verge of doing it two or three times since."

"Don't go any farther than the verge," he said.

"I don't intend to," she answered. "I don't like even the verge. I resent it with all my strength. I should like to invent some kind of horrible torture to pay myself for — for what I did."

He was watching her very closely, but she was not aware of it. She had arrested his attention completely enough by this time, and the fact made itself evident in his intent and rather startled expression.

"I hope it was nothing very serious," he said.

"It was serious enough for me," she replied. "Nobody else was hurt, but it was serious enough for me — the mere knowing that for a few minutes I had lost my hold on myself. I didn't like it —I didn't like it!"

There was an intensity in her manner, in her voice, in her face, in her very figure itself, which was curiously disproportionate to her words. She leaned forward a little, and laid her small, clenched hand upon her knee.

"In all my life," she said, slowly, — "in all my life, I have never had a feeling which was as strong as myself. I have been that fortunate. I have been angry, but never so angry that I could not seem perfectly still and calm; I have been happy, but never so happy that I could not have hidden it if I chose; I have been unhappy — for a moment or so — but never so unhappy that I had the horrible anguish of being found out. I am not capable of strong, real emotions. I am too shallow and — and light. I have been light all my life, and I *will* be light until the end."

"Only the children could make me suffer, really," she said after it, — "only the children, and all women are like that. Through Janey, or Jack, or Meg, my heart could be torn in two, if they were in pain, or badly treated, or taken from me, — that is nothing but common nature; but nothing else could hurt me so that I should cry out — nothing and nobody — not even Richard!"

She stopped herself, and opened her fan again.

"There!" she exclaimed. "Why did I say so much then, and say it so vehemently, as if it was of consequence? Nothing is of consequence — nothing, nothing!" And she laughed, and rose and began to take up and set down again some trifles on the mantel.

Arbuthnot still watched her.

"No," he said, "you are quite right; nothing is of consequence really, and the sooner one learns that, the better for one's peace of mind. The worst pain you could have to bear could not last you more than a few score years, and you would get used to it in that time; the greatest happiness you could yearn for would not last any longer, and you would get tired of it in time, too."

"Tired of it!" she echoed. "One could tire of anything in threescore years and ten. How tired one must be of one's self before it is over — how tired! how tired!" and she threw up her hands in a sudden, desperate gesture.

"No," he answered, in a tone whose level coolness was a forcible contrast to her own. "Not necessarily, if one doesn't expect too much. If we take things for what they are worth, and don't let ourselves be deceived by them, there is plenty of rational entertainment to be had by the way. We mayn't like it quite as well as what we set out with expecting, but we can manage to subsist upon it. I hope I am logical. I know I am not eloquent." He said it bitterly.

"No," she returned, without looking at him, "you are not eloquent, perhaps, but you are speaking the truth — and I like to hear it. I want to hear it. It is good for me. It is always good for people to hear the truth; the bare, unvarnished, unadorned truth. Go on."

"If I go on," he said, still bitterly, "I shall begin to drag myself in, and I don't care to do it. It is natural that I should feel the temptation. I never knew the man yet who could talk in this strain and not drag himself in."

"Drag yourself in as much as you like," she said, even fiercely, "and be an example to me."

"I should be example enough if I said all I could," he replied. "Am I a happy man?"

She turned, and for a moment they looked into each other's eyes; his were stern, hard, and miserable.

"No," she cried out, "you are not. No one is happy in the world!" And she dropped her face upon her hands as she leaned upon the mantel.

"I might have been happier if I had begun right, I suppose," he said.

"Begun!" she repeated. "Does any one ever begin right? One ought to begin at the end and go backward, and then one might make something of it all."

"I didn't make much of it," he said. "I was not as wise as you. I began with emotions, and follies, and fires, — and the rest of it, and the enjoyment I derived from them was scarcely what I anticipated it would be. The emotions didn't last, and the follies didn't pay, and the fires burnt out — and that was the worst of all. And they always do — and that is worse still. It is in the nature of things. Look at that grate," pointing to it. "It looked different a week ago, when we had a rainy night and sat around it. We could have burned ourselves at it then if we had been feeble-minded enough to try it; we couldn't do it now; and yet a few days ago it was hot enough. The fire has burned out, and even the ashes are gone."

She stooped down, picked up her fan, and reseated herself upon the sofa. She did not look quite like herself, — her face was very pale but for the two red spots Tredennis had seen on her cheeks when her display of feeling had startled him; but all at once a change had taken place in her manner. There was a sort of deadly stillness in it.

"We are a long way from my temper," she said, — "a long way."

"Yes," he replied, "about as far as we could get in the space of time allowed us; and we have been a trifle emotional."

"And it was my fault," she continued. "Isn't it time I went somewhere cool and bracing? I think you must admit it is."

"Yes," he said, "it is time. Take my advice, and go."

"I'll go," she said, steadily, "the day after to-morrow. And I'll not go to Fortress Munroe. I'll go into the mountains of Virginia, — to a farmhouse I know of, where one has forests, and silence, and nature — and nothing else. I'll take the children, and live out-of-doors with them, and read to them, and talk to them, and sew for them when I want anything to do. I always was happy and natural when I was sewing and doing things for them. I like it. Living in that simple, natural way, and having the children with me, will rest and cure me if anything will on earth; the children always — the children"—

She stopped and sat perfectly still; her voice had broken, and she had turned her face a little away.

Arbuthnot got up. He stood a moment, as he always did before going, but he did not look directly at her, though he did not seem to avoid her in his glance.

"It is the best thing you can do," he said, — "the very best thing. You will be thoroughly rested when you come home, and that is what you need. I will go now; I hear Richard, and I want to speak to him alone."

And by the time the door opened and Richard stood on the threshold, he had reached him and turned him around, throwing his arm boyishly over his shoulder.

"You are just in time," he said. "Take me into the museum, or the library. I want to have a confidential chat with you."

And they went out together.

Chapter 13

The following day Richard presented himself to Tredennis in the morning, looking a little disturbed, and scarcely in such excellent spirits as usual.

"Bertha and the children are going away to-morrow," he said. "And if you have no other engagement you are to come and dine with us this evening and say good-by."

"I have no other engagement," Tredennis answered. "I shall be glad to come. They are really going to Fortress Monroe to-morrow?"

Richard threw himself into a chair with a rather discontented air. "They are not going to Fortress Munroe at all," he said. "They are going to bury themselves in the mountains of Virginia. It is a queer fancy of Bertha's. I think she is making a mistake. She won't like it, really, when she tries it."

"If she needs rest," said Tredennis, "certainly the mountains of Virginia" —

"The mountains of Virginia," interrupted Richard, "were not made for Bertha. She will tire of them in a week. I wish she would not go!" he said, with the faintest possible touch of petulance.

"You will miss her very much, of course," said Tredennis.

"Oh, yes, I shall miss her. I always miss her — and I shall miss her specially just now."

"Just now?" said Tredennis.

"Oh," said Richard, straightening himself somewhat and clearing his slightly knitted brow, "I was only thinking of two or three plans which had half-formed themselves in my mind. I was looking at it from a selfish point of view, which I had no right to do. I suppose things might wait — until she comes back."

"Are you going with her?" said Tredennis.

"I!" exclaimed Richard. "No, I could not do that. My business would not allow of it. I have more than usual on hand just now. I shall run down to see them once a week, if possible. I must confess," with a laugh, "that I could not make up my mind to three months of it. Bertha knows that."

Taking all things into consideration, he bore the prospect of his approaching loneliness very well. He soon began to speak of other matters, and before he took his departure had quite recovered his usual gayety. As he talked Tredennis regarded him with some curiosity.

"He has a fortunate temperament," he was thinking. "He would have been happy if she had remained, but he is not unhappy because she goes. There are men who would take it less lightly — though, after all, he is the one to be envied."

Tredennis did not feel that he himself was greatly to be envied. He had said that she ought to go, and had been anxious and unhappy because she had not gone; but now that she was going he was scarcely happier. There were things he should miss every day. As he remembered them, he knew he had not allowed himself to admit what their value had been to him. The very fact that they had not been better friends made it harder. From the first he had been aware that a barrier stood between them, and in the interview which had revealed to him something of its nature he had received some sharp wounds.

"There was truth in what she said," he had often pondered since, "though she put it in a woman's way. I have resented what she has said and done, often enough, and have contrasted it bitterly with what I remembered — God knows why! I had no right to do it, and it was all folly; but I did it, and made myself wretched through it — and she saw the folly, and not the wretchedness."

But now that her presence would no longer color and animate the familiar rooms he realized what their emptiness would be. He could not endure the thought of what it would be to go into them for the first time and sit alone with Richard, — no bright figure moving before them, or sitting in its chair by the table, or the window, or the hearth. The absence of the very things which had angered and disturbed him would leave a blank. It would actually be a wretchedness to see no longer that she often chose to be flippant, and mocked for mere mocking's sake.

"What!" he said, savagely, "am I beginning to care for her very faults? Then it is best that she should go."

But his savageness was not against Bertha, but against himself and his weakness.

When he arrived at the house in the evening he found Bertha in the parlor, with Jack and Janey, who were to be allowed to share the farewell dinner.

As she advanced to meet him with a child on either side, he was struck by certain changes which he observed in her dress and manner. She wore a dark, simple gown, her hair was dressed a trifle more closely and plainly than usual, and there was no color about her. When she gave him her hand, and stood with the other resting on Jack's shoulder, her eyes uplifted to his own, he was bewildered by a feeling that he was suddenly brought face to face with a creature quite strange to him. He could not have said that she was actually cold and reserved, but there was that in the quiet of her manner which suggested both reserve and coldness.

"I have allowed the children to stay downstairs," she said, "and they are to dine with us if they will be good. They wished very much to see as much of you as possible — as it will be some time before they return — and I think they will be quiet."

"If you will seat one on each side of me," said Tredennis, "I will keep them quiet."

"You are very kind," she answered, "but I should scarcely like to do that."

And then she returned to her seat by the window, and he sat opposite her on the end of a sofa, with Janey leaning against his knee.

"You are not going to Fortress Monroe?" he said.

"No," she replied; "I am going to the Virginia mountains."

"I should think that would be better," he said, putting an arm around Janey.

"I thought so," she answered, "upon reflection. I am not as strong as I should be, and I think I dislike ill-health even more than most people do."

She held Jack's hand, and spoke in a quiet tone of common things, — of her plans for the summer, of the children, of Richard; and Tredennis listened like a man in a dream, missing the color and vivacity from her manner as he had known he should miss her presence from the rooms when she was gone.

"Tell Uncle Philip something of what we are going to do," she said to Jack. "Tell him about the hammocks, and the spades we are to dig with, and the books. We are to live out of doors and enjoy ourselves immensely," she added, with a faint smile.

"Mamma is going to play with us every day," said Jack, triumphantly. "And we are going to lie in our hammocks while she reads to us and tells us stories."

"And there will be no parties and no company," added Janey. "Only we are to be the company."

"And Jack is to take care of me," said Bertha, "because I am growing old, and he is so big."

Jack regarded her dubiously.

"You haven't any wrinkles," he said.

"Yes, I have, Jack," she answered; "but they don't show." And a little laugh broke from her, and she let her cheek rest against his dark love-locks for a moment in a light caress.

Glancing up at the colonel's face at this juncture, Janey found cause in it for serious dissatisfaction. She raised her hand, and drew a small forefinger across his forehead.

"Uncle Philip," she said, "you are bad again. The black marks have come back, and you are quite ugly; and you promised you would try not to let them come any more."

"I beg your pardon, Janey," he answered, and then turned to Bertha. "She does not like my black face," he said, "and no wonder. I am rather an unfortunate fellow to have my faults branded upon me so plainly that even a child can see them."

There was a touch of bitterness in the words, and in his manner of uttering them. Bertha answered him in a soft, level voice.

"You are severe upon yourself," she said. "It is much safer to be severe upon other people."

It was rather cruel, but she did not object to being cruel. There come to most women moments when to be cruel is their only refuge against themselves and others; and such a moment had come to her.

In looking back upon the evening, when it was over, the feeling that it had been unreal was stronger in Tredennis's mind than any other. It was all unreal from beginning to end, — the half-hour before dinner, when Arbuthnot and Richard and the professor came in, and Bertha stood near her father's chair and talked to him, and Tredennis, holding Janey on his knee and trying to answer her remarks lucidly, was aware only of the presence of the dark, slender figure near him, and the strange quiet of the low voice; the dinner itself, during which Richard was in the most attractive mood, and the professor was rather silent, and Arbuthnot's vivacity was a little fitful at first and afterward seemed to recover itself and rise to the occasion; while Bertha, with Jack on one hand and Janey on the other, cared for their wants and answered Richard's sallies, and aided him in them, and yet was not herself at all, but a new being.

"And you think," said the professor, later in the evening, when they had returned to the parlors, — "you think that you will like the quiet of the mountains?"

"I think it will be good for me," she answered, "and the children will like it."

"She will not like it at all," said Richard. "She will abhor it in ten days, and she will rush off to Fortress Monroe, and dance every night to make up for her temporary mental aberration."

"No, she will not," said Arbuthnot. "She has made preparations to enjoy her seclusion in its dramatic aspects. She is going to retire from the world in the character of a graceful anchorite, and she has already begun to dress the part. She is going to be simple and serious, and a trifle severe; and it even now expresses itself in the lines and color of her gown."

She turned toward him, with the sudden gleam of some new expression in her eyes.

"How well you understand me!" she said. "No one else would have understood me so well. I never can deceive you, at least. Yes, you are quite right. I am going to enjoy the thing dramatically. I don't want to go, but as I feel it discreet I intend to amuse myself, and make the best of it. I am going to play at being maternal and amiable, and even domesticated. I have a costume for it, as I have one for bathing and dining and making calls. "This," she said, touching her dress, "is part of it. Upstairs I have a little mob-cap and an apron, and a work-basket to carry on my arm. They are not unbecoming, either. Shall I run up into the nursery and put them on, and show them to you? Then you can be sure that I comprehend the part."

"Have you a mob-cap and an apron?" asked Richard. "Have you, really?"

"Yes, really," she answered. "Don't you remember that I told you that it was my dresses that were of consequence, and not myself? Shall I go and put them on?"

Her tone was soft no longer; it was a little hard, and so was the look which half hid itself behind the brightness of the eyes she turned toward him.

"Yes," he answered. "Put them on, and let us see them."

She turned round and went out of the room, and Arbuthnot followed her with a rather anxious glance. The professor stirred his tea as usual, and Tredennis turned his attention to Janey, while Richard laughed.

"I have no doubt she has all three," he said. "And they will be well worth seeing."

They were worth seeing. In a few minutes she returned, — the little work-basket on her arm, the mob-cap upon her head, the apron around her waist, and a plain square of white muslin crossed upon her bosom. She stopped in the door-way, and made a courtesy.

"There ought to be a curtain, and somebody ought to ring it up," she said. "Enter the domestic virtues."

And she came and stood before them, her eyes shining still, and her head erect, but — perhaps through the rather severe black and white of her costume — seeming to have a shade less color than before.

"I did not make them for this occasion," she said. "They have appeared before. You don't remember them, Richard, but I had them when Jack was a baby — and a novelty. I tried being maternal then."

"Why, yes," said Richard, "to be sure I remember them, — and very becoming they were, too."

"Oh, yes," she answered. "I knew they were becoming!"

She turned and fronted Tredennis.

"I hope they are becoming now," she said, and made her little courtesy again.

"They are very becoming," he answered, looking at her steadily. "I like them better than — the silks and brocades."

"Thank you," she said. "I thought you would — or I would not have put them on. Jack and Janey, come and stand on each side of me while I sit down. I have always congratulated myself that you were becoming. This is what we shall be constrained to do when we are in Virginia, only we shall not have the incentive of being looked at."

"We will make up a party," said Richard, "and come down once a week to look at you. Planefield would enjoy it, I am sure."

"Thank you," said Bertha. "And I will always bring out the work-basket, with a lace-collar for Meg in it. Lace-collars are more becoming than small aprons or stocking-mending. Do you remember the little shirt Mrs. Eawdon Crawley was making for her boy, and which was always produced when she was in virtuous company? Poor Eawdon was quite a big boy, and very much too large for it, by the time it was finished. I wonder if Meg will be grown up before she gets her collar."

She produced a needle, threaded it, and took a few stitches, bending her head over her task with a serious air.

"Does it look as if I had done it before?" she said. "I hope it does. I really have, you know. Once I sewed on a button for Richard."

But she did not sew many minutes. Soon she laid her work down in the basket.

"There!" she said, "that is enough! I have made my impression, and that is all I care for — or I *should* have made my impression if you had been strangers. If you had not known me you would have had time to say to one another: 'What a simple, affectionate little creature she must be! After all, there is nothing which becomes a woman so well as to sit at her work in that quiet, natural way, with her children about her!' Come, Jack and Janey, it is time for you to say good-night, and let me make a pretty exit with you, in my mob-cap and apron."

She took them away, and remained upstairs with them until they were in bed. When she came back she did not bring the work-basket, but she had not taken off the cap and handkerchief. She held an open letter in her hand, and went to Richard and sat down by him. Her manner had changed again entirely. It was as if she had left upstairs something more than the work-basket.

"Richard," she said, "I did not tell you I had had a letter from Agnes Sylvestre."

"From Agnes Sylvestre!" he exclaimed. "Why, no, you didn't! But it is good news. Laurence, you must remember Agnes Sylvestre!"

"Perfectly," was the answer. "She was not the kind of person you forget."

"She was a beautiful creature," said Richard, "and I always regretted that we lost sight of her as we did after her marriage. Where is she now, Bertha?"

"When she wrote she was at Castellamare. She went abroad, you know , immediately after her husband's death."

"He was not the nicest fellow in the world, — that Sylvestre," said Richard. "He was not the man for a woman like that to marry. I wonder if she did not find out that she had made a mistake?"

"If she did," said Bertha, "she bore it very well, and it has been all over for more than two years."

She turned suddenly to Tredennis.

"Did not you once tell me" — she began.

"Yes," he replied. "I met her in Chicago, and Mr. Sylvestre was with her."

"It must have been two or three weeks before his death," said Bertha. "He died quite suddenly, and they were in Chicago at the time. Do you remember how she looked, and if you liked her? — but of course you liked her."

"I saw her only for a short time," he answered. "We talked principally of you. She was very handsome, and had a sweet voice and large, calm eyes."

Bertha was silent a moment.

"Yes," she said next, "she has beautiful eyes. They are large and clear, like a child's, but they are not childish eyes. She sees a great deal with them. I think there was never anything more effective than a way she has of looking at you quietly and directly for a few seconds, without saying anything at all."

"You wonder what she is thinking of," said Arbuthnot. "And you hope she is thinking of yourself, and are inclined to believe she is, when there are ten chances to one that she is not at all."

"But she generally is," said Bertha. "The trouble is that perhaps she is not thinking exactly what you would like best, though she will never tell you so, and you would not discover it from her manner. She had an adorable manner; it is soft and well-bred, but she never wastes herself."

"I remember," said Tredennis, "that I thought her very attractive."

Bertha turned more directly toward him.

"She is exactly what you would like," she said, — "exactly. When I said just now that her way of looking at people was effective, I used the worst possible word, and did her an injustice. She is never effective — in that way. To be effective, it seems to me, you must apply yourself. Agnes Sylvestre never applies herself. Trifles do not amuse her as they amuse me. I entertain myself with my whims and with all sorts of people; she has no whims, and cares only for the people she is fond of. If she were here to-night she would look calmly at my mob-cap and apron, and wonder what I meant by them, and what mental process I had gone through to reach the point of finding it worth while to wear them."

"Oh," said Arbuthnot, "I should not think she was slow at following mental processes."

"No," answered Bertha, "I did not mean that. She would reason clearly enough, after she had looked at me a few moments and asked herself the question. But in talking of her I am forgetting to tell you that she is coming home, and will spend next winter in Washington."

"Congratulate yourself, Laurence," said Richard. "We may all congratulate ourselves. It will be something more to live for."

"As to congratulating myself," said Arbuthnot, "I should have no objection to devoting the remainder of the evening to it, but I am afraid —"

"Of what?" demanded Bertha.

"Oh," he answered, "she will see through *me* with her calm eyes; and, as you say, she never wastes herself."

"No," said Bertha, "she never wastes herself. And, after all, it is Colonel Tredennis who has most reason to congratulate himself. He has not thrown away his time. I am obliged to admit that she once said to me of you, 'Why does he throw away his time? Does he never think at all?' Yes, it is Colonel Tredennis who must be congratulated."

It was chiefly of Agnes Sylvestre they talked during the rest of the evening.

"She is a person who says very little of herself," was Bertha's comment, "but there is a great deal to say of her."

And so there seemed to be. There were anecdotes to be related of her, the charm of her beauty and manner was to be analyzed, and all of her attributes were found worth touching upon.

It was Tredennis who took his departure first. When he rose to go, Bertha, who was talking to Arbuthnot, did not at first observe his movement, and when he approached her she turned with an involuntary start.

"You — are going now?" she said.

"Yes," he answered. "I wish you a pleasant summer and all the rest you require."

She stood up and gave him her hand.

"Thank you," she replied. "I shall be sure to have the rest."

It scarcely seemed more than the ordinary conventional parting for the night; to Tredennis it seemed something less. There were only a few words more, and he dropped her hand and went out of the room.

He had certainly felt that this was the last, and only a powerful effort of will held in check a feeling whose strength he would have been loath to acknowledge.

"Such things are always a wrench," he said, mentally. "I never bore them well."

And he had barely said it when he heard Bertha cross the parlor quickly and pass through the door. He had bent to take up a paper he had left on the hat-stand, and when he turned she was close to him.

Something in her look was so unusual that he recognized it with an inward start. Her eyes were a little dilated, and her breath came with soft quickness, as if she had moved rapidly and impulsively. She put out both her hands with a simple, sudden gesture, and with an action as simple and unpremeditated he took them and held them in his own.

"I came," she said, "to say good-by again. All at once I seemed to — to realize that it would be months before I — we saw you again. And so many things happen, and — "She stopped a second, but went on after it. "When I come back," she said, "I shall be well and strong, and like a new person. Say good-by to this person;" and a smile came and went as she said it.

"A moment ago," he answered, "I was telling myself that good-byes were hard upon me."

"They — they are not easy," she said.

This, at least, was not easy for him. Her hands were trembling in his clasp. The thought came to him that perhaps some agitation she wished to hide had driven her from the room within, and she had come to him for momentary refuge because he was near. She looked up at him for a second with a touch of desperation in her eyes, and then he saw her get over it, and she spoke.

"Jack and Janey will miss you very much," she said. "You have been very kind to them. I think — it is your way to be good to every one."

"My opportunities of being good have been limited," he said. "If — if one should present itself," — and he held her hands a little closer, — "you won't let me miss my chance, will you? There is no reason for my saying so much, of course, but — but you will try to remember that I am here and always ready to come when I am called."

"Yes," she said, "I think you would come if I called you. And I thank you very much. And good-by — good-by."

And she drew her hands away and stood with them hanging clasped before her, as if she meant to steady them, and so she stood until he was gone.

He was breathing quickly himself when he reached the street.

"Yes," he said, "the professor was right. It is Arbuthnot — it is Arbuthnot."

Chapter 14

When he passed the house the next day they were gone. The nursery windows were thrown open, and he fancied that the place wore a deserted look. The very streets seemed empty, and the glare of sunshine, whose heat increased with every hour, added to the air of desolateness he imagined.

"It *is* imagination," he said. "And the feeling will die away all the more quickly because I recognize the unreality of it. By to-morrow or the day after I shall have got over it."

And yet a week later, when he dropped in upon the professor, one sultry evening, to spend an hour with him, his old friend found cause for anxious inspection of him.

"What," he said, "the hot weather begins to tell on you already! You are not acclimatized yet, — that's it. You must spare yourself as much as possible. It doesn't promise well that you look fagged so soon. I should say you had not slept well."

"I don't sleep well," Tredennis answered.

"You are working too hard," said the professor; "that is it, perhaps."

"I am not working hard enough," replied Tredennis, with a slight knitting of the brows. "I wish I had more to do. Leisure does not agree with me."

"One must occupy one's self!" said the professor. He spoke half-absently, and yet with a touch of significance in his tone which — combined with the fact that he had heard the words before — caused Tredennis to glance at him quickly.

He smiled slightly, in answer to the glance.

"Bertha?" he said. "Oh, yes, I am quoting Bertha. Your manner is not as light as hers, but it reminded me of her in some way; perhaps because I had a letter from her to-day, and she was in my thoughts."

"I hope she is well," said Tredennis, "and does not find her farm-house too dull."

"She does not complain of it," the professor answered. "And she says nothing of her own health, but tells me she is a little anxious about Janey, who does not seem quite herself."

Tredennis looked out into the darkening street. They were sitting by the opened window.

"She was not well when she went away," he said, a trifle abstractedly.

"Janey?" asked the professor, as if the idea was new to him; "I did not know that."

Tredennis roused himself.

"I — was thinking of Bertha," he said.

"Oh, of Bertha," said the professor, and then he lapsed into a reverie himself for a few moments: and seemed to watch the trees on the street without seeing them.

"No, she was not well," he said, at length; "but I think she will be better when she comes back."

"The rest and quiet" — began Tredennis.

"I think she had determined to be better," said the professor.

"Determined?" repeated Tredennis.

"She has a strong will," returned the professor, "though it is a thing she is never suspected of. She does not suspect herself of it, and yet she has relied upon its strength from the first, and is relying upon it now. I am convinced that she went away with the determination to conquer a restlessness whose significance she is just awakening to. And she deliberately chose nature and the society of her children as the best means of cure."

"Do you think," asked Tredennis, in a low voice, "that she will get over it?"

The professor turned to look at him.

"I don't know," he answered, with a slight tone of surprise. "Why did you fancy I would?"

"You seem to understand her," said Tredennis.

The professor sighed.

"I have studied her so long," he replied, "that I imagine I know what she is *doing*, but you can't safely go beyond that with women; you can't say what they are *going* to do, — with any degree of certainty. They are absorbingly interesting as a study, but they are not to be relied on. And they rarely compliment your intelligence by doing what you expect of them. *She* has not done what I expected. She has lived longer than I thought she would without finding herself out. A year ago she believed that she had proved to herself that such an emotion as —as this was impossible to her. It was a very innocent belief, and she was entirely sincere in it, and congratulated herself upon it." He turned to Tredennis again with a sudden movement and a curious look of pain in his face. "I am afraid it's a great mistake," he said.

"What?" Tredennis asked.

"This — this feeling," he said, in a tremulous and troubled voice. "I don't mean in her alone, but in any one, everywhere. I am not sure that it ever brings happiness really in the end. I am afraid there always is an end. If there wasn't, it might be different; but I am afraid there is. There are those of us who try to believe there is none, but — but I am afraid those are happiest who lose all but their ideal. There are many who lose even that, and Fate has done her worst by them." He checked himself, and sank back in his chair.

"Ah!" he said, smiling half sadly. "I am an old man — an old man, — and it is an old man's fancy, that the best thing in life is death. And Fate did not do her worst by me; she left me my ideal. She had gray eyes," he added, "and a bright face, like Bertha's. Perhaps, after all, if I had won what I wanted, I should not feel so old to-night, and so tired. Her face was very bright."

He had not been wholly well for some days, and to-night seemed fatigued by the heat and languor in the air, but he was somewhat more hopeful when he spoke of Bertha than he had been.

"I have confidence in the strength of her will," he said, "and I like her pride and courage. She does not give away to her emotions; she resents them fiercely, and refuses to acknowledge their powers over her. She insists to herself that her restlessness is nervousness, and her sadness morbid."

"She said as much to me," said Tredennis.

"Did she?" exclaimed the professor. "That is a good sign; it shows that she has confidence in you, and that it is a feeling strong enough to induce her to use you as a defence against her own weakness. She would never have spoken if she had not believed that you were a sort of stronghold. It is the old feeling of her girlhood ruling her again. Thank Heaven for that!"

There was a ring at the front-door bell as he spoke, and a moment or so later it was answered by a servant; buoyant feet were heard in the hall, and paused a second on the threshold.

"Are you here, Professor?" some one inquired. "And may I come in?"

Professor Herrick turned his head.

"Come in, Richard," he said; "come in, by all means." And Amory entered and advanced toward them.

The slight depression of manner Tredennis had fancied he had seen in him on the last two occasions of their meeting had disappeared altogether. He seemed even in gayer spirits than usual.

"I have come to tell you," he said to the professor, "that I am going away for a short time. It is a matter of business connected with the Westoria lands. I may be away a week or two."

"Isn't it rather a long journey?" asked the professor.

"Oh, yes," he replied, with no air of being daunted by the prospect, — "and a tiresome one, but it is important that I should make it, and I shall not be alone."

"Who is to be your companion?"

"Planefield — and he's rather an entertaining fellow, in his way — Planefield. Oh, it won't be so bad, on the whole."

"It is Planefield who is interested in the lands, if I remember rightly," suggested the professor.

"Oh, Planefield?" Richard replied, carelessly. "Well, more or less. He is given to interesting himself in things, and, by Jove!" he added with a laugh, "this promises to be a good thing to be interested in. I shouldn't mind if I" —

"My dear Richard," interposed the professor, "allow me to advise you not to do so. You'll really find it best. Such things rarely end well."

Richard laughed again.

"My dear Professor," he answered, with much good-humor, "you may rely upon me. I haven't any money of my own."

"And if you had money?" said the professor.

"I think I should risk it. I really do. Though why I should say risk, I hardly know. There is scarcely enough risk to make it exciting."

He was very sanguine, and once or twice became quite brilliant on the subject. The great railroad, which was to give the lands an enormous value, was almost an established fact; everything was being laid in train: a man influenced here, a touch given there, a vigorous move made in this direction, an interest awakened in that, and the thing was done.

"There isn't a doubt of the termination," he said, "not a doubt. It's a brilliant sort of thing that is its own impetus, one might say, and the right men are at work for it, and the right worn —"

"Were you going to say women?" asked Tredennis, when he pulled himself up somewhat abruptly.

"Well, yes," Richard said, blithely. "After all, why not? I must confess to finding the fact lend color and vivacity to the thing. And the delightful cleverness the clever ones show is a marvellous power for or against a thing, though I think the feminine tendency is to work for a thing, not against it."

"I should like to know," said Tredennis, "how they begin it."

For a moment he thought he did not know why he asked the question; but the self-delusion did not last long. He felt an instant later that he did know, and wished that he did not.

"In nine cases out of ten," Richard replied, giving himself up at once to an enjoyable analysis of the subject, — "in nine cases out of ten it is my impression they begin with almost entire lack of serious intention, and rarely, if ever, even in the end, admit to themselves that they have done what they are accused of. Given a clever and pretty woman whose husband or other male relative needs her assistance: why should she be less clever and pretty in the society of one political dignitary than in that of another, whose admiration of her charms may not be of such importance? I suppose that is the beginning, and then come the sense of power and the fascination of excitement. What woman does not like both? What woman is better and more charming than Bertha, and Bertha does not hesitate to admit, in her own delightful way, that there must have been a fascination in the lives of those historical charmers before whom prime ministers trembled, and who could make and unmake a cabinet with a smile."

"What," was the thought that leaped into Tredennis' mind, "do we begin to compare Bertha with a king's favorite!" But he did not say it aloud — it was not for him to defend her against her husband's lightness; and were they not her own words, after all? And so he could only sit silent in the shadow of his darkening corner and knit his heavy brows with hot resentment in his heart, while Richard went on:

"There are some few who make a profession of it," he said; "but they do not carry the most power. The woman who is ambitious for her husband, or eager for her son, or who wishes to escape from herself and find refuge in some absorbing excitement, necessarily is more powerful than the more sordid element. If I were going in for that kind of thing," he went on, settling himself in his favorite graceful, lounging posture, and throwing his arm lightly behind his head, — "if I were going in for it, and might make a deliberate choice, I think I should choose a woman who had something to forget, — a woman who had reached an emotional crisis — who was young, and yet who could not take refuge in girlish forgetfulness, and who, in spite of her youth, had lived beyond trusting in the future — a woman who represented beauty, and wit, and despair (the despair would be the strongest lever of all). There isn't a doubt of it that such a woman, taken at such a turning-point in her existence, could move — the world, if you like — the world itself;" and he arranged himself a trifle more comfortably, and half-laughed again.

"But," suggested the professor, "you are not going in for that sort of thing, my dear Richard."

"Oh, no, no!" answered Richard; "but if I were, I must confess it would have a fascination for me which would not permit of my regarding it in cold blood. I am like Bertha, you know — I like my little drama."

"And, speaking of Bertha," said the professor, "if anything should happen while you are away" —

"Now, really," said Richard, "that shows what a careless fellow I am! Do you know, it never once occurred to me that anything could happen. We have such an admirable record to look back upon, Bertha and I, though I think I usually refer the fact to Bertha's tact and executive ability; nothing ever has happened, and I feel that we have established a precedent. But, if anything should happen, you had better telegraph to Merritsville. In any ordinary event, however, I feel quite safe in leaving Bertha in your hands and Tredennis's," he said, smiling at the large shadow in the corner. "One is always sure, in the midst of the ruling frivolity, that Tredennis is to be relied on."

He went away soon after, and Tredennis, bidding the professor good-night, left the house with him.

As they passed down the steps Richard put his arm through his companion's with caressing friendliness.

"It wouldn't do you any harm to take a run up into Virginia yourself, once in a while," he said. "You have been losing ground since the heat set in, and we can't submit to that. We need your muscular development in its highest form, as an example to our modern deterioration. Kill two birds with one stone when you have a day's leisure, — go and see Bertha and the children, and lay in a new supply of that delightful robustness we envy and admire."

"I should be glad to see Bertha," said Tredennis.

"She would be glad to see you," Richard answered. "And, while I am away, it will be a relief to me to feel that she has you to call upon in case of need. The professor — dear old fellow — is not as strong as he was. And you — as I said before — one naturally takes the liberty of relying upon your silent substantiality."

"Thank you," said Tredennis. "If it is a matter of avoirdupois" —

Richard turned quickly to look at him.

"Ah, no," he said, "not that; though, being human, we respect the avoirdupois. It's something else, you know. Upon my word, I can't exactly say what, but something which makes a man feel instinctively that he can shift his responsibilities upon you and they will be in good hands. Perhaps it is not an enviable quality in one's self, after all. Here am I, you see, shifting Bertha and the children off on your shoulders."

"If I can be of any use to Bertha and the children, why not?" said Tredennis, tersely.

"Oh, but one might also say 'Why?'" returned Richard. "We haven't any claim on you, really, and yet we do it, or, rather, *I* do it, which speaks all the more strongly for your generosity and trustworthiness."

"And you will be away" — Tredennis began.

"Two or three weeks. It might be more, but I think not. We separate here, I think, as I am going to drop in on Planefield. Good-night, and thanks."

"Good-night," responded Tredennis, and they shook hands and parted.

Chapter 15

During the hot days and nights of the next few weeks Tredennis found life rather a dreary affair. Gradually the familiar faces he met on the avenue became fewer and fewer; the houses he knew one after another assumed their air of summer desertion, offering as their only evidences of life an occasional colored servant sunning him or herself on the steps; the crowds of nursery-maids, with their charges, thinned out in the parks, and the freshness of the leaves was lost under a coating of dust, while the countenances of those for whom there was no prospect of relief expressed either a languid sense of injury or the patience of despair.

"But, after all," Tredennis said, on two or three occasions, as he sat in one of the parks in the evening, — "after all, I suppose most of them have — an object," adding the last two words with a faint smile.

He was obliged to confess to himself that of late he found that the work which he had regarded as his object had ceased to satisfy him. He gave his attention to it with stern persistence, and refused to spare himself when he found his attention wandering; he even undertook additional labor, writing in his moments of leisure several notable articles upon various important questions of the day, and yet he had time left to hang heavily on his hands and fill him with weariness; and at last there came an evening when, after sitting in one of the parks until the lamps were lighted, he rose suddenly from his seat, and spoke as if to the silence and shadow about him.

"Why should I try to hide the truth from myself?" he said. "It is too late for that. I may as well face it like a man, and bear it like one. Many a brave fellow has carried a bullet in his body down to his grave, and seldom winced. This is something like that, I suppose, only that pain" — And he drew a sharp, hard breath, and walked away down the deserted path without ending the sentence.

He made a struggle after this to resist one poor temptation which beset him daily, — the temptation to pass through the street in which stood the familiar house, with its drawn blinds and closed doors. Sometimes, when he rose in the morning, he was so filled with an unreasoning yearning for a sight of its blankness that he was overwhelmed by it, and went out before he breakfasted.

"It is weakness and self-indulgence," he would say; "but it is a very little thing, and it can hurt no one — it is only a little thing, after all." And he found a piteous pleasure — at which at first he tried to smile, but at which before long he ceased even to try to smile — in the slow walk down the street, on which he could see this window or that, and remember' some day when he had caught a glimpse of Bertha through it, or some night he had spent in the room within when she had been gayer than usual, or quieter, — when she had given him some new wound, perhaps, or when she had half-healed an old one in some mood of relenting he had not understood.

"There is no reason why I should understand any woman," was his simple thought. "And why should I understand her, unless she chose to let me? She is like no other woman."

He was quite sure of this. In his thoughts of her he found every word and act of hers worth remembering and even repeating mentally again and again for the sake of the magnetic grace which belonged only to herself, and it never once occurred to him that his own deep sympathy and tender fancy might brighten all she did.

"When she speaks," he thought, "how the dullest of them stir and listen! When she moves across a room, how natural it is to turn and look at her, and be interested in what she is going to do! What life I have seen her put in some poor, awkward wretch by only seating herself near him and speaking to him of some common thing! One does not know what her gift is, and whether it is well for her or ill that it was given her, but one sees it in the simplest thing she does."

It was hard to avoid giving himself up to such thoughts as these, and when he most needed refuge from them he always sought it in the society of the professor; so there were few evenings when he did not spend an hour or so with him, and their friendship grew and waxed strong until there could scarcely have been a closer bond between them.

About two weeks after Richard Amory's departure, making his call later than usual one evening, he met, coming down the steps, Mr. Arbuthnot, who stopped, with his usual civility, to shake hands with him.

"It is some weeks since we have crossed each other's paths, colonel," he said, scrutinizing him rather closely: "and, in the meantime, I am afraid you have not been well."

"Amory called my attention to the fact a short time ago," responded Tredennis, "and so did the professor. So, perhaps, there is some truth in it. I hadn't noticed it myself."

"You will presently, I assure you," said Arbuthnot, still regarding him with an air of interest. "Perhaps Washington doesn't agree with you. I have heard of people who couldn't stand it. They usually called it malaria, but I think there was generally something" — He checked himself somewhat abruptly, which was a rather unusual demonstration on his part, as it was his habit to weigh his speech with laudable care and deliberation. "You are going to see the professor?" he inquired.

"Yes," answered Tredennis. The idea was presenting itself to his mind that there was a suggestion of something unusual in the questioner's manner; that it was not so entirely serene as was customary; that there was even a hint of some inward excitement strong enough to be repressed only by an effort. And the consciousness of this impressed itself upon him even while a flow of light talk went on, and Arbuthnot smiled at him from his upper step.

"I have been to see the professor, too," he was saying, "and I felt it was something of an audacity. His invitations to me have always been of the most general nature; but I thought I would take the liberty of pretending that I fancied he regarded them seriously. He was very good to me, and exhibited wonderful presence of mind in not revealing that he was surprised to see me. I tried not to stay long enough to tire him, and he was sufficiently amiable to ask me to come again. He evidently appreciated the desolation of my circumstances."

"You are finding it dull?" said Tredennis.

"Dull!" repeated Arbuthnot. "Yes; I think you might call it dull. The people who kindly condescend to notice me in the winter have gone away, and my dress-coat is packed in camphor. I have ceased to be useful; and, even if Fate had permitted me to be ornamental, where should I air my charms? There seems really no reason why I should exist, until next winter, when I may be useful again, and receive in return my modicum of entertainment. To be merely a superior young man in a department is not remunerative in summer, as one ceases to glean the results of one's superiority. At present I might as well be inferior, and neither dance, nor talk, nor sing, and be utterly incapacitated by nature for either carrying wraps or picking up handkerchiefs; and you cannot disport yourself at the watering-places of the rich and great on a salary of a hundred dollars a month; and you could only get your sordid 'month's leave,' if such a thing were possible."

"I — have been dull myself," said Tredennis, hesitantly.

"If it should ever occur to you to drop in and see a fellow-sufferer," said Arbuthnot, "it would relieve the monotony of *my* lot, at least, and might awaken in me some generous emotions."

Tredennis looked up at him.

"It never has occurred to you so far, I see," was Arbuthnot's light reply to the look; "but, if it should, don't resist the impulse. I can assure you it is a laudable one. And my humble apartment has the advantage of comparative coolness."

When Tredennis entered the library he found the professor sitting in his usual summer seat, near the window. A newspaper lay open on his knee, but he was not reading it; he seemed, indeed, to have fallen into a reverie of a rather puzzling kind.

"Did you meet any one as you came in?" he asked of Tredennis, as soon as they had exchanged greetings.

"I met Mr. Arbuthnot," Tredennis answered, "and stopped a few moments on the steps to talk to him."

"He has been entertaining me for the last hour," said the professor, taking off his glasses and beginning to polish them. "Now, will you tell me," he asked, with his quiet air of reflective inquiry into an interesting subject, — "will you tell me why he comes to entertain *me*?"

"He gave me the impression," answered Tredennis, "that his object in coming was that you might entertain him, and he added that you were very good to him, and he appeared to have enjoyed his call very much."

"That is his way," responded the professor, impartially. "And a most agreeable way it is. To be born with such a way as a natural heritage is to be a social millionnaire. And the worst of it is, that it may be a gift entirely apart from all morals and substantial virtues. Bertha has it. I don't know where she got it. Not from me, and not from her poor mother. I say it *may be* apart from all morals and substantial virtues. I don't say it always is. I haven't at all made up my mind what attributes go along with it in Arbuthnot's case. I should like to decide. But it would be an agreeable way in a criminal of the deepest dye. It is certainly agreeable that he should in some subtle manner be able to place me in the picturesque attitude of a dignified and entertaining host. I didn't entertain him at all," he added, simply. "I sat and listened to him."

"He is frequently well worth listening to," commented Tredennis.

"He was well worth listening to this evening," said the professor. "And yet he was light enough. He had two or three English periodicals under his arm, — one of them was 'Punch,' — and — and I found myself laughing quite heartily over it. And then there was something about a new comic opera, and he seemed to know the libretto by heart, and ran over an air or so on the piano. And he had been reading a new book, and was rather clever about it — in his way, of course, but still it was cleverness. And then he went to the piano again and sang a captivating little love-song very well, and, after it, got up and said good-night — and on the whole I regretted it. I liked his pictures, I liked his opera, I liked his talk of the book, and I liked his little love-song. And how should he know that an old dry-bones would like a tender little ballad and be touched by it, and pleased because his sentiment was discovered and pandered to? Oh, it is the old story. It's his way — it's the way."

"I am beginning to think," said Tredennis, slowly, "that 'his way' might be called sympathy and good feeling and fine tact, if one wanted to be specially fair to him."

The professor looked up rather quickly,

"I thought you did not like him," he said.

Tredennis paused a moment, looking down at the carpet as if deliberating.

"I don't think I do," he said at length; "but it's no fault of his — the fault lies in me. I haven't the way, and I am at a disadvantage with him. He is never at a loss, and I am; he is ready-witted and self-possessed; I am slow and rigid, and I suppose it is human that I should try to imagine at times that I am at a disadvantage only because my virtues are more solid than his. They are not more solid; they are only more clumsy and less available."

"You don't spare yourself," said the professor.

"Why should I spare myself?" said Tredennis, knitting his brows. "After all, *he* never spares himself. He knows better. He would be just to me. Why should I let him place me at a disadvantage again by being unjust to him? And why should we insist that the only good qualities are those which are unornamental? It is a popular fallacy. We like to believe it. It is very easy to suspect a man of being shallow because we are sure we are deep and he is unlike us. This Arbuthnot" —

"'This Arbuthnot,'" interposed the professor, with a smile. "It is curious enough to hear you entering upon a defence of 'this Arbuthnot.' You don't like him, Philip. You don't like him."

"I don't like myself," said Tredennis, "when I am compared with him; and I don't like the tendency I discover in myself, the tendency to disparage him. I should like to be fair to him, and I find it difficult."

"Upon my word," said the professor, "it is rather fine in you to make the effort, but" — giving him one of the old admiring looks — "you are always rather fine, Philip."

"It would be finer, sir," said Tredennis, coloring, "if it were not an effort."

"No," said the professor, quietly, "it would not be half so fine." And he put out his hand and let it rest upon the arm of the chair in which Tredennis sat, and so it rested as long as their talk went on.

In the meantime Arbuthnot walked rather slowly down the street, quite conscious of finding it necessary to make something of an effort to compose himself. It was his recognition of this necessity which had caused him to change his first intention of returning to his bachelor apartment after having made his call upon Professor Herrick. And he felt the necessity all the more strongly after his brief encounter with Colonel Tredennis.

"I will go into the park and think it over," he said to himself. "I'll give myself time."

He turned into Lafayette Park, found a quiet seat, and took out a very excellent cigar. He was not entirely surprised to see that, as he held the match to it, his hand was not as steady as usual. Tredennis had thought him a little pale.

The subject of his reflections, as he smoked his cigar, was a comparatively trivial incident; taken by itself, but he had not taken it by itself, because in a flash it had connected itself with a score of others, which at the times of their occurring had borne no significance whatever to him.

His visit to the professor had not been made without reasons; but they had been such reasons as, simply stated to the majority of his ordinary acquaintance, would have been received with open amazement or polite discredit, and this principally because they were such very simple reasons indeed. If such persons had been told that, finding himself without any vestige of entertainment, he had wandered in upon the professor as a last resource, or that he had wished to ask of him some trivial favor, or that he had made his call without any reason whatever, they would have felt such a state of affairs probable enough; but being informed that while sitting in the easiest of chairs, in the coolest possible *negligée*, reading an agreeable piece of light literature, and smoking a cigar before his open window, he had caught sight of the professor at *his* window, sitting with his head resting on his hand, and being struck vaguely by some air of desolateness and lassitude in the solitary old figure, had calmly laid aside book and cigar, had put himself into conventional attire, and had walked across the street with no other intention than that of making the best of gifts of entertainment it was certainly not his habit to overvalue, —

those to whom the explanation had been made would have taken the liberty of feeling it somewhat insufficient, and would, in nine cases out of ten, privately have provided themselves with a more complicated one, cautiously insuring themselves against imposture by rejecting at the outset the simple and unvarnished truth.

Upon the whole, the visit had been a success. On entering, it is true, he found himself called upon to admire the rapidity with which the professor recovered from his surprise at seeing him; but, as he had not been deluded by any hope that his first appearance would awaken unmistakable delight, he managed to make the best of the situation. His opening remarks upon the subject of the weather were not altogether infelicitous, and then he produced his late number of "Punch," and the professor laughed, and, the ice being broken, conversation flourished, and there was no further difficulty. He discovered, somewhat to his surprise, that he was in better conversational trim than usual.

"It is a delusive condition to be in," he explained to the professor; "but experience has taught me not to be taken in by it and expect future development. It won't continue, as you no doubt suspect. It is the result of entire social stagnation for several weeks. I am merely letting off all my fireworks at once, inspired to the improvidence by your presence. I am a poor creature, as you know; but even a poor creature is likely to suffer from an idea a day. The mental accumulations of this summer, carefully economized, will support me in penury during the entire ensuing season. I only conjure you not to betray me when you hear me repeat the same things by instalments at Mrs. Amory's evenings."

And, saying it, he saw the professor's face change in some subtle way as he looked at him. What there was in this look and change to make him conscious of an inward start he could not have told. It was the merest lifting of the lids, combined with an almost imperceptible movement of the muscles about the mouth; and yet he found it difficult to avoid pausing for a moment. But he accomplished the feat, and felt he had reason to be rather proud of it. "Though what there is to startle him in my mention of Mrs. Amory's evenings," he reflected, "it would require an intellect to explain."

Being somewhat given to finding entertainment in quiet speculation upon passing events, he would doubtless have given some attention to the incident, even if it had remained a solitary unexplained and mystifying trifle. But it was not left to stand alone in his mind.

It was not fifteen minutes before, in drawing his handkerchief from his breast-pocket, he accidentally drew forth with it a letter, which fell upon the newspaper lying upon the professor's lap, and for a moment rested there with the address upward.

And the instant he glanced from the pretty feminine envelope to the professor's face Arbuthnot recognized the fact that something altogether unexpected had occurred again.

As he had looked from the envelope to the professor, so the professor looked from the envelope to him. Then he picked the letter up and returned it.

"It is a letter," Arbuthnot began, — "a letter" — and paused ignominiously.

"Yes," said the professor, as if he had lost something of his own gentle self-possession. "I see it is a letter."

It was not a happy remark, nor did Arbuthnot feel his own next effort a particularly successful one.

"It is a letter from Mrs. Amory," he said. "She is kind enough to write to me occasionally."

"Yes," responded the professor. "I saw that it was from Bertha. Her hand is easily recognized."

"It is an unusual hand," said Arbuthnot. "And her letters are very like herself. When it occurs to her to remember me — which doesn't happen as frequently as I could wish — I consider myself fortunate. She writes as she talks, and very few people do that."

He ended with a greater degree of composure than he had begun with, but to his surprise he felt that his pulses had quickened, and that there had risen to his face a touch of warmth suggestive of some increase of color, and he did not enjoy the sensation. He began to open the letter.

"Shall I" — he said, and then suddenly stopped.

He knew why he had stopped, but the professor did not; and to make the pause and return the letter to its envelope and its place in his pocket without an explanation required something like hardihood.

"She is well, and seems to be taking advantage of the opportunity to rest," he said, and picked up his "Punch" again, returning to his half-finished comment upon its cartoon as if no interruption had taken place.

As he sat on his seat in the park, apparently given up to undivided enjoyment of his cigar, his mind was filled with a tumult of thought. He had not been under the influence of such mental excitement for years. Suddenly he found himself confronting a revelation perfectly astounding to him.

"And so *I* am the man!" he said, at last. "*I* am the man!"

He took his cigar out of his mouth and looked at the end of it with an air of deliberate reflection, as is the masculine habit.

"It doesn't say much for me," he added, "that I never once suspected it — not once."

Then he replaced his cigar, with something like a sigh.

"We are a blind lot," he said.

He did not feel the situation a pleasant one; there were circumstances under which he would have resented it with a vigor and happy ingenuity of resource which would have stood him in good stead; but there was no resentment in his present mood. From the moment the truth had dawned upon him, he had treated it without even the most indirect reference to his own very natural feelings, and there had been more sacrifice of himself and his own peculiarities in his action when he had returned the letter to his pocket than even he himself realized.

"It was not the letter to show him," was his thought. "She does not know how much she tells me. He would have understood it as I do."

He went over a good deal of ground mentally as he sat in the deepening dusk, and he thought clearly and dispassionately, as was his habit when he allowed himself to think at all. By the time he had arrived at his conclusions it was quite dark. Then he threw the end of his last cigar away and arose, and there was no denying that he was pale still, and wore a curiously intense expression.

"If there is one thing neither man nor devil can put a stop to," he said, "it is an experience such as that. It will go on to one of two ends, — it will kill her, or she will kill it. The wider of the mark they shoot, the easier for her; and as for me," he added, with a rather faint and dreary smile, "perhaps it suits me well enough to be merely an alleviating circumstance. It's all I'm good for. Let them think as they please."

And he brushed an atom of cigar-ash from his sleeve with his rather too finely feminine hand, and walked away.

Chapter 16

He paid the professor another visit a few days later, and afterwards another, and another.

"What," said the professor, at the end of his second visit, "is it ten o'clock? I assure you it is usually much later than this when it strikes ten."

"Thank you," said Arbuthnot. "I never heard that civility accomplished so dexterously before. It is perfectly easy to explain the preternatural adroitness of speech on which Mrs. Amory prides herself. But don't be too kind to me, professor, and weaken my resolution not to present myself unless I have just appropriated an idea from somewhere. If I should appear some day *au naturel*, not having taken the precaution to attire myself in the mature reflections of my acquaintance, I shouldn't pay you for the wear and tear of seeing me, I'll confess beforehand."

"I once told you," said the professor to Tredennis, after the fourth visit, "that I was not fond of him, but there had been times when I had been threatened with it. This is one of the times. Ah!" with a sigh of fatigue, "I understand the attraction — I understand it."

The following week Tredennis arrived at the house one evening to find it in some confusion. The *coupé* of a prominent medical man stood before the pavement, and the servant who opened the door looked agitated.

"The professor, sir," he said, "has had a fall. We hope he ain't much hurt, and Mr. Arbuthnot and the doctor are with him."

"Ask if I may go upstairs," said Tredennis; and, as he asked it, Arbuthnot appeared on the landing above, and, seeing who was below, came down at once.

"There is no real cause for alarm," he said, "though he has had a shock. He had been out, and the heat must have been too much for him. As he was coming up the steps he felt giddy and lost his footing, and fell. Doctor Malcom is with him, and says he needs nothing but entire quiet. I am glad you have come. Did you receive my message?"

"No," answered Tredennis. "I have not been to my room."

"Come into the library," said Arbuthnot. "I have something to say to you."

He led the way into the room, and Tredennis followed him, wondering. When they got inside Arbuthnot turned and closed the door.

"I suppose," he said, "you know no more certainly than I do where Mr. Amory is to be found." And as he spoke he took a telegram from his pocket.

"What is the matter?" demanded Tredennis. "What has" —

"This came almost immediately after the professor's accident," said Arbuthnot. "It is from Mrs. Amory, asking him to come to her. Janey is very ill."

"What!" exclaimed Tredennis. "And she alone, and probably without any physician she relies on!"

"Some one must go to her," said Arbuthnot, "and the professor must know nothing of it. If we knew of any woman friend of hers we might appeal to her; but everybody is out of town."

He paused a second, his eyes fixed on Tredennis's changing face.

"If you will remain with the professor," he said, "I will go myself, and take Doctor Wentworth with me."

"You!" said Tredennis.

"I shall be better than nothing," replied Arbuthnot, quietly. "I can do what I am told to do, and she mustn't be left alone. If her mother had been alive, she would have gone; if her father had been well, he would have gone; if her husband had been here" —

"But he is not here," said Tredennis, with a bitterness not strictly just. "Heaven only knows where he is."

"It would be rather hazardous to trust to a telegram reaching him at Merrittsville," said Arbuthnot. "We are not going to leave her alone even until we have tried Merrittsville. What must be done must be done now. I will go and see Doctor Wentworth at once, and we can leave in an hour if I find him. You can tell the professor I was called away."

He made a step toward the door, and as he did so Tredennis turned suddenly.

"Wait a moment," he said.

Arbuthnot came back.

"What is it?" he asked.

There was a curious pause, which, though it lasted scarcely longer than a second, was still a pause.

"If *I* go," said Tredennis, "it will be easier to explain my absence to the professor." And then there was a pause again, and each man looked at the other, and each was a trifle pale.

It was Arbuthnot who spoke first.

"I think," he said, without moving a muscle, "that you had better let me go."

"Why?" said Tredennis, and the unnatural quality of his voice startled himself.

"Because," said Arbuthnot, as calmly as before, "you will be conferring a favor on me, if you do. I want an excuse for getting out of town, and — I want an opportunity to be of some slight service to Mrs. Amory."

Before the dignity of the stalwart figure towering above his slighter proportions he knew he appeared to no advantage as he said the words; but to have made the best of himself he must have relinquished his point at the outset, and this he had no intention of doing, though he was not enjoying himself. A certain cold-blooded pertinacity which he had acquired after many battles with himself was very useful to him at the moment.

"The worst thing that could happen to her just now," he had said to himself, ten minutes before, "would be that he should go to her in her trouble." And upon this conviction he took his stand.

In placing himself in the breach he knew that he had no means of defence whatever; that any reasons for his course he might offer must appear, by their flimsiness, to betray in him entire inadequacy to the situation in which he seemed to stand, and that he must present himself in the character of a victim to his own bold but shallow devices, and simply brazen the matter out; and when one reflects upon human weakness it is certainly not to his discredit that he had calmly resigned himself to this before entering the room. There was no triviality in Tredennis's mood, and he made no pretence of any. The half darkness of the room, which had been shaded from the sun during the day, added to the significance of every line in his face. As he stood, with folded arms, the shadows seemed to make him look larger, to mark his pallor, and deepen the intensity of his expression.

"Give me a better reason," he said.

Arbuthnot paused. What he saw in the man moved him strongly. In the light of that past of his, which was a mystery to his friends, he often saw with terrible clearness much he was not suspected of seeing at all, and here he recognized what awakened in him both pity and respect.

"I have no better one," he answered. "I tell you I miss the exhilaration of Mrs. Amory's society and want to see her, and hope she will not be sorry to see me." And, having said it, he paused again before making his *coup d'etat*. Then he spoke deliberately, looking Tredennis in the eyes. "That you should think anything detrimental to Mrs. Amory, even in the most shadowy way, is out of the question," he said. "Think of me what you please."

"I shall think nothing that is detrimental to any man who is her friend," said Tredennis, and there was passion in the words, though he had tried to repress it.

"Her friendship would be a good defence for a man against any wrong that was in him," said Arbuthnot, and this time the sudden stir of feeling in him was not altogether concealed. Let me have my way," he ended. "It will do no harm."

"It will do no good," said Tredennis.

"No," answered Arbuthnot, recovering his impervious air, "it will do no good, but one has to be sanguine to expect good. Perhaps I need pity," he added. "Suppose you are generous and show it me."

He could not help seeing the dramatic side of the situation, and with half-conscious irony abandoning himself to it. All at once he seemed to have deserted the well-regulated and decently arranged commonplaces of his ordinary life, and to be taking part in a theatrical performance of rather fine and subtle quality, and he waited with intense interest to see what Tredennis would do.

What he did was characteristic of him. He had unconsciously taken two or three hurried steps across the room, and he turned and stood still.

"It is I who must go," he said.

"You are sure of that?" said Arbuthnot.

"We have never found it easy to understand each other," Tredennis answered, "though perhaps you have understood me better than I have understood you. You are quicker and more subtle than I am. I only seem able to see one thing at a time, and do one thing. I only see one thing now. It is better that I should go."

"You mean," said Arbuthnot, "better for me?"

Tredennis looked down at the floor.

"Yes," he answered.

A second or so of silence followed, in which Arbuthnot simply stood and looked at him. The utter uselessness of the effort he had made was borne in upon him in a manner which overpowered him.

"Then," he remarked at length, "if you are considering me, there seems nothing more to be said. Will you go and tell the professor that you are called away, or shall I?"

"I will go myself," replied Tredennis.

He turned to leave the room, and Arbuthnot walked slowly toward the window. The next moment Tredennis turned from the door and followed him.

"If I have ever done you injustice," he said, "the time is past for it, and I ask your pardon."

"Perhaps it is not justice I need," said Arbuthnot, "but mercy — and I don't think you have ever been unjust to me. It wouldn't have been easy."

"In my place," said Tredennis, with a visible effort, "you would find it easier than I do to say what you wished. I" —

"You mean that you pity me," Arbuthnot interposed. "As I said before, perhaps I need pity. Sometimes I think I do;" and the slight touch of dreariness in his tone echoed in Tredennis's ear long after he had left him and gone on his way.

Chapter 17

It was ten o'clock and bright moonlight when Tredennis reached his destination, the train having brought him to a way-side station two miles distant, where he had hired a horse, and struck out into the county road. In those good old days when the dwelling of every Virginia gentleman was his "mansion," the substantial pile of red brick before whose gate-way he dismounted had been a mansion too, and had not been disposed to trifle with its title, but had insisted upon it with a dignified squareness which scorned all architectural devices to attract attention. Its first owner had chosen its site with a view to the young "shade-trees" upon it, and while he had lived upon his property had been almost as proud of his trees as of his "mansion"; and when, long afterward, changes had taken place, and the objects of his pride fell into degenerate hands, as the glories of the mansion faded, its old friends, the trees, grew and flourished, and seemed to close kindly in about it, as if to soften and shadow its decay.

On each side of the drive which led down to the gateway grew an irregular line of these trees, here and there shading the way from side to side, and again leaving a space for the moonlight to stream upon. As he tied his horse Tredennis glanced up this drive-way toward the house.

"There is a light burning in one of the rooms," he said. "It must be there that" — He broke off in the midst of a sentence, his attention suddenly attracted by a figure which flitted across one of the patches of moonlight.

He knew it at once, though he had had no thought of seeing it before entering the house. It was Bertha, in a white dress, and with two large dogs following her, leaping and panting, when she spoke in a hushed voice, as if to quiet them.

She came down toward the gate with a light, hurried tread, and, when she was within a few feet of it, spoke.

"Doctor," she said, "oh, how glad I am — how glad !" and, as she said it, came out into the broad moonlight again, and found herself face to face with Tredennis.

She fell back from him as if a blow had been struck her, — fell back trembling, and as white as the moonlight itself.

"What!" she cried, "is it *you* — *you?*"

He looked at her, bewildered by the shock his presence seemed to her.

"I did not think I should frighten you," he said. "I came to-night because the professor was not well enough to make the journey. Doctor Wentworth will be here in the morning. He would have come with me, but he had an important case to attend."

"I did not think *you* would come," she said, breathlessly, and put out her hand, groping for the support of the swinging gate, which she caught and held.

"There was no one else," he answered.

He felt as if he were part of some strange dream. The stillness, the moonlight, the heavy shadows of the great trees, all added to the unreality of the moment; but most unreal of all was Bertha herself, clinging with one trembling hand to the gate, and looking up at him with dilated eyes.

"I did not think *you* would come," she said again, "and it startled me — and" — She paused with a poor little effort at a smile, which the next instant died away. "Don't — don't look at me!" she said, and, turning away from him, laid her face on the hand clinging to the gate.

He looked down at her slight white figure and bent head, and a great tremor passed over him. The next instant she felt him standing close at her side.

"You must not — do that," he said, and put out his hand and touched her shoulder.

His voice was almost a whisper; he was scarcely conscious of what his words were; he had scarcely any consciousness of his touch. The feeling which swept over him needed no sense of touch or sound; the one thing which overpowered him was his sudden sense of a nearness to her which was not physical nearness at all.

"Perhaps I was wrong to come," he went on; "but I could not leave you alone — I could not leave you alone. I knew that you were suffering, and I could not bear that."

She did not speak or lift her head.

"Has it been desolate?" he asked.

"Yes," she answered, in a hushed voice.

"I was afraid so," he said. "You have been alone so long — I thought of it almost every hour of the day; you are not used to being alone. Perhaps it was a mistake. Why do you tremble so?"

"I don't know," she answered.

"My poor child!" he said. "My poor child!" And then there was a pause which seemed to hold a lifetime of utter silence.

It was Bertha who ended it. She stirred a little, and then lifted her face. She looked as he remembered her looking when he had first known her, only that she was paler, and there was a wearied softness in her eyes. She made no attempt at hiding the traces of tears in them, and she spoke as simply as a child.

"I thought it was the doctor, when I heard the horse's feet," she said; "and I was afraid the dogs would bark and waken Janey. She has just fallen asleep, and she has slept so little. She has been very ill."

"You have not slept," he said.

"No," she replied. "This is the first time I have left her."

He took her hand and drew it gently through his arm.

"I will take you up to the house," he said, "so that you can hear every sound; but you must stay outside for a little while. The fresh air will do you good, and we can walk up and down while I tell you the reason the professor did not come."

All the ordinary conventional barriers had fallen away from between them. He did not know why or how, and he did not ask. Suddenly he found himself once again side by side with the Bertha he had fancied lost forever. All that had bewildered him was gone. The brilliant little figure, with its tinkling ornaments, the unemotional little smile, the light laugh, were only parts of a feverish dream. It was Bertha whose hand rested on his arm — whose fair, young face was pale with watching over her child — whose soft voice was tremulous and tender with innocent, natural tears. She spoke very little. When they had walked to and fro before the house for a short time, she said:

"Let us go and sit down on the steps of the porch," and they went and sat there together, — he upon a lower step, and she a few steps above, her hands clasped on her knee, her face turned half away from him. She rarely looked at him, he noticed, even when he spoke to her or she spoke to him; her eyes rested oftener than not upon some far-away point under the trees.

"You are no better than you were when you went away," he said, looking at her cheek where the moonlight whitened it.

"No," she answered.

"I did not think to find you looking like this," he said.

"Perhaps," she said, still with her eyes fixed on the far-away shadows, "perhaps I have not had time enough. You must give me time."

"You have had two months," he returned.

"Two months," she said, "is not so long as it seems." And between the words there came a curious little catch of the breath.

"It has seemed long to you?" he asked.

"Yes."

She turned her face slowly and looked at him.

"Has it seemed long to you?" she said.

"Yes,", he replied, "long and dreary."

She swayed a little toward him with a sort of unconscious movement; her eyes were fixed upon his face with a wistful questioning; he had seen her look at her children so.

"Was it very hot?" she said. "Were you tired? Why did you not go away?"

"I did not want to go away," he answered.

"But you ought to have gone away," she said. "You were not used to the heat, and — Let the light fall on your face so that I can see it!"

He came a little nearer to her, and as she looked at him the wistfulness in her eyes changed to something else.

"Oh," she cried, "it has done you harm. Your face is quite changed. Why didn't I see it before? What have you been doing?"

"Nothing," he answered.

He did not stir, or want to stir, but sat almost breathlessly still, watching her, the sudden soft anxiousness in her eyes setting every pulse in his body throbbing.

"Oh," she said, "you are ill — you are ill! How could you be so careless? Why did not papa"—

She faltered — her voice fell and broke. She even drew back a little, though her eyes still rested upon his.

"You were angry with me when you thought I did not take care of myself," she said; "and you have been as bad as I was, and worse. You had not so many temptations." And she turned away, and he found himself looking only at her cheek again, and the soft side-curve of her mouth.

"There is less reason why I should take care of myself," he said.

"You mean"— she asked, without moving —"that there are fewer people who would miss you?"

"I do not —not know of any one who would miss me."

Her hands stirred slightly, as they lay in her lap.

"That is underrating your friends," she said, slowly. "But" — altering her tone — "it is true, I have the children and Richard."

"Where is Richard?" he asked.

"I don't know."

"When you heard from him last," he began.

"He is a bad correspondent," she said.

"He always finds so much to fill his time when he is away. There is an understanding between us that he shall write very few letters. I am responsible for it myself, because I know it spoils everything for him when he has an unwritten letter on his conscience. I haven't heard from him first yet since he went West."

She arose from her seat on the step.

"I will go in now," she said. "I must speak to Mrs. Lucas about giving you a room, and then I will go to Janey. She is sleeping very well."

He arose, too, and stood below her, looking up.

You must promise not to think of me," he said. "I did not come here to be considered. Do you think an old soldier, who has slept under the open sky many a night, cannot provide for himself?"

"Have you slept so often?" she asked, the very triviality of the question giving it a strange sweetness to his ears.

"Yes," he answered. "And often with no surety of wakening with my scalp on."

"Oh!" she exclaimed, and made an involuntary movement toward him.

He barely restrained his impulse to put out his hands, but hers fell at her sides the next instant.

"I am a great coward," she said. "It fills me with terror to hear of things like that. Is it at all likely that you will be ordered back?"

"I don't know," he replied, his uplifted eyes devouring all the sweetness of her face. "Would that"—

The very madness of the question forming itself on his lips was his own check.

"I don't want to think of it," he said. Then he added, "As I stand here I look up at you. I never looked up at you before."

"Nor I down at you," she returned. "You are always so high above me. It seems strange to look down at you."

It was all so simple and inconsequent, but every word seemed full of the mystery and emotion of the hour. When he tried afterward to recall what they had said he was bewildered by the slightness of what had been uttered, even though the thrill of it had not yet passed away.

He went up the steps and stood beside her.

"Yes," he said, speaking as gently as he might have spoken to a child. "You make me feel what a heavy-limbed, clumsy fellow I am. All women make me feel it, but you more than all the rest. You look almost like a child."

"But I am not very little," she said; "it is only because I am standing near you."

"I always think of you as a small creature," he said. "I used to think, long ago, that some one should care for you."

"You were very good, long ago," she answered softly, "And you are very good now to have come to try to help me. Will you come in?"

"No," he said, "not now. It might only excite the child to-night if she saw me, and so long as she is quiet I will not run the risk of disturbing her. I will tell you what I am going to do. I am not going to leave you alone. I shall walk up and down beneath your window, and if you need me you will know I am there, and you have only to speak in your lowest voice. If she should be worse, my horse is at the gate, and I can go for the doctor at once."

She looked up at him with a kind of wonder.

"Do you mean that you intend to stand sentinel all night?" she said.

"I have stood sentinel before," was his reply. "I came to stand sentinel. All that I can do is to be ready if I am wanted."

"But I cannot let you stay up all night," she began.

"You said it had been desolate," he answered. "Won't it be less desolate to know that — that some one is near you?"

"Oh, yes! Oh, yes!" she said. "But"—

"Go upstairs," he said, "and promise me that, if she still sleeps, you will lie down and let your nurse watch her."

The gentle authority of his manner seemed to impress her curiously. She hesitated as if she scarcely understood it.

"I — don't — know," she faltered.

"You will be better for it to-morrow," he persisted, "and so will she."

"I never did such a thing before," she said, slowly.

"I shall be beneath the open window," he said, "and I have the ears of an Indian. I shall know if she stirs."

She drew a soft, troubled breath.

"Well," she said, "I will — go."

And, without another word, she turned away. He stood and watched her as she moved slowly across the wide porch. At the door she stopped and turned toward him.

"But," she said, faint lines showing themselves on her forehead, "I shall be remembering that you — are not asleep."

"You must not remember me at all," he answered.

And then he stood still and watched her again until she had entered the house and noiselessly ascended the staircase, which was a few yards from the open door, and then, when he could see her white figure in the darkness no more, he went out to his place beneath the window, and strode silently to and fro, keeping watch and listening until after the moon had gone down and the birds were beginning to stir in the trees.

Chapter 18

At six o'clock in the morning Bertha came down the stairs again. Her simple white gown was a fresh one, and there was a tinge of color in her cheeks.

"She slept nearly all night," she said to Tredennis, when he joined her, "and so did I. I am sure she is better." Then she put out her hand for him to take. "It is all because you are here," she said. "When I wakened for a moment, once or twice, and heard your footsteps, it seemed to give me courage and make everything quieter. Are you very tired?"

"No," he answered, "I am not tired at all."

"I am afraid you would not tell me if you were," she said. "You must come with me now and let me give you some breakfast."

She led him into a room at the side of the hall. When the house had been a "mansion" it had been considered a very imposing apartment, and, with the assistance of a few Washingtonian luxuries, which she had dexterously grafted upon its bareness, it was by no means unpicturesque even now.

"I think I should know that you had lived here," he said, as he glanced around.

"Have I made it so personal?" she replied. "I did not mean to do that. It was so bare at first, and, as I had nothing to do, it amused me to arrange it. Richard sent me the rugs, and odds and ends, and I found the spindle-legged furniture in the neighborhood. I am afraid it won't be safe for you to sit down too suddenly in the chairs, or to lean heavily on the table. I think you had better choose that leathern arm-chair and abide by it. It is quite substantial."

He took the seat, and gave himself up to the pleasure of watching her as she moved to and fro between the table and an antique sideboard, from whose recesses she produced some pretty cups and saucers.

"What are you going to do?" he asked.

"I am going to set the table for your breakfast," she said, "because Maria is busy with the children, and the other nurse is with Janey, and the woman of the house is making your coffee and rolls."

"You are going to set the table!" he exclaimed.

"It doesn't require preternatural intelligence," she answered. "It is rather a simple thing, on the whole."

It seemed a very simple thing as she did it, and a very pretty thing. As he leaned against the leathern back of his chair, beginning vaguely to realize by a dawning sense of weariness that he had been up all night, he felt that he had not awakened from his dream yet, or that the visions of the past months were too far away and too unreal to move him.

The early morning sunlight made its way through the vines embowering the window, and cast lace-like shadows of their swaying leaves upon the floor, and upon Bertha's dress when she passed near. The softness of the light mellowed everything, and intensified the touches of color in the fans and ornaments on the walls and mantel, and in the bits of drapery thrown here and there as if by accident; and in the midst of this color and mellowed light Bertha moved before him, a slender, quiet figure, making the picture complete.

It was her quietness which impressed itself upon him more than all else. After the first moments, when she had uttered her cry on seeing him, and had given way in her momentary agitation, he had noticed that a curious change fell upon her. When she lifted her face from the gate all emotion seemed to have died out of it; her voice was quiet. One of the things he remembered of their talk was that they had both spoken in voices so low as to be scarcely above a whisper.

When the breakfast was brought in she took a seat at the table to pour out his coffee and attend to his wants. She ate very little herself, but he rarely looked up without finding her eyes resting upon him with wistful interest.

"At least," she said once, "I must see that you have a good breakfast.

The kindest thing you can do this morning is to be hungry. Please be hungry if you can."

The consciousness that she was caring for him was a wonderful and touching thins; to him. The little house-wifely acts with which most men are familiar were bewilderingly new to him. He had never been on sufficiently intimate social terms with women to receive many of these pretty services at their hands. His unsophisticated reverence for everything feminine had worked against him, with the reserve which was one of its results. It had been his habit to feel that there was no reason why he should be singled out for the bestowal of favors, and he had perhaps ignored many through the sheer ignorance of simple and somewhat exaggerated humility.

To find himself sitting at the table alone with Bertha, in her new mood, — Bertha quiet and beautiful, — was a moving experience to him. It was as if they two must have sat there every day for years, and had the prospect of sitting so together indefinitely. It was the very simplicity and naturalness of it all which stirred him most. Her old vivid gayety was missing; she did not laugh once, but her smile was very sweet. They talked principally of the children, and of the common things about them; but there was never a word which did not seem a thing to be cherished and remembered. After a while the children were brought down, and she took Meg upon her knee, and Jack leaned against her while she told Tredennis what they had been doing, and the sun creeping through the vines touched her hair and the child's and made a picture of them. When she went upstairs she took Meg with her, holding her little hand and talking to her in pretty maternal fashion; and, after the two had vanished, Tredennis found it necessary to pull himself together with a strong effort, that he might prove himself equal to the conversational demands made upon him by Master Jack, who had remained behind.

"I will go and see Janey again," she had said. "And then, perhaps, you will pay her a visit."

When he went up, a quarter of an hour later, he found his small favorite touchingly glad to see him. The lever from which she had been suffering for several days had left her languid and perishable-looking, but she roused wonderfully at the sight of him, and when he seated himself at her bedside regarded him with adoring admiration, finally expressing her innocent conviction that he had grown very much since their last meeting.

"But it doesn't matter," she hastened to assure him, "because I don't mind it, and mamma doesn't, either."

When, in the course of the morning, Doctor Wentworth arrived, he discovered him still sitting by the bedside, only Janey had crept close to him and fallen asleep, clasping both her small hands about his large one, and laying her face upon his palm.

"What!" said the doctor. "Can you do that sort of thing?"

"I don't know," answered Tredennis, slowly. "I never did it before."

He looked down at the small, frail creature, and the color showed itself under his bronzed skin.

"I think she's rather fond of me — or something," he added with *naïvete*, "and I like it."

"She likes it, that's evident," said the doctor.

He turned away to have an interview with Bertha, whom he took to the window at the opposite end of the room, and after it was over they came back together.

"She is not so ill as she was yesterday," he said; "and she was not so ill then as you thought her." He turned and looked at Bertha herself. "She doesn't need as much care now as you do," he said, "that's my impression. What have you been doing with yourself?"

"Taking care of her," she answered, "since she began to complain of not feeling well."

He was a bluff, kindly fellow, with a bluff, kindly way, and he shook a big forefinger at her.

"You have been carrying her up and down in your arms," he said. "Don't deny it."

"No," she answered, "I won't deny it."

"Of course," he said. "I know you — carrying her up and down in your arms, and singing to her and telling her stories, and holding her on your knee when you weren't doing anything worse. You'd do it if she were three times the size."

She blushed guiltily, and looked at Janey.

"Good Heaven!" he said. "You women will drive me mad! Don't

let me hear any more about fashionable mothers who kill their children! I find my difficulty in fashionable children who kill their mothers, and in little simpletons who break down under the sheer weight of their maternal nonsense. Who was it who nearly died of the measles?"

"But — but," she faltered, deprecatingly, "I don't think I ever had the measles."

"They weren't your measles," he said, with amiable sternness. "They were Jack's, and Janey's, and Meg's, and so much the worse."

"But," she interposed, with a very pretty eagerness, "they got through them beautifully, and there wasn't a cold among them."

"There wouldn't have been a cold among them if you'd let a couple of sensible nurses take care of them. Do you suppose I'm not equal to bringing three children through the measles? It's all nonsense, and sentiment, and self-indulgence. You like to do it, and you do it, and, as a natural consequence, you die of somebody else's measles — or come as near it as possible."

She blushed as guiltily as before, and looked at Janey again.

"I think she is very much better," she said.

"Yes," he answered, "she is better, and I want to see you better. Who is going to help you to take care of her?"

"I came to try to do that," said Tredennis.

Bertha turned to look at him.

"You?" she exclaimed. "Oh, no! You are very good; but now the worst is over, I couldn't"—

"Should I be in the way?" he asked.

She drew back a little. For a moment she had changed again, and returned to the ordinary conventional atmosphere.

"No," she said, "you know that you would not be in the way, but I should scarcely be likely to encroach upon your time in such a manner."

The doctor laughed.

"He is exactly what you need," he said. "And he would be of more use to you than a dozen nurses. He won't stand any of your maternal weakness, and he will see that my orders are carried out. He'll domineer over you, and you'll be afraid of him. You had better let him stay. But you must settle it between you after I am gone."

Bertha went downstairs with him to receive a few final directions, and when she returned Tredennis had gently released himself from Janey, and had gone to the window, where he stood evidently awaiting her.

"Do you know," he said, with his disproportionately stern air, when she joined him, — "do you know why I came here?"

"You came," she answered, "because I alarmed you unnecessarily, and it seemed that some one must come, and you were kind enough to assume the responsibility."

"I came because there was no one else," he began.

She stopped him with a question she had not asked before, and he felt that she asked it inadvertently.

"Where was Laurence Arbuthnot?" she said.

"That is true," he replied, grimly. "Laurence Arbuthnot would have been better."

"No," she said, "he would not have been better."

She looked up at him with a curious mixture of questioning and defiance in her eyes.

"I don't know why it is that I always manage to make you angry," she said; "I must be very stupid. I always know you will be angry before you have done with me. When we were downstairs"—

"When we were downstairs," he put in, hotly, "we were two honest human beings, without any barriers of conventional pretence between us, and you allowed me to think you meant to take what I had to offer, and then, suddenly, all is changed, and the barrier is between us again, because you choose to place it there, and profess that you must regard me, in your pretty, civil way, as a creature to be considered and treated with form and ceremony."

"Thank you for calling it a pretty way," she said.

And yet there was a tone in her low voice which softened his wrath somehow, — a rather helpless tone, which suggested that she had said the words only because she had no other resource, and still must utter her faint protest.

"It is for *me*," he went on, "to come to you with a civil pretence instead of an honest intention? I am not sufficiently used to conventionalities to make myself bearable. I am always blundering and stumbling. No one can feel that more bitterly than I do; but you have no right to ignore my claim to do what I can when I might be of use. I might be of use, because the child is fond of me, and in my awkward fashion I can quiet and amuse her as you say no one but yourself can."

"Will you tell me?" she asked, frigidly, "what right I have to permit you to make of yourself a — a nurse-maid to my child?"

"Call it what you like," he answered. "Speak of it as you like. What right does it need? I came because" —

His recollection of her desolateness checked him. It was not for him to remind her again by his recklessness of speech that her husband had not felt it necessary to provide against contingencies. But she filled up the sentence.

"Yes, you are right," she said. "As you said before, there was no one else — no one."

"It chanced to be so," he said; "and why should I not be allowed to fill up the breach for the time being?"

"Because it is almost absurd," she said, inconsequently. "Don't you see that?"

"No," he answered, obstinately.

Their eyes met, and rested upon each other.

"You don't care?" she said.

"No."

"I knew you wouldn't," she said. "You never care for anything. That is what I like in you — and dread."

"Dread?" he said; and in the instant he saw that she had changed again. Her cheeks had flushed, and there was upon her lips a smile, half-bitter, half-sweet.

"I knew you would not go," she said, "as well as I knew that it was only civil in me to suggest that you should. You are generous enough to care for me in a way I am not quite used to — and you always have your own way. Have it now; have it as long as you are here. Until you go away I shall do everything you tell me to do, and never once oppose you again; and — perhaps I shall enjoy the novelty."

There was a chair near her, and she put her hand against it as if to steady herself, and the color in her face died out as quickly as it had risen.

"I did not want you to go," she said.

"You did not want me to go?"

"No," she answered, in a manner more baffling than all the rest. "More than anything in the world I wanted you to stay. There, Janey is awakening!"

And she went to the bed and kneeled down beside it, and drew the child into her arms against her bosom.

Chapter 19

From that day until they separated there was no change in her. It was scarcely two weeks before their paths diverged again; but, in looking back upon it afterward, it always seemed to Tredennis that some vaguely extending length of time must have elapsed between the night when he dismounted at the gate in the moonlight, and the morning when he turned to look his last at Bertha, standing in the sun. Each morning when she gave him his breakfast in the old-fashioned room, and he watched her as she moved about, or poured out his coffee, or talked to Meg or Jack, who breakfasted with them; each afternoon when Janey was brought down to lie on the sofa, and she sat beside her singing pretty, foolish songs to her, and telling her stories; each evening, when the child fell asleep in her arms, as she sang; each brief hour, later on, when the air had cooled, and she went out to sit on the porch, or walk under the trees, — seemed an experience of indefinite length, not to be marked by hours, nor by sunrise and sunset, but by emotions. Her gentle interest in his comfort continued just what it had been the first day he had been so moved by it, and his care for her she accepted with a gratitude which might have been sweet to any man. Having long since established his rank in Janey's affections it was easy for him to make himself useful, in his masculine fashion. During her convalescence his strong arms became the child's favorite resting-place; when she was tired of her couch he could carry her up and down the room without wearying; she liked his long, steady strides, and the sound of his deep voice, and his unconscious air of command disposed of many a difficulty. When Bertha herself was the nurse he watched her faithfully, and when he saw in her any signs of fatigue he took her place at once, and from the first she made no protest against his quietly persistent determination to lighten her burdens. Perhaps, through the fact that they were so lightened, or through her relief from her previous anxiety, she seemed to grow stronger as the child did. Her color became brighter and steadier, and her look of lassitude and weariness left her. One morning, having been beguiled out of doors by Jack and Meg, Tredennis heard her laugh in a tone that made him rise from his chair by Janey, and go to the open window.

He reached it just in time to see her run like a deer across the sun-dappled grass, after a bright ball Meg had thrown to her, with an infantile aimlessness which precluded all possibility of its being caught. She made a graceful dart at it, picked it up, and came back under the trees, tossing it in the air, and catching it again with a deft turn of hand and wrist. She was flushed with the exercise, and, for the moment, almost radiant; she held her dress closely about her figure, her face was upturned and her eyes were uplifted, and she was as unconscious as Meg herself.

When she saw him she threw the ball to the children, and came forward to the window.

"Does Janey want me?" she asked.

"No. She is asleep."

"Do you want me?"

"I want to see you go on with your game."

"It is not my game," she answered, smiling. "It is Jack's and Meg's. Suppose you come and join them. It will fill them with rapture, and I shall like to look on."

When he came out she sat down under a tree leaning against the trunk, and watched him, her eyes following the swift flight of the ball high into the blue above them, as he flung it upward among the delighted clamor of the children. He had always excelled in sports and feats of strength, and in this simple feat of throwing the ball his physical force and grace displayed themselves to decided advantage. The ball went up, as an arrow flies from the bow, hurtling through the air, until it was little more than a black speck to the eye. When it came back to earth he picked it up and threw it again, and each time it seemed to reach a greater height than the last.

"That is very fine," she said. "I like to see you do it."

"Why?" he asked, pausing.

"I like the force you put into it," she answered. "It scarcely seems like play."

"I did not know that," he said; "but I am afraid I am always in earnest. That is my misfortune."

"It is a great misfortune," she said. "Don't be in earnest," with a gesture as if she would sweep the suggestion away with her hand. "Go on with your game. Let us be like children, and play. Our holiday will be over soon enough, and we shall have to return to Washington and effete civilization."

"Is it a holiday?" he asked her.

"Yes," she answered. "Now that Janey is getting better I am deliberately taking a holiday. Nothing rests me so much as forgetting things."

"Are you forgetting things?" he asked.

"Yes," she replied, looking away; "everything."

Then the children demanded his attention, and he returned to his ball-throwing.

If she was taking a holiday with deliberate intention she did it well. In a few days Janey was well enough to be carried out and laid on one of the two hammocks swung beneath the trees, and then far the greater part of the day was spent in the open air. To Tredennis it seemed that Bertha made the most of every hour, whether she swung in her hammock with her face upturned to the trees, or sat reading, or talking as she worked with the decorous little basket, at which she had jeered, upon her knee.

He was often reminded in these days of what the professor had said of her tenderness for her children. It revealed itself in a hundred trifling ways, in her touch, in her voice, in her almost unconscious habit of caring for them, and, more than all, in a certain pretty, inconvenient fashion they had of getting close to her, and clinging about her, at all sorts of inopportune moments. Once when she had run to comfort Meg who had fallen down, and had come back to the hammock, carrying her in her arms, he was betrayed into speaking.

"I did not think," — he began, and then he checked himself guiltily.

"You did not think?" she repeated.

He began to recognize his indiscretion.

"I beg your pardon," he said, "I was going to make a blunder."

She sat down in the hammock, with the child in her arms.

"You were going to say that you did not think I cared so much for my children," she said, gently. "Do you suppose I did not know that? Well, perhaps it was not a blunder. Perhaps it is only one of my pretences."

"Don't speak like that," he implored.

The next instant he saw that tears had risen in her eyes.

"No," she said. "I will not. Why should I? It is not true. I love them very much. However bad you are, I think you must love your children. Of course, my saying that I loved them might go for nothing; but don't you see," she went on with a pathetic thrill in her voice, "that they love *me*? They would not love me, if I did not care for them."

"I know that," he returned remorsefully. "It was only one of my blunders, as I said. But you have so bewildered me sometimes. When I first returned I could not understand you. It was as if I found myself face to face with a creature I had never seen before."

"You did," she said. "That was it. Perhaps I never was the creature you fancied me."

"Don't say that," he replied. "Since I have been here I have seen you as I used to dream of you, when I sat by the fire in my quarters in the long winter nights."

"Did you ever think of me like that?" she said slowly, and with surprise in her face.

He had not thought of what he was revealing, and he did not think of it now.

"I never forgot you," he said. "Never."

"It seems very strange — to hear that now," she said. "I never dreamed of your thinking of me — afterwards. You seemed to take so little notice of me."

"It is my good fortune," he said, with a touch of bitterness, "that I never *seem* to take notice of anything."

"I suppose," she went on, "that you remembered me because you were lonely at first, and there was no one else to think of."

"Perhaps that was it," he answered.

"After all," she said, "it was natural — only I never thought"—

"It was as natural that you should forget as that I should remember," he said.

Her face had been slightly averted, and she turned it toward him.

"But I did not forget," she said.

"You did not?"

"No. At first, it is true, I scarcely seemed to have time for anything, but to be happy and enjoy the days, as they went by. Oh! what bright days they were, and how far away they seem! Perhaps, if I had known that they would come to an end really, I might have tried to make them pass more slowly."

"They went slowly for me," he said. "I was glad when they were over."

"Were you so very lonely?" she asked.

"Yes."

"Would it have pleased you, if I had written to you when papa did?"

"Did you ever think of doing it?" he asked.

The expression dawning in her eyes was a curious one — there was a suggestion of dread in it.

"Once," she replied. "I began a letter to you. It was on a dull day, when I was restless and unhappy for the first time in my life; and suddenly I thought of you, and I felt as if I should like to speak to you again, — and I began the letter."

"But you did not finish it."

"No. I only wrote a few lines, and then stopped. I said to myself that it was not likely that you had remembered me in the way I had remembered you, so I laid my letter aside. I saw it only a few days ago among some old papers in my trunk."

"You have it yet?"

"I did not know that I had it, until I saw it the other day. It seems strange that it should have lain hidden all these years, and then have come to light. I laid it away thinking I might find courage to finish it sometime. There are only a few lines, but they prove that my memory was not so bad as you thought."

He had been lying on the grass a few feet away from her. As she talked he had looked not at her, but at the bits of blue sky showing through the interlacing greenness of the trees above him. Now he suddenly half rose and leaned upon his elbow.

"Will you give it to me?" he said.

"Do you want it? It is only a yellow scrap of paper."

"I think it belongs to me," he said. "I have a right to it."

She got up without a word and went toward the house, leading Meg by the hand. Tredennis watched her retreating figure in silence until she went in at the door. His face set, and his lips pressed together, then he flung himself backward and lay at full length again, seeing only the bright green of the leaves and the bits of intense blue between. It was well that he was alone. His sense of impotent anguish was more than he had strength to bear, and it wrung a cry from him.

"My God!" he said; "my God!" He was still lying so when Bertha returned. She had not been away many minutes, and she came back alone with the unfinished letter in her hand.

He took it from her without comment, and looked at it. The faint odor of heliotrope he knew so well floated up to him as he bent over the paper. As she had said, there were only a few lines, and she had evidently been dissatisfied with them, and irresolute about them, for several words were erased as if with girlish impatience. At the head of the page was written first: *Dear Philip*, and then *Dear Captain Tredennis*, and there were two or three different opening sentences. As he read each one through the erasures, he thought he understood the innocent, unconscious appeal in it, and he seemed to see the girl-face bending above it, changing from eagerness to uncertainty, and from uncertainty to the timidity which had made her despair.

"I wish you had finished it," he said.

"I wish I had," she answered, and then she added vaguely, "if it would have pleased you."

He folded it, and put it in his breast-pocket and laid down once more, and it was not referred to again.

It seemed to Tredennis, at least, that there never before had been such a day as the one which followed. After a night of rain the intense heat subsided, leaving freshness of verdure, skies of the deepest, clearest blue, and a balmy, luxurious sweetness in the air, deliciously pungent with the odors of cedar and pine.

When he came down in the morning, and entered the breakfast room, he found it empty. The sunlight streamed through the lattice-work of vines, and the cloth was laid, with the pretty blue cups and saucers in waiting; but Bertha was not there, and, fancying she had risen later than usual, he went out into the open air.

The next morning he was to return to Washington. There was no absolute need of his remaining longer. The child had so far recovered that, at the doctor's suggestion, in a few days she was to be removed to the seaside. Nevertheless, it had cost him a struggle to arrive at his decision, and it had required resolution to announce it to Bertha. It would have been far easier to let the days slip by as they would, and when he told her of his intended departure, and she received the news with little more than a few words of regret at it, and gratitude for the services he had rendered, he felt it rather hard to bear.

"If it had been Arbuthnot," he thought, "she would not have borne it so calmly." And then he reproached himself bitterly for his inconsistency.

"Did I come here to make her regret me, when I left her?" he said. "What a fool a man can make of himself, if he gives way to his folly!"

As he descended the steps of the porch he saw her, and he had scarcely caught sight of her before she turned and came toward him. He recognized at once that she had made a change in her dress; that it was no longer such as she had worn while in attendance upon Janey, and that it had a delicate holiday air about it, notwithstanding its simplicity.

"Was there ever such a day before?" she said, as she came to him.

"I thought not, as Hooked out of my window," he replied.

"It is your last," she said, "and I should like you to remember it as being pleasanter than all the rest; though," she added, thoughtfully, "the rest have been pleasant."

Then she looked up at him, with a smile.

"Do you see my gala attire?" she said. "It was Janey who suggested it. She thinks I have not been doing myself justice since you have been here."

"That," he said, regarding her seriously, "is a very beautiful gown, but"— with an entirely respectful sense of inadequacy of expression —"you always wear beautiful gowns, I believe."

"Did Mr. Arbuthnot tell you so?" she said, "or was it Miss Jessup?"

They breakfasted together in the sunny room, and after breakfast they rambled out together. It was she who led, and he who followed, with a curious, dreamy pleasure in all he did, and in every beauty around him, even in the unreal passiveness of his very mood itself. He had never been so keenly conscious of things before; everything impressed itself upon him, — the blue of the sky, the indolent sway of the leaves, the warmth of the air, and the sweet odors in it, the broken song of the birds, the very sound of Bertha's light tread as they walked.

"I am going to give the day to you," she had said. "And you shall see the children's favorite camping-ground on the hill. Before Janey was ill we used to go there almost every day."

Behind the house was a wood-covered hill, and half-way up was the favored spot. It was a sort of bower formed by the clambering of a great vine from one tree to another, making a canopy, under which, through a break in the trees, could be seen the most perfect view of the country below, and the bend of the river. The ground was carpeted with moss, and there was a moss-covered rock to lean against, which was still ornamented with the acorn cups and saucers with which the children had entertained their family of dolls on their last visit.

"See," said Bertha, taking one of them up when she sat down. "When we were here last we had a tea-party, and it was poor Janey's headache which brought it to a close. At the height of the festivities she laid down her best doll, and came to me to cry, and we were obliged to carry her home."

"Poor child!" said Tredennis. He saw only her face upturned under the shadow of the white hat, — a pretty hat, with small, soft, downy plumes upon it, and a general air of belonging to the great world.

"Sit down," said Bertha, "or you may lie down, if you like, and look at the river, and not speak to me at all." He lay down, stretching his great length upon the soft moss, and clasping his hands beneath his head. Bertha clasped her hands about her knee and leaned slightly forward, looking at the view as if she had never seen it before.

"Is this a dream?" Tredennis said, languidly, at last. "I think it must be."

"Yes," she answered, "that is why the air is so warm and fragrant, and the sky so blue, and the scent of the pines so delicious. It is all different when one is awake. That is why I am making the most of every second, and am determined to enjoy it to the very utmost."

"That is what I am doing," he said.

"It is not a good plan, as a rule," she began, and then checked herself. "No," she said, "I won't say that. It is a worldly and Washingtonian sentiment. I will save it until next winter."

"Don't save it at all," he said; "it is an unnatural sentiment. It isn't true, and you do not really believe it."

"It is safer," she said.

He lay still a moment, looking down the hillside through the trees at the broad sweep of the river bend and the purple hills beyond.

"Bertha," he said, at last, "sometimes I hate the man who has taught you all this."

She plucked at the red-tipped moss at her side for a second or so before she replied; she showed no surprise or hurry when she spoke.

"Laurence Arbuthnot!" she said. "Sometimes I hate him, too; but it is only for a moment, — when he tells me the simple, deadly truth, and I know it is the truth, and wish I did not."

She threw the little handful of moss down the hill as if she threw something away with it.

"But this is not being happy," she said. "Let us be happy. I *will* be happy. Janey is better, and all my anxiety is over, and it is such a lovely day, and I have put on my favorite gown to celebrate it in. Look at the color of the hills over there — listen to those doves in the pines. How warm and soft the wind is, and how the scent of my carnations fills the air! Ah, what a bright world it is, after all!"

She broke into singing softly, and half under breath, a snatch of a gay little song. Tredennis had never heard her sing it before, and thought it wonderfully sweet. But she sang no more than a line or two, and then turned to him, with a smile in her eyes.

"Now," she said, "it is your turn. Talk to me. Tell me about your life in the West; tell me all you did the first year, and begin — begin just where you left me the night you bade me good-by at the carriage-door."

"I am afraid it would not be a very interesting story," he said.

"It would interest me," she answered. "There are camp-fires in it, and scalps, and Indians, and probably war-paths." And her voice falling a little, "I want to discover why it was that you always seemed to be so much alone, and sat and thought in that dreary way by the fire in your quarters. It seems to me that you have been a great deal alone."

"I have been a great deal alone," he said; "that is true."

"It must have been so even when you were a child," she went on. "I heard you tell Janey once that when you were her age you belonged to no one. I don't like to think of that. It touches the maternal side of me. It makes me think of Jack. Suppose Jack belonged to no one; and you were not so old as Jack. I wonder if you were at all like him, and how you looked. I wish there was a picture of you I could see."

He had never regarded himself as an object likely to interest in any degree, and had lost many of the consolations and excitements of the more personal kind thereby; and to find that she had even given a sympathetic thought to the far-away childhood whose desolalateness he himself had never quite analyzed, at once touched and bewildered him.

"I have not been without friends," he said, "but I am sure no one ever gave much special thought to me. Perhaps it is because men are scarcely likely to give such thoughts to men, and I have not known women. My parents died before I was a year old, and I don't think any one was ever particularly fond of me. People did not dislike me, but they passed me over. I never wondered at it, but I saw it. I knew there was something a little wrong with me; but I could not understand what it was. I know now: I was silent, and could not express what I thought and felt."

"Oh!" she cried; "and was there no one to help you?"

There was no thought of him as a full-grown person in the exclamation; it was a womanish outcry for the child, whose desolate childhood seemed for the moment to be an existence which had never ended.

"I know about children," she said, "and what suffering there is for them if they are left alone. They can say so little, and we can say so much. Haven't I seen them try to explain things when they were at a disadvantage and overpowered by the sheer strength of some full-grown creature? Haven't I seen them make their impotent little struggle for words and fail, and look up with their helpless eyes and see the uselessness of it, and break down into their poor little shrieks of wrath and grief? The happiest of them go through it sometimes, and those who are left alone — Why didn't some woman see and understand? — some woman ought to have seen and cared for you."

Tredennis found himself absorbed in contemplation of her. He was not sure that there were not tears in her eyes, and yet he could hardly believe it possible.

"That is all true," he said; "you understand it better than I did. I understood the feeling no better than I understood the reason for it."

"I understand it because I have children," she answered. "And because I have watched them and loved them, and would give my heart's blood for them. To have children makes one like a tiger, at times. The passion one can feel through the wrongs of a child is something *awful*. One can feel it for any child — for all children. But for one's own"—

She ended with a sharply drawn breath. The sudden uncontrollable fierceness, which seemed to have made her in a second, — in her soft white gown and lace, and her pretty hat, with its air of good society, — a small, wild creature, whom no law of man could touch, affected him like an electric shock; perhaps the thrill it gave him revealed itself in his look, and she saw it, for she seemed to become conscious of herself and her mood, with a start. She made a quick, uneasy movement and effort to recover herself.

"I beg your pardon," she said, with a half laugh. "But I couldn't help it. It was" — and she paused a second for reflection, —"it was the primeval savage in me." And she turned and clasped her hands about her knee again, resuming her attitude of attention, even while the folds of lace on her bosom were still stirred by her quick breathing.

But, though she might resume her attitude, it was not so easy to resume the calmness of her mood. Having been stirred once, it was less difficult to be stirred again. When he began, at last, to tell the story of his life on the frontier, if his vanity had been concerned he would have felt that she made a good listener. But his vanity had nothing to do with his obedience to her wish. He made as plain a story as his material would allow, and also made persistent, though scarcely successful, efforts to avoid figuring as a hero. He was, indeed, rather abashed to find, on recurring to facts, that he had done so much to bring himself to the front. He even found himself at last taking refuge in the subterfuge of speaking of himself in the third person as "one of the party," when recounting a specially thrilling adventure in which he discovered that he had unblushingly distinguished himself. It was an exciting story of the capture of some white women by the Indians at a critical juncture, when but few men could be spared from the fort, and the fact that the deadly determination of "one of the party" that no harm should befall them was not once referred to in words, and only expressed itself in daring and endurance, for which every one but himself was supposed to be responsible, did not detract from its force. This "one of the party," who seemed to have sworn a silent oath that he would neither eat, nor sleep, nor rest until he had accomplished his end of rescuing the captives, and who had been upon the track almost as soon as the news had reached the fort, and who had followed it night and day, with his hastily gathered and altogether insufficient little band, and at last had overtaken the captors, and through sheer courage and desperate valor had overpowered them, and brought back their prisoners unharmed, — this "one of the party," silent, and would be insignificant, was, in spite of himself, a figure to stir the blood.

"It was *you* who did that?" she said, when he had finished.

"I was only one of the company," he answered, abashed, "and obeyed orders. Of course a man obeys orders."

Chapter 20

When he took her hand to assist her to rise he felt it tremble in his own.

"It was not a pleasant story," he said. "I ought not to have told it to you."

They scarcely spoke at all as they descended. He did not understand his own unreasoning happiness. What reason was there for it, after all? If he had argued the matter, he was in the mood to have said that what he gained in the strange sweetness of the flying moments could only hurt himself, and was enough in itself to repay him for any sense of pain and loss which might follow. But he did not argue at all. In Laurence Arbuthnot's place he would scarcely have given himself the latitude he was giving himself now.

"It is safe enough for *me*," was the sharp-edged thought which had cut through all others once or twice. "It is safe enough for *me* to be as happy as I may."

But he forgot this as they went down the hill, side by side. For the time being he only felt, and each glance he turned upon Bertha's downcast face gave him cause to realize, what intensity his feelings had reached, and wakened him to that sudden starting of pulse and heart which is almost a pain. When they reached the house Bertha went in search of Janey. She remained with her for about half an hour, and then came out to the hammock with her work-basket. The carnations at her waist were crushed a little, and something of the first freshness of her holiday air was gone. She held a letter in her hand, which she had evidently been reading. She had not returned it to its envelope, and it was still half open.

"It is from Richard," she said, after she had taken her seat in the hammock. "It was brought in from the post-office at Lowville about an hour ago."

"From Richard?" he said. "He is coming home, I suppose."

"No," she answered, looking down at the closely written sheets, —"he is not coming yet. He was wise enough not to take a serious view of Janey's case. He is very encouraging, and expresses his usual confidence in my management."

There was nothing like bitterness in her voice, and it struck him that he had never seen so little expression of any kind in her face. She opened the letter and looked over the first page of it.

"He has a great many interesting things to say," she went on; "and he is very enthusiastic."

"About what?" Tredennis asked. She looked up.

"About the Westoria lands," she answered. "He finds all sorts of complications of good fortune connected with them. I don't understand them all, by any means. I am not good at business. But it seems as though the persons who own the Westoria lands will be able to command the resources of the entire surrounding country, — if the railroad is carried through; of course it all depends upon the railroad."

"And the railroad," suggested Tredennis, "depends upon"—

"I don't know," she replied. "On several people, I suppose. I wish it depended on me."

"Why?" said Tredennis.

She smiled slightly and rather languidly.

"I should like to feel that anything so important depended on me," she said. "I should like the sense of power. I am very fond of power."

"I once heard it said that you had a great deal of it," Tredennis said; "far more than most women."

She smiled again, a trifle less languidly.

"That is Laurence Arbuthnot," she observed. "I always recognize his remarks when I hear them. He did not mean a compliment exactly, either, though it sounds rather like one. He has a theory that I affect people strongly, and he chooses to call that power. But it is too trivial. It is only a matter of pleasing or displeasing, and I am obliged to exert myself. It does not enable me to bestow things, and be a potentate. I think that to be a potentate might console one for a great many things, — and for the lack of a great many. If you can't take, it must distract your attention to be able to give."

"I do not like to hear you speak as if the chief thing to be desired was the ability to distract one's self," Tredennis said.

She paused a second.

"Then," she said, "I will not speak so now. To-day I will do nothing you do not like." Then she added, "As it is your last day, I wish to retrieve myself."

"What have you to retrieve?" he asked.

"Myself," she answered, "as I said."

She spread the letter upon her lap, and gave her attention to it.

"Isn't it rather like Richard," she said, "that, when he begins to write, he invariably writes a letter like that? Theoretically he detests correspondence, but when he once begins, his letter always interests him, and even awakens him to a kind of enthusiasm, so that instead of being brief he tells one everything. He has written twelve pages here, and it is all delightful."

"That is a wonderful thing to do," remarked Tredennis; "but it does not surprise me in Richard."

"No," she replied, "Richard can always interest himself; or, rather, he does not interest *himself*, — it is that he is interested without making an effort; that is his strong point."

She replaced the letter in the envelope and laid it in the basket, from which she took a strip of lace-work, beginning to employ herself with it in a manner more suggestive of graceful leisure than of industrious intention. It seemed to accentuate the fact that they had nothing to do but let the day drift by in luxurious idleness.

But Tredennis could not help seeing that for a while the tone of her mood, so to speak, was lowered. And yet, curiously enough, nothing of his own dreamy exaltation died away. The subtle shadow which seemed to have touched her, for a moment, only intensified his feeling of tenderness. In fact there were few things which would not have so intensified it; his mental condition was one which must advance by steady, silent steps of development to its climax. He was not by nature a reckless man, but he was by no means unconscious that there was something very like recklessness in his humor this last day.

As for the day itself, it also advanced by steady steps to its climax, unfolding its beauties like a perfect flower. The fresh, rain-washed morning drifted into a warm, languorous noon, followed by an afternoon so long and golden that it seemed to hold within itself the flower and sun, shade and perfume, of a whole summer. Tredennis had never known so long an afternoon, he thought, and yet it was only lengthened by the strange delight each hour brought with it, and was all too short when it was over. It seemed full of minute details, which presented themselves to his mind at the time as discoveries. Bertha worked upon her lace, and he watched her, waiting for the moment when she would look up at him, and then look down again with a quick or slow droop of the lids, which impressed itself upon him as a charm in itself. There was a little ring she wore which made itself a memory to him, — a simple turquoise, which set upon the whiteness of her hand like a blue flower. He saw, with a new sense of recognition, every fold and line of her thin, white drapery, the slight, girlish roundness of her figure, the dashes of brightness in the color of her hair, the smallness of the gold thimble on her finger, her grace when she rose or sat down, or rested a little against the red cushions in her hammock, touching the ground now and then with her slender slipper and swaying lightly to and fro.

"Do you know," he said to her once, as he watched her do this, "do you know," — with absorbed hesitation, —"that I feel as if — as if I had never really seen you until to-day — until this afternoon. You seem somehow to look different."

"I am not sure," she answered, "that I have ever seen you before; but it is not because you look different."

"Why is it?" he asked, quite ready to relinquish any idea of his own in the pursuit of one of hers.

She looked down a moment.

"To-day," she said, "I don't think you have anything against me."

"You think," he returned, "that I have usually something against you?"

"Yes," she answered.

"Will you tell me what you think it is?"

"I do not need to tell you," she said. "You know so well — and it would rather hurt me to put it into words."

"Hurt you?" he repeated.

"I should be harder than I am," she returned, "if it had not hurt me to know it myself — though I would not tell you that at any other time than now. I dare say I shall repent it to-morrow," she said.

"No," he answered, "you won't repent it. Don't repent it."

He felt the vehemence of his speech too late to check it. When he ended she was silent, and it was as if suddenly a light veil had fallen upon her face, and he felt that, too, and tried to be calmer.

"No," he repeated, "you must not repent. It is I who must repent that I have given you even a little pain. It is hard on me to know that I have done that."

The afternoon stretched its golden length to a sunset which cast deep, velvet shadows upon the grass and filled the air with an enchanted mellow radiance. Everything took a tinge of gold, — the green of the pines and the broad-leaved chestnut trees, the gray and brown of their trunks, the red of the old house, the honeysuckle and Virginia creeper clambering about it, the birds flying homeward to their nests. When the rich clearness and depth of color reached its greatest beauty Bertha folded her strip of lace and laid it in the little basket.

"We ought simply to sit and watch this," she said. "I don't think we ought even to speak. It will be all over in a few minutes, and we shall never see it again."

"No," said Tredennis, with a sad prescience; "nor anything at all like it."

"Ah!" was Bertha's rejoinder, "to *me* it has always seemed that it is not the best of such hours that one *does* see others like them. I have seen the sun set like this before."

"*I* have not," he said.

As he stood silent in the stillness and glow a faint, rather bitter, smile touched his lips and faded out. He found himself, he fancied, face to face with Laurence Arbuthnot again. He was sharing the sunset with him; there were ten chances against one that he had shared the day with him also.

Bertha sat in the deepening enchanted light with a soft, dreamy look. He thought it meant that she remembered something; but he felt that the memory was one to which she yielded herself without reluctance, or that she was happy in it. At last she lifted her eyes to his, and their expression was very sweet in its entire gentleness and submission to the spell of the moment.

"See!" she said, "the sun has slipped behind the pines already. We have only a few seconds left."

And then, even as they looked at the great fire, made brighter by the dark branches through which they saw it, it sank a little lower, and a little lower, and with an expiring flame was gone.

Bertha drew a quick breath, there was a second or so of silence, and then she stirred.

"It is over," she said; "and it has been like watching some one die, only sadder."

She took up the little work-basket and rose from her seat.

"It seems a pity to speak of mundane things," she said; "but I think we must go in to tea."

When the children were taken upstairs for the night Bertha went with them. It had been her habit to do this during their sojourn in the country, and naturally Janey had been her special care of late.

"I cannot often do such things when I am in Washington," she had explained once to Tredennis. "And I really like it as much as they do. It is part of the holiday."

As he sat on the porch in the starlight Tredennis could hear her voice mingling with the children's. The windows were wide open; she was moving from one room to the other, and two or three times she laughed in answer to some childish speech.

It was one of these laughs which, at last, caused Tredennis to leave his seat and go to the place under the trees where the hammocks were swung, and which was far more the place of general rendezvous than the parlor windows. From this point he could see the corner of the brightly lighted room, near the window where it was Bertha's custom to sit in her low chair, and rock Janey to sleep when she was restless.

She was doing it to-night. He could see the child's head lying on her bosom, and her own bent so that her cheek rested against the bright hair. In a few moments all was quiet, and she began to sing, and as she sang, swaying to and fro, Tredennis looked and listened without stirring.

But, though it was gay no longer, he liked to hear her song, and to his mind the moments in which he stood in the odorous dark, looking upward at the picture framed by the vine-hung window, were among the tenderest of the day. It was his fate to be full of a homely sentiment, which found its pleasure in unsophisticated primary virtues and affections. Any deep passion he might be moved by would necessarily have its foundation in such elements. He was slow at the subtle analysis whose final result is frequently to rob such simplicities of their value. His tendency was to reverence for age, tenderness to womanhood and childhood, faithfulness to all things. There was something boyish and quixotic in his readiness to kindle in defence of any womanly weakness or pain. Nothing he had ever said, or done, had so keenly touched and delighted Professor Herrick as his fiery denunciation, one night, of a man who was the hero of a scandalous story. There had been no qualifications of his sweeping assertion that in such cases it must be the man who had earned the right to bear the blame.

"It is *always* the man who is in the wrong," he had cried, flushing fiercely, "coward and devil — it is in the nature of things that he should be. Let him stand at the front and take what follows, if he has ever been a man for an hour!" And the professor had flushed also, — the fainter flush of age, — and had given some silent moments to reflection afterwards, as he sat gazing at the fire.

It was these primitive beliefs and sentiments which stirred within him now. He would not have lost one low note of the little song for the world, and he had left his seat only that he might see what he saw now, — her arm about her child, her cheek pressed against its hair.

It was not long before her little burden fell asleep he saw, but she did not rise as soon as this happened. She sat longer, and her song went on, finally dying away into brooding silence, which reigned for some time before she moved.

At length she lifted her face gently. She looked down at the child a few seconds, and slowly changed the position in which she lay, with an indescribably tender and cautious movement. Then she rose, and after standing an instant, holding her in her folding arms, crossed the room and passed out of sight.

Tredennis turned and began mechanically to arrange the cushions in the hammock. He felt sure she would come to-night and talk to him, for a little while at least.

It was not very long before he recognized her white figure in the door-way, and went toward it.

"They are all asleep," she said, in a voice whose hushed tone seemed to belong half to the slumber she had left and half to the stillness of the hour.

"Will you come out to the hammock," he said, "or will you sit here?"

She came forward and descended the steps.

"I will sit in the hammock," she replied. "I like the trees above me."

They went down the path together, and reaching the hammock she took her usual seat among its cushions, and he his upon a rough rustic bench near her.

"I was thinking before you came," he said, "of what you said this afternoon of my having something against you. I won't deny that there has been something in my thoughts of you that often has been miserable, and you were right in saying it was not in them to-day. It has not been in them for several days. What I was thinking just now was that it could never be in them again."

She did not stir.

"Don't you see," he went on, "I can't go back. If there had been nothing but to-day, I could not go back — beyond to-day. It would always be a factor in my arguments about you. I should always say to myself when things seemed to go wrong: 'There was no mistake about that day, — she was real then,' and I should trust you against everything. To-day — and in the other days too — I have seen you as you are, and because of that I should trust you in spite of everything."

"Oh!" she cried. "Don't trust me too much!" There was anguish in the sound, and he recognized it.

"I can't trust you too much," he answered, with obstinacy. "No honest human being can trust another honest human being too much."

"Am I an honest human being?" she said.

"I shall believe you one until the end," he returned.

"That is saying a great deal," was her reply.

"Listen," he said. "You know I am not like Arbuthnot and the rest. If I were to try to be like them I should only fail. But, though you never told me that I could be of any use to you, and you never will, I shall know if the time should come — and I shall wait for it. Have we not all of us something that belongs to ourselves, and not to the world, — it may be a pleasure or a pain, it does not matter which?"

"No," she put in, "it does not matter which."

"It does not matter to those on the outside," he went on; "it only matters to us, and I think we all have it to bear. Even I"—

"What," she said, "you, too?"

"Yes," he answered, "I, too; but it does not matter, if no one is hurt but ourselves."

"There are so many things that 'do not matter,'" she said. "To say that, only means that there is no help."

"That is true," was his reply, "and I did not intend to speak of myself, but of you."

"No," she said, "don't speak of me, — don't speak of me!"

"Why not?" he asked.

"Because I tell you that you are trusting me too much."

"Go on," he said.

She had covered her face with her hands, and held them so for a little while, then she let them fall slowly to her lap.

"If I tell you the truth," she said, "it will not be my fault if you still trust me too much. I don't want it to be my fault. The worst of me is, that I am neither bad nor good, and that I cannot live without excitement. I am always changing and trying experiments. When one experiment fails, I try another. They all fail after a while, or I get tired of them."

"Poor child!" he said.

She stirred slightly; one of the flowers fell from her belt upon her lap, and she let it lie there.

"It does not matter," she answered. "All that matters is, that you should know the truth about me, — that I am not to be depended upon, and that, above all, you need not be surprised at any change you see in me."

"When we meet again in Washington?" he suggested.

She hesitated a moment and then made her response.

"When we meet again in Washington, or at any time."

"Are you warning me?" he inquired.

"Yes," was her reply, and he recognized that in spite of her effort it was faintly given. "I am warning you."

He looked down at the grass and then at her. The determined squareness of chin, which was one of the chief characteristics of his face, struck her as being more marked than she had ever seen it.

"It is unnecessary," he said. "I won't profit by it."

He rose abruptly from his seat, and there was meaning in the movement, and in his eyes looking down upon her deep and dark in the faint light.

"You cannot change *me*," he said. "And you would have to change me before your warning would carry weight. Change yourself as you like — try as many experiments as you like — you cannot change the last ten days."

Even as the words were uttered, the day was ended for them as they had never once thought of its ending. There fell upon the quiet the sound of horses' feet approaching at a rapid pace and coming to a stop before the gate. The dogs came bounding and baying from the house, and above their deep-mouthed barking a voice made itself heard, calling to some one to come out, — a voice they both knew.

Tredennis turned toward it with a sharp movement.

"Do you hear that?" he exclaimed.

"Yes," said Bertha; and suddenly her manner was calm almost to coldness, — "it is Laurence Arbuthnot, and papa is with him. Let us go and meet them."

And in a few seconds they were at the gate, and the professor was explaining their unexpected appearance.

"It is all Mr. Arbuthnot's fault, my dear," he said; "he knew that I wished to see you, and, having an idea that I was not strong enough to make the journey alone, he suddenly affected to have business in this vicinity. It was entirely untrue, and I was not in the least deceived; but I humored him, as I begin to find it best to do, and allowed him to bring me to you."

Arbuthnot had dismounted, and was fastening his horse to the gate, and he replied by one of the gayest and most discriminatingly pitched of the invaluable laughs.

"It is no use," he said; "the professor does not believe in me. He refuses to recognize in me anything but hollow mockery."

Bertha went to him. There was something hurried in her movement; it was as if she was strangely, almost feverishly, glad to see him. She went to his horse's head and laid her hand on the creature's neck.

"That takes me back to Washington," she said: "to Washington. It was like you to come, and I am glad, but — you should have come a little sooner."

And, as she stood there, faintly smiling up at him, her hand was trembling like a leaf.

Chapter 21

It was New-Year's day, and His Excellency the President had had several months in which to endeavor to adjust himself to the exigencies of his position; though whether he had accomplished this with a result of entire satisfaction to himself and all parties concerned and unconcerned, had, perhaps unfortunately, not been a matter of record. According to a time-honored custom, he had been placed at the slight disadvantage of being called upon to receive, from time to time, the opinions of the nation concerning himself without the opportunity of expressing, with any degree of publicity, his own opinions regarding the nation; no bold spirit having as yet suggested that such a line of procedure might at least be embellished with the advantage of entire novelty, apart from the possibility of its calling forth such originality and force of statement as would present to the national mind questions never before discussed, and perhaps not wholly unimportant. All had, however, been done which could be done by a nation justly distinguished for its patriotic consideration for, and courtesy toward, the fortunate persons elevated to the position of representing its dignity at home and abroad. Nothing, which could add to that dignity had been neglected; no effort which could place it in its proper light, and remove all difficulty from the pathway of the figure endeavoring creditably to support it, had been spared. The character of the successful candidate for presidential office having been, during the campaign, effectually disposed of, — his morals having been impugned, his honor rent to tatters, his intellectual capacity pronounced far below the lowest average, — united good feeling was the result, and there seemed little more to attain. His past had been exhausted. Every event of his political career and domestic life had been held up to public derision, laudation, and criticism. It had been successfully proved that his education had been entirely neglected, and that his advantages had been marvellous; that he had read Greek at the tender age of four years, and that he had not learned to read at all until he attained his majority; that his wife had taught him his letters, and that he had taught his wife to spell; that he was a liar, a forger, and a thief; that he was a model of virtue, probity, and honor, — each and all of which incontrovertible facts had been public property and a source of national pride and delight.

After the election, however, the fact that he had had a past at all had ceased to be of any moment whatever. A future — of four years — lay before him, and must be utilized; after that, the Deluge. The opposing party sneered, vilified, and vaunted themselves in the truth of their predictions concerning his incapacity; the non-opposing party advised, lauded, cautioned, mildly discouraged, and in a most human revulsion of feeling showed their unprejudiced frankness by openly condemning on frequent occasions. The head of the nation having appointed an official from among his immediate supporters, there arose a clamor of adverse criticism upon a course which lowered the gifts of his sacred office to the grade of mere payment for value received. Having made a choice from without the circle, he called down upon himself frantic accusations of ingratitude to those to whom he owed all. There lay before him the agreeable alternatives of being a renegade or a monument of bribery and corruption, and if occasionally these alternatives lost for a moment their attractiveness, and the head of the nation gave way to a sense of perplexity, and was guilty of forming in secret a vague wish that the head of the nation was on some other individual's shoulders, or even went to the length of wishing that the head upon his own shoulders was his own property, and not a football for the vivacious strength of the nation to expend itself upon, — if this occurred, though it is by no means likely, it certainly revealed a weakness of character and inadequacy to the situation which the nation could not have failed to condemn. The very reasonable prophecy, — made by the party whose candidate had not been elected, — that the government must inevitably go to destruction and the country to perdition, had, through some singular oversight on the part of the powers threatened, not been fulfilled. After waiting in breathless suspense for the occurrence of these catastrophes, and finding that they had apparently been postponed until the next election, the government had drawn a sigh of relief, and the country had gained courage to bestir itself cheerfully, with a view to such perquisites as might be obtained by active effort and a strong sense of general personal worthiness and fitness for any position.

There had descended upon the newly elected ruler an avalanche of seekers for office, a respectable number of whom laid in his hands the future salvation of their souls and bodies, and generously left to him the result. He found himself suddenly established as the guardian of the widow, the orphan, and the friendless, and required to repair fortunes or provide them, as the case might be, at a moment's notice; his sympathies were appealed to, his interests, his generosity, as an altogether omnipotent power in whose hands all things lay, and whose word was naturally law upon all occasions, great or small; and any failure on his part to respond to the entirely reasonable requests preferred was very properly laid to a tendency to abandoned scheming or to the heartless indifference of the great, which decision disposed of all difficulties in the argument, apart from such trivial ones as were left to the portion of the delinquent and were not referred to. Being called upon in his selection of his cabinet to display the judgment of Solomon, the diplomacy of Talleyrand, and the daring of Napoleon, and above all to combine like powers in each official chosen, he might have faltered but for the assistance proffered him from all sides. This, and the fact that there was no lack of the qualifications required, supported him. Each day some monument of said qualifications, and others too numerous to mention, was presented to his notice. To propitiate the South it was suggested that he should appoint A; to secure the North, B; to control the East, C; to sweep the West, D; and to unite the country, E. Circumstances having finally led him to decide upon G, the government appeared to be in jeopardy again; but — possibly through having made use of its numerous opportunities of indulging in acrobatic efforts in the direction of losing its balance and regaining it again in an almost incredible manner — it recovered from the shock, and even retained its equilibrium, upon finding itself in the end saddled with a cabinet whose selection was universally acknowledged to be a failure when it was not denounced as a crime.

On this particular New Year's day there were few traces on the social surface of the disasters which so short a time before had threatened to engulf all. Washington wore an aspect even gayer than usual. The presidential reception began the day in its most imposing manner. Lines of carriages thronged the drive before the White House, and the diplomatists, statesmen, officials, and glittering beings in naval and military uniform, who descended from them, were possibly cheered and encouraged by the comments of the lookers-on, who knew them and their glories and their shortcomings by heart. The comments were not specially loud, however. That which in an English crowd takes the form of amiable or unamiable clamor, in an American gathering of a like order resolves itself into a serene readiness of remark, which exalts or disposes of a dignity with equal impartiality, and an ingenuous fearlessness of any consequence whatever, which would seem to argue that all men are born free and some equal, though the last depends entirely upon circumstances. Each vehicle, having drawn up, deposited upon the stone steps of the broad portico a more or less picturesque or interesting personage. Now it was the starred and ribboned representative of some European court; again, a calm-visaged Japanese or Chinese official, in all the splendor of flowing robes and brilliant color; and, again, a man in citizen's clothes, whose unimposing figure represented such political eminence as to create more stir among the lookers-on than all the rest. Among equipages, there drove up at length a rather elegant little coupe, from which, when its door was opened, there sprang lightly to the stone steps the graceful figure of a young man, followed by an elder one. The young fellow, who was talking with much animation, turned an exhilaratingly bright face upon the crowd about him.

"On the whole, I rather like it," he said.

"Oh!" responded his companion, "as to that, you like everything. I never saw such a fellow."

The younger man laughed quite joyously.

"There is a great deal of truth in that," he said, "and I don't suppose you will deny that it is an advantage."

"An advantage!" repeated the other. "By Jupiter, I should think it was an advantage! Now, how long do you think this fellow will keep us waiting when we want him?"

"Oh!" was the answer; "he is Mrs. Amory's coach-man, you know, and there isn't a doubt that he has had excellent training. She isn't fond of waiting."

"No," said the other, with a peculiar smile. "I should fancy she wasn't. Well, I guess we'll go in."

They turned to do so, and found themselves near a tall man in uniform, who almost immediately turned also, and revealed the soldierly visage of Colonel Tredennis.

He made a quick movement forward, which seemed to express some surprise.

"What, Amory!" he exclaimed. "You here, too? I was not at all sure that you had returned."

"I am scarcely sure myself yet," answered Richard, as he shook hands. "It only happened last night; but Bertha has been home a week. Is it possible you haven't seen her?"

"I have not seen anybody lately," said Tredennis, "and I did not know that she had returned until I read her name in the list of those who would receive."

"Oh, of course she will receive," said Richard. "And Planefield and I — you have met Senator Planefield?"

"How do you do?" said Senator Planefield, without any special manifestation of delight.

Tredennis bowed, and Richard went on airily, as they made their way in:

"Planefield and I have been sent out to do duty, and our list extends from Capitol Hill to Georgetown Heights."

"And he," said Senator Planefield, "professes to enjoy the prospect."

"Why not?" said Richard. "It is a bright, bracing day, and there is something exhilarating in driving from house to house, to find one's self greeted at each by a roomful of charming women, — most of them pretty, some of them brilliant, all of them well dressed and in holiday spirits. It is delightful."

"Do *you* find it delightful?" inquired Planefield, turning with some abruptness to Tredennis.

"I am obliged to own that I don't shine in society," answered Tredennis.

He knew there was nothing to resent in the question, but he was conscious of resenting something in the man himself. His big, prosperous-looking body and darkly florid face, with its heavy, handsome outlines, and keen, bold eyes, had impressed him unpleasantly from the first, and on each occasion of their meeting the impression seemed to deepen.

"Well, Amory shines," was his response, "and so does Mrs. Amory. We are to drop in and see her shine, as often as we happen to be in the neighborhood through the day."

They had reached the threshold of the reception-room by this time, and Richard, catching the last words, turned and spoke.

"Of course you will be there yourself in the course of the day," he said. "We shall possibly meet you — and, by-the-by, you will see Mrs. Sylvestre. She arrived two days ago."

When they came out again Richard was in more buoyant spirits than before. The lighted rooms, the brilliant dresses, the many faces he knew or did not know, the very crush itself, had acted upon him like a fine wind. He issued forth into the light of day again, girded and eager for his day's work.

"There is nothing like Washington," he announced, "and especially nothing like Washington at the beginning of the season. Just at the outset, when one is meeting people for the first time since their return, they actually have the air of being glad to see one, and a man has a delightful evanescent sense of being somehow positively popular."

"Does it make *you* feel popular?" demanded Planefield of Tredennis, in his unceremonious fashion.

Tredennis presented to him an entirely immovable front.

"How do *you* find it?" he inquired.

The man laughed.

"Not as Amory does," he answered.

When the *coupé* appeared and he took his place at Richard's side, he bent forward to bestow on Tredennis, as they drove away, a glance expressive of but little favor.

"I don't like that fellow," he said. "Confound him!"

Richard settled himself in his corner of the carriage, folding his fur-trimmed coat about him quite luxuriously.

"Oh, no. Not confound him," he replied. "He is a delightful fellow — in his way."

"Confound his way, then," responded Planefield. "There's too much of it."

Richard leaned slightly forward to look at the tall, motionless figure himself, and the faintest possible change passed over his face as he did so.

"He is not exactly a malleable sort of fellow," he remarked, "and I suppose there might arise occasions when he would be a little in the way; but there is no denying that he is picturesque."

"Oh!" exclaimed his companion, with more fervor than grace. "The devil take his picturesqueness!"

In the meantime Colonel Tredennis awaited the arrival of his own carriage, which had fallen back in the line. The surging of the crowd about him, the shouts of the policemen as they called up the vehicles, the rolling of vehicles and opening and shutting of doors, united themselves in an uproar which seemed to afford him a kind of seclusion. The subject of his thoughts as he stood in the midst of the throng was not a new one; it was one from whose presence he had ceased to expect to free himself; but as the information in the morning paper had accelerated the pulse of emotion in him, so his brief interview with Richard Amory had quickened it again. Since the day when he had left her in Virginia, five months before, he had not seen Bertha at all, and had only heard from her directly once. She had been at Long Branch, Saratoga, Newport, and afterward visiting friends in the northern cities. After his return from the West, Richard had frequently been with her, and their letters to the professor had informed him that they were well and were involved in a round of gayeties.

How the time had passed for Tredennis he could not himself have told. When he had returned to Washington he had lived and moved as a man in a dream. The familiar streets and buildings wore an unfamiliar look. It was a relief to find the places more deserted than before; his chief desire was to be, if possible, entirely alone. In the first vivid freshness of his impressions it seemed incredible that the days he had been living through had come to an end, and that absolutely nothing remained but the strange memory of them. At times it appeared that something must happen, — some impossible thing which would give reality to the past and motive to the future. If in any of his nightly walks before the closed and silent house he had suddenly seen that the shutters were opened and lights were shining within; if Bertha herself had, without warning, stood at the window and smiled upon him, he would have felt it at first only natural, even though he knew she was hundreds of miles away.

This for a few weeks, and then his exaltation died a gradual death for want of sustenance, and there remained only the long, sultry days to be lived through and their work to be done. They were lived through, and their work was not neglected; but there was no one of them which dragged its slow length by without leaving marks upon him which neither time nor change could erase in any future that might come.

"Five months," he said, as he waited with the clamor about him, "is longer than it seems — it is longer."

And Miss Jessup, passing him at the moment and looking up, found herself so utterly at a loss for an adjective adequate to the description of his expression, that her own bright and alert little countenance fell, and existence temporarily palled upon her.

It was late in the day when he reached the Amorys. When he drove up several carriages stood before the door, one of them Bertha's own, from which Richard and Planefield had just descended. Two or three men were going into the house, and one or two were leaving it. Through the open door were to be seen the lighted hall, and glimpses of bright rooms beyond, from which came the sound of voices, laughter, and the clink of glass. ,

Richard entered the house with Tredennis, and flung off his rather sumptuous outer garment with a laugh of relief.

"We have made fifty calls so far," he said, "and have enjoyed them enormously. What have you accomplished?"

"Not fifty, by any means," Tredennis answered, and then the man-servant took his coat, and they went into the parlors.

They seemed to be full of men, — young men, middle-aged men, old men; even a half-grown boy or two had timorously presented themselves, with large hopes of finding dazzling entertainment in the convivialities of the day. The shutters were closed and the rooms brilliantly alight; there were flowers in every available corner, and three or four charmingly dressed women, each forming a bright central figure in a group of black coats, gave themselves to their task of entertainment with delightful animation.

For a moment Tredennis stood still. He did not see Bertha at once, though he fancied he heard her voice in the room adjoining, where, through the half-drawn *portières*, were to be seen men standing, with coffee-cups, wine-glasses, or little plates in their hands, about a table bright with flowers, fruits, and all the usual glittering appurtenances. The next instant, amid a fresh burst of laughter, which she seemed to leave behind her, she appeared upon the threshold.

As she paused a second between the heavy curtains Tredennis thought suddenly of a brilliant tropical bird he had once seen somewhere, and the fancy had scarcely formed itself in his mind before she recognized him and came forward.

He had never seen her so brilliantly dressed before. The wonderful combination of rich and soft reds in her costume, the flash of the little jewelled bands clasped close about her bare throat and arms, their pendants trembling and glowing in the light, the color on her cheeks, the look in her eyes, had a curiously bewildering effect upon him. When she gave him her hand he scarcely knew what to do with it, and could only wait for her to speak. And she spoke as if they had parted only an hour ago.

"At last," she said. "And it was very nice in you to leave me until the last, because now I know you will not feel obliged to go away so soon." And she withdrew her hand and opened her fan, and stood smiling up at him over its plumy border. "You see," she said, "that we have returned to our native atmosphere and may begin to breathe freely. Now we are real creatures again."

"Are we?" he answered. "Is that it?" and he glanced over the crowd, and then came back to her and looked her over from the glittering buckle on her slipper to the scintillating arrow in her hair. "I suppose we have," he added. "I begin to realize it."

"If you need anything to assist you to realize it," she said, "cast your eye upon Mr. Arbuthnot, and I think you will find him sufficient; for me, everything crystallized itself and all my doubts disappeared the moment I saw his opera hat, and heard his first remark about the weather. It is a very fine day," she added, with a serene air of originality, "a little cold, but fine and clear. Delightful weather for those of you who are making calls. It has often struck me that it must be unpleasant to undertake so much when the weather is against you. It is colder to-day than it was yesterday, but it will be likely to be warmer to-morrow. It is to be hoped that we shall have an agreeable winter."

"You might," he said, looking at her over the top of her fan, "induce them to mention it in the churches."

"That," she answered, "is the inspiration of true genius, and it shall be attended to at once, or — here is Senator Planefield; perhaps he might accomplish something by means of a bill?"

The senator joined them in his usual manner, which was not always an engaging manner, and was at times a little suggestive of a disposition to appropriate the community, and was also a somewhat loud-voiced manner, and florid in its decorative style. It was, on the whole, less engaging than usual upon the present occasion. The fact that he was for some reason not entirely at ease expressed itself in his appearing to be very wonderfully at ease; indeed, metaphorically speaking, he appeared to have his hands in his pockets.

"A bill!" he said. "You have the floor, and I stand ready to second any motion you choose to make. I think we might put it through together. What can we do for you?"

"We want an appropriation," Bertha answered, — "an appropriation of fine weather, which will enable Colonel Tredennis to be as giddy a butterfly of fashion as his natural inclination would lead him to desire to be."

Planefield glanced at Tredennis with a suggestion of grudging the momentary attention.

"Is he a butterfly of fashion?" he asked.

"What!" exclaimed Bertha, —"is it possible that you have not detected it? It is the fatal flaw upon his almost perfect character. Can it be that you have been taking him seriously, and mistakenly imagining that it was Mr. Arbuthnot who was frivolous?"

"Arbuthnot," repeated the senator. "Which is Arbuthnot? How is a man to tell one from the other? There are too many of them!"

"What an agreeable way of saying that Colonel Tredennis is a host in himself!" said Bertha. "But I have certainly not found that there were too many of him, and I assure you that you would know Mr. Arbuthnot from the other after you had exchanged remarks with him. He has just been beguiled into the next room by Mrs. Sylvestre, who is going to give him some coffee."

"Mrs. Sylvestre," said Tredennis. "Richard told me she was with you, and I was wondering why I did not see her."

"You did not see her," said Bertha, "because I wished her to dawn upon you slowly, and, having that end in view, I arranged that Mr. Arbuthnot should occupy her attention when I saw you enter."

"He couldn't stand it all at once, could he?" remarked Planefield, whose manner of giving *her* his attention was certainly not grudging. He kept his eyes fixed on her face, and apparently found entertainment in her most trivial speech.

"It was not that, exactly," she answered. Then she spoke to Tredennis.

"She is ten times as beautiful as she was," she said, "and it would not be possible to calculate how many times more charming."

"That was not necessary," responded Tredennis.

He could not remove his own eyes from her face, even while he was resenting the fact that Planefield looked at her; he himself watched her every movement and change of expression.

"It was entirely unnecessary," she returned; "but it is the truth."

"You are trying to prejudice him against her," said Planefield.

"She is my ideal of all that a beautiful woman ought to be," she replied, "and I should like to form myself upon her."

"Oh, we don't want any of that," put in Planefield. "You are good enough for us."

She turned her attention to him. Her eyes met his with the most ingenuous candor, and yet the little smile in them was too steady not to carry suggestion with it.

"Quite?" she said.

"Yes, quite," he answered, not so entirely at ease as before.

Her little smile did not waver in the least.

"Do you know," she said, "it seems almost incredible, but I will try to believe it. Now," she said to Tredennis, "if Senator Planefield will excuse me for a moment, I will take you into the other room. You shall speak to Mrs. Sylvestre. He has already seen her. Will you come?"

"I shall be very glad," he answered. He followed as she led him to the adjoining room. On its threshold she paused an instant.

"Exactly as I expected," she said. "She is listening to Mr. Arbuthnot."

Mr. Arbuthnot was standing at the end of the low mantel. He held a cup of coffee in his hand, but had apparently forgotten it in giving his attention to his very charming companion. This companion was, of course, Mrs. Sylvestre herself. Tredennis recognized her clear, faintly tinted face and light, willowy figure at once. She wore a dress of black lace, with purple passion-flowers, and she was looking at Arbuthnot with reflective eyes, almost the color of the flowers. She did not seem to be talking herself, but she was listening beautifully, with a graceful, receptive attention. Arbuthnot evidently felt it, and was improving his shining hour with a sense of enjoyment tampered by no lack of ability to avail himself of its fleeting pleasure.

It is possible, however, that his rapture at seeing Tredennis may have been tempered by the natural weakness of man, but he bore himself with his usual unperturbed equanimity.

"There," he remarked to Mrs. Sylvestre, "is the most objectionable creature in Washington."

"Objectionable!" Mrs. Sylvestre repeated. "Bertha is bringing him here."

"Yes," responded Arbuthnot, "that is the objection to him, and it leaves him without a redeeming quality."

Mrs. Sylvestre gave him a charmingly interested glance, and the next instant made a slight movement forward.

"Ah!" she exclaimed, "it is Colonel Tredennis!" and she held out her hand with the most graceful gesture of welcome imaginable.

"It is very good of you to remember me," Tredennis said.

"It was not difficult," she answered, with a smile. And they fell, in the most natural manner, a step apart from the others, and she stood and looked at him as he spoke just as she had looked at Arbuthnot a moment before. Arbuthnot began to give mild attention to his coffee.

"It is quite cold," he said to Bertha. "Will you give me another cup?"

"Yes," she answered, and took it from his hand to carry it to the table. He followed her, and stood at her side as she poured the fresh cup out.

"It is my impression," he said, with serene illiberality, "that she did not remember him at all."

"Yes, she did," Bertha replied. "She remembers everybody. That is one of her gifts. She has a great many gifts."

"I did not place implicit confidence in her intimation that she remembered me," he proceeded, still serenely. "I liked the statement, and saw the good taste of it, and the excellent reasons for its being true; but I managed to restrain the naive impulses of a trusting nature. And it doesn't strike me as being so entirely plausible that she should have remembered Tredennis."

He paused suddenly and looked at Bertha's hand, in which she held the sugar-tongs and a lump of sugar.

"Will you have one lump, or two?" she asked.

Then he looked from her hand to her face. Her hand was trembling and her face was entirely without color. The look of strained steadiness in her uplifted eyes was a shock to him. It seemed to him that any one who chanced to glance at her must see it.

"You have been standing too long," he said. "You have tired yourself out again."

He took the cup of coffee from her.

"It is too late for you to expect many calls now," he said, "and if any one comes you can easily be found in the conservatory. I am going to take you there, and let you sit down for a few seconds, at least."

He gave her his arm and carried the cup of coffee with him.

"You will have to drink this yourself," he said. "Have you eaten anything to-day?"

"No," she replied.

"I thought not. And then you are surprised to find your hand trembling. Don't you see what nonsense it is?"

"Yes."

He stepped with her into the tiny conservatory at the end of the room, and gave her a seat behind a substantial palm on a red stand. His eyes never left her face, though he went on talking in the most matter-of-fact tone.

"Drink that coffee," he said, "and then I will bring you a glass of wine and a sandwich."

She put out her hand as if to take the cup, but it fell, shaking, upon her lap.

"I can't," she said.

"You must," he replied.

The inflexibility of his manner affected her, as he had known it would. When he sat down in the low seat at her side, and held out the cup, she took it.

"Go and get the wine," she said, without looking at him.

He went at once, neither speaking nor glancing back at her. He was glad of the opportunity of turning his face away from her, since he felt that, in spite of his determination, it was losing something of its expressionless calm.

When he entered the room Mrs. Sylvestre still stood where he had left her. It was she who was speaking now, and Tredennis, who was listening, looking down upon her with an expression of much interest.

When he had procured a glass of wine and a sandwich Arbuthnot went to her.

"I have secreted Mrs. Amory in the conservatory," he said, "with a view of inducing her to take something in the form of sustenance. I can produce her at a moment's notice if she is needed."

"That was consideration," she replied.

"It was humanity," he answered, and went away.

Bertha had finished the coffee when he returned to her. The blanched look had left her, and her voice, when she spoke, sounded more natural and steady.

"It did me good," she said, and this time she looked at him, and there was something in her uplifted eyes which touched him.

"I knew it would," he answered.

"You always know," she said. "There is no one who knows so well what is good for me"; and she said it with great gentleness.

He took refuge from himself, as he sometimes found it discreet to do, in his usual airy lightness.

"I am all soul myself," he remarked, "as you may have observed, and I understand the temptation to scorn earthly food and endeavor to subsist wholly upon the plaudits of the multitude. You will, perhaps, permit me to remark that though the new gown"— with an approving glance at it —"is an immense and unqualified success, I doubt its power to sustain nature during the six or eight hours of a New Year's reception."

Bertha glanced down at it herself.

"Do you think it is pretty?" she asked.

"I shouldn't call it pretty," he replied. "I should call it something more impressive."

She still looked at it.

"It is a flaring thing," she said.

"No, it isn't," he returned, promptly. "Not in the least. You might call it brilliant — if you insist on an adjective. It is a brilliant thing, and it is not like you in the least."

She turned toward him. "No," she said, "it isn't like me in the least."

"It looks," remarked Arbuthnot, giving it some lightly critical attention, "as if you had taken a new departure."

"That is it exactly," she returned. "You always say the right thing. I have taken a new departure."

"Might I ask in what direction?" he inquired.

"Yes," she responded. "I will tell you, as a fair warning. I am going to be a dazzling and worldly creature."

"You are?" he said. "Now that is entirely sensible, though I should scarcely call it a new departure. You know you tried it last winter, with the most satisfying results. When Lent came on you had lost several pounds in weight and all your color; you had refined existence until neither rest nor food appeared necessary to you, and the future was naturally full of promise. Be gay, by all means; you'll find it pay, I assure you. Go to a lunch-party at one, and a reception at four, a dinner in the evening, and drop in at a German or so on your way home, taking precautions at the same time against neglecting your calling-list in the intervals these slight recreations allow you. Oh, I should certainly advise you to be gay."

"Laurence," she said, "do you think if one should do that *every* day, *every* day, and give one's self no rest, that after a while it would *kill* one?"

He regarded her fixedly for an instant.

"Do you want to die?" he asked, at last.

She sat perfectly still, and something terribly like, and yet terribly unlike, a smile crept slowly into her eyes as they met his. Then she replied, without flinching in the least, or moving her gaze:

"No."

He held up a long, slender forefinger, and shook it at her, slowly, in his favorite gesture of warning.

"No," he said, "you don't; but, even if you fancied you did, don't flatter yourself that it would happen. Shall I tell you what would occur? You would simply break down. You would lose your self-control and do things you did not wish to do; you would find it a physical impossibility to be equal to the occasion, and you would end by being pale and haggard — haggard, and discovering that your gowns were not becoming to you. How does the thing strike you?"

"It is very brutal," she said, with a little shudder; "but it is true."

"When you make ten remarks that are true," he returned, "nine of them are brutal. That is the charm of life."

"I don't think," she said, with inconsequent resentment, "that you very much mind being brutal to me."

"A few minutes ago you said I knew what was good for you," he responded.

"You do," she said, "that is it, and it is only like me that I should hate you because you do. You must think," with a pathetic tone of appeal for herself in her voice, "that I do not mind being brutal to you; but I don't want to be. I don't want to do any of the things I am doing now."

She picked up the bouquet of Jacqueminot roses she had been carrying and had laid down near her.

"Don't talk about me," she said. "Let us talk about something else, — these, for instance. Do you know where they came from?"

"I could scarcely guess."

"Senator Planefield sent them to me."

He regarded them in silence.

"They match the dress," she said, "and they belong to it."

"Yes," he answered, "they match the dress."

Then he was silent again.

"Well," she said, restlessly, "why don't you say something to me?"

"There isn't anything to say," he replied.

"You are thinking that I am very bad?" she said.

"You are trying to persuade yourself that you are very bad, and are finding a fictitious excitement in it; but it is all a mistake. It won't prove the consolation you expect it to," he answered. "Suppose you give it up before it gives rise to complications."

"We are talking of Bertha Amory again," she said. "Let us talk about Agnes Sylvestre. Don't you find her very beautiful?"

"Yes," he replied.

"Why don't you say more than 'yes'?" she asked. "You mean more."

"I couldn't mean more," he answered. "I should think it was enough to mean that much; there are even circumstances under which it might be too much."

"She is lovelier than she used to be," said Bertha, reflectively; "and more fascinating."

"Yes to that also," he responded.

"Any one might love her," she went on, in the same tone. "*Any* one."

"I should think so," he replied, quietly.

"I do not see how it would be possible," she added, "for any one — who was thrown with her — to resist her — unless it was some one like you."

She turned a faint smile upon him.

"I am glad," she said, "that *you* are not susceptible."

"So am I," he said, with some dryness.

"If you were susceptible you would go too," she ended. "And I don't want *every* one to leave me."

"Every one?" he repeated.

She rose as if to go, giving a light touch to the folds of her dress, and still smiling a little.

"Colonel Tredennis has fallen a victim," she said, "in the most natural and proper manner. I knew he would, and he has distinguished himself by at once carrying out my plans for him. Now we must go back to the parlors. I have rested long enough."

They returned just in time to meet a fresh party of callers, and Arbuthnot was of necessity thrown for the time being upon his own resources. These did not fail him. He found entertainment in his surroundings until a certain opportunity he had rather desired presented itself to him. He observed that Mrs. Sylvestre was once more near him, and that the men occupying her attention were on the point of taking their leave. By the time they had done so he had dexterously brought to a close his conversation with his male companion, and had unobtrusively forwarded himself, in an entirely incidental manner, as an aspirant for her notice.

She received him with a quiet suggestion of pleasure in her smile.

"Have you enjoyed the day?" he asked.

"Yes," she replied. "I am almost sorry that it is so nearly over. It has been very agreeable."

Then he found her eyes resting upon him in the quiet and rather incomprehensible way which Bertha had counted among her chiefest charms.

"Have you enjoyed it?" she inquired.

"If I had not," he said, "I should feel rather like a defeated candidate. One may always enjoy things if one applies one's self."

She seemed to reflect upon him an instant again.

"You see a great deal of Bertha?" she said.

"Yes, a great deal. Would you mind telling me why you ask?"

"Because that remark was so entirely like her," she replied.

"Well," he returned, "there is no denying that I have formed myself upon her, and though the fact reveals me in all my shallow imitative weakness, I can offer the apology that the means justifies the end. Upon the whole, I am glad to be detected, as it points to a measure of success in the attempt."

"But," she went on, "she tells me that she has formed herself upon you."

"Ah!" he said; "she meant you to repeat it to me, her design being to betray me into a display of intoxicated vanity."

"She is very fond of you," she remarked.

"I am very fond of her," he answered, quickly — and then relapsing into his usual manner —"though that is not a qualification sufficiently rare to distinguish me."

"No," she said, "it is not."

Then she gave Bertha one of the glances.

"It was very thoughtful in you to take her into the conservatory," she said. "I was startled to see how pale she looked as you left the room."

"She is not strong," he said, "and she insists on ignoring the fact."

"Do you know," said Mrs. Sylvestre, "that was what struck me when we met for the first time in the autumn — that she was not strong. She used to be strong."

"If she would accept the fact she would get over it," he said; "but she won't."

"I met her first at Newport," said Mrs. Sylvestre, "just after Janey's illness. For a day or so I felt that I did not know her at all; but in course of time I got over the feeling; or she changed — I scarcely know which. I suppose the strain during the little girl's illness had been very severe?"

"There is no doubt of that," said Arbuthnot; "and her anxiety had been much exaggerated."

"I shall see a great deal of her this winter," she returned, "and perhaps I may persuade her to take care of herself."

He spoke with a touch of eager seriousness in his manner.

"I wish you would," he said. "It is what she needs, that some woman should call her attention to the mistake she is making."

"I will try to do it," she responded, gently. "I am fond of her too."

"And you intend remaining in Washington?" he asked.

"Yes. I have had no plans for three years. When first it dawned on me that it would interest me to make plans again, I thought of Washington. I have found a house in Lafayette Square, and I think I shall be established in it, with the assistance of my aunt, who is to live with me, in about three weeks."

"That sounds very agreeable," he remarked.

"I shall hope to make it sufficiently so," she said. "Will you come sometimes to see if my efforts are successful?"

"If you knew how unworthy I am," he responded, "even my abject gratitude for your kindness would not repay you for it."

"Are you so very unworthy?" she was beginning, when her eyes appeared to be caught by some object at the other side of the room.

It was not a particularly interesting object. It was merely the figure of an unprepossessing boy, whose provincial homeliness was rendered doubly impressive by his frightful embarrassment. He had arrived a few moments before, with two more finished youths, whose mother Bertha knew, and, having been basely deserted by them at the outset, had stranded upon the treacherous shores of inexperience as soon as he had shaken hands.

Mrs. Sylvestre's beautiful eyes dwelt upon him a moment with sympathy and interest.

"Will you excuse me," she said to Arbuthnot, "if I go and talk to that boy? Bertha is too busy to attend to him, and he seems to know no one."

Arbuthnot gave the boy a glance. He would not have regretted any comparatively harmless incident which would have removed him, but his own very naturally ignoble desire not to appear to a disadvantage restrained the impulse prompting a derisive remark. And while he objected to the boy in his most pronounced manner, he did not object in the least to what he was clever enough to see in his companion's words and the ready sympathy they expressed. Indeed, there was a side of him which derived definite pleasure from it.

"I will excuse you," he answered; "but I need you more than the boy does, and I cannot help believing that I am more worthy of you;

though, of course, I only use the word in its relative sense. As I remarked before, I am unworthy, but as compared to the boy — He is a frightful boy," he added, seeming to take him in more fully; "but I dare say his crimes are unpremeditated. Let me go with you and find out if I know his mother. I frequently know their mothers."

"If you do know his mother, I am sure it will be a great relief to him, and it will assist me," said Mrs. Sylvestre.

They crossed the room together, and, seeing them approach, the boy blushed vermilion and moved uneasily from one foot to the other. Gradually, however, his aspect changed a little. Here were rather attractive worldlings whose bearing expressed no consciousness whatever of his crime of boyhood. He met Mrs. Sylvestre's eyes and blushed less; he glanced furtively at Arbuthnot, and suddenly forgot his hands and became almost unconscious of his legs.

"I have been asking Mrs. Sylvestre," said Arbuthnot, with civil mendacity, "if you did not come with the Bartletts. I thought I saw you come in together."

"Yes," responded the boy. "I am a cousin of theirs."

"Then I have heard them speak of you," Arbuthnot returned. "And I think I had the pleasure of meeting your sister several times last winter, — Miss Hemmingway?"

"Yes," said the boy; "she was here on a visit."

In two minutes he found himself conversing almost fluently, and it was Arbuthnot who was his inspiration equally with Mrs. Sylvestre. He was a modest and inoffensive youth, and overestimated the brilliance of the scenes surrounding him, and the gifts and charms of his new-found friends, with all the ardor of his tender years. To him, Arbuthnot's pale, well-bred face and simple, immaculate attire represented luxury, fashion, and the whirling vortex of society. The kindly imagination of simplicity bestowed upon him an unlimited income and an exalted position in the diplomatic corps, at least; his ease of manner and readiness of speech seeming gifts only possible of attainment through familiarity with foreign courts and effete civilizations. When he was asked how he liked Washington, if he intended to spend the season with his relations, if he had made many calls, and if the day did not seem to be an unusually gay one, he accomplished the feat of answering each question, even adding an original remark or so of his own. The conversation seemed to assume a tone of almost feverish brilliancy in view of the social atmosphere surrounding these queries. When he was led into the adjoining room to partake of refreshments he ate his lobster-salad with an honest young appetite, much aided by the fact that Mrs. Sylvestre gave him his coffee, and, taking a cup herself, sat down by him on a sofa. As he watched her, Arbuthnot was thinking her manner very soft and pretty, and, inspired by it, his own became all that could be desired in the way of dexterity and tact. As he exercised himself in his entertainment, his first objections to the boy gradually vanished; he plied him with refreshments, and encouraged him to renewed conversational effort, deriving finally some satisfaction from finding himself able to bring to bear upon him with successful results his neatly arranged and classified social gifts. When the young Bartletts — who had been enjoying themselves immensely in the next room — suddenly remembered their charge, and came in search of him, their frank countenances expressed some surprise at the position they found him occupying. He was relating with some spirit the story of a boat-race, and Mrs. Sylvestre, who sat at his side, was listening with the most perfect air of attention and pleasure, while Arbuthnot stood near, apparently bent upon losing nothing of the history. He ended the story with some natural precipitation and rose to go, a trifle of his embarrassment returning as he found himself once more, as it were, exposed to the glare of day. He was not quite sure what conventionality demanded of him in the way of adieus; but when Mrs. Sylvestre relieved him by extending her hand, nature got the better of him, and he seized it with ardor.

"I've had a splendid time," he said, blushing. "This is the nicest reception I've been to yet. The house is so pretty and — and everything. I was thinking I shouldn't go anywhere else; but I believe I shall now."

When he shook hands with Arbuthnot he regarded him with admiration and awe.

"I'm much obliged to you," he said, his vague sense of indebtedness taking form. "If you ever come to Whippleville I'm sure my father would like to — to see you."

And he retired with his young relatives, blushing still, and occasionally treading on their feet, but his modesty, notwithstanding, bearing with him an inoffensive air of self-respect, which would be more than likely to last him through the day, and perhaps a little beyond it.

Mrs. Sylvestre's eyes met Arbuthnot's when he was gone.

"You were *very* kind to him," she said.

"I am obliged to confess," he replied, "that it was nothing but the low promptings of vanity which inspired me. It dawned upon me that he was impressed by my superior ease and elegance, and I seized the opportunity of exhibiting them."

"You knew just what to say to him," she added.

"That," he replied, "was entirely owing to the fact that I was a boy myself in the early part of the last century."

"He was an appreciative boy," she said, "and a grateful one; but I am sure I could not have made him comfortable if you had not been so kind."

And she once again bestowed upon him the subtle flattery of appearing to lose herself an instant in reflection upon him.

There were no more callers after this. Later on an unconventional little dinner was served, during which Mrs. Sylvestre was placed between Arbuthnot and Tredennis, Planefield loomed up massive and florid at Bertha's side, and Richard devoted himself with delightful ardor to discussing French politics with the young woman who fell to his share.

This young woman, whose attire was perfect and whose manner was admirable, and who was furthermore endowed with a piquant, irregular face and a captivating voice, had attracted Tredennis's attention early in the evening. She had been talking to Richard when he had seen her first, and she had been talking to Richard at intervals ever since, and evidently talking very well.

"I don't know your friend," he said to Bertha, after dinner, "and I did not hear her name when I was presented."

"Then you have hitherto lived in vain," said Bertha, glancing at her. "That is what Richard would tell you. Her name is Helen Varien."

"It is a very pretty name," remarked Tredennis.

"Ah!" said Bertha. "You certainly might trust her not to have an ugly one. She has attained that state of finish in the matter of her appendages which insures her being invariably to be relied on. I think she must even have invented her relatives — or have ordered them, giving *carte blanche*."

She watched her a moment with a smile of interest.

"Do you see how her sleeves fit?" she asked. "It was her sleeves which first attracted my attention. I saw them at a luncheon in New York, and they gave me new theories of life. When a woman can accomplish sleeves like those, society need ask nothing further of her."

Tredennis glanced down at her own.

"Have you accomplished"— he suggested.

"In moments of rashness and folly," she answered, "I have occasionally been betrayed into being proud of my sleeves; but now I realize that the feeling was simply impious."

He waited with grim patience until she had finished, and then turned his back upon Miss Varien's sleeves.

"Will you tell me about Janey?" he said.

"When last I saw her, which was this morning," she replied, "she was as well as usual, and so were the others. Now I have no doubt they are all in bed."

"May I come and see them to-morrow, or the day after?"

"Yes," she answered. "And at anytime. I hope you will come often. Mrs. Sylvestre will be with me until her house is ready for her, and, as I said before, I wish you to know her well."

"I shall feel it a great privilege," he responded.

She leaned back a little in her chair, and regarded her with an expression of interest even greater than she had been aroused to by the contemplation of Miss Varien's sleeves.

"Have you found out yet," she inquired, "what her greatest charm is?"

"Is it by any chance a matter of sleeves?" he asked; and he made the suggestion stolidly.

"No," she answered, "it is not sleeves. One's difficulty is to decide what it is. A week ago I thought it was her voice. Yesterday I was sure it was her eyelashes and the soft shadow they make about her eyes. About an hour ago I was convinced it was her smile, and now

I think it must be her power of fixing her attention upon you. See how it matters Mr. Arbuthnot, and how, though he is conscious of his weakness, he succumbs to it. It will be very pleasant occupation during the winter to watch his struggles."

"Will he struggle?" said Tredennis, still immovably. "I don't think I would in his place."

"Oh, no," she answered. "You mustn't struggle."

"I will not," he returned.

She went on with a smile, as if he had spoken in the most responsive manner possible.

"Mr. Arbuthnot's struggles will not be of the usual order," she remarked. "He will not be struggling with his emotions, but with his vanity. He knows that she will not fall in love with him, and he has no intention of falling in love with her. He knows better — and he does not like affairs. But he will find that she is able to do things which will flatter him, and that it will require all his self-control to refrain from displaying his masculine delight in himself and the good-fortune which he has the secret anguish of knowing does not depend upon his merits. And his struggles at a decently composed demeanor, entirely untinged by weak demonstrations of pleasure or consciousness of himself, will be a very edifying spectacle."

She turned her glance from Arbuthnot and Mrs. Sylvestre, whom she had been watching as she spoke, and looked up at Tredennis. She did so because he had made a rather sudden movement, and placed himself immediately before her.

"Bertha," he said, "I am going away."

Her Jacqueminot roses had been lying upon her lap. She picked them up before she answered him.

"You have made too many calls," she said. "You are tired."

"I have not made too many calls," he replied; "but I am tired. I am tired of this."

"I was afraid you were," she said, and kept her eyes fixed upon the roses.

"You were very fair to me," he said, "and you gave I told you I should not profit by it, and I. did not. I don't know what I expected when I came here to-day, but it was not exactly this. You are too agile for me; I cannot keep up with you."

"You are not modern," she said. "You must learn to adjust yourself rapidly to changes of mental attitude."

"No, I am not modern," he returned; "and I am always behindhand. I do not enjoy myself when you tell me it is a fine day, and that it was colder yesterday, and will be warmer to-morrow; and I am at a loss when you analyze Mr. Arbuthnot's struggles with his vanity."

"I am not serious enough," she interrupted. "You would prefer that I should be more serious."

"It would avail me but little to tell you what I should prefer," he said, obstinately. "I will tell you a simple thing before I go, — all this counts for nothing."

She moved slightly.

"All this," she repeated, "counts for nothing."

"For nothing," he repeated. "You cannot change me. I told you that. You may give me some sharp wounds, — I know you won't spare those, — and because I am only a man I shall show that I smart under them; but they will not move me otherwise. Be as frivolous as you like, mock at everything human if you choose; bat don't expect me to believe you."

She put the flowers to her face and held them there a second.

"The one thing I should warn you against," she said, "would be against believing me. I don't make the mistake of believing myself."

She put the flowers down.

"You think I am trying to deceive you," she said. "There would have to be a reason for my doing it. What should you think would be the reason?"

"So help me God!" he answered, "I don't know."

"Neither do I," she said.

Then she glanced about her over the room, — at Planefield, rather restively professing to occupy himself with a pretty girl; at Miss Varien, turned a trifle sidewise in her large chair so that her beautiful sleeve was displayed to the most perfect advantage, and her vivacious face was a little uplifted as she spoke to Richard, who leaned on the high back of her seat; at Arbuthnot, talking to Agnes Sylvestre, and plainly at no loss of words; at the lights and flowers and ornamented tables seen through the *portières*, — and then she spoke again.

"I tell you," she said, "it is *this* that is real — this. The other was only a kind of dream."

She made a sudden movement and sat upright on her chair, as if she meant to shake herself free from something.

"There was no other," she said. "It wasn't even a dream. There never was anything but this."

She left her chair and stood up before him, smiling.

"The sky was not blue," she said, "nor the hills purple; there were no chestnut trees, and no carnations. Let us go and sit with the rest, and listen to Mr. Arbuthnot and admire Miss Varien's sleeves."

But he stood perfectly still.

"I told you I was going away," he said, "and I am going. To-morrow I shall come and see the children — unless you tell me that you do not wish to see me again."

"I shall not tell you that," she returned, "because it would be at once uncivil and untrue."

"Then I shall come," he said.

"That will be kind of you," she responded, and gave him her hand, and after he had made his bow over it, and his adieus to the rest of the company, he left them.

Bertha crossed the room and stood near the fire, putting one foot on the fender, and shivering a little.

"Are you cold?" asked Miss Varien.

"Yes — no," she answered. "If I did not know better, I should think I was."

"Allow me," said Miss Varien, "to make the cheerful suggestion that that sounds quite like malaria."

"Thank you," said Bertha; "that seems plausible, and I don't rebel against it. It has an air of dealing with glittering generalities, and yet it seems to decide matters for one. We will call it malaria."

Chapter 22

The room which Mrs. Sylvestre occupied in her friend's house was a very pretty one. It had been one of Mrs. Amory's caprices at the time she had fitted it up, and she had amused herself with it for two or three months, arranging it at her leisure, reflecting upon it, and making additions to its charms every day as soon as they suggested themselves to her.

"It is to be a purely feminine apartment," she had said to Richard and Arbuthnot. "And I have a sentiment about it. When it is complete you shall go and stand outside the door and look in, but nothing would induce me to allow you to cross the threshold."

When this moment had arrived, and they had been admitted to the private view from the corridor, they had evidently been somewhat impressed.

"It is very pretty," Mr. Arbuthnot had remarked, with amiable tolerance; "but I don't approve of it. Its object is plainly to pamper and foster those tendencies of the feminine temperament which are most prominent and least desirable. Nothing could be more apparent than its intention to pander to a taste for luxury and self-indulgence, combined in the most shameless manner with vanity and lightness of mind. It will be becoming to the frivolous creatures, and will exalt and inflate them to that extent that they will spend the greater portion of their time in it, utterly ignoring the superior opportunities for cultivating and improving their minds they might enjoy downstairs on occasions when Richard remains at home, and my own multifarious duties permit me to drop in. It strikes me as offering a premium to feminine depravity and crime."

"That expresses it exactly," agreed Richard.

Arbuthnot turned him round.

"Will you," he said, "kindly give your attention to the length and position of that mirror, and the peculiar advantages to be derived from the fact that the light falls upon it from that particular point, and that its effects are softened by the lace draperies and suggestions of pink and blue? The pink and blue idea is merely of a piece with all the rest, and is prompted by the artfulness of the serpent. If it had been all pink the blondes would have suffered, and if it had been all blue the brunettes would have felt that they were not at their best; this ineffably wily combination, however, truckles to either, and intimates that each combines the attractions of both. Take me away, Richard; it is not for the ingenuous and serious mind to view such spectacles as these. Take me away, — first, however, making a mental inventory of the entirely debasing sofas and chairs and the flagrant and openly sentimental nature of the pictures, all depicting or insinuating the drivelling imbecility and slavery of man, — 'The Huguenot Lovers,' you observe, 'The Black Brunswicker,' and others of like nature."

Mrs. Sylvestre had thought the room very pretty indeed when she had first taken possession of it, and its prettiness and comfort impressed her anew when, the excitement of the New Year's day at last at an end, she retired to it for the night.

When she found herself within the closed doors she did not go to bed at once. Too many impressions had been crowded into the last ten hours to have left her in an entirely reposeful condition of mind and body, and, though of too calm a temperament for actual excitement, she was still not inclined to sleep.

So, having partly undressed and thrown on a loose wrap, she turned down the light and went to the fire. It was an open wood-fire, and burned cheerily behind a brass fender; a large rug .of white fur was spread upon the hearth before it; a low, broad sofa, luxurious with cushions, was drawn up at one side of it, and upon the rug, at the other, stood a deep easy-chair. It was this chair she took, and, having taken it, she glanced up at an oval mirror which was among the ornaments on the opposite wall. In it she saw reflected that portion of the room which seemed to have arranged itself about her own graceful figure, — the faint pinks and blues, the flowered drapery, the puffed and padded furniture, and the hundred and one entirely feminine devices of ornamentation; and she was faintly aware that an expression less thoughtful than the one she wore would have been more in keeping with her surroundings.

"I look too serious to harmonize," she said. "If Bertha were here she would detect the incongruity and deplore it."

But she was in a thoughtful mood, which was not an uncommon experience with her, and the faint smile the words gave rise to died away as she turned to the fire again. What she thought of as she sat and looked into it, it would have been difficult to tell; but there was evidence that she was mentally well occupied in the fact that she sat entirely still and gazed at its flickering flame for nearly half an hour. She would not have moved then, perhaps, if she had not been roused from her reverie by a sound at the door, — a low knock, and a voice speaking to her.

"Ames!" it said. "Ames!"

She knew it at once as Bertha's, and rose to reply to the summons almost as if she had expected or even waited for it. When she unlocked the door, and opened it, Bertha was standing on the threshold. She had partly undressed, too. She had laid aside the red dress, and put on a long white *negligée*, bordered with white fur; there was no color about her, and it made her look cold. Perhaps she was cold, for Agnes thought she seemed to shiver a little.

"May I come in?" she asked. "I know it is very inconsiderate, but I had a sort of conviction that you would not be asleep."

"I was not thinking of going to sleep yet," said Agnes. "I am glad you have come."

Bertha entered, and, the door being closed, crossed the room to the fire. She did not take a chair, but sat down upon the hearth-rug.

"This is very feminine," she said, "and we ought to be in bed; but the day would not be complete without it."

Then she turned toward Agnes.

"You must have a great deal to think of to-night," she said.

Agnes Sylvestre looked at the fire.

"Yes," she answered, "I have a great deal to think of."

"Are they things you like to think of?"

"Some of them — not all."

"It must be a curious experience," said Bertha, "to find yourself here again after so many years — with all your life changed for you."

Mrs. Sylvestre did not reply.

"You have not been here," Bertha continued, "since you went away on your wedding journey. You were nineteen or twenty then, — only a girl."

"I was young," said Mrs. Sylvestre, "but I was rather mature for my years. I did not feel as if I was exactly a girl."

Then she added, in a lower voice:

"I had experienced something which had ripened me."

"You mean," said Bertha, "that you knew what love was."

She had not intended to say the words, and their abrupt directness grated upon her as she spoke; but she could not have avoided uttering them.

Mrs. Sylvestre paused a moment.

"The experience I passed through," she said, "did not belong to my age. It was not a girl's feelings. I think it came too soon."

"You had two alternatives to choose from," said Bertha, — "that it should come too soon or too late."

Mrs. Sylvestre paused again.

"You do not think," she said, "that it ever comes to any one at the right time?"

Bertha had been sitting with her hands folded about her knee. She unclasped and clasped them with a sharply vehement movement.

"It is a false thing from beginning to end," she said. "I do not believe in it."

"Ah," said Mrs. Sylvestre, softly, "I believe it. I wish I did not."

"What is there to be gained by it?" said Bertha; "a feeling that is not to be reasoned about or controlled; a miserable, feverish emotion you cannot understand, and can only resent and struggle against blindly. When you let it conquer you, how can you respect yourself or the object of it? What do women love men for? Who knows? It is like madness! All you can say is, 'I love him. He is life or death to me.' It is so unreasoning — so unreasoning."

She stopped suddenly, as if all at once she became conscious that her companion was looking at herself instead of at the fire.

"You love a man generally," said Mrs. Sylvestre, in her tenderly modulated voice, — "at least I have thought so, — because he is the one human creature who is capable of causing you the greatest amount of suffering. I don't know of any other reason, and I have thought of it a great deal."

"It is a good reason," said Bertha, — "a good reason."

Then she laughed.

"This is just a little tragic, isn't it?" she said. "What a delightfully emotional condition we must be in to have reached tragedy in less than five minutes, and entirely without intention! I did not come to be tragic; I came to be analytical. I want you to tell me carefully how we strike you."

"We?" said Mrs. Sylvestre.

Bertha touched herself on the breast.

"We," she said, —"I, Richard, Laurence Arbuthnot, Colonel Tredennis, Senator Planefield, the two hundred men callers, — Washington, in short. How does Washington strike you, now that you have come to it again?"

"Won't you give me two weeks to reflect upon it?" said Agnes.

"No. I want impressions, not reflections. Is it all very much changed?"

"I am very much changed," was the reply.

"And we?" said Bertha. "Suppose — suppose you begin with Laurence Arbuthnot."

"I do not think I could. He is not one of the persons I have remembered."

"Agnes," said Bertha, "only wait with patience for one of those occasions when you feel it necessary to efface him, and then tell him that, in exactly that tone of voice, and he will in that instant secretly atone for the crimes of a lifetime. He won't wince, and he will probably reply in the most brilliant and impersonal manner; but, figuratively speaking, you will have reduced him to powder and cast him to the breeze."

"We shall not be sufficiently intimate to render such a thing possible," said Mrs. Sylvestre. "One must be intimate with a man to be angry enough with him to wish to avenge one's self."

Bertha smiled.

"You don't like him," she said. "Poor Larry!"

"On the contrary," was her friend's reply. "But it would not occur to me to ' begin with him,' as you suggested just now."

"With whom, then," said Bertha, "would you begin."

Her guest gave a moment to reflection, during which Bertha regarded her intently.

"If I were going to begin at all," she said, rather slowly, "I think it would be with Colonel Tredennis."

There was a moment of silence, and then Bertha spoke, in a somewhat cold and rigid voice,

"What do you like about him?" she asked.

"I think I like everything."

"If you were any one else," said Bertha, "I should say that you simply like his size. I think that is generally it. Women invariably fall victims to men who are big and a little lumbering. They like to persuade themselves that they are overawed and subjected. I never understood it myself. Big men never pleased me very much — they are so apt to tread on you."

"I like his eyes," said Agnes, apparently reflecting aloud; "they are very kind. And I like his voice"—

"It is rather too deep," remarked Bertha, "and sometimes I am a little afraid it will degenerate into a growl, though I have never heard it do so yet."

Mrs. Sylvestre went on:

"When he bends his head a little and looks down at you as you talk," she said, "he is very nice. He is really thinking of you and regarding you seriously. I do not think he is given to trifling."

"No," returned Bertha; "I do not think he is given to anything special but being massive. That is what you are thinking, — that he is massive."

"There is no denying," said her friend, "that that is one of the things I like."

"Ah!" said Bertha, "you find the rest of us very flippant and trivial. *That* is how we strike you!"

A fatigued little sigh escaped her lips.

"After all," she said, "it is true. And we have obliged ourselves to be trivial for so long that we are incapable of seriousness. Sometimes — generally toward Lent, after I have been out a great deal — I wonder if the other would not be interesting for a change; but, at the same time, I know I could not be serious if I tried."

"Your seriousness will be deeper," said Mrs. Sylvestre, "when you accomplish it without trying."

She was serious herself as she spoke, but her seriousness was extremely gentle. She looked at Bertha even tenderly, and her clear eyes were very expressive.

"We are both changed since we met here last," she said, with simple directness, "and it is only natural that what we have lived through should have affected us differently. We are of very different temperaments. You were always more vivid and intense than I, and suffering — if you had suffered"—

Her soft voice faltered a little, and she paused. Bertha turned and looked her unflinchingly in the face.

"I — have not suffered," she said.

Agnes spoke as simply as before.

"I have," she said.

Bertha turned sharply away.

"I was afraid so," was her response.

"If we are to be as near to each other as I hope," Agnes continued, "it would be useless for me to try to conceal from you the one thing which has made me what I am. The effort to hide it would always stand between us and our confidence in each other. It is much simpler to let you know the truth."

She put her hands up to her face an instant, and Bertha broke the silence with a curiously incisive question.

"Was he very cruel to you?"

Agnes withdrew her hands, and if her shadow of a smile had not been so infinitely sad, it would have been bitter.

"He could not help it," she said; "and when I was calm enough to reason I knew he was not to blame for my imagination. It was all over in a few months, and he would have been quite content to bear what followed philosophically. When the worst came to the worst, he told me that he had known it could not last, because such things never did; but that he had also known that, even after the inevitable termination, I should always please him and display good taste. He had lived through so much, and I had known so little. I only spoke openly to him once, — one awful day, and after that I scarcely know what happened to me for months. I asked him to let me go away alone, and I went to the sea-side. Since then the sound of the sea has been a terror to me, and yet there are times when I long to hear it. I used to tell myself that, on one of those days when I sat on the sand and looked at the sea, I died, and that I have never really lived since. Something happened to me — I don't know what. It was one brilliant morning, when the sun beat on the blue water and the white sand, and everything was a dazzling glare. I sat on the beach for hours without moving, and when I got up and walked away I remember hearing myself saying, 'I have left you behind, — I have left you behind, — I shall never see you again.' I was ill for several days afterward, and when I recovered I seemed to have become a new creature. When my husband came I was able to meet him so calmly that I think it was even a kind of shock to him."

"And that was the end?" said Bertha.

"Yes, that was the end — for me."

"And for him?"

"Once or twice afterward it interested him to try experiments with me, and when they failed he was not pleased."

"Were you never afraid," said Bertha, "that they would not fail?"

"No. There is nothing so final as the ending of such a feeling. There is nothing to come after it, because it has taken everything with it, — passion, bitterness, sorrow, — even regret. I never wished that it might return after the day I spoke of. I have thought if, by stretching forth my hand, I could have brought it all back just as it was at first, I should not have wished to do it. It had been too much."

"It is a false thing," said Bertha, — "a false thing, and there must always be some such end to it."

Agnes Sylvestre was silent again, and because of her silence Bertha repeated her words with feverish eagerness.

"It must always end so," she said.

"*You* know that — you *must* know it."

"I am only one person," was the characteristic answer. "And I do not know. I do not want to know. I only want quiet now. I have learned enough."

"Agnes," said Bertha, "that is very pathetic."

"Yes," Agnes answered. "I know it is pathetic, when I allow myself to think of it." And for the first time her voice broke a little, and was all the sweeter for the break in it. But it was over in a moment, and she spoke as she had spoken before.

"But I did not mean to be pathetic," she said. "I only wanted to tell you the entire truth, so that there should be nothing between us, and nothing to avoid. There can be nothing now. You know of me all that is past, and you can guess what is to come."

"No, I cannot do that," said Bertha.

Agnes smiled.

"It is very easy," she responded. "I shall have a pretty house, and I shall amuse myself by buying new or old things for it, and by moving the furniture. I shall give so much thought to it that after a while it will be quite celebrated, in a small way, and Miss Jessup will refer to it as 'unique.' Mrs. Merriam will be with me, and I shall have my reception day, and perhaps my 'evening,' and I shall see as many of the charming people who come to Washington as is possible. You will be very good to me, and come to see me often, and — so I hope will Mr. Arbuthnot, and Colonel Tredennis"—

"Agnes," interposed Bertha, with an oddly hard manner, "if they do, one or both of them will fall in love with you."

"If it is either," responded Mrs. Sylvestre, serenely, "I hope it will be Mr. Arbuthnot, as he would have less difficulty in recovering."

"You think," said Bertha, "that nothing could ever touch you again, — nothing?"

"Think!" was the response; "my safety lies in the fact that I do not think of it at all. If I were twenty I might do so, and everything would be different. Life is very short. It is not long enough to run risks in. I shall not trifle with what is left to me."

"Oh," cried Bertha, "how calm you are — how calm you are!"

"Yes," she answered, "I am calm now."

But she put her hands up to her face again for an instant, and her eyelashes were wet when she withdrew them.

"It was a horribly dangerous thing," she said, brokenly. "There were so many temptations; the temptation to find excitement in avenging myself on others was strongest of all. I suppose it is the natural savage impulse. There were times when I longed to be cruel. And then I began to think — and there seemed so much suffering in life — and everything seemed so pitiful. And I could not bear the thought of it." And she ended with the sob of a child.

"It is very womanish to cry," she whispered, "and I did not mean to do it, but — you look at me so." And she laid her cheek against the cushioned back of her chair, and, for a little while, was more pathetic in her silence than she could have been in any words she might have uttered. It was true that Bertha had looked at her. There were no tears in her own eyes. Her feeling was one of obstinate resistance to all emotion in herself; but she did not resent her friend's; on the contrary, she felt a strange enjoyment of it.

"Don't stop crying because I am here," she said. "I like to see you do it."

Mrs. Sylvestre recovered herself at once. She sat up, smiling a little. There were no disfiguring traces of her emotion on her fair face.

"Thank you," she answered; "but I do not like it myself so much, and I have not done it before for a long time."

It was, perhaps, because Mr. Arbuthnot presented himself as an entirely safe topic, with no tendency whatever to develop the sensibilities, that she chose him as the subject of her next remarks.

"I do not see much change in your friend," she observed.

"If you mean Laurence," Bertha replied, "I dare say not. He does not allow things to happen to him. He knows better."

"And he has done nothing whatever during the last seven years?"

"He has been to a great many parties," said Bertha, "and he has read a book or so, and sung several songs."

"I hope he has sung them well," was her friend's comment.

"It always depends upon his mood," Bertha returned; "but there have been times when he has sung them very well indeed."

"It can scarcely have been a great tax to have done it occasionally," said Mrs. Sylvestre; "but I should always be rather inclined to think it was the result of chance, and not effort. Still" — with a sudden conscientious scruple brought about by her recollection of the fact that these marks of disapproval had not expressed themselves in her manner earlier in the day —"still he is very agreeable, one cannot deny that."

"It is always safe not to attempt to deny it, even if you feel inclined," was Bertha's comment, "because, if you do, he will inevitably prove to you that you were in the wrong before he has done with you."

"He did one thing I rather liked," her companion proceeded. "He was very nice — in that peculiar, impartial way of his — to a boy"—

"The boy who came with the Bartletts?" Bertha interposed. "I saw him, and was positively unhappy about him, because I could not attend to him. Did he take him in hand?" she asked, brightening visibly. "I knew he would, if he noticed him particularly. It was just like him to do it."

"I saw him first," Mrs. Sylvestre explained; "but I am afraid I should not have been equal to the occasion if Mr. Arbuthnot had not assisted me. It certainly surprised me that he should do it. He knew the Bartletts, and had met the boy's sister, and in the most wonderful, yet the most uneffusive and natural, way he utilized his material until the boy felt himself quite at home, and not out of place at all. One of the nicest things was the way in which he talked about Whippleville, — the boy came from Whippleville. He seemed to give it a kind of interest and importance, and even picturesqueness. He did not pretend to have been there; but he knew something of the country, which is pretty, and he was very clever in saying neither too much nor too little. Of course that was nice."

"Colonel Tredennis could not have done it," said Bertha.

Agnes paused. She felt there was something of truth in the statement, but she was reluctant to admit it.

"Why not?" she inquired.

"By reason of the very thing which is his attraction for you, — because he is too massive to be adroit."

Agnes was silent.

"Was it not Colonel Tredennis who went to Virginia when your little girl was ill?" she asked, in a few moments.

"Yes," was Bertha's response. "He came because Richard was away and papa was ill."

"It was Janey who told me of it," said Agnes, quietly. "And she made a very pretty story of it, in her childish way. She said that he carried her up and down the room when she was tired, and that when her head ached he helped her not to cry. He must be very gentle. I like to think of it. It is very picturesque; the idea of that great soldierly fellow nursing a frail little creature, and making her pain easier to bear. Do you know, I find myself imagining that I know how he looked."

Bertha sat perfectly still. She, too, knew how he had looked. But there was no reason, she told herself, for the sudden horrible revulsion of feeling which rushed upon her with the remembrance. A little while before, when Agnes had told her story, there had been a reason why she should be threatened by her emotions; but now it was different, — now that there was, so to speak, no pathos in the air; now that they were merely talking of commonplace, unemotional things. But she remembered so well; if she could have forced herself to forget for one instant she might have overcome the passion of unreasoning anguish which seized her; but it was no use, and as she made the effort Agnes sat and watched her, a strange questioning dawning slowly in her eyes.

"He looked — very large"—

She stopped short, and her hands clutched each other hard and close. A wild thought of getting up and leaving the room came to her, and then she knew it was too late.

A light nickered up from the wood-fire and fell upon her face as she slowly turned it to Agnes.

For an instant Agnes simply looked at her, then she uttered a terror-stricken exclamation.

"Bertha!" she cried.

"Well," said Bertha; "well!" But at her next breath she began to tremble, and left her place on the hearth and stood up, trembling still. "I am tired out," she said. "I must go away. I ought not to have come here."

But Agnes rose and went to her, laying her hand on her arm. She had grown pale herself, and there was a thrill of almost passionate feeling in her words when she spoke.

"No," she said. "You were right to come. *This* is the place for you."

She drew her down upon the sofa and held both her hands.

"Do you think I would let you go now," she said, "until you had told me everything? Do you think I did not know there was something you were struggling with? When I told you of my own unhappiness, it was because I hoped it would help you to speak. If you had not known that I had suffered you could not have told me. You *must* tell me now. What barrier could there be between us, — two women who have — who have been hurt, and who should know how to be true to each other?"

Bertha slipped from her grasp and fell upon her knees by the sofa, covering her face.

"Agnes," she panted, "I never thought of this — I don't know how it has come about. I never meant to speak. Almost the worst of it all is that my power over myself is gone, and that it has even come to this, — that I am speaking when I meant to be silent. Don't look at me! I don't know what it all means! All my life has been so different — it is so unlike me — that I say to myself it cannot be true. Perhaps it is not. I have never believed in such things. I don't think I believe now; I don't know what it means, I say, or whether it will last, and if it is not only a sort of illness that I shall get better of. I am trying with all my strength to believe that, and to get better; but while it lasts" —

"Go on," said Agnes, in a hushed voice.

Bertha threw out her hands and wrung them, the pretty baubles she had not removed when she undressed jingling on her wrists.

"It is worse for me than for any one else," she cried. "Worse, worse! It is not fair. I was not prepared for it. I was so sure it was not true; I can't understand it. But, whether it is true or not, while it lasts,

237

Agnes, while it lasts"— And she hid her face again and the bangles and serpents of silver and gold jingled more merrily than ever.

"You think," said Agnes, "that you will get over it?"

"Get over it!" she cried. "How often do you suppose I have said to myself that I *must* get over it? How many thousand times? I *must* get over it. Is it a thing to trifle with and be sentimental over? It is a degradation. I don't spare myself. No one could say to me more than I say to myself. I cannot spare it, and I *must* get over it; but I don't — I don't — I don't. And sometimes the horrible thought comes to me that it is a thing you can't get over, and it drives me mad, but — but" —

"But what?" said Agnes.

Her hands dropped away from her face.

"If I tell you this," she said, breathlessly, "you will despise me. I think I am going to tell it to you that you *may* despise me. The torture of it will be a sort of penance. When the thought comes to me that I *may* get over it, that it will go out of my life in time, and be lost forever, then I know that, compared to that, all the rest is nothing — nothing; and that I could bear it for an eternity, the anguish and the shame and the bitterness, if only it might not be taken away."

"Oh!" cried Agnes, "I can believe it! I can believe it!"

"You can believe it?" said Bertha, fiercely. "You? Yes. But I— I cannot!"

For some minutes after this Agnes did not speak. She sat still and looked down at Bertha's cowering figure. There came back to her, with terrible distinctness, times when she herself must have looked so, — only she had always been alone, — and there mingled with the deep feeling of the moment a far-away pity for her own helpless youth and despair.

"Will you tell me," she said, at last, "how it began?"

She was struck, when Bertha lifted her face from its cushions, by the change which had come upon her. All traces of intense and passionate feeling were gone; it was as if her weeping had swept them away, and left only a weariness, which made her look pathetically young and helpless. As she watched her Agnes wondered if she had ever looked up at Tredennis with such eyes.

"I think," she said, "that it was long before I knew. If I had not been so young and so thoughtless I think I should have known that I began to care for him before he went away the first time. But I was very young, and he was so quiet. There was one day, when he brought me some heliotrope, when I wondered why I liked the quiet things he said; and after he went away I used to wonder, in a sort of fitful way, what he was doing. And the first time I found myself face to face with a trouble I thought of him, and wished for him, without knowing why. I even began a letter to him; but I was too timid to send it."

"Oh, if you had sent it!" Agnes exclaimed, involuntarily.

"Yes — if I had sent it! But I did not. Perhaps it would not have made much difference if I had, only when I told him of it"—

"You told him of it?" said Agnes. "Yes — in Virginia. All the wrong I have done, all the indulgence I have allowed myself, is the wrong I did and the indulgence I allowed myself in Virginia. There were days in Virginia when I suppose I was bad enough"—

"Tell me that afterward," said Agnes. "I want to know how you reached it."

"I reached it," answered Bertha, "in this way: the thing that was my first trouble grew until it was too strong for me — or I was too weak for it. It was my own fault. Perhaps I ought to have known, but I did not. I don't think that I have let any one but myself suffer for my mistake. I couldn't do that. When I found out what a mistake it was, I told myself that it was mine, and that I must abide by it. And in time I thought I had grown quite hard, and I amused myself, and said that nothing mattered; and I did not believe in emotion, and thought I enjoyed living on the surface. I disliked to hear stories of any strong feeling. I tried to avoid reading them, and I was always glad when I heard clever worldly speeches made. I liked Laurence first, because he said such clever, cold-blooded things. He was at his worst when I first knew him. He had lost all his money, and some one had been false to him, and he believed nothing."

"I did not know," said Agnes, "that *he* had a story." And then she added, a trifle hurriedly, "But it does not matter."

"It mattered to him," said Bertha. "And we all have a story — even poor Larry — and even I — even I!"

Then she went on again.

"There was one thing," she said, "that I told myself oftener than anything else, and that was that I was not unhappy. I was always saying that and giving myself reasons. When my dresses were becoming, and I went out a great deal, and people seemed to admire me, I used to say, 'How few women are as happy! How many things I have to make me happy!' and when a horrible moment of leisure came, and I could not bear it, I would say, 'How tired I must be to feel as I do; and what nonsense it is!' The one thing Richard has liked most in me has been that I have not given way to my moods, and have always reasoned about them. Ah! Agnes, if I had been happier I might have given way to them just a little sometimes, and have been less tired. If I were to die now I know what they would remember of me: that I laughed a great deal, and made the house gay."

She went on without tears.

"I think," she said, "that I never felt so sure of myself as I did last winter, — so sure that I had lived past things and was quite safe. It was a very gay season, and there were several people here who amused me and made things seem brilliant and enjoyable. When I was not going out the parlors were always crowded with clever men and women; and when I did go out I danced and talked and interested myself more than I had ever seemed to do before. I shall never forget the inauguration ball. Laurence and Richard were both with me, and I danced every dance, and had the most brilliant night. I don't think one expects to be actually brilliant at an inauguration ball, but that night I think we were, and when we were going away we turned to look back, and Laurence said, 'What a night it has been! We couldn't possibly have had such a night if we had tried. I wonder if we shall ever have such a night again'; and I said, ' Scores of them, I haven't a doubt "but that was the last night of all."

"The last night of all?" repeated Agnes.

"There have been no more nights at all like it, and no more days. The next night but one the Winter Gardners gave a party, and I was there. Laurence brought me some roses and heliotrope, and I carried them; and I remember how the scent of the heliotrope reminded me of the night I sat and talked to Philip Tredennis by the fire. It came back all the more strongly because I had heard from papa of his return. I was not glad that he had come to Washington, and I did not care to see him. He seemed to belong to a time I wanted to forget. I did not know he was to be at the Gardners' until he came in, and I looked up and saw him at the door. You know how he looks when he comes into a room, — so tall, and strong, and different from all the rest. Does he look different from all the rest, Agnes —or is it only that I think so?"

"He is different," said Agnes. "Even I could see that."

"Oh!" said Bertha, despairingly, "I don't know what it is that makes it so; but sometimes I have thought that, perhaps, when first men were on earth they were like that, — strong and earnest, and simple and brave, — never trifling with themselves or others, and always ready to be tender with those who suffer or are weak. If you only knew the stories we have heard of his courage and determination and endurance! I do not think he ever remembers them himself; but how can the rest of us forget!"

"The first thought I had when I saw him was that it was odd that the mere sight of him should startle me so. And then I watched him pass through the crowds, and tried to make a paltry satirical comment to myself upon his size and his grave face. And then, against my will, I began to wonder what he would do when he saw me, and if he would see what had happened to me since he had given me the flowers for my first party; and I wished he had stayed away — and I began to feel tired — and just then he turned and saw me."

She paused and sank into a wearied sitting posture, resting her cheek against the sofa cushion.

"It seems so long ago — so long ago," she said; "and yet it is not one short year since."

She went on almost monotonously.

"He saw the change in me, — I knew that, — though he did not know what it meant. I suppose he thought the bad side of me had developed instead of the good, because the bad had predominated in the first place."

"He never thought that," Agnes interposed. "Never!"

"Don't you think so?" said Bertha. "Well, it was not my fault if he didn't. I don't know whether it was natural or not that I should always make the worst of myself before him; but I always did. I did not want him to come to the house; but Richard brought him again and again, until he had been so often that there must have been some serious reasons if he had stayed away. And then — and then"—

"What then?" said Agnes.

She made a gesture of passionate impatience.

"Oh, I don't know," she said, "I don't know! I began to be restless and unhappy. I did not care for going out, and I dared not stay at home. When I was alone I used to sit and think of that first winter, and compare myself with the Bertha who lived then as if she had been another creature, — some one I had been fond of, and who had died in some sad, unexpected way while she was very young. I used to be angry because I found myself so easily moved, — things touched me which had never touched me before; and one day, as I was singing a little German song of farewell, — that poor little, piteous 'Auf Wiedersehn' we all know, — suddenly my voice broke, and I gave a helpless sob, and the tears streamed down my cheeks. It filled me with terror. I have never been a crying woman, and I have rather disliked people who cried. When I cried I knew that some terrible change had come upon me, and I hated myself for it. I told myself I was ill, and I said I would go away; but Richard wished me to remain. And every day it was worse and worse. And when I was angry with myself I revenged myself on the person I should have spared. When I said things of myself which were false he had a way of looking at me as if he was simply waiting to hear what I would say next, and I never knew whether he believed me or not, and I resented that more than all the rest."

She broke off for an instant, and then began again hurriedly.

"Why should I make such a long story of it?" she said. "I could not tell it all, nor the half of it, if I talked until to-morrow. If I had been given to sentiments and emotions I could not have deceived myself so long as I did, that is all. I have known women who have had experiences and sentiments all their lives, one after another. I used to know girls, when I was a girl, who were always passing through some sentimental adventure; but I was not like that, and I never understood them. But I think it is better to be so than to live unmoved so long that you feel you are quite safe, and then to waken up to face the feeling of a lifetime all at once. It is better to take it by instalments. If I had been more experienced I should have been safer. But I deceived myself, and called what I suffered by every name but the right one. I said it was resentment and wounded vanity and weakness; but it was not — it was not. There was one person who knew it was not, though he let me call it what I pleased" —

"He?" said Agnes.

"It was Laurence Arbuthnot who knew. He had been wretched himself once, and while he laughed at me and talked nonsense, he cared enough for me to watch me and understand."

"It would never have occurred to me," remarked Agnes, "to say he did not care for you. I think he cares for you very much."

"Yes, he cares for me," said Bertha, "and I can see now that he was kinder to me than I knew. He stood between me and many a miserable moment, and warded off things I could not have warded off myself. I think he hoped at first that I would get over it. It was he who helped me to make up my mind to go away. It seemed the best thing, but it would have been better if I had not gone."

"Better?" Agnes repeated.

"There was a Fate in it," she said. "Everything was against me. When I said good-by to — to the person I wished to escape from — though I did not admit to myself then that it was from him I wished to escape — when I said good-by, I thought it was almost the same thing as saying good-by forever. I had always told myself that I was too superficial to be troubled by anything long, and that I could always forget anything I was determined to put behind me. I had done it before, and I fancied I could do it then, and that when I came back in the winter I should have got over my moods, and be stronger physically, and not be emotional any more. I meant to take the children and give them every hour of my days, and live out-of-doors in a simple, natural way, until I was well. I always called it getting well. But when he came to say good-by — it was very hard. It was so hard that I was terrified again. He spent the evening with us, and the hours slipped away — slipped away, and every time the clock struck my heart beat so fast that, at last, instead of beating, it seemed only to tremble and make me weak. And at last he got up to go; and I could not believe that it was true, that he was really going, until he went out of the door. And then so much seemed to go with him, and we had only said a few commonplace words — and it was the last — last time. And it all rushed upon me, and my heart leaped in my side, and — and I went to him. There was no other way. And, O Agnes"—

"I know — I know!" said Agnes, brokenly. "But — try not to do that! It is the worst thing you can do — to cry so."

"He did not know why I came," Bertha said. "I don't know what he thought. I don't know what I said. He looked pale and startled at first, and then he took my hand in both his and spoke to me. I have seen him hold Janey's hand so — as if he could not be gentle enough. And he said it was always hard to say good-by, and would I remember — and his voice was quite unsteady — would I remember that if I should ever need any help he was ready to be called. I had treated him badly and coldly that very evening, but it was as if he forgot it. And I forgot, too, and for just one little moment we were near each other, and there was nothing in our hearts but sadness and kindness, as if we had been friends who had the right to be sad at parting. And we said good-by again — and he went away.

"I fought very hard in those next two months, and I was very determined. I never allowed myself time to think in the daytime. I played with the children and read to them and walked with them, and when night came I used to be tired out; but I did not sleep. I laid awake trying to force my thoughts back, and when morning broke it seemed as if all my strength was spent. And I did not get well. And, when it all seemed at the worst, suddenly Janey was taken ill, and I thought she would die, and I was all alone, and I sent for papa"—

She broke off with the ghost of a bitter little laugh.

"I have heard a great deal said about fate," she went on. "Perhaps it was fate; I don't know. I don't care now — it doesn't matter. That very day papa was ill himself, and Philip Tredennis came to me — Philip Tredennis!"

"Oh!" cried Agnes, "it was very cruel!"

"Was it cruel?" said Bertha. "It was something. Perhaps it would do to call it cruel. I had been up with Janey for two or three nights. She had suffered a great deal for a little creature, and I was worn out with seeing her pain and not being able to help it. I was expecting the doctor from Washington, and when she fell asleep at last I went to the window to listen, so that I might go down and keep the dogs quiet if he came. It was one of those still, white moonlight nights — the most beautiful night. After a while I fancied I heard the far-away hoof-beat of a horse on the road, and I ran down. The dogs knew me, and seemed to understand I wished them to be quiet when I spoke to them. As the noise came nearer I went down to the gate. I was trembling with eagerness and anxiety, and I spoke before I reached it. I was sure it was Doctor Malcolm; but it was some one larger and taller, and the figure came out into the moonlight, and I was looking up at Philip Tredennis!"

Agnes laid her hand on her arm.

"Wait a moment before you go on," she said. "Give yourself time."

"No," said Bertha, hurrying, "I will go on to the end. Agnes, I have never lied to myself since that minute — never once. Where would have been the use? I thought he was forty miles away, and there he stood, and the terror, and joy, and anguish of seeing him swept everything else away, and I broke down. I don't know what he felt and thought. There was one strange moment when he stood quite close to me and touched my shoulder with his strong, kind hand. He seemed overwhelmed by what I did, and his voice was only a whisper. There seemed no one in all the world but ourselves, and when I lifted my face from the gate I knew what all I had suffered meant. As he talked to me afterward I was saying over to myself, as if it was a lesson I was learning, 'You are mad with joy just because this man is near you. All your pain has gone away. Everything is as it was before, but you don't care — you don't care.' I said that because I wished to make it sound as wicked as I could. But it was of no use. I have even thought since then that if he had been a bad man, thinking of himself, I might have been saved that night by finding it out. But he was not thinking of himself — only of me. He came, not for his own sake, but for mine and Janey's. He came to help us and stand by us and care for us; to do any common, simple service for us, as well as any great one. We were not to think of him; he was to think of us. And he sent me away upstairs to sleep, and walked outside below the window all night. And I slept like a child. I should not have slept if it had been any one else, but it seemed as if he had brought strength and quietness with him, and I need not stay awake, because everything was so safe. That has been his power over me from the first — that he rested me. Sometimes I have been so tired of the feverish, restless way we have of continually amusing ourselves, as if we dare not stop, and of reasoning and wondering and arguing to no end. We are all introspection and retrospection, and we call it being analytical and clever. If it is being clever, then we are too clever. One gets so tired of it; one wishes one could stop thinking and know less — or more. He was not like that, and he rested me. That was it. He made life seem more simple."

"Well, he rested me then, and, though I made one effort to send him away, I knew he would not go, and I did not try very hard. I did not want him to go. So when he refused to be sent away, an obstinate feeling came over me, and I said to myself that I would not do or say one unkind thing to him while he was there. I would be as gentle and natural with him as if — as if he had been some slight, paltry creature who was nothing, and less than nothing, to me. I should have been amiable enough to such a man if I had been indebted to him for such service."

"Ah!" sighed Agnes, "but it could not end there!"

"End!" said Bertha. "There is no end, there never will be! Do you think I do not see the bitter truth? One may call it what one likes, and make it as pathetic and as tragic and hopeless as words can paint it, but it is only the old, miserable, undignified story of a woman who is married, and who cares for a man who is not her husband. Nothing can be worse than that. It is a curious thing, isn't it, that somehow one always feels as if the woman must be bad?"

Agnes Sylvestre laid a hand on her again without speaking.

"I suppose I was bad in those days," Bertha continued. "I did not feel as if I was — though I dare say that only makes it worse. I deliberately let myself be happy. I let him be kind to me. I tried to amuse and please him. Janey got well, and the days were beautiful. I did all he wished me to do, and he was as good to me as he was to Janey. When you spoke of his being so gentle it brought everything back to me in a rush, — his voice, and his look, and his touch. There are so many people who, when they touch you, seem to take something from you; he always seemed to give you something, — protection, and sympathy, and generous help. He had none of the gallant tricks of other men, and he was often a little shy and restrained, but the night he held my hand in both his, and the moment he touched my shoulder, when I broke down so at the gate, I could not forget if I tried."

"But, perhaps," said Agnes, sadly, "you had better try."

Bertha looked up at her.

"When I have tried for a whole year," she said, "I will tell you what success I have had."

"Oh!" Agnes cried, desperately, "it will take more than a year."

"I have thought it might," said Bertha; "perhaps it may take even two."

The fire gave a fitful leap of flame, and she turned to look at it.

"The fire is going out," she said, "and I have almost finished. Do you care to hear the rest? You have been very patient to listen so long."

"Go on," Agnes said.

"Well, much as I indulged myself then I knew where I must stop, and I never really forgot that I was going to stop at a certain point. I said that I would be happy just so long as he was there, and that when we parted that would be the end of it. I even laid out my plans, and the night before he was to go away — in the evening, after the long, beautiful day was over — I said things to him which I meant should make him distrust me. The shallowest man on earth will hate you if you make him think you are shallow, and capable of trifling as he does himself. The less a man intends to remember you the more he intends you shall remember him. It will be his religious belief that women should be true, — some one should be true, you know, and it is easier to let it be the woman. What I tried to suggest that night was that my treatment of him had only been a caprice, — that what he had seen of me in Washington had been the real side of my life, and that he would see it again and need not be surprised."

"O Bertha!" her friend cried. "O Bertha!"

And she threw both arms about her with an intensely feminine swiftness and expressiveness.

"Yes," said Bertha, "it was not easy. I never tried anything quite so difficult before, and perhaps I did not do it well, for — he would not believe me."

There was quite a long pause, in which she leaned against Agnes, breathing quickly.

"I think that is really the end," she said at last. "It seems rather abrupt, but there is very little more. He is a great deal stronger than I am, and he is too true himself to believe lies at the first telling. One must tell them to him obstinately and often. I shall have to be persistent and consistent too."

"What do you mean?" exclaimed Agnes. "What are you thinking of doing?"

"There will be a great deal to be done," she answered, — "a great deal. There is only one thing which will make him throw me aside"—

"Throw you aside — you?"

"Yes. I have always been very proud, — it was the worst of my faults that I was so deadly proud, — but I want him to throw me aside — me! Surely one could not care for a man when he was tired and did not want one any more. That *must* end it. And there is something else. I don't know — I am not sure — I could not trust myself — but there have been times when I thought that he was beginning to care too — whether he knew it or not. I don't judge him by the other men I have known, but sometimes there was such a look in his eyes that it made me tremble with fear and joy. And he shall not spoil his life for me. It would be a poor thing that he should give all he might give — to Bertha Amory. He bad better give it to — to you, Agnes," she said, with a little tightening grasp.

"I do not want it," said Agnes, calmly. "I have done with such things, and he is not the man to change."

"He must," said Bertha, "in time — if I am very unflinching and clever. They always said I was clever, you know, and that I had wonderful control over myself. But I shall have to be very clever. The only thing which will make him throw me aside is the firm belief that I am worth nothing, — the belief that I am false, and shallow, and selfish, and as wicked as such a slight creature can be. Let me hide the little that is good in me, and show him always, day by day, what is bad. There is enough of that, and in the end he must get tired of me, and show me that he has done with me forever."

"You cannot do it," said Agnes, breathlessly.

"I cannot do it for long, I know that; but I can do it for a while, and then I will make Richard let me go away — to Europe. I have asked him before, but he seemed so anxious to keep me — I cannot tell why — and I have never opposed or disobeyed him. I try to be a good wife in such things as that. I ought to be a good wife in something. Just now he has some reason for wishing me to remain here. He does not always tell me his reasons. But perhaps in the spring he will not object to my going, and one can always spend a year or so abroad; and when he joins us, as he will afterward, he will be sure to be fascinated, and in the end we might stay away for years, and if we ever come back all will be over, and — and I shall be forgotten."

She withdrew herself from her friend's arms, and rose to her feet.

"I shall be forgotten — forgotten!" she said. "Oh! how *can* I be! How can such pain pass away and end in nothing! Just while everything is at the worst, it is not easy to remember that one only counts for one, after all, and that a life is such a little thing. It seems so much to one's self. And yet what does it matter that Bertha Amory's life went all wrong, and was only a bubble that was tossed away and broken? There are such millions and millions of people that it means nothing, only to Bertha Amory, and it cannot mean anything to her very long. Only just while it lasts — and before one gets used to — to the torture of it"—

She turned away and crossed the room to the window, drawing aside the curtain.

"There is a little streak of light in the East," she said. "It is the day, and you have not slept at all."

Agnes went to her, and they stood and looked at it together, — a faint, thin line of gray tinged with palest yellow.

"To-morrow has come," said Bertha. "And we must begin the New Year properly. I must make up my visiting-book and arrange my lists. Don't — don't call any one, Agnes — it is only — faintness." And with the little protesting smile on her lips she sank to the floor.

Agnes knelt down at her side, and began to loosen her wrapper at the throat and chafe her hands.

"Yes, it is only faintness," she said, in a low voice; "but if it were something more you would be saved a great deal."

Chapter 23

"*On dit* that the charming Mrs. Silvestre, so well known and so greatly admired in society circles as Miss Agnes Wentworth, has, after several years of absence, much deplored by her numberless friends, returned to make 'her home in Washington, having taken a house on Lafayette Square. The three years of Mrs. Sylvestre's widowhood have been spent abroad, chiefly in Italy, — the land of love and beauty, — where Tasso sang and Raphael dreamed of the Immortals."

Thus, the society column of a daily paper, and a week later Mrs. Merriam arrived, and the house on Lafayette Square was taken possession of.

It was one of the older houses, — a large and substantial one, whose rather rigorous exterior still held forth promises of possibilities in the way of interior development. Arbuthnot heard Bertha mention one day that one of Mrs. Sylvestre's chief reasons for selecting it was that it "looked quiet," and he reflected upon this afterward as being rather unusual as the reason of a young and beautiful woman.

"Though, after all, she 'looks quiet' herself," was his mental comment. "If I felt called upon to remark upon her at all, I should certainly say that she was a perfectly composed person. Perhaps that is the groove she chooses to live in, or it may be simply her nature. I shouldn't mind knowing which."

He was rather desirous of seeing what she would make of the place inside, but the desire was by no means strong enough to lead him to make his first call upon her an hour earlier than he might have been expected according to the strictest canons of good taste.

On her part Mrs. Sylvestre found great pleasure in the days spent in establishing herself. For years her life had been an unsettled one, and the prospect of arranging a home according to her own tastes — and especially a home in Washington — was very agreeable to her. Her fortune was large, her time was her own, and as in the course of her rambling she had collected innumerable charming and interesting odds and ends, there was no reason why her house should not be a delightful one.

For several days she was quite busy and greatly interested. She found her pictures, plaques, and hangings even more absorbing than she had imagined they would be. She spent her mornings in arranging and rear-ranging cabinets, walls, and mantels, and moved about her rooms wearing a faint smile of pleasure on her lips, and a faint tinge of color on her cheeks.

"Really," she said to Bertha, who dropped in to see her one morning, and found her standing in the middle of the room reflecting upon a pretty old blue cup and saucer, "I am quite happy in a quiet way. I seem to be shut in from the world and life, and all busy things, and to find interest enough in the color of a bit of china, or the folds of a *portière*. It seems almost exciting to put a thing on a shelf, and then take it down and put it somewhere else."

When Arbuthnot passed the house he saw that rich Eastern-looking stuffs curtained the windows, and great Indian jars stood on the steps and balconies, as if ready for plants. In exhausting the resources of the universe Mr. Sylvestre had given some attention to India, and, being a man of caprices, had not returned from his explorings empty-handed. A carriage stood before the house, and the door being open, revealed glimpses of pictures and hangings in the hall, which were pleasantly suggestive.

"She will make it attractive," Arbuthnot said to himself. "That goes without saying. And she will be rather perilously so herself."

His first call upon her was always a very distinct memory to him. It was made on a rather chill and unpleasant evening, and, being admitted by a servant into the hall he had before caught a glimpse of, its picturesque comfort and warmth impressed themselves upon him in the strongest possible contrast to the raw dampness and darkness of the night. Through half-drawn *portières* he had a flitting glance at two or three rooms and a passing impression of some bright or deep point of color on drapery, bric-a-brac, or pictures, and then he was ushered into the room in which Mrs. Sylvestre sat herself. She had been sitting before the fire with a book upon her lap, and she rose to meet him, still holding the volume in her hand. She was dressed in violet and wore a large cluster of violets loosely at her waist. She looked very slender, and tall, and fair, and the rich, darkly glowing colors of the furniture and hangings formed themselves into a background for her, as if the accomplishment of that end had been the sole design of their existence. Arbuthnot even wondered if it was possible that she would ever again look so well as she did just at the instant she rose and moved forward, though he recognized the folly of the thought before ten minutes had passed.

She looked quite as well when she reseated herself, and even better when she became interested in the conversation which followed. It was a conversation which dealt principally with the changes which had taken place in Washington during her absence from it. She found a great many.

"It strikes me as a little singular that you do not resent them more," said Arbuthnot.

"Most of them are changes for the better," she answered.

"Ah!" he returned; "but that would not make any difference to the ordinary mind — unless it awakened additional resentment. There is a sense of personal injury in recognizing that improvements have been made entirely without our assistance."

"I do not feel it," was her reply, "or it is lost in my pleasure in being at home again."

"She has always thought of it as 'home,' then," was Arbuthnot's mental comment. "That is an inadvertent speech which tells a story."

His impressions of the late Mr. Sylvestre were not agreeable ones. He had heard him discussed frequently by men who had known him, and the stories told of him were not pleasant. After fifteen minutes in the crucible of impartial public opinion, his manifold brilliant gifts and undeniable graces and attainments had a habit of disappearing in vapor, and leaving behind them a residuum of cold-blooded selfishness and fine disregard of all human feelings in others, not easily disposed of. Arbuthnot had also noticed that there was but one opinion expressed on the subject of his marriage.

"He married a lovely girl twelve or fifteen years younger than himself," he had heard a man say once. "I should like to see what he has made of her."

"You would!" ejaculated an older man. "I shouldn't! Heaven forbid!"

It added greatly to Arbuthnot's interest in her that she bore no outward signs of any conflict she might have passed through. Whatever it had been, she had borne it with courage, and kept her secret her own. The quiet of her manner was not suggestive either of sadness or self-repression, and she made no apparent effort to evade mention of her married life, though, as she spoke of herself but seldom, it seemed entirely natural that she should refer rarely to the years she had passed away from Washington.

When, a little later, Mrs. Merriam came in, she proved to be as satisfactory as all other appurtenances to the household. She was a picturesque, elderly woman, with a small, elegant figure, an acute little countenance, and large, dark eyes, which sparkled in the most amazing manner at times. She was an old Washingtonian herself, had lived through several administrations, and had made the most of her experience. She seemed to have personally known the notabilities of half a century, and her reminiscences gave Arbuthnot a feeling of being surpassingly youthful and modern. She had been living abroad for the last seven years, and, finding herself at home once more, seemed to settle down with a sense of relief.

"It is a bad habit to get into — this of living abroad," she said. "It is a habit, and it grows on one. I went away intending to remain a year, and I should probably have ended my existence in Europe if Mrs. Sylvestre had not brought me home. I was always a little homesick, too, and continually felt the need of a new administration; but I lacked the resolution it required to leave behind me the things I had become accustomed to."

When he went away Arbuthnot discovered that it was with her he had talked more than with Mrs. Sylvestre, and yet, while he had been in the room, it had not occurred to him that Mrs. Sylvestre was silent. Her silence was not unresponsiveness. When he looked back upon it he found that there was even something delicately inspiring in it. "It is that expression of gentle attentiveness in her eyes," he said. "It makes your most trivial remark of consequence, and convinces you that, if she spoke, she would be sure to say what it would please you most to hear. It is a great charm."

For a few moments before returning to his rooms he dropped in upon the Amory household.

There was no one in the parlor when he entered but Colonel Tredennis, who stood with his back to the fire, apparently plunged deep in thought, his glance fixed upon the rug at his feet. He was in evening dress, and held a pair of white gloves in his hand, but he did not wear a festive countenance. Arbuthnot thought that he looked jaded and worn. Certainly there were deep lines left on his forehead, even when he glanced up and straightened it.

"I am waiting for Mrs. Amory," he said. "Amory is out of town, and, as we were both going to the reception at the Secretary of State's, I am to accompany her. I think she will be down directly. Yes, there she is."

They saw her through the *portières* descending the staircase as he spoke. She was gleaming in creamy satin and lace, and carried a wrap over her arm. She came into the room with a soft rustle of trailing draperies, and Tredennis stirred slightly, and then stood still.

"Did I keep you waiting very long?" she said. "I hope not," and then turned to Arbuthnot, as she buttoned her long glove deliberately.

"Richard has gone to Baltimore with a theatre party," she explained. "Miss Varien went and half-a-dozen others. I did not care to go; and Richard persuaded Colonel Tredennis to assume his responsibilities for the evening and take me to the Secretary of State's. The President is to be there, and as I have not yet told him that I approve of his Cabinet and don't object to his message, I feel I ought not to keep him in suspense any longer."

"Your approval will naturally remove a load of anxiety from his mind," said Arbuthnot. "Can I be of any assistance to you in buttoning that glove?"

She hesitated a second and then extended her wrist. To Arbuthnot, who had occasionally performed the service for her before, there was something novel both in the hesitation and the delicate suggestion of coquettish surrender in her gesture. It had been the chief of her charms for him that her coquetries were of the finer and more reserved sort, and that they had never expended themselves upon him. This was something so new that his momentary bewilderment did not add to his dexterity, and the glove-buttoning was of longer duration than it would otherwise have been.

While it was being accomplished Colonel Tredennis looked on in silence. He had never buttoned a woman's glove in his life. It seemed to him that it was scarcely the thing for a man who was neither husband, brother, nor lover to do. If there was any deep feeling in his heart, how could this careless, conventional fellow stand there and hold her little wrist and meet her lifted eyes without betraying himself? His reasoning was not very logical in its nature: it was the reasoning of pain and hot anger, and other uneasy and masterful emotions, which so got the better of him that he turned suddenly away that he might not see, scarcely knowing what he did. It was an abrupt movement and attracted Arbuthnot's attention, as also did something else, — a movement of Bertha's, — an unsteadiness of the gloved hand which, however, was speedily controlled or ended. He glanced at her, but only to find her smiling, though her breath came a little quickly, and her eyes looked exceedingly bright.

"I am afraid you find it rather troublesome," she said.

"Extremely," he replied; "but I look upon it in the light of moral training, and, sustained by a sense of duty, will endeavor to persevere."

He felt the absurdity and triviality of the words all the more, perhaps, because as he uttered them he caught a glimpse of Tredennis' half-averted face. There was that in its jaded look which formed too sharp a contrast to inconsequent jesting.

"It is not getting easier for him," was his thought. "It won't until it has driven him harder even than it does now."

Perhaps there was something in his own humor which made him a trifle more susceptible to outward influences than usual. As has been already intimated, he had his moods, and he had felt one of them creeping upon him like a shadow during his brief walk through the dark streets.

"I hear the carriage at the door," he said, when he had buttoned the glove. "Don't let me detain you, I am on my way home."

"You have been?" — questioned Bertha, suddenly awakening to a new interest on her own part.

"I called upon Mrs. Sylvestre," he answered.

And then he assisted her to put on her wrap and they all went out to the carriage together. When she was seated and the door closed, Bertha leaned forward and spoke through the open window.

"Don't you think the house very pretty?" she inquired.

"Very," was his brief reply, and though she seemed to expect him to add more, he did not do so, and the carriage drove away and left him standing upon the sidewalk.

"Ah!" said Bertha, leaning back, with a faint smile, "he will go again and again, and yet again."

"Will he?" said the colonel. "Let us hope he will enjoy it." But the truth was that the subject did not awaken in him any absorbing interest.

"Oh! he will enjoy it," she responded.

"And Mrs. Sylvestre?" suggested Tredennis.

"He will never be sure what she thinks of him, or what she wishes him to think of her, though she will have no caprices, and will always treat him beautifully, and the uncertainty will make him enjoy himself more than ever."

"Such a state of bliss," said the colonel, "is indeed greatly to be envied."

He was always conscious of a rather dreary sense of bewilderment when he heard himself giving voice in his deep tones to such small change as the above remark. Under such circumstances there was suggested to him the idea that for the moment he had changed places with some more luckily facile creature and represented him but awkwardly. And yet, of late, he had found himself gradually bereft of all other conversational resource. Since the New Year's day, when Bertha had called his attention to the weather, he had seen in her no vestige of what had so moved him in the brief summer holiday in which she had seemed to forget to arm herself against him.

It appeared that his place was fixed for him, and that nothing remained but to occupy it with as good a grace as possible. But he knew he had not borne it well at the outset. It was but nature that he should have borne it ill, and have made some effort at least to understand the meaning of the change in her.

"All this goes for nothing," he had said to her; but it had not gone for nothing, after all. A man who loves a woman with the whole force of his being, whether it is happily or unhappily, is not a well-regulated creature wholly under his own control. His imagination will play him bitter tricks and taunt him many an hour, both in the bright day and in the dead watches of the night, when he wakens to face his misery alone. He will see things as they are not, and be haunted by phantoms whose vague outlines torture him, while he knows their unreality.

"It is not true," he will say. "It cannot be — and yet if it should be — though it is not."

A word, a smile, the simplest glance or tone, will distort themselves until their very slightness seems the most damning proof. But that he saw his own folly and danger, there were times on those first days when Tredennis might have been betrayed by his fierce sense of injury into mistakes which it would have been impossible for him to retrieve by any after effort. But even in the moments of his greatest weakness he refused to trifle with himself. On the night of the New Year's day when Bertha and Agnes had sat together, he had kept a vigil too. The occupant of the room below his had heard him walking to and fro, and had laid his restlessness to a great number of New Year's calls instead of to a guilty conscience. But the colonel had been less lenient with himself, and had fought a desperate battle in the silent hours.

"What rights have I," he had said, in anguish and humiliation, —"what rights have I at the best? If her heart was as tender toward me as it seems hard, that would be worse than all. It would seem then that I must tear myself from her for her sake as well as for my own. As it is I can at least be near her, and torture myself and let her torture me, and perhaps some day do her some poor kindness of which she knows nothing. Only I must face the truth that I have no claim upon her — none. If she chooses to change her mood, why should I expect or demand an explanation? The wife of one man, the — the beloved of another — O Bertha! Bertha!" And he buried his face in his hands and sat so in the darkness, and in the midst of his misery he seemed to hear again the snatch of song she had sung as she sat on the hillside, with her face half upturned to the blue sky.

The memory of that day, and of some of those which had gone before it, cost him more than all else. It came back to him suddenly when he had reduced himself to a dead level of feeling; once or twice, when he was with Bertha herself, it returned to him with such freshness and vivid truth, that it seemed for a moment that a single word would sweep every barrier away, and they would stand face to face, speaking the simple truth, whatever it might be.

"Why not?" he thought. "Why not, after all, if she is unhappy and needs a friend, why should it not be the man who would bear either death or life for her?" But he said nothing of this when he spoke to her. After their first two or three interviews he said less than ever. Each of those interviews was like the first. She talked to him as she talked to Arbuthnot, to Planefield, to the *attachés* of the legations, to the clever newspaper man from New York or Boston, who was brought in by a friend on one of her evenings, because he wished to see if the paragraphists had overrated her attractions. She paid him graceful conventional attentions; she met him with a smile when he entered; if he was grave, she hoped he was not unwell or out of spirits; she made fine, feathery, jesting little speeches, as if she expected them to amuse him; she gave him his share of her presence, of her conversation, of her laugh, and went her way to some one else to whom she gave the same things.

"And why should I complain?" he said.

But he did complain, or some feverish, bitter ache in his soul complained for him, and wrought him all sorts of evil, and wore him out, and deepened the lines on his face, and made him feel old and hopeless. He was very kind to Janey in those days and spent a great deal of time with her. It was Janey who was his favorite, though he was immensely liberal to Jack, and bestowed upon Meg, who was too young for him, elaborate and expensive toys, which she reduced to fragments and dissected and analyzed with her brother's assistance. He used to go to see Janey in the nursery and take her out to walk and drive, and at such times felt rather glad that she was not like her mother. She bore no likeness to Bertha, and was indeed thought to resemble the professor, who was given to wondering at her as he had long ago wondered at her mother. The colonel fancied that it rested him to ramble about in company with this small creature. They went to the parks, hand in hand, so often that the nurse-maids who took their charges there began to know them quite well, the popular theory among them being that the colonel was an interesting widower, and the little one his motherless child. The winter was a specially mild one, even for Washington, and it was generally pleasant out of doors, and frequently Janey's escort sat on one of the green benches and read his paper while she disported herself on the grass near him, or found entertainment in propelling her family of dolls up and down the walk in their carriage. They had long and interesting conversations together, and once or twice even went to the Capitol itself, and visited the House and the Senate, deriving much pleasure and benefit from looking down upon the rulers of their country "rising to points of order" in their customary awe-inspiring way. On one of these occasions, possibly overpowered by the majesty of the scene, Janey fell asleep, and an hour later, as Bertha stepped from her carriage, with cards and calling-list in hand, she encountered a large, well-known figure, bearing in its arms, with the most astonishing accustomed gentleness and care, a supine little form, whose head confidingly reposed on the broadest of shoulders.

"She went to sleep," said the colonel, with quite a paternal demeanor.

He thought at first that Bertha was going to kiss the child. She made a step forward, an eager tenderness kindling in her eyes, then checked herself and laughed, half shrugging her shoulders.

"May I ask if you carried her the entire length of the avenue in the face of the multitude?" she said. "You were very good, and displayed most delightful moral courage if you did; but it must not occur again. She must not go out without a nurse, if she is so much trouble."

"She is no trouble," he answered, "and it was not necessary to carry her the length of the avenue."

Bertha went into the house before him.

"I will ring for a nurse," she said at the parlor door. "She will be attended to — and you are extremely amiable. I have been calling all the afternoon and have just dropped in for Richard, who is going with me to the Drummonds' *musicale*."

But Tredennis did not wait for the nurse. He knew the way to the nursery well enough, and bore off his little burden to her own domains *sans cérémonie*, while Bertha stood and watched him from below.

If she had been gay the winter before, she was gayer still now. She had her afternoon for reception and her evening at home, and gave, also, a series of more elaborate and formal entertainments. At these festivities the political element was represented quite brilliantly. She professed to have begun at last to regard politics seriously, and, though this statement was not received with the most entire confidence, the most liberal encouragement was bestowed upon her. Richard, especially, seemed to find entertainment in her whim. He even admitted that he himself took an interest in the affairs of the nation this winter. He had been awakened to it by his intimacy with Planefield, which increased as the business connected with the Westoria lands grew upon him. There was a great deal of this business to be transacted, it appeared, though his references to the particular form of his share of it were never very definite, being marked chiefly by a brilliant vagueness which, Bertha was wont to observe, added interest to the subject.

"I should not understand if you explained it, of course," she said. "And, as I don't understand, I can give play to a naturally vivid imagination. All sorts of events may depend upon you. Perhaps it is even necessary of you to 'lobby,' and you are engaged in all sorts of machinations. How do people 'lobby,' Richard, and is there an opening in the profession for a young person of undeniable gifts and charms?"

In these days Planefield presented himself more frequently than ever. People began to expect to see his large, florid figure at the "evenings" and dinner-parties, and gradually he and his friends formed an element in them. It was a new element, and not altogether the most delightful one. Some of the friends were not remarkable for polish of manner and familiarity with the *convenances*, and one or two of them, after they began to feel at ease, talked a good deal in rather pronounced tones, and occasionally enjoyed themselves with a freedom from the shackles of ceremony which seemed rather to belong to some atmosphere other than that of the pretty, bright parlors. But it would not have been easy to determine what Bertha thought of the matter.

She accepted Richard's first rather apologetic mention of it gracefully enough, and, after a few evenings, he no longer apologized.

"They may be a trifle uncouth," he had said; "but some of them are tremendous fellows when you understand them, — shrewd, far-seeing politicians, who may astonish the world any day by some sudden, brilliant move. Such men nearly always work their way from the ranks, and have had no time to study the graces; but they are very interesting, and will appreciate the attention you show them. There is that man Bowman, for instance, — began life as a boy in a blacksmith's shop, and has been in Congress for years. They would send him to the Senate if they could spare him. He is a positive mine of political information, and knows the Westoria business from beginning to end."

"They all seem to know more or less of it," said Bertha. "That is our atmosphere now. I am gradually assimilating information myself."

But Tredennis did not reconcile himself to the invasion. He looked on in restless resentment. What right had such men to be near her, was his bitter thought. Being a man himself, he knew more of some of them than he could remember without anger or distaste. He could not regard them impartially as mere forces, forgetting all else. When he saw Planefield at her side, bold, fulsome, bent on absorbing her attention and frequently succeeding through sheer thick-skinned pertinacity, he was filled with wrathful repulsion. This man at least he knew had no right to claim consideration from her, and yet somehow he seemed to have established himself in an intimacy which appeared gradually to become a part of her everyday life. This evening, on entering the house, he had met him leaving it, and when he went into the parlor he had seen upon Bertha's little work-table the customary sumptuous offering of Jacqueminot roses. She carried the flowers in her hand now — their heavy perfume filled the carriage.

"There is no use in asking why she does it," he was thinking. "I have given up expecting to understand her. I suppose she has a reason. I won't believe it is as poor a one as common vanity or coquetry. Such things are beneath her."

He understood himself as little as he understood her. There were times when he wondered how long his unhappiness would last, and if it would not die a natural death. No man's affection and tenderness could feed upon nothing and survive, he told himself again and again. And what was there to sustain his? This was not the woman he had dreamed of, — from her it should be easy enough for him to shake himself free. What to him were her cleverness, her bright eyes, her power over herself and others, the subtle charms and graces which were shared by all who came near her? They were only the gift of a finer order of coquette, who was a greater success than the rest because nature had been lavish with her. It was not these things which could have changed and colored all life for him. If all his thoughts of her had been mere fancies it would be only natural that he should outlive his experience, and in time look back upon it as simply an episode which might have formed a part of the existence of any man. There had been nights when he had left the house, thinking it would be far better for him never to return if he could remain away without awakening comment; but, once in the quiet of his room, there always came back to him memories and fancies he could not rid himself of, and which made the scenes he had left behind unreal. He used to think it must be this which kept his tenderness from dying a lingering death. When he was alone it seemed as if he found himself face to face again with the old, innocent ideal that followed him with tender, appealing eyes and would not leave him. He began to have an odd fancy about the feeling. It was as if, when he left the silent room, he left in it the truth and reality of his dream and found them there when he returned.

"Why do you look at me so?" Bertha said to him one night, turning suddenly aside from the group she bad been the central figure of. "You look at me as if — as if I were a ghost, and you were ready to see me vanish into thin air."

He made a slight movement as if rousing himself.

"That is it," he answered. "I am waiting to see you vanish."

"But you will not see it," she said. "You will be disappointed. I am real — real! A ghost could not laugh as I do — and enjoy itself. Its laugh would have a hollow sound. I assure you I am very real indeed."

But he did not answer her, and, after looking at him with a faint smile for a second or so, she turned to her group again. To-night, as they drove to their destination, once or twice, in passing a street-lamp, the light, flashing into the carriage, showed him that Bertha leaned back in her corner with closed eyes, her flowers lying untouched on her lap. He thought she seemed languid and pale, though she had not appeared so before they left the house. And this touched him, as such things always did. There was no moment, however deep and fierce his bewildered sense of injury might have been before it, when a shade of pallor on her cheek, or of sadness in her eyes, a look or tone of weariness, would not undo everything, and stir all his great heart with sympathy and the tender longing to be kind to her. The signs of sadness or pain in any human creature would have moved him, but such signs in her overwhelmed him and swept away every other feeling but this yearning desire to shield and care for her. He looked at her now with anxious eyes and bent forward to draw up her Wrap which had slipped from her shoulders.

"Are you warm enough, Bertha?" he said, with awkward gentleness. "It is a raw night. You should have had more — more shawls — or whatever they are."

She opened her eyes with a smile.

"More shawls!" she said. "We don't wear shawls now when we go to receptions. They are not becoming enough, even when they are very grand indeed. This is not a shawl, — it is a sortie du bal, and a very pretty one; but I think I am warm enough, thank you, and it was very good in you to ask." And though he had not known that his own voice was gentle, he recognized that hers was.

"Somebody ought to ask," he answered. And just then they turned the corner into a street already crowded with carriages, and their own drew up before the lighted front of a large house. Tredennis got out and gave Bertha his hand. As she emerged from the shadow of the carriage, the light fell upon her again, and he was impressed even more forcibly than before with her pallor.

"You would have been a great deal better at home," he said, impetuously. "Why did you come here?"

She paused a second, and it seemed to him as if she suddenly gave up some tense hold she had previously kept upon her external self. There was only the pathetic little ghost of a smile in her lifted eyes.

"Yes, I should be better at home," she said, almost in a whisper. "I would rather be asleep with — with the children."

"Then why in Heaven's name do you go?" he protested. "Bertha, let me take you home and leave you to rest. It must be so — I"—

But the conventionalities did not permit that he should give way to the fine masculine impulse which might have prompted him in the heat of his emotions to return her to the carriage by the sheer strength of his unaided arm, and he recognized his own tone of command, and checked himself with a rueful sense of helplessness.

"There is the carriage of the French minister," said Bertha, "and madame wonders who detains her. But — if I were a regiment of soldiers, I am sure I should obey you when you spoke to me in such a tone as that."

And as if by magic she was herself again, and, taking her roses from him, went up the carpeted steps lightly, and with a gay rustle of trailing silk and lace.

The large rooms inside were crowded with a distinguished company, made up of the material which forms the foundation of every select Washingtonian assemblage. There were the politicians, military and naval men, *attachés* of legations, foreign ministers and members of the Cabinet, with their wives and daughters, or other female relatives. A distinguished scientist loomed up in one corner, looking disproportionately modest; a well-known newspaper man chatted in another. The Chinese minister, accompanied by his interpreter, received with a slightly wearied air of quiet patience the conversational attentions proffered him. The wife of the Secretary of State stood near the door with her daughter, receiving her guests as they entered. She was a kindly and graceful woman, whose good breeding and self-poise had tided her safely over the occasionally somewhat ruffled social waters of two administrations. She had received a hundred or so of callers each Wednesday, — the majority of them strangers, and in the moments of her greatest fatigue and lassitude had endeavored to remember that each one of them was a human being, endowed with human vanity and sensitiveness; she had not flinched before the innocent presumption of guileless ignorance; she had done her best by timorousness and simplicity; she had endeavored to remember hundreds of totally uninteresting people, and if she had forgotten one of them who modestly expected a place in her memory had made an effort to repair the injury with aptness and grace. She had given up pleasures she enjoyed and repose she needed, and had managed to glean entertainment and interesting experience by the way, and in course of time, having occupied for years one of the highest social positions in the land, and done some of the most difficult and laborious work, would retire simply and gracefully, more regretted than regretting, and would look back upon her experience more as an episode in her husband's career' than her own.

She was one of the few women who produced in Professor Herrick neither mild perturbation nor mental bewilderment. He had been a friend of her husband's in his youth, and during their residence in Washington it had been his habit to desert his books and entomological specimens once or twice in the season for the purpose of appearing in their parlors. There was a legend that he had once presented himself with a large and valuable beetle pinned to the lapel of his coat, he having absentmindedly placed it in that conspicuous position in mistake for the flower Bertha had suggested he should decorate himself with.

He was among the guests to-night, her hostess told Bertha, as she shook hands with her.

"We were very much pleased to see him, though we do not think he looks very well," she said. "I think you will find him talking to Professor Borrowdale, who has just returned from Central America."

She gave Bertha a kind glance of scrutiny.

"Are *you* looking very well?" she said. "I am afraid you are not. That is not a good way to begin a season."

"I am afraid," said Bertha, laughing, "that I have not chosen my dress well. Colonel Tredennis told me, a few moments ago, that I ought to be at home."

They passed on shortly afterward, and, on the way to the other room, Bertha was unusually silent. Tredennis wondered what she was thinking of, until she suddenly looked up at him and spoke.

"Am I so very haggard?" she said,

"I should not call it haggard," he answered. "You don't look very well."

She gave her cheek a little rub with her gloved hand.

"No; you should not call it haggard," she said, "that is true. It is bad enough not to look well. One should always have a little rouge in one's pocket. But you will see that the excitement will do me good."

"Will it, Bertha?" said the colonel.

But, whether the effect it produced upon her was a good or bad one, it was certainly strong enough. The room was full of people she knew or wished to know. She was stopped at every step by those who spoke to her, exchanging gay speeches with her, paying her compliments, giving her greeting. Dazzling young dandies forgot their indifference to the adulation of the multitude, in their eagerness to make their bows and their *bon mots* before her; their elders and superiors were as little backward as themselves, and in a short time she had gathered quite a little court about her, in which there was laughter and badinage, and an exhilarating exchange of gaycties. The celebrated scientist joined the circle, the newspaper man made his way into it, and a stately, gray-haired member of the Supreme Bench relaxed his grave face in it, and made more clever and gallant speeches than all his younger rivals put together; it was even remarked that the Oriental visage of the Chinese ambassador himself exhibited an expression of more than slight curiosity and interest. He addressed a few words to his interpreter as he passed. But somehow Colonel Tredennis found himself on the outer edge of the enchanted ground. It was his own fault, perhaps. Yes, it was his own fault, without a doubt. Such changes were too rapid for him, as he himself had said before. He did not understand them; they bewildered and wounded him, and gave him a sense of insecurity, seeming to leave him nothing to rely on. Was it possible that sadness or fatigue which could be so soon set aside and lost sight of could be very real? And if these things which had so touched his heart were unreal and caprices of the moment, what was there left which might not be unreal too? Could she look pale, and make her voice and her little hand tremulous at will when she chose to produce an effect, and why should it please her to produce effects upon him? She had never cared for him, or shown kindness or friendly feeling for him, but in those few brief days in Virginia. Was she so flippant, such a coquette and trifler that, when there was no one else to play her pretty tricks upon, she must try them on him and work upon his sympathies in default of being able to teach him the flatteries and follies of men who loved her less? He had heard of women who were so insatiable in their desire for sensation that they would stoop to such things, but he did not believe he had ever met one. Perhaps he had met several, and had been too ingenuous and generous to understand their, wiles and arts. At any rate, they had always been myths to him, and it seemed to him that he himself, as well as all existence, must have changed when he could even wonder if such a thing might be true of Bertha. But nothing could be more certain than that there were no longer any traces of her weariness about her. A brilliant color glowed in her cheeks, her eyes were as bright as diamonds, there was something, — some vividness about her before which every other woman in the room paled a little, though there were two or three great beauties present, and she had never taken the attitude of a beauty at all. The colonel began to see, at last, that there was a shade of something else, too, in her manner, from which it had always before been free. In the midst of all her frivolities she had never been reckless, and there had never been any possibility that the looker-on could bear away with him any memory which had not the charm of fineness about it. But to-night, as one man hung over her chair, and others stood around and about it, one holding her fan, another wearing in his coat a rose which had fallen from her bouquet, all sharing her smiles and vying in their efforts to win them, Tredennis turned away more than once with a heavy heart.

"I would go home if I could leave her," he said. "I don't want to see this. I don't know what it means. This is no place for me."

But he could not leave her, and so lingered about and looked on, and when he was spoken to answered briefly and abstractedly, scarcely knowing what he said. There was no need that he should have felt himself desolate, since there were numbers of pretty and charming women in the rooms who would have been pleased to talk to him, and who, indeed, showed something of this kindly inclination when they found themselves near him; his big, soldierly figure, his fine sun-browned face, his grave manner, and the stories they heard of him, made him an object of deep interest to women, though he had never recognized the fact. They talked of him and wondered about him, and made up suitable little romances which accounted for his silence and rather stern air of sadness. The favorite theory was that he had been badly treated in his early youth by some soulless young person totally unworthy of the feeling he had lavished upon her, and there were two or three young persons — perhaps even a larger number — who, secretly conscious of their own worthiness of any depth of affection, would not have been loath to bind up his wounds and pour oil upon them and frankincense and myrrh, if such applications would have proved effectual. There were among these some very beautiful and attractive young creatures indeed, and as their parents usually shared their interest in the colonel, he was invited to kettledrums and musicales, and theatre parties and dinners, and always welcomed warmly when he was encountered anywhere. But though he received these attentions with the simple courtesy and modest appreciation of all kindness which were second nature with him, and though he paid his party calls with the most unflinching, conventional promptness, and endeavored to return the hospitalities in masculine fashion by impartially sending bouquets to mammas and daughters alike, it frequently happened that various reasons prevented his appearing at the parties; or if he appeared he disappeared quite early; and, indeed, if he had been any other man he would have found it difficult to make his peace with the young lady who discovered that the previous engagement which had kept him away from her kettledrum had been a promise made to little Janey Amory that he would take her to see Tom Thumb.

"It is very kind in you to give us any of your time at all," Bertha had said to him once, "when you are in such demand. Richard tells me your table is strewn with invitations, and there is not a belle of his acquaintance who is so besieged with attentions. Mr. Arbuthnot is filled with envy. He has half-a-dozen new songs which he plays without music, and he has learned all the new dances, and yet is not invited half so much."

"It is my conversational powers they want," was the colonel's sardonic reply.

"That goes without saying," responded Bertha. "And if you would only condescend to waltz, poor Laurence's days of usefulness would be over. Won't you be persuaded to let me give you a lesson?"

And she came toward him with mocking in her eyes and her hands extended.

But the colonel blushed up to the roots of his hair and did not take them.

"I should tread on your slippers, and knock off the buckles, and grind them into powder," he said. "I should tear your gown and lacerate your feelings, and you could not go to the German to-night. I am afraid I am not the size for waltzing."

"You are the size for anything and everything," said Bertha, with an exaggerated little obeisance. "It is we who are so small that we appear insignificant by contrast."

This, indeed, was the general opinion, that his stalwart proportions were greatly to his advantage, and only to be admired. Among those who admired them most were graceful young waltzers, who would have given up that delightful and exhilarating exercise on any occasion, if Colonel Tredennis would have sat out with them in some quiet corner, where the eyes of a censorious world might be escaped. Several such were present to-night, and cast slightly wistful glances at him as they passed to and fro, or deftly managed to arrange little opportunities for conversations which, however, did not nourish and grow strong even when the opportunities were made. It was not entertainment of this sort — innocent and agreeable as it might be — that Colonel Tredennis *wanted*. It would be difficult to say exactly what he wanted, indeed, or what satisfaction he obtained from standing gnawing his great mustache among Mrs. Amory's more versatile and socially gifted adorers.

He did not want to be a witness of her coquetries — they were coquetries, though to the sophisticated they might appear only delightful ones, and a very proper exercise of feminine fascination upon their natural prey; but to this masculine prude, who unhappily loved her and had no honest rights in her, and whose very affection was an emotion against which his honor must struggle, it was a humiliation that others should look on and see that she could so amuse herself.

So he stood on the outer edge of the little circle, and was so standing when he first caught sight of the professor at the opposite end of the room. He left his place then and went over to him. "The sight of the refined, gentle, old face brought to him something bordering on a sense of relief. It removed a little of his totally unreasonable feeling of friendlessness and isolation.

"I have been watching you across the room," the professor said, kindly. "I wondered what you were thinking about? You looked fierce, my boy, and melancholy. I think there were two or three young ladies who thought you very picturesque as you stared at the floor and pulled your mustache, but it seemed to me that your air was hardly gay enough for a brilliant occasion."

"I was thinking I was out of place and wishing I was at home," replied the colonel, with a short laugh, unconsciously pulling his mustache again. "And I dare say I was wishing I had Mrs. Amory's versatility of gifts and humor. I thought she was tired and unwell when I helped her out of the carriage; but it seems that I was mistaken, or that the atmosphere of the great world has a most inspiring effect."

The professor turned his spectacles upon the corner Tredennis had just left.

"Ah!" he remarked quietly; "it is Bertha, is it? I fancied it might be, though it was not easy to see her face, on account of the breadth of Commander Barnacles' back. And it was you who came with her?"

"Yes," said Tredennis.

"I rather expected to see Mr. Arbuthnot," said the professor. "I think Richard gave me the impression that I should."

"We saw Mr. Arbuthnot just before we left the house," returned the colonel. "He had been calling: upon Mrs. Sylvestre."

"Upon Mrs. Sylvestre!" echoed the professor, and then he added, rather softly, "Ah, she is another."

"Another!" Tredennis repeated.

"I only mean," said the professor, "that I am at my old tricks again. I am wondering what will happen now to that beautiful, graceful young woman."

He turned his glance a little suddenly upon Tredennis' face.

"Have you been to see her?" he inquired.

"Not yet."

"Why not yet?"

"Perhaps because she is too beautiful and graceful," Tredennis answered. "I don't know of any other reason. I have not sufficient courage."

"Mr. Arbuthnot has sufficient courage," said the professor. "And some of those gentlemen across the room would not shrink from the ordeal. They will all go to see her, — Commander Barnacles included, — and she will be kind to them every one. She would be kind to me if I went to see her — and some day I think I shall."

He glanced across at Bertha. She was talking to Commander Barnacles, who was exhibiting as much chivalric vivacity as his breadth would allow. The rest of her circle were listening and laughing, people outside it were looking at her with interest and curiosity.

"She is very gay to-night," the professor added. "And I dare say Mrs. Sylvestre could give us a better reason for her gayety than we can see on the surface."

"Is there always a reason?" said the colonel. For the moment he was pleasing himself with the fancy that he was hardening his heart.

But just at this moment a slight stir at one of the entrances attracted universal attention. The President had come in, and was being welcomed by his host and hostess. He presented to the inspection of those to whom he was not already a familiar object, the unimposing figure of a man past middle life, his hair grizzled, his face lined, his expression a somewhat fatigued one.

"Yes, he looks tired," said Bertha to the newspaper man who stood near her, "though it is rather unreasonable in him. He has nothing to do but satisfy the demands of two political parties who hate each other, and to retrieve the blunders made during a few score years by his predecessors, and he has four years to do it in — and every one will give him advice. I wonder how he likes it, and if he realizes what has happened to him. If he were a king and had a crown to look at and try on in his moments of uncertainty, or if he were obliged to attire himself in velvet and ermine occasionally, he might persuade himself that he was real; but how can he do so when he never wears anything but an ordinary coat, and cannot cut people's heads off, or bow-string them, and hasn't a dungeon about him? Perhaps he feels as if he is imposing on us and is secretly a little ashamed of himself. I wonder if he is not haunted by a disagreeable ghost who persists in reminding him of the day when he will only be an abject ex-President and we shall pity where we don't condemn him; and he will be dragged to the Capitol in the triumphal car of the new one and know that he has awakened from his dream; or, perhaps, he will call it a nightmare and be glad it is over."

"That is Planefield who came in with him," said her companion. "He would not object to suffer from a nightmare of the same description."

"Would he be willing to dine off the indigestibles most likely to produce it?" said Bertha. "You have indigestibles on your political *menu*, I suppose. I have heard so, and that they are not always easy to swallow because the cooks at the Capitol differ so about the flavoring."

"Planefield would not differ," was the answer. "And he would dine off them, and breakfast and sup off them, and get up in the night to enjoy them, if he could only bring about the nightmare."

"Is there any possibility that he will accomplish it?" Bertha inquired. "If there is, I must be very kind to him when he comes to speak to me. I feel a sort of eagerness to catch his eye and nod and beck and bestow wreathed smiles upon him already; but don't let my modest thrift waste itself upon a mere phantasy if the prospect is that the indigestibles will simply disagree with him and will *not* produce the nightmare." And the colonel, who was just approaching with the professor, heard her and was not more greatly elated than before.

It was not very long, of course, before there was an addition to the group. Senator Planefield found his way to it, — to the very centre of it, indeed, — and so long as it remained a group formed a permanent feature in its attractions. When he presented himself Bertha gave him her hand with a most bewitching little smile, whose suggestion of archness was somehow made to include the gentleman with whom she had previously been talking. Her manner was so gracious and inspiring that Planefield was intoxicated by it and wondered what it meant. He was obliged to confess to himself that there were many occasions when she was not so gracious, and if he had been easily rebuffed, the wounds his nourishing and robust vanity received might have led him to retire from the field. Frequently, when he was most filled with admiration of her cleverness and spirit, he was conscious of an uneasy sense of distrust, not only of her, but of himself. There was one special, innocent, and direct gaze of which her limpid eyes were capable, which sometimes made him turn hot and cold with uncertainty, and there was also a peculiarly soft and quiet tone in her voice which invariably filled him with perturbation.

"She's such a confounded cool little devil," he had said, gracefully, to a friend on one occasion when he was in a bad humor. "She's afraid of nothing, and she's got such a hold on herself that she can say anything she likes, with a voice as soft as silk, and look you straight in the eyes like a baby while she does so; and when you say the words over to yourself you can't find a thing to complain of, while you know they drove home like knives when she said them herself. She looks like a school-girl half the time; but she's made up of steel and iron, and — the devil knows what."

She did not look like a school-girl this evening, — she was far too brilliant and self-possessed and entertaining; but he had nothing to complain of and plenty to congratulate himself upon. She allowed him to take the chair near her which its occupant reluctantly vacated for him; she placed no obstacles in the way of his conversational desires, and she received all his jokes with the most exhilarating laughter. Perhaps it was because of all this that he thought he had never seen her so pretty, so well dressed, and so inspiring. When he told her so, in a clumsy whisper, a sudden red flushed her cheek, her eyes fell, and she did not reply, as he had feared she would, with a keen little two-edged jest far more discouraging than any displeasure at his boldness would have been. He could scarcely believe the evidence of his senses, and found it necessary to remain silent a few seconds to give himself time to recover his equilibrium. It was he who was with her when Tredennis saw her presentation to the President, who, it was said, had observed her previously and was pleased, after the interview was over, to comment admiringly upon her and ask various questions concerning her. It doubtless befell His Excellency to be called upon to be gracious and ready of speech when confronted with objects less inspiring than this young person, and it might have been something of this sort which caused him to wear a more relaxed countenance and smile more frequently than before when conversing with her, and also to appear to be in no degree eager to allow her to make her bow and withdraw.

It was just after she had been permitted to make this obeisance and retire that Colonel Tredennis, standing near a group of three persons, heard her name mentioned and had his ears quickened by the sound.

The speakers were a man and two women.

"Her name," he heard a feminine voice say, "is Amory. She is a little married woman who flirts."

"Oh!" exclaimed the man, "that is Mrs. Amory, is it — the little Mrs. Amory? And — yes — that is Plancfield with her now. He generally is with her, isn't he?"

"At present," was the answer. "Yes."

The colonel felt his blood warming. He began to think he recognized the voice of the first speaker, and when he turned found he was not mistaken. It belonged to the "great lady" who had figured prominently in the cheery little encounter whose story had been related with such vivacity the first evening he had dined with the Amorys. She had, perhaps, not enjoyed this encounter as impartially as had her opponent, and had probably not forgotten it so soon. She wore the countenance of a woman with an excellent memory, and not totally devoid of feminine prejudice. Perhaps she had been carrying her polished little stone in her pocket, and turning it occasionally ever since the memorable occasion when justice had been meted out to her not so largely tempered with mercy as the faultless in character might have desired.

"The matter gives rise to all the more comment," she remarked, "because it is something no one would have expected. Her family is entirely respectable. She was a Miss Herrick, and though she has always been a gay little person, she has been quite cleverly prudent. Her acquaintances are only just beginning to realize the state of affairs, and there is a great division of opinion, of course. The Westoria lands have dazzled the husband, it is supposed, as he is a person given to projects, and he has dazzled her — and the admirer is to be made use of."

The man — a quiet, elderly man, with an astutely humorous countenance — glanced after Bertha as she disappeared into the supper-room. She held her roses to her face, and her eyes smiled over them as Planefield bent to speak to her.

"It is a tremendous affair, — that Westoria business," he said. "And it is evident she has dazzled the admirers. There is a good deal of life and color, and — audacity about her, isn't there?"

"There is plenty of audacity," responded his companion with calmness. "I think that would be universally admitted, though it is occasionally referred to as wit and self-possession."

"But she has been very much liked," timorously suggested the third member of the group, who was younger and much less imposing. "And — and I feel sure I have heard women admire her as often as men."

"A great deal may be accomplished by cleverness and prudence of that particular kind," was the answer. "And, as I said, she has been both prudent and clever."

"It isn't pleasant to think about," remarked the man. "She will lose her friends and — and all the rest of it, and ma} r gain nothing in the end. But I suppose there is a good deal of that sort of thing going on here. We outsiders hear it said so, and are given to believing the statement."

"It does not usually occur in the class to which this case belongs," was the response. "The female lobbyist is generally not so — not so"—

"Not so picturesque as she is painted," ended her companion with a laugh. "Well, I consider myself all the more fortunate in having seen this one who is picturesque, and has quite a charming natural color of her own."

Chapter 24

They moved away and went to the supper-room themselves, leaving Tredennis to his reflections. What these were he scarcely knew himself for a few seconds. The murmur of voices and passing to and fro confused him. For half an hour of quiet in some friendly corner, where none could see his face, he felt that he would have given a year or so of his life — perhaps a greater number of years than a happier man would have been willing to part with. It was of Bertha these people had been speaking — of Bertha, and it was Bertha he could see through the open doors of the supper-room, eating ices, listening to compliment and laughter and jest! It was Planefield who was holding her flowers, and the man who had just picked up her fan was one of his friends; in two or three others near her, Tredennis recognized his associates: it seemed as if the ground had been ceded to them by those who had at first formed her little court.

Tredennis was seized with a wild desire to make his way into their midst, take her hand in his arm, and compel her to come away — to leave them all, to let him take her home — to safety and honor and her children. He was so filled with the absurd impulse that he took half a step forward, stopping and smiling bitterly, when he realized what he was prompted to do.

"How she would like it," he thought, "and like me for doing it; and what a paragraph it would make for the society column!"

Incidents which had occurred within the last few weeks came back to him with a significance they had never before borne. Speeches and moods of Richard's, things he had done, occasional unconscious displays of eagerness to please Planefield and cultivate him, his manner toward Bertha, and certain touches of uneasiness when she was not at her best.

From the first the colonel had not felt himself as entirely prepossessed by this amiable and charming young man as he desired to be, and he had been compelled to admit that he was not always pleased by his gay good-humor, evanescent enthusiasms, and by his happy, irresponsible fashion of looking at life. When he had at last made this confession to himself he had not shrunk from giving himself an explanation of the matter, from which a nature more sparing of itself would have flinched. He had said that his prejudice was one to blush at and conquer by persistent effort, and he had done his sternly honest best to subdue it. But he had not succeeded as he had hoped he should. When he fancied he was making progress and learning to be fair, some trifle continually occurred which made itself an obstacle in his path. He saw things he did not wish to see, and heard things he did not wish to hear, — little things which made him doubt and ponder, and which somehow he could not shake off, even when he tried to forget them and persuade himself that, after all, they were of slight significance. And as he had seen more of the gay good-humor and readiness to be moved, his first shadowy feeling had assumed more definite form. He had found himself confronted by a distrust which grew upon him; he had met the young man's smiling eyes with a sense of being repelled by their very candor and brightness; he had learned that they were not so candid as they seemed, and that his boyish frankness was not always to be relied upon. He had discovered that he was ready to make a promise and forget it; that his impressionable mind could shift itself and change its color, and that somehow its quickness of action had a fashion of invariably tending toward the accomplishment of some personal end, — a mere vagary or graceful whim, perhaps, but always a fancy pertaining to the indulgence of self. Tredennis had heard him lie, — not wickedly or awkwardly, so far; but with grace and freedom from embarrassment. It was his accidental detection of one of the most trivial and ready of these falsehoods which had first roused him to distrust. He remembered now, as by a flash, that it had been a lie about Planefield, and that it had been told to Bertha. He had wondered at the time what its object could be; now he thought he saw, and in a measure comprehended the short-sighted folly which had caused the weak, easily swayed nature to drift into such danger.

"He does not realize what he is doing," was his thought. "He would lie to me if I accused him of it."

Of these two things he was convinced: that the first step had been merely one of many whims, whatever the results following might be, and that no statement or promise Amory might make could be relied on. There was no knowing what he had done or what he would do. As he had found entertainment in the contents of the "museum," so it was as probable he had, at the outset, amused himself with his fancies concerning the Westoria lands, which had, at last, so far fascinated and dazed him as to lead him into the committal of follies he had not paused to excuse even to himself. He had not thought it necessary to excuse them. Why should he not take the legal business in hand, and since there was no reason against that, why should he not also interest himself in the investigations and be on intimate terms with the men who were a part of the brilliant project? Why should not his wife entertain them, as she entertained the rest of her friends and acquaintances? Tredennis felt that he had learned enough of the man's mental habits to follow him pretty closely in his reasoning — when he reasoned. While he had looked on silently, the colonel had learned a great deal and grown worldly-wise and quicker of perception than he could have believed possible in times gone by. He was only half conscious that this was because he had now an object in view which he had not had before; that he was alert and watchful because there was some one he wished to shield; that he was no longer indifferent to the world and its ways, — no longer given to underrating its strength and weaknesses, its faults and follies, because he wished to be able to defend himself against them, if such a thing should become necessary. He had gained wisdom enough to appreciate the full significance of the low-voiced, apparently carelessly uttered words he had just heard; and to feel his own almost entire helplessness in the matter. To appeal to Amory would be useless; to go to the professor impossible; how could he carry to him such a story, unless it assumed proportions such as to make the step a last terrible resource? He had been looking older and acknowledging himself frailer during the last year; certainly he was neither mentally nor physically in the condition to meet such a blow, if it was possible to spare it to him.

Tredennis looked across the room at Bertha again. It seemed that there was only one very simple thing he could do now.

"She will probably be angry and think I have come to interfere, if I go to her," he said; "but I will go nevertheless. At least, I am not one of them, — every one knows that, — and perhaps it will occur to her to go home."

There was resolution on his face when he approached her. He wore the look which never failed to move her more strongly than any other thing on earth had ever done before, and whose power over her cost her all the resistance of which she was capable. It had sometimes made her wonder if, after all, it was true that women liked to be subdued — to be ruled a little — if their rulers were gentle as well as strong. She had heard it said so, and had often laughed at the sentiment of the popular fallacy. She used to smile at it when it presented itself to her even in this manner; but there had been occasions — times perhaps when she was very tired — when she had known that she would have been glad to give way before this look, to obey it, to feel the relief of deciding for herself no more.

Such a feeling rose within her now. She looked neither tired nor worn; but a certain deadly sense of fatigue, which was becoming a physical habit with her, had been growing upon her all the evening. The color on her cheeks was feverish, her limbs ached, her eyes were bright with her desperate eagerness to sustain herself. Once or twice, when she had laughed or spoken, she had been conscious of such an unnatural tone in her voice that her heart had trembled with fear lest others should have heard it too. It seemed impossible to her that they should not, and that these men who listened and applauded her should not see that often she scarcely heard them, and that she dare not stop for fear of forgetting them altogether and breaking down in some dreadful way, which would show that all her spirit and gayety was a lie, and only a lie poorly acted, after all.

She thought she knew what Tredennis had come to her for. She had not lost sight of him at any time. She had known where he stood or sat, and whom he spoke to, and had known that he had seen her also. She had met his eyes now and then, and smiled and looked away again, beginning to talk to her admirers with more spirit than ever each time. What else was there to do but go on as she had begun? She knew only too well what reason there was in herself that she should not falter. If it had been strong yesterday, it was ten times stronger to-day, and would be stronger to-morrow and for many a bitter day to come. But when he came to her she only smiled up at him, as she would have smiled at Planefield, or the gallant and spacious Barnacles, or any other of the men she knew.

"I hope you have had a pleasant evening," she said. "You enjoy things of this sort so much, however, that you are always safe. I saw you talking in the most vivacious manner to that pretty Miss Stapleton, — the one with the eyelashes, — or rather you were listening vivaciously. You are such a good listener."

"That's an accomplishment, isn't it?" said Planefield, with his easy air.

"It is a gift of the gods," she answered. "And it was bestowed on Colonel Tredennis."

"There *are* talkers, you know," suggested the Senator, "who would make a good listener of a man without the assistance of the gods."

"Do you mean the Miss Stapleton with the eyelashes?" inquired Bertha, blandly.

"Oh, come now," was the response. "I think you know I don't mean the Miss Stapleton with the eyelashes. If I did, it would be more economical to make the remark to her."

"Ah!" said Bertha, blandly again. "You mean me? I hoped so. Thank you very much. And I am glad you said it before Colonel Tredennis, because it may increase his confidence in me, which is not great. I am always glad when any one pays me a compliment in his presence."

"Does he never pay you compliments himself?" asked Planefield.

Bertha gave Tredennis a bright, full glance.

"Did you ever pay me a compliment?" she said. "Will you ever pay me a compliment — if I should chance to deserve one?"

"Yes," he answered, his face unsmiling, his voice inflexible. "May I begin now? You always deserve them. My only reason for failing to pay them is because I am not equal to inventing such as would be worthy of you. Your eyes are like stars — your dress is the prettiest in the room — every man present is your slave and every woman pales before you — the President is going home now only because you have ceased to smile upon him."

The color on Bertha's cheek faded a little, but her smile did not. She checked him with a gesture.

"Thank you," she said, "that will do! You are even better than Senator Planefield. My eyes are like stars — my dress is perfection! I myself am as brilliant as — as the chandelier! Really, there seems nothing left for me to do but to follow the President, who, as you said, has been good enough to take his leave and give us permission to retire." And she rose from her chair.

She made her adieus to Planefield, who bestowed upon Tredennis a sidelong scowl, thinking that it was he who was taking her away. It consoled him but little that she gave him her hand — in a most gracious farewell. He had been enjoying himself as he did not often enjoy himself, and the sight of the colonel's unresponsive countenance filled him with silent rage. It happened that it was not the first time, or even the second, that this gentleman had presented himself inopportunely.

"The devil take his grim airs!" was his cordial mental exclamation. "What does he mean by them, and what is he always turning up for when no one wants to see him?"

Something of this amiable sentiment was in his expression, but the colonel did not seem to see it; his countenance was as unmoved, as ever when he led his charge away, her little hand resting on his arm. In truth, he was thinking of other things. Suddenly he had made up his mind that there was one effort he could make: that, if he could conquer himself and his own natural feeling of reluctance, he might speak to Bertha herself in such words as she would be willing to listen to and reflect upon. It seemed impossible to tell her all, but surely he might frame such an appeal as would have some small weight with her. It was not an easy thing to do. He must present himself to her in the role of an individual who, having no right to interfere with her actions, still took upon himself to do so; who spoke when it would have seemed better taste to be silent; who delivered homilies with the manner of one who thought himself faultless, and so privileged to preach and advise.

"But what of that?" he said, checking himself impatiently in the midst of these thoughts. "I am always thinking of myself, and of how I shall appear in her eyes! Am I a boy lover trying to please her, or a man who would spare and shield her? Let her think poorly of me if she chooses, if she will only listen and realize her danger when her anger is over."

The standard for his own conduct which he had set up was not low, it will be observed. All that he demanded of himself was utter freedom from all human weakness, and even liability to temptation; an unselfishness without blemish, a self-control without flaw; that he should bear his own generous anguish without the movement of a muscle; that he should wholly ignore the throbbing of his own wounds, remembering only the task he had set himself; that his watchfulness over himself should never falter, and his courage never be shaken. It was, perhaps, indicative of a certain degree of noble simplicity that he demanded this of himself, which he would have asked of no other human creature, and that at no time did the thought cross his mind that the thing he demanded was impossible of attainment. When he failed, as he knew he often did; when he found it difficult to efface himself utterly from his own thoughts and was guilty of the weakness of allowing himself to become a factor in them; when his unhappiness was stronger than himself; when he was stirred to resentment, or conscious of weariness, and the longing to utter some word which would betray him and ask for pity, — he never failed to condemn himself in bitterness of spirit as ignoble and unworthy.

"Let her be angry with me if she chooses," he thought now. "It is for me to say my say, and leave the rest to her — and I will try to say it kindly."

He would set aside the bitter feeling and resentment of her trifling which had beset him more than once during the evening; he would forget them, as it was but right and just that they should be forgotten. When he spoke, as they went up the staircase together, his tone was so kind that Bertha glanced up at him, and saw that his face had changed, and, though still grave, was kind, too. When she joined him after leaving the cloak-room, he spoke to her of her wrap again, and asked her to draw it more closely about her; when he helped her into the carriage, there was that in his light touch which brought back to her with more than its usual strength the familiar sense of quiet protection and support.

"It would be easier," she thought, "if he would be angry. Why is he not angry? He was an hour ago — and surely I have done enough."

But he showed no signs of disapproval, — he was determined that he would not do that, — though their drive was rather a silent one again. And yet, by the time they reached home, Bertha was in some indefinite way prepared for the question he put to her as he assisted her to alight.

"May I come in for a little while?" he asked . "I know it is late, but — there is something I must say to you."

"Something you must say to me?" she repeated. "I am sure it must be something interesting and something I should like to hear. Come in, by all means."

So they entered the house together, and went into the parlor. They found a fire burning there, and Bertha's chair drawn up before it. She loosened her wrap rather deliberately and threw it off, and then sat down as deliberately, arranging her footstool and draperies until she had attained the desired amount of languid comfort in her position. Tredennis did not speak until she was settled. He leaned against the mantel, his eyes bent on the fire.

Being fairly arranged, Bertha held out her hand.

"Will you give me that feather screen, if you please?" she said, — "the one made of peacock feathers. When one attains years of discretion, one has some care for one's complexion. Did it ever occur to you how serious such matters are, and that the difference between being eighteen and eighty is almost wholly a matter of complexion? If one could remain pink and smooth, one might possibly overcome the rest, and there would be no such thing as growing old. It is not a single plank which is between ourselves and eternity, but a — Would the figure of speech appear appropriate if one said ' a single cuticle'? I am afraid not."

He took the screen from its place and regarded it a little absently.

"You had this in your hand the first night I came here," he said, "when you told the story of your great lady."

She took it from him.

"That was a pretty little story," she said. "It was a dear little story. My great lady was present to-night. "We passed and repassed each other, and gazed placidly at each other's eyebrows. We were vaguely haunted by a faint fancy that we might have met before; but the faculties become dimmed with advancing years, and we could not remember where or how it happened. One often feels that one has met people, you know."

She balanced her gleaming screen gracefully, looking at him from under its shadow.

"And it is not only on account of my complexion that I want my peacock feathers," she continued, dropping her great lady by the way as if she had not picked her up in the interim. "I want them to conceal my emotions if your revelations surprise me. Have you never seen me use them when receiving the compliments of Senator Planefield and his friends? A little turn to the right or the left — the least graceful little turn — and I can look as I please, and they will see nothing and only hear my voice, which, I trust, is always sufficiently under control."

She wondered if it was sufficiently under control now. She was not sure, and because she was not sure she made the most reckless speeches she could think of. There was a story she had heard of a diplomatist, who once so entirely bewildered his fellow-diplomats that they found it impossible to cope with him; they were invariably outwitted by him: the greatest subtlety, the most wondrous *coup d'état*, he baffled alike; mystery surrounded him; his every act was enshrouded in it; with such diplomatic methods it was madness to combat. When his brilliant and marvellous career was at an end his secret was discovered; on every occasion he had told the simple, exact truth. As she leaned back in her chair and played with her screen Bertha thought of this story. She had applied it to herself before this. The one thing which would be incredible to him at this moment, the one thing it would appear more than incredible that she should tell him, would be the truth — if he realized what that truth was. Any other story, however wild, might have its air or suggestion of plausibility; but that, being what it was, she should have the nerve, the daring, the iron strength of self-control, which it would require to make a fearless jest of the simple, terrible truth, it would seem to him the folly of a madman to believe, she knew. To look him in the eye with a smile, and tell him that she feared his glance and dreaded his words, would place the statement without the pale of probability. She had told him things as true before, and he had not once thought of believing them. "It is never difficult to persuade him not to believe me," she thought. There was no one of her many moods of which she felt such terror, in her more natural moments, as of the one which held possession of her now; and yet there was none she felt to be so safe, which roused her to such mental exhilaration while its hour lasted, or resulted in such reaction when it had passed. "I am never afraid then," she said to Agnes once. "There is nothing I could not bear. It seems as if I were made of steel, and had never been soft or timid in my life. Everything is gone but my power over myself, and — yes, it intoxicates me. Until it is over I am not really hurt, I think. There was something I read once about a man who was broken on the wheel, and while it was being done he laughed, and shrieked, and sang. I think all women are like that sometimes: while they are being broken they laugh, and shriek, and sing; but afterward — afterward"—

So now she spoke the simple truth.

"I shall have you at a disadvantage, you may observe," she said. "I shall see your face, and you will not see mine — unless I wish you to do so. A little turn of my wrist, and you have only my voice to rely upon. Do you wish to speak to me before Richard comes in? If so, I am afraid you must waste no time, as his train is due at twelve. You were going to say" —

"I am afraid it is something you will not like to hear," he answered, "though I did not contradict you when you suggested that it was."

"You were outside then," she replied, "and I might not have let you come in."

"No," he said, "you might not."

He looked at the feather screen which she had inclined a trifle.

"Your screen reminded me of your great lady, Bertha," he said, "because I saw her to-night, and — and heard her — and she was speaking of you."

"Of me!" she replied. "That was kind indeed."

"No," he returned, "it was not. She was neither generous nor lenient; she did not even speak the truth; and yet, as I heard her, I was obliged to confess that, to those who did not know you and only saw you as you were to-night, what she said might not appear so false."

Bertha turned her screen aside and looked at him composedly.

"She was speaking of Senator Planefield," she remarked, "and Judge Ballard, and Commander Barnacles. She reprehended my frivolity and deplored the tendency of the age."

"She was speaking of Senator Planefield," he answered.

She moved the screen a little.

"Has Senator Planefield been neglecting her?" she said. "I hope not."

"Lay your screen aside, Bertha," he commanded, hotly. "You don't need it. What I have to say will not disturb you, as I feared it would — no, I should say as I hoped it would. It is only this: that these people were speaking lightly of you — that they connected your name with Planefield's as — as no honest man is willing that the name of his wife should be connected with that of another man. That was all; and I, who am always interfering with your pleasures, could not bear it, and so have made the blunder of interfering again."

There were many things she had borne, of which she had said nothing to Agnes Sylvestre in telling her story, — things she had forced herself to ignore or pass by; but just now some sudden, passionate realization of them was too much for her, and she answered him in words she felt it was madness to utter even as they leaped to her lips.

"Richard has not been unwilling," she said. "Richard has not resented it!"

"If he had been in my place," he began, feeling ill at ease —"if he understood"—

She dropped her screen upon her lap and looked at him with steady eyes.

"No," she interposed, "that is a mistake. He would not have looked upon the matter as you do. It is only a trifle, after all. You are overestimating its importance."

"Am I?" he said. "Do you regard it in that light?"

"Yes," she replied, "you are too fastidious. Is the spiteful comment of an ill-natured, unattractive woman, upon a woman who chances to be more fortunate than herself, of such weight that it is likely to influence people greatly? Women are always saying such things of one another when they are angry. I cannot say them of our friend, it is true, because — because she is so fortunate as to be placed by nature beyond reproach. If I had her charms, and her manner, and her years, I should, perhaps, be beyond reproach too."

She wondered if he would deign to answer her at all. It seemed as if the execrable bad taste of her words must overwhelm him. If he had turned his back upon her and left the room, she would have felt no surprise. To have seen him do so would have been almost a relief. But, for him, he merely stood perfectly still and watched her.

"Go on," he said, at length.

She faintly smiled.

"Do you want me to say more?" she asked. "Is not that enough? My great lady was angry, and was stupid enough to proclaim the fact." She made a quick turn toward him. "To whom was she speaking?" she demanded. "To a man or a woman?"

"To a man," he answered.

She sank back into her chair and smiled again.

"Ah," she said, "then it is of less consequence even than I imagined. It is pleasant to reflect that it was a man. One is not afraid of men."

She lifted the screen from her lap, and for a moment he could not see her face.

"Now he will go," she was saying to herself breathlessly behind it. "Now he must go. He will go now — and he will not come back."

But he did not go. It was the irony of fate that he should spare her nothing. In the few moments of silence which followed he had a great struggle with himself. It was such a struggle that, when it was at an end, he was pale and looked subdued. There was a chair near her. He went to it and sat down at her side.

"Bertha," he said, "there has been one thing in the midst of all —

all this, to which you have been true. You have loved your children when it has seemed that nothing else would touch you. I say 'seemed,' because I swear to you I am unmoved in my disbelief in what you persist in holding before me — for what reason you know best. You love your children; you don't lie to me about that — you don't lie to yourself about it. Perhaps it is only nature, as you said once, and not tenderness; I don't know. I don't understand you; but give yourself a few moments to think of them now."

He saw the hand holding the screen tremble; he could not see her face.

"What — must I think of them?"

He looked down at the floor, knitting his brows and dragging at his great mustache.

"I overestimate the importance of things," he said. "I don't seem to know much about the standards society sets up for itself; but it does not seem a trifle to me that their mother should be spoken of lightly. There was a girl I knew once — long ago" — He stopped and looked up at her with sudden, sad candor. "It is you I am thinking of, Bertha," he said; "you, as I remember you first when you came home from school. I was thinking of your mother and your dependence upon her, and the tenderness there was between you."

"And you were thinking," she added, "that Janey's mother would not be so good and worthy of trust. That is true."

"I have no answer to make to that, Bertha," he said. "None."

She laid the screen upon her lap once more.

"But it *is* true," she said; "it is *true*. Why do you refuse to believe it? Are you so good that you cannot? Yes, you are! As for me — what did I tell you? I am neither good nor bad, and I want excitement. Nine people out of ten are so, and I am no worse than the rest of the nine. One must be amused. If I were religious, I should have Dorcas societies and missions.

As I am not, I have" — she paused one second, no more — "I have Senator Planefield."

She could bear the inaction of sitting still no longer. She got up.

"You have an ideal for everything," she said, "for men, women, and children, — especially for women, I think. You are always telling yourself that they are good, and pure, and loving, and faithful; that they adore their children, and are true to their friends. It is very pretty, but it is not always the fact. You try to believe it is true of me; but it is not. I am not your ideal woman. I have told you so. Have you not found out yet that Bertha Amory is not what you were so sure Bertha Herrick would be?"

"Yes," he answered. "You — you have convinced me of that."

"It was inevitable," she continued. "I was very young then. I knew nothing of the world or of its distractions and temptations. A thousand things have happened to change me. And, after all, what right had you to expect so much of me? I was neither one thing nor the other, even then; I was only ignorant. You could not expect me to be ignorant always."

"Bertha," he demanded, "what are you trying to prove to me?"

"Only a little thing," she answered; "that I need my amusements, and cannot live without them."

He rose from his seat also.

"That you cannot live without Senator Planefield?" he said.

"Go and tell him so," was her reply. "It would please him, and perhaps this evening he would be inclined to place some confidence in the statement."

She turned and walked to the end of the room; then she came back and stood quite still before him.

"I am going to tell you something I would rather keep to myself," she said. "It may save us both trouble if I don't spare myself as my vanity prompts me to do. I said I was no worse than the other nine; but I am — a little. I am not very fond of anything or any one. Not so fond even of — Richard and the children, as I seem. I know that, though they do not. If they were not attractive and amiable, or if they interfered with my pleasures, my affection would not stand many shocks. In a certain way I am emotional enough always to appear better than I am. Things touch me for a moment. I was touched a little just now when you spoke of remembering my being a girl. I was moved when Janey was ill and you were so good to me. I almost persuaded myself that I was good too, and faithful and affectionate, and yet at the same time I knew it was only a fancy, and I should get over it. It is easy for me to laugh and cry when I choose. There are tears in my eyes now, but — they don't deceive me."

"They look like real tears, Bertha," he said. "They would have deceived me — if you had not given me warning."

"They always *look* real," she answered. "And is not there a sort of merit in my not allowing you to believe in them? Call it a merit, won't you?"

His face became like a mask. For several seconds he did not speak. The habit he had of taking refuge in utter silence was the strongest weapon he could use against her. He did not know its strength; he only knew that it was the signal of his own desperate helplessness; but it left her without defence or resource.

"Won't you?" she said, feeling that she must say something,

He hesitated before replying.

"No," he answered, stonily, after the pause. "I won't call it a merit. I wish you would leave me — something."

That was very hard.

"It is true," she returned, "that I do not — leave you very much."

The words cost her such an effort that there were breaks between them.

"No," he said, "not much."

There was something almost dogged in his manner. He could not bear a great deal more, and his consciousness of this truth forced him to brace himself to outward hardness.

"I don't ask very much," he said. "I only ask you to spare yourself and your children. I only ask you to keep out of danger. It is yourself I ask you to think of, not me. Treat me as you like, but don't — don't be cruel to yourself. I am afraid it does not do for a woman — even a woman as cool as you are — to trifle with herself and her name. I have heard it said so, and I could not remain silent after hearing what I did tonight."

He turned as if to move away.

"You are going?" she said.

"Yes," he replied. "It is very late, and it would be useless to say any more."

"You have not shaken hands with me," she said when he was half way to the door. The words forced themselves from her. Her power of endurance failed her at the last moment, as it had done before and would do again.

He came back to her.

"You will never hold out your hand to me when I shall not be ready to take it, Bertha," he said. "You know that."

She did not speak.

"You are chilled," he said. "Your hand is quite cold."

"Yes," she replied. "I shall lie down on the sofa by the fire a little while before going upstairs."

Without saying anything he left her, drew the sofa nearer to the hearth and arranged the cushions.

"I would advise you not to fall asleep," he said when this was done.

"I shall not fall asleep," she answered. She went to the sofa and sat down on it.

"Good-night," she said.

And he answered her "Good-night," and went out of the room.

She sat still a few seconds after he was gone, and then lay down. Her eyes wandered over the room. She saw the ornaments, the pictures on the wall, the design of the rug, every minute object, with a clearness which seemed to magnify its importance and significance. There was a little Cloissone jar whose pattern she never seemed to have seen before; she was looking at it when at last she spoke.

"It is very hard to live," she said. "I wish it was not — so hard. I wish there was some way of helping one's self, but there is not. One can only go on — and on — and there is always something worse coming."

She put her hand upon her breast. Something rose beneath it which gave her suffocating pain. She staggered to her feet, pressing one hand on the other to crush this pain down. No woman who has suffered such a moment but has done the same thing, and done it in vain. She fell, half-kneeling, half-sitting, upon the rug, her body against her chair, her arms flung out.

"Why do you struggle with me?" she cried, between her sobs. "Why do you look at me so? You — hurt me! I love you! Oh! let me go — let me go! Don't you know — I can't bear it!"

In the street she heard the carriages rolling homeward from some gay gathering. One of them stopped a few doors away, and the people got out of it laughing and talking.

"Don't laugh!" she said, shuddering. "No one — should laugh! I laugh! O God! O God!"

In half an hour Richard came in. He had taken Miss Varien home, and remained to talk with her a short time. As he entered the house Bertha was going up the staircase, her gleaming dress trailing behind her, her feather-trimmed wrap over her arm. She turned and smiled down at him.

"Your charms will desert you if you keep such hours as these," she said. "How did you enjoy yourself, or, rather, how did you enjoy Miss Varien, and how many dazzling remarks did she make?"

"More than I could count," he said, laughing. "Wait a moment for me — I am coming up." And he ran up the steps lightly and joined her, slipping his arm about her waist.

"You look tired," he said, "but your charms never desert you. Was that the shudder of guilt? Whose peace of mind have you been destroying?"

"Colonel Tredennis'," she answered.

"Then it was not the shudder of guilt," he returned, laughing again. And, as she leaned gently against him, he bent and kissed her.

Chapter 25

It was generally conceded that nothing could be more agreeable than Mrs. Sylvestre's position and surroundings. Those of her acquaintance who had known her before her marriage, seeking her out, pronounced her more full of charm than ever; those who saw her for the first time could scarcely express with too much warmth their pleasure in her grace, gentleness, and beauty. Her house was only less admired than herself, and Mrs. Merriam, promptly gathering a coterie of old friends about her, established herself most enviably at once. It became known to the world, through the medium of the social colums of the dailies, that Mrs. Sylvestre was at home on Tuesday afternoons, and that she also received her friends each Wednesday evening. On these occasions her parlors were always well filled, and with society so agreeable that it was not long before they were counted among the most attractive social features of the week. Professor Herrick himself appeared on several Wednesdays, and it was gradually remarked that Colonel Tredennis presented himself upon the scene more frequently than their own previous knowledge of his habits would have led the observers to expect. On seeing Mrs. Sylvestre in the midst of her guests and admirers, Miss Jessup was reminded of Madame Recamier and the *salons* of Paris, and wrote almost an entire letter on the subject, which was printed by the "Wabash Times," under the heading of "A Recent Recamier," and described Mrs. Sylvestre's violet eyes, soft voice, and willowy figure, with nothing short of enthusiasm.

Under these honors Mrs. Sylvestre bore herself very calmly. If she had a fault, an impetuous acquaintance once remarked, it was that she was too calm. She found her life even more interesting than she had hoped it would be; there was pleasure in the renewal of old friendships and habits and the formation of new ones, and in time it became less difficult to hold regrets and memories in check with a steady hand. She neither gave herself to retrospection nor to feverish gayety; she felt she had outlived her need of the latter and her inclination for the former. Without filling her life with excitement, she enjoyed the recreations of each day as they came, and felt no resulting fatigue. When Professor Herrick came to spend an evening hour with her and sat by the fire gently admiring her as he was led on to talk, and also gently admiring Mrs. Merriam, who was in a bright, shrewd humor, she herself was filled with pleasure in them both. She liked their ripeness of thought and their impartial judgment of the life whose prejudices they had outlived. And as genuinely as she liked this she enjoyed Colonel Tredennis, who now and then came too. In the first place he came because he was asked, but afterwards because, at the end of his first visit, he left the house with a sense of being in some vague way the better for it. Agnes' manner to-ward him bad been very kind. She had shown an interest in himself and his pursuits, which had somehow beguiled him out of his usual reticence and brought the best of his gifts to the surface, though nothing could have been more unstrained and quiet than the tone of their conversation. He was at no disadvantage when they talked together; he could keep pace with her and understand her gentle thoughts; she did not bewilder him or place him on the defensive. Once, as he looked at her sweet, reposeful face, he remembered what Bertha had said of his ideal woman and the thought rose in his mind that this was she — fair, feminine, full of all tender sympathy and kindly thought; not ignorant of the world nor bitter against it, only bearing no stain of it upon her. "All women should be so," he thought, sadly. And Agnes saw the shadow fall upon his face, and wondered what he was thinking of.

She began to speak to him of Bertha soon afterward, and, perhaps, if the whole truth were told, it was while she so spoke that he felt her grace and sweetness most movingly. The figure her words brought before him was the innocent one he loved, the one he only saw in memory and dreams, and whose eyes followed him with an appeal which was sad truth itself. At first Agnes spoke of the time when they had been girls together, making their *entrée* into society, with others as young and untried as themselves — Bertha the happiest and brightest of them all.

"She was always a success," she said. "She had that quality. One don't know how to analyze it. People remembered her and were attracted, and she never made them angry or envious. Men who had been in love with her remained her friends. It was because she was so true to them. She was always a true friend."

She remembered so many incidents of those early days, and in her relation of them Bertha appeared again and again the same graceful, touching young presence, always generous and impetuous, ready of wit, bright of spirit, and tender of heart.

"We all loved her," said Agnes. "She was worth loving; and she is not changed."

"Not changed," said Tredennis, involuntarily.

"Did you think her so?" she asked, gently.

"Sometimes," he answered, looking down. "I am not sure that I know her very well."

But he knew that he took comfort with him when he went away, and that he was full of heartfelt gratitude to the woman who had defended him against himself. When he sat among his books that night his mind was calmer than it had been for many a day, and he felt his loneliness less. What wonder that he went to the house again and again, and oftener to spend a quiet hour than when others were there! When his burdens weighed most heavily upon him, and his skies looked darkest, Agnes Sylvestre rarely failed to give him help. When he noted her thoughtfulness for others, he did not know what method there was in her thoughtfulness for himself, and with what skilful tact and delicate care she chose the words in which she spoke to him of Bertha; he only felt that, after she had talked to him, the shadow which was his companion was less a shadow, and more a fair truth to be believed in and to draw faith and courage from.

The professor, who met him once or twice during his informal calls, spoke of the fact to Arbuthnot with evident pleasure.

"He was at his best," he said, "and I have noticed that it is always so when he is there. The truth is, it would be impossible to resist the influence of that beautiful young woman."

His acquaintance with Mr. Arbuthnot had taken upon itself something of the character of an intimacy. They saw each other almost daily. The professor had indeed made many discoveries concerning the younger man, but none which caused him to like him less. He had got over his first inclination towards surprise at finding they had many things in common, having early composed himself to meet with calmness any source of momentary wonder which might present itself, deciding, at length, that he, himself, was either younger or his new acquaintance older than he had imagined, without making the matter an affair of years. The two fell into a comfortable habit of discussing the problems of the day, and, though their methods were entirely different, and Arbuthnot was, at the outset, much given to a light treatment of argument, they always understood each other in the end, and were drawn a trifle nearer by the debate. It was actually discovered that Laurence had gone so far as to initiate the unwary professor into the evil practice of smoking, having gradually seduced him by the insidious temptings of the most delicate cigars. The discussions, it was observed, were always more enjoyable when, the professor, having his easy-chair placed in exactly the right position with regard to light and fire, found himself, with his cigar in hand, carefully smoking it, and making the most of its aroma. His tranquil enjoyment of and respect for the rite were agreeable things to see.

"It soothes me," he would say to Arbuthnot. "It even inspires and elevates me. I feel as if I had discovered a new sense. I am really quite grateful."

It was Arbuthnot who generally arranged his easy-chair, showing a remarkable instinct in the matter of knowing exactly what was necessary to comfort. Among his discoveries concerning him the professor counted this one, that he had in such things the silent quickness of perception and deft-handedness of a woman, and perhaps it had at first surprised him more than all else.

It may have been for some private reason of his own that the professor occasionally gave to the conversation a lighter tone, even giving a friendly and discursive attention to social topics, and showing an interest in the doings of pleasure-lovers and the butterfly of fashion. At such times Arbuthnot noticed that, beginning with a reception at the British Embassy, they not unfrequently ended with Bertha; or, opening with the last dinner at the White House, closed with Richard and the weekly "evenings" adorned by the presence of Senator Planefield and his colleague. So it was perfectly natural that they should not neglect Mrs. Sylvestre, to whom the professor had taken a great fancy, and whose progress he watched with much interest. He frequently spoke of her to Arbuthnot, dwelling upon the charm which made her what she was, and analyzing it and its influence upon others. It appeared to have specially impressed itself upon him on the occasion of his seeing Tredennis, and having said that it would be impossible to resist this "beautiful young woman,"— as he had fallen into the unconscious habit of calling her, — he went on to discourse further.

"She is too tranquil to make any apparent effort," he said. "And yet the coldest and most reserved person must be warmed and moved by her. You have seen that, though you are neither the most reserved nor the coldest."

Arbuthnot was smoking the most perfectly flavored of cigars, and giving a good deal of delicate attention to it. At this he took it from his mouth, looked at the end, and removed the ash with a touch of his finger, in doing which he naturally kept his eyes upon the cigar, and not upon the professor.

"Yes," he said, "I have recognized it, of course."

"You see her rather often, I think?" said the professor.

"I am happy to be permitted that privilege," was the answer; "though I am aware I am indebted for it far more to Mrs. Amory than to my own fascinations, numberless and powerful though they may be."

"It is a privilege," said the professor; "but it is more of one to Philip than to you — even more of one than he knows. He needs what such a woman might give him."

"Does he?" said Arbuthnot. "Might I ask what that is?"

And he was angry with himself because he did not say it with more ease and less of a sense of unreasonable irritation. The professor seemed to forget his cigar, he held it in the hand which rested on his chair-arm, and neglected it while he gave himself up to thought.

"He has changed very much during the past year," he said. "In the few last months I have noticed it specially. I miss something from his manner, and he looks fagged and worn. It has struck me that he rather needs an interest, and feels his loneliness without being conscious that he does so. After all, it is only natural. A man who leads an isolated life inevitably reaches a period when his isolation wearies him, and he broods over it a little."

"And you think," said Arbuthnot, "that Mrs. Sylvestre might supply the interest?"

"Don't you think so yourself?" suggested the professor, mildly.

"Oh," said Laurence, "*I* think the man would be hard to please who did not find she could supply him with anything and everything."

And he laughed and made a few rings of smoke, watching them float upward toward the ceiling.

"He would have a great deal to bring her," said the professor, speaking for the moment rather as if to himself than to any audience. "And she would have a great deal in return for what she could bestow. He has always been what he is to-day, and only such a man is worthy of her. No man who has trifled with himself and his past could offer what is due to her."

"That is true," said Laurence.

He made more rings of smoke and blew them away.

"As for Tredennis," he said, with a deliberateness he felt necessary to his outward composure, "his advantage is that he does not exactly belong to the nineteenth century. He has no place in parlors; when he enters one, without the least pretension or consciousness of himself, he towers over the rest of us with a gigantic modesty it is useless to endeavor to bear up against. He ought to wear a red cross, and carry a battle-axe, and go on a crusade, or right the wrongs of the weak by unhorsing the oppressor in single combat. He might found a Round Table. His crush hat should be a helmet, and he should appear in armor."

The professor smiled.

"That is a very nice figure," he said, "though you don't treat it respectfully. It pleases my fancy."

Arbuthnot laughed again, not the gayest laugh possible.

"It is he who is a nice figure," he returned. "And, though he little suspects it, he is the one most admired of women. He could win anything he wanted and would deserve all he won. Oh, I'm respectful enough. I'm obliged to be. There's the rub!"

"Is it a rub?" asked the professor, a little disturbed by an illogical fancy which at the moment presented itself without a shadow of warning.

"*You* don't want the kind of thing he might care for." This time Laurence's laugh had recovered its usual delightful tone. He got up and went to the mantel for a match to light a new cigar.

"I!" he said. "I want nothing but the assurance that I shall be permitted to retain my position in the Treasury until I don't need it. It is a modest ambition, isn't it? And yet I am afraid it will be thwarted. And then — in the next administration, perhaps — I shall be seedy and out at elbows, and Mrs. Amory won't like to invite me to her Thursday evenings, because she will know it will make me uncomfortable, and then — then I shall disappear."

"Something has disturbed you," commented the professor, rather seriously. "You are talking nonsense."

And as he said it the thought occurred to him that he had heard more of that kind of nonsense than usual of late, and that the fact was likely to be of some significance. "It is the old story," he thought, "and it is beginning to wear upon him until he does not control himself quite so completely as he did at first. That is natural too. Perhaps Bertha herself has been a little cruel to him, in her woman's way. She has not been bearing it so well either."

"My dear professor," said Laurence, "everything is relative, and what you call nonsense I regard as my most successful conversational efforts. *I* could not wield Excalibur. Don't expect it of me, I beg you."

If he had made an effort to evade any further discussion of Mrs. Sylvestre and the possibilities of her future, he had not failed in it. They talked of her no more; in fact, they talked very little at all. A shade had fallen upon the professor's face and did not pass away. He lighted his cigar again, but scarcely seemed to enjoy finishing it. If Arbuthnot had been in as alert a mental condition as usual, his attention would have been attracted by the anxious thoughtfulness of his old friend's manner; but he himself was preoccupied and rather glad of the opportunity to be silent. When the cigars were finished, and he was on the point of taking his departure, the professor seemed to rouse himself as if from a reverie.

"That modest ambition of yours" — he began slowly.

"Thank you for thinking of it," said Arbuthnot, as he paused.

"It interests me," replied the professor. "You are continually finding something to interest me. There is no reason why it should be thwarted, you know."

"I wish I did," returned Laurence. "But I don't, you see. They are shaky pieces of architecture, those government buildings. The foundation-stones are changed too often to insure a sense of security to the occupants. No; my trouble is that I don't know."

"You have a great many friends," said the professor.

"I have a sufficient number of invitations to make myself generally useful," said Laurence, "and of course they imply an appreciation of my social gifts which gratifies me; but a great deal depends on a man's wardrobe. I might as well be without talents as minus a dress-coat. It interests me sometimes to recognize a brother in the 'song and dance artist' who is open to engagements. I, my dear professor, am the 'song and dance artist.' When I am agile and in good voice I am recalled; but they would not want me if I were hoarse and out of spirits, and had no spangles."

"You might get something better than you have," said the professor, reflectively. "You ought to get something."

"To whom shall I apply?" said Laurence. "Do you think the President would receive me to-morrow?"

Perhaps he has already mentioned his anxiety to see me." Then, his manner changing, he added, with some hurry, "You are very good, but I think it is of no use. The mistake was in letting myself drift as I did. It would not have happened if — if I hadn't been a fool. It was my own fault. Thank you! Don't think of me. It wouldn't pay me to do it myself, and you may be sure it would not pay you."

And he shook the professor's hand and left him.

He was not in the best of humor when he reached the street, and was obliged to acknowledge that of late the experience had not been as rare a one as discretion should have made it. His equable enjoyment of his irresponsible existence had not held its own entirely this winter.

It had been disturbed by irrational moods and touches of irritability. He had broken, in spite of himself, the strict rules he had laid down against introspection and retrospection; he had found himself deviating in the direction of shadowy regrets and discontents; and this in the face of the fact that no previous season had presented to him greater opportunities for enjoyment than this one. Certainly he counted as the most enviable of his privileges those bestowed upon him by the inmates of the new establishment in Lafayette Place. His intimacy with the Amorys had placed him upon a more familiar footing than he could have hoped to attain under ordinary circumstances, and, this much gained, his social gifts and appreciation of the favor showed him did the rest.

"Your Mr. Arbuthnot," remarked Mrs. Merriam, after having conversed with him once or twice, "or, I suppose, I ought rather to say little Mrs. Amory's Mr. Arbuthnot, is a wonderfully suitable person."

"Suitable?" repeated Agues. "For what?"

"For anything — for everything. He would never be out of place, and his civility is absolute genius."

Mrs. Sylvestre's smile was for her relative's originality of statement, and apparently bore not the slightest reference to Mr. Arbuthnot himself.

"People are never entirely impersonal," Mrs. Merriam went on. "But an appearance of being so may be cultivated, as this gentleman has cultivated his, until it is almost perfection. He never projects himself into the future. When he picks up your handkerchief he does not appear to be thinking how you will estimate his civility; he simply restores you an article you would miss. He does nothing with an air, and he never forgets things. Perhaps the best part of his secret is that he never forgets himself."

"I am afraid he must find that rather tiresome," Agnes remarked.

"My dear," said Mrs. Merriam, "no one could forget herself less often than you do. That is the secret of your repose of manner. Privately you are always on guard, and your unconsciousness of the fact arises from the innocence of youth. You are younger than you think."

"Ah!" said Mrs. Sylvestre, rising and crossing the room to move a yellow vase on the top of a cabinet, "don't make me begin life over again."

"You have reached the second stage of existence," said the older woman, her bright eyes sparkling. "There are three: the first, when one believes everything is white; the second, when one is sure everything is black; the third, when one knows that the majority of things are simply gray."

"If I were called upon to find a color for your favorite," said Agnes, bestowing a soft, abstracted smile on the yellow vase, "I think I should choose gray. He is certainly neutral."

"He is a very good color," replied Mrs. Merriam; "the best of colors. He matches everything, — one's tempers, one's moods, one's circumstances. He is a very excellent color indeed."

"Yes," said Agnes, quietly.

And she carried her vase to another part of the room, and set it on a little ebony stand.

It had become an understood thing, indeed, that her relative found Laurence Arbuthnot entertaining, and was disposed to be very gracious toward him. On his part he found her the cleverest and most piquant of elderly personages. When he entered the room where she sat it was her habit to make a place for him at her own side, and to enjoy a little agreeable gossip with him before letting him go. After they had had a few such conversations together Arbuthnot began to discover that his replies to her references to himself and his past had not been so entirely marked by reticence as he had imagined when he had made them. His friend had a talent for putting the most adroit leading questions, which did not betray their significance upon the surface; and once or twice, after answering such a one, he had seen a look in her sparkling old eyes which led him to ponder over his own words as well as hers. Still, she was always astute and vivacious, and endowed him for the time being with a delightful sense of being at his best, for which he was experienced enough to be grateful. He had also sufficient experience to render him alive to the fact that he preferred to be at his best when it was his good fortune to adorn this particular drawing-room with his presence. He knew, before long, that when he had made a speech upon which he privately prided himself, after the manner of weak humanity, he found it agreeable to be flattered by the consciousness that Mrs. Sylvestre's passion-flower-colored eyes were resting upon him with that delicious suggestion of reflection. He was not rendered happier by the knowledge of this susceptibility, but he was obliged to admit its existence in himself. Few men of his years were as little prone to such natural weaknesses, and he had not attained his somewhat abnormal state of composure without paying its price. Perhaps the capital had been too large.

"If one has less, one is apt to be more economical," Bertha had heard him remark, "and, at least, retain a small annuity to exist upon in one's maturer years. I did not retain such an annuity."

Certainly there was one period of his life upon which he never looked back without a shudder; and this being the case, he had taught himself, as time passed, not to look back upon it at all. He had also taught himself not to look forward, finding the one almost as bad as the other. As Bertha had said, he was not fond of affairs, and even his enemies were obliged to admit that he was ordinarily too discreet or too cold to engage in the most trivial of such agreeable entanglements.

"If I pick up a red-hot coal," he said, "I shall burn my fingers, even if I throw it away quickly. Why should a man expose himself to the chance of being obliged to bear a blister about with him for a day or so? If I may be permitted, I prefer to stand before the fire and enjoy an agreeable warmth without personal interference with the blaze."

Nothing could have been farther from his intentions than interference with the blaze, where Mrs. Sylvestre was concerned; though he had congratulated himself upon the glow her grace and beauty diffused, certainly no folly could have been nearer akin to madness than such folly, if he had been sufficiently unsophisticated to indulge in it. And he was not unsophisticated; few were less so. His perfect and just appreciation of his position bounded him on every side, and it would have been impossible for him to lose sight of it. He had never blamed any one but himself for the fact that he had accomplished nothing particular in life, and had no prospect of accomplishing anything. It had been his own fault, he had always said; if he had been a better and stronger fellow he would not have been beaten down by one blow, however sharp and heavy. He had given up because he chose to give up and let himself drift. His life since then had been agreeable enough; he had had his moments of action and reaction; he had laughed one day and felt a little glum the next, and had let one mood pay for the next, and trained himself to expect nothing better. He had not had any inclination for marriage, and had indeed frequently imagined that he had a strong disinclination for it; his position in the Amory household had given him an abiding-place, which was like having a home without bearing the responsibility of such an incumbrance.

"I regard myself," Bertha sometimes said to him, "as having been a positive boon to you. If I had not been so good to you there would have been moments when you would have almost wished you were married; and if you had had such moments the day of your security would have been at an end."

"Perfectly true," he invariably responded, "and I am grateful accordingly."

He began to think of this refuge of his, after he had walked a few minutes. He became conscious that, the longer he was alone with himself, the less agreeable he found the situation. There was a sentence of the professor's which repeated itself again and again, and made him feel restive; somehow he could not rid himself of the memory of it.

"No man who had trifled with himself and his past could offer what is due to her." It was a simple enough truth, and he found nothing in it to complain of; but it was not an exhilarating thing to dwell upon and be haunted by.

He stopped suddenly in the street and threw his cigar away. A half-laugh broke from him.

"I am resenting it," he said. "It is making me as uncomfortable as if I was a human being, instead of a mechanical invention in the employ of the government. My works are getting out of order. I will go and see Mrs. Amory; she will give me something to think of. She always does."

A few minutes later he entered the familiar parlor. The first object which met his eye was the figure of Bertha, and, as he had anticipated would be the case, she gave him something to think of. But it was not exactly the kind of thing he had hoped for, though it was something, it is true, which he had found himself confronted with once or twice before. It was something in herself, which on his first sight of her presented itself to him so forcibly that it gave him something very near a shock.

He had evidently broken in upon some moment of absorbed thought. She was standing near the mantel, her hands clasped behind her head, her eyes seeming fixed on space. The strangeness of her attitude struck him first, and then the unusualness of her dress, whose straight, long lines of unadorned black revealed, as he had never seen it revealed before, the change which had taken place in her.

She dropped her hands when she saw him, but did not move toward him.

"Did you meet Richard?" she said.

"No," he replied. "Did he want to see me?"

"He said something of the kind, though I am not quite sure what it was."

Their eyes rested on each other as he approached her. In the questioning of hers there was a touch of defiance, but he knew its meaning too well to be daunted by it.

"I would not advise you to wear that dress again," he said.

"Why not?" she asked.

"Go to the mirror and look at yourself," he said.

She turned, walked across the room with a slow, careless step, as if the effort was scarcely worth while. There was an antique mirror on the wall, and she stopped before it and looked herself over.

"It isn't wise, is it?" she said. "It makes me look like a ghost. No, it doesn't *make* me look like one; it simply shows me as I am. It couldn't be said of me just now that I am at my best, could it?"

Then she turned around.

"I don't seem to care!" she said. "*Don't* I care? That would be a bad sign in *me*, wouldn't it?"

"I should consider it one," he answered. "It is only in novels that people can afford not to care. You cannot afford it. Don't wear a dress again which calls attention to the fact that you are so ill and worn as to seem only a shadow of yourself. It isn't wise."

"Why should one object to being ill?" she said. "It is not such a bad idea to be something of an invalid, after all; it insures one a great many privileges. It is not demanded of invalids that they shall always be brilliant. They are permitted to be pale, and silent, and heavy-eyed, and lapses are not treasured up against them." She paused an instant. "When one is ill," she said, "nothing one does or leaves undone is of any special significance. It is like having a holiday."

"Do you want to take such a holiday?" he asked. "Do you need it?"

She stood quite still a moment, and he knew she did it because she wished to steady her voice.

"Sometimes," she said at last, "I think I do."

Since he had first known her there had been many times when she had touched him without being in the least conscious that she did so. He had often found her laughter as pathetic as other people's tears, even while he had joined in it himself. Perhaps there was something in his own mood which made her seem in those few words more touching than she had ever been before.

"Suppose you begin to take it now," he said, "while I am with you."

She paused a few seconds again before answering. Then she looked up.

"When people ask you how I am," she said, "you might tell them that I am not very well, that I have not been well for some time, and that I am not getting better."

"Are you getting — worse?" he asked.

Her reply — if reply it was — was a singular one.

She pushed the sleeve of her black dress a little way from her wrist, and stood looking down at it without speaking. There were no bangles on the wrist this morning, and without these adornments its slenderness seemed startling. The small, delicate bones marked themselves, and every blue vein was traceable.

Neither of them spoke, and in a moment she drew the sleeve down again, and went back to her place by the fire. To tell the truth,

Arbuthnot could not have spoken at first. It was she who at length broke the silence, turning to look at him as he sat in the seat he had taken, his head supported by his hand.

"Will you tell me," she said, "what has hurt *you*?"

"Why should you ask that?" he said.

"I should be very blind and careless of you if I had not seen that something had happened to you," she answered. "You are always caring for me, and — understanding me. It is only natural that I should have learned to understand you a little. This has not been a good winter for you. What is it, Larry?"

"I wish it was something interesting," he answered; "but it is not. It is the old story. I am out of humor. I'm dissatisfied. I have been guilty of the folly of not enjoying myself on one or two occasions, and the consciousness of it irritates me."

"It is always indiscreet not to enjoy one's self," she said.

And then there was silence for a moment, while she looked at him again.

Suddenly she broke into a laugh, — a laugh almost hard in its tone. He glanced up to see what it meant.

"Do you want to know what makes me laugh?" she said. "I am thinking how like all this is the old-fashioned tragedy, where all the *dramatis personæ* are disposed of in the last act. We go over one by one, don't we? Soon there will be no one left to tell the tale. Even Colonel Tredennis and Richard show signs of their approaching doom. And you — some one has shown you your dagger, I think, and you know you cannot escape it."

"I am the ghost," he answered; "the ghost who was disposed of before the tragedy began, and whose business it is to haunt the earth, and remind the rest of you that once I had blood in my veins too."

He broke off suddenly and left his seat. The expression of his face had altogether changed.

"We always talk in this strain," he exclaimed. "We are always jeering! Is there anything on earth, any suffering or human feeling, we could treat seriously? If there is, for God's sake let us speak of it just for one hour."

She fixed her eyes on him, and there was a sad little smile in their depths.

"Yes, you have seen your dagger," she said. "You have seen it. Poor Larry! Poor Larry!"

She turned away and sat down, clasping her hands on her knee, and he saw that suddenly her lashes were wet, and thought that it was very like her that, though she had no tears for herself, she had them for him.

"Don't be afraid that I will ask you any questions," she said. "I won't. You never asked me any. Perhaps words would not do you any good."

"Nothing would do me any good just now," he answered. "Let it go at that. It mayn't be as bad as it seems just for the moment — such things seldom are. If it gets really worse, I suppose I shall find myself coming to you some day to make my plaint; but it's very good in you to look at me like that. And I was a fool to fancy I wanted to be serious. I don't, on the whole."

"No, you were not a fool," she said. "There is no reason why *you* should not be what you want. Laurence," with something like sudden determination in her tone, "there is something I want to say to you."

"What is it?" he asked.

"I have got into a bad habit lately," she said, — "a bad habit of thinking. When I lie awake at night" —

"Do you lie awake at night?" he interrupted.

She turned her face a little away, as if she did not wish to meet Ms inquiring gaze.

"Yes," she answered, after a pause. "I suppose it is because of this — habit. I can't help it; but it doesn't matter."

"Oh," he exclaimed, "it does matter! You can't stand it."

"Is there anything people 'cannot stand'?" she said. "If there is, I should like to try it."

"You may well look as you do," he said.

"Yes, I may well," she answered. "And it is the result of the evil practice of thinking. When once you begin, it is not easy to stop. And I think you have begun."

"I shall endeavor to get over it," he replied.

"No," she said, "don't!"

She rose from her seat and stood up before him, trembling, and with two large tears falling upon her cheeks.

"Larry," she said, "that is what I wanted to say — that is what I have been thinking of. I shall not say it well, because we have laughed at each other so long that it is not easy to speak of anything seriously; but I must try. See! I am tired of laughing. I have come to the time when there seems to be nothing left but tears — and there is no help; but you are different, and if you are tired too, and if there is anything you want, even if you could not be sure of having it, it would be better to be trying to earn it, and to be worthy of it."

He rested his forehead on his hands, and kept his eyes fixed on the carpet.

"That is a very exalted way of looking at things," he said, in a low voice. "I am afraid I am not equal to it."

"In the long nights, when I have lain awake and thought so," she went on, "I have seemed to find out that — there were things worth altering all one's life for. I did not want to believe in them at first, but now it is different with me. I could not say so to any one but you — and perhaps not to you to-morrow or the day after — and you will hear me laugh and jeer many a time again. That is my fate; but it need not be yours. Your life is your own. If mine were my own — oh, if mine were my own!" She checked the passionate exclamation with an effort. "When one's life belongs to one's self," she added, '" one can do almost anything with it!"

"I have not found it so," he replied.

"You have never tried it," she said. "One does not think of these things until the day comes when there is a reason — a reason for everything — for pain and gladness, for hope and despair, for the longing to be better and the struggle against being worse. Oh, how can one give up when there is such a reason, and one's life is in one's own hands! I am saying it very badly, Larry, I know that. Agnes Sylvestre could say it better, though she could not mean it more."

"She would not take the trouble to say it at all," he said.

Bertha drew back a pace with an involuntary movement. The repressed ring of bitterness in the words had said a great deal.

"Is it — ?" she exclaimed, involuntarily, as she had moved, and then stopped. "I said I would not ask questions," she added, and clasped her hands behind her back, standing quite still, in an attitude curiously expressive of agitation and suspense.

"What!" he said; "have I told you? I was afraid I should. Yes, it is Mrs. Sylvestre who has disturbed me; it is Mrs. Sylvestre who has stirred the calm of ages."

She was silent a second, and when she spoke her eyes looked very large and bright.

"I suppose," she said, slowly, "that it is very womanish in me, — that I almost wish it had been some one else."

"Why?" he asked.

"You *all* have been moved by Mrs. Sylvestre," she replied, more slowly than before, — "*all* of you."

"How many of us are there?" he inquired.

"Colonel Tredennis has been moved, too," she said. "Not long before you came in he paid me a brief visit. He does not come often now, and his visits are usually for Janey, and not for me. I displeased him the night he went with me to the reception of the Secretary of State, and he has not been able to resign himself to seeing me often; but this evening he came in, and we talked of Mrs. Sylvestre. He had been calling upon her, and her perfections were fresh in his memory. He finds her beautiful and generous and sincere; she is not frivolous or capricious. I think that was what I gathered from the few remarks he made. I asked him questions; you see, I wanted to know. And she has this advantage, — she has all the virtues which the rest of us have not."

"You are very hard on Tredennis sometimes," he said, answering in this vague way the look on her face which he knew needed answer.

"Sometimes," she said; "sometimes he is hard on me."

"He has not been easy on *me* to-day," he returned.

"Poor Larry!" she said again. "Poor Larry!"

He smiled a little.

"You see what chance I should be likely to have against such a rival," he said. "I wonder if it ought to be a consolation to me to reflect that my position is such that it cannot be affected by rivals. If

I had the field to myself I should stand exactly where I do at this moment. It saves me from the risk of suffering, don't you see? I know my place too well to allow myself to reach that point. I am uncomfortable only because circumstances have placed it before me in a strong light, and I don't like to look at it."

"What is your place?" she asked.

"It is in the Treasury," he replied. "The salary is not large. I am slightly in debt — to my tailor and hosier, who are, however, patient, because they think I am to be relied on through this administration."

"I wish I knew what to say to you 1" she exclaimed. "I wish I knew!"

"I wish you did," he answered. "You have said all you could. I wish I believed what you say. It would be more dignified than to be simply out of humor with one's self, and resentful."

"Larry," she said, gently, "I believe you are something more."

"No! no! Nothing more!" he exclaimed. "Nothing more, for Heaven's sake!" And he made a quick gesture, as if he was intolerant of the thought, and would like to move it away. So they said no more on this subject, and began soon after to talk about Richard.

"What did you mean," Arbuthnot asked, "by saying that Richard showed signs of his approaching doom? Isn't he in good spirits?"

"It seems incredible," she answered, "that Richard should not be in good spirits; but it has actually seemed to me lately that he was not. The Westoria lands appear to have worried him."

"The Westoria lands," he repeated, slowly.

"He has interested himself in them too much," she said. "Things don't go as easily as he imagined they would, and it annoys him. To-day" —

"What happened to-day?" Laurence asked, as she stopped.

"It was not very much," she said; "but it was unlike him. He was a little angry."

"With whom?"

"With me, I think. Lately I have thought I would like to go abroad, and I have spoken of it to him once or twice, and he has rather put it off; and to-day I wanted to speak of it again, and it seemed the wrong time, somehow, and he was a trifle irritable about it. He has not always been quite himself this winter, but he has never been irritable with me. That isn't like him, you know."

"No, it isn't like him," was Laurence's comment.

Afterward, when he was going away, he asked her a question:

"Do you wish very much to go abroad?" he said.

"Yes," she answered.

"You think the change would do you good?"

"Change often does one good," she replied. "I should like to try it."

"I should like to try it myself," he said. "Go, if you can, though no one will miss you more than I shall."

And, having said it, he took his departure.

Chapter 26

But Bertha did not go abroad, and the season reached its height and its wane, and, though Miss Jessup began to refer occasionally to the much-to-be- regretted delicacy of the charming Mrs. Amory's health, there seemed but little alteration in her mode of life.

"I will confide to you," she said to Colonel Tredennis, "that I have set up this effective little air of extreme delicacy as I might set up a carriage, — if I needed one. It is one of my luxuries. Do you remember Lord Farintosh's tooth, which always ached when he was invited out to dinner and did not want to go, — the tooth which Ethel Newcome said nothing would induce him to part with? My indisposition is like that. I refuse to become convalescent. Don't prescribe for me, I beg of you."

It was true, as she had said, that the colonel presented himself at the house less often than had been his wont, and that his visits were more frequently for Janey than for herself. "You will never hold out your hand to me when I shall not be ready to take it," he had said; but she did not hold out her hand, and there was nothing that he could do, and if he went to her he must find himself confronted with things he could not bear to see, and so he told himself that, until he was needed, it was best that he should stay away, or go only now and then.

But he always knew what she was doing. The morning papers told him that she was involved in the old, unceasing round of excitement, — announcing that she was among the afternoon callers; that she received at home; that she dined, lunched, danced, appeared at charitable entertainments, and was seen at the theatre. It became his habit to turn unconsciously to the society column before he read anything else, though he certainly found himself none the happier for its perusal.

But, though he saw Bertha less frequently, he did not forget Richard. At this time he managed to see him rather often, and took some pains to renew the bloom of their first acquaintance, which had, perhaps, shown itself a little on the wane, as Richard's friendships usually did in course of time. And, perhaps, this waning having set in, Richard was not at first invariably so enthusiastically glad to see the large military figure present itself in his office. He had reasons of his own for not always feeling entirely at ease before his whilom favorite. As he had remarked to Planefield, Philip Tredennis was not a malleable fellow. He had unflinching habits of truth, and remorseless ideas of what a man's integrity should be, and would not be likely to look with lenient or half-seeing eyes upon any palterings with falsehood and dishonor, however colored or disguised. And he did not always appear at the most convenient moment; there were occasions, indeed, when his unexpected entrance had put an end to business conferences of a very interesting and slightly exciting nature. These conferences had, it is true, some connection with the matter of the Westoria lands, and the colonel had lately developed an interest in the project in question which he had not shown at the outset. He had even begun to ask questions about it, and shown a desire to inform himself as to the methods most likely to be employed in manipulating the great scheme. He amassed, in one way and another, a large capital of information concerning subsidies and land grants, and exhibited remarkable intelligence in his mental investment of it. Indeed, there were times when he awakened in Richard a rather uneasy sense of admiration by the clearness of his insight and the practical readiness of his views.

"He has always been given to digging into things," Amory said to Planefield, after one of their interviews. "That is his habit of mind, and he has a steady business capacity you don't expect to fill."

"What is he dicing into this thing for?" Planefield asked. "He will be digging up something, one of these days, that we are not particularly anxious to have dug up. I am not overfond of the fellow myself. I never was."

Richard laughed a trifle uneasily.

"Oh, he's well enough," he said; "though I'll admit he has been a little in the way once or twice."

It is quite possible that the colonel himself had not been entirely unaware of this latter fact, though he had exhibited no signs of his knowledge, either in his countenance or bearing; indeed, it would be difficult, for one so easily swayed by every passing interest as Richard Amory was, to have long resisted his manly courtesy and good nature. Men always found him an agreeable companion, and he made the most of his powers on the occasions which threw him, or in which he threw himself, in Amory's way. Even Planefield admitted reluctantly, once or twice, that the fellow had plenty in him. It was not long before Richard succumbed to his personal influence with pleasurable indolence. It would have cost him too much effort to combat against it; and, besides this, it was rather agreeable to count among one's friends and supporters a man strong enough to depend on and desirable enough to be proud of. There had been times during the last few months when there would have been a sense of relief in the feeling that there was within reach a stronger nature than his own, — one on whose strength he knew he could rely. As their intimacy appeared to establish itself, if he did not openly confide in Tredennis, he more than once approached the borders of a confidence in his moments of depression. That he had such moments had become plain. He did not even look so bright as he had looked; something of his care-free, joyous air had deserted him, and now and then there were to be seen faint lines on his forehead.

"There is a great deal of responsibility to be borne in a matter like this," he said to Tredennis, "and it wears on a man." To which he added, a few seconds later, with a delightfully unconscious mixture of petulance and protest: "Confound it! why can't things as well turn out right as wrong?"

"Have things been turning out wrong?" the colonel ventured.

Richard put his elbows on the table before him, and rested his forehead on his hands a second.

"Well, yes," he admitted; "several things, and just at the wrong time, too. There seems a kind of fate in it, — as if when one thing began the rest must follow."

The colonel began to bite one end of his long mustache reflectively as he looked at the young man's knitted brow.

"There is one thing you must understand at the outset," he said, at length. "When I can be made useful — supposing such a thing were possible — I am here."

Richard glanced up at him quickly. He looked a little haggard for the moment.

"What a steady, reliable fellow you are!" he said. "Yes, I should be sure of you if — if the worst came to the worst."

The colonel bit the ends of his mustache all the way home, and more than one passer-by on the avenue was aroused to wonder what the subject of his reflections might be, he strode along with so absorbed an air, and frowned so fiercely.

"I should like to know what the worst is," he was saying to himself. "I should like to know what that means."

It was perhaps his desire to know what it meant which led him to cultivate Richard more faithfully still, to join him on the street, to make agreeable bachelor-dinners for him, to carry him off to the theatres, and, in a quiet way, to learn something of what he was doing each day. It was, in fact, a delicate diplomatic position the colonel occupied in these days, and it cannot be said that he greatly enjoyed it or liked himself in it. He was too honest by nature to find pleasure in diplomacy, and what he did for another he would never have done for himself. For the sake of the woman who rewarded his generosity and care with frivolous coldness and slight, he had undertaken a task whose weight lay heavily upon him. Since his first suspicions of her danger had been aroused he had been upon the alert continually, and had seen many things to which the more indifferent or less practical were blind. As Richard had casually remarked, he was possessed of a strong business sense and faculty of which he was not usually suspected, and he had seen signs in the air which he felt boded no good for Richard Amory or those who relied on his discretion in business affairs. That the professor had innocently relied upon it when he gave his daughter into his hands he had finally learned; that Bertha never gave other than a transient thought — more than half a jest — to money matters he knew. Her good fortune it had been to be trammelled neither by the weight of money nor the want of it, — a truly enviable condition, which had, not unnaturally, engendered in her a confidence at once unquestioning and somewhat perilous. Tredennis had recalled more than once of late a little scene he had taken part in on one occasion of her signing a legal document Richard had brought to her.

"Shall I sign it here?" she had said, with exaggerated seriousness, "or shall I sign it there? What would happen to me if I wrote on the wrong line? Could not Laurence sign it for me in his government hand, and give it an air of distinction? Suppose my hand trembled and I made a blot? I am not obliged to read it, am I?"

"I think I should insist that she read it," the colonel had said to Richard, with some abruptness.

Bertha had looked up and smiled.

"Shall you insist that I read it?" she said; "I know what it says. It says 'whereas' and 'moreover' and 'in accordance ' with 'said agreement ' and 'in consideration of.' Those are the prevailing sentiments, and I am either the ' party of the first part' or the 'party of the second part '; and if it was written in Sanskrit, it would be far clearer to my benighted mind than it is in its present lucid form. But I will read it if you prefer it, even though delirium should supervene."

It was never pleasant to Colonel Tredennis to remember this trivial episode, and the memory of it became a special burden to him as time progressed and he saw more of Amory's methods and tendencies. But it was scarcely for him to go to her, and tell her that her husband was not as practical a business man as he should be; that he was visionary and too easily allured by glitter and speciousness. He could not warn her against him and reveal to her the faults and follies she seemed not to have discovered. But he could revive something of Richard's first fancy for him, and make himself in a measure necessary to him, and perhaps gain an influence over him which might be used to good purpose. Possibly, despite his modesty, he had a half-conscious knowledge of the power of his own strong will and nature over weaker ones, and was resolved that this weak one should be moved by them, if the thing were possible.

Nor was this all. There were other duties he undertook, for reasons best known to himself. He became less of a recluse socially, and presented himself more frequently in the fashionable world. He was no fonder of gayety than he had been before, but he faced it with patience and courage. He went to great parties, and made himself generally useful. He talked to matrons who showed a fancy for his company, and was the best and most respectful of listeners; he was courteous and attentive to both chaperones and their charges, and by quietly persistent good conduct won additional laurels upon each occasion of his social appearance. Those who had been wont to stand somewhat in awe of him, finding nothing to fear on more intimate acquaintance, added themselves to the list of his admirers. Before the season was over he had made many a stanch friend among matronly leaders of fashion, whose word was law. If such a thing could be spoken of a person of habits so grave, it might have been said that he danced attendance upon these ladies; but, though such a phrase would seem unfitting, it may certainly be remarked that he walked attendance on them, and sought their favor and did their bidding with a silent faithfulness wonderful to behold. He accepted their invitations and attended their receptions; he escorted them to their carriages, found their wraps, and carried their light burdens with an imperturbable demeanor.

"What!" said Bertha, one night, when she had seen him in attendance on the wife of the Secretary of State, whose liking for him was at once strong and warm; "what! is it Colonel Tredennis who curries the favor of the rich and great? It has seemed so lately. Is there any little thing in foreign missions you desire, or do you think of an Assistant-Secretaryship?"

"There is some dissatisfaction expressed with regard to the Minister to the Court of St. James," was his reply. "It is possible that he will be recalled. In that case may I hope to command your influence?"

But, many a time as he carried his shawls, or made his grave bow over the hand of a stately dowager, a half-sad smile crossed his face as he thought of the true reason for his efforts, and realized with a generous pang the depth of his unselfish perfidy. They were all kind to him, and he was grateful for their favors; but he would rather have been in his room at work, or trying to read, or marching up and down, thinking, in his solitude. Janey entertained him with far more success than the prettiest *débutante* of the season could hope to attain, though there was no *débutante* among them who did not think well of him and admire him not a little. But the reason which brought him upon this brightly lighted stage of action? Well, there was only one reason for everything now, he knew full well; for his being sadder than usual, or a shade less heavy of heart; for his wearing a darker face or a brighter one; for his interest in society, or his lack of interest in it; for his listening anxiously and being upon the alert. The reason was Bertha. When he heard her name mentioned he waited in silent anxiety for what followed; when he did not hear it he felt ill at ease, lest it had been avoided from some special cause.

"What she will not do for herself," he said, "I must try to do for her. If I make friends and win their good opinions I may use their influence in the future, if the worst should come to the worst, and she should need to be upheld. It is women who sustain women or condemn them. God forbid that she should ever lack their protection!"

And so he worked to earn the power to call upon this protection, if it should be required, and performed his part with such steadfastness of purpose that he made a place for himself such as few men are fortunate enough to make.

There was one friendship he made in these days, which he felt would not be likely to fade out or diminish in value. It was a friendship for a woman almost old enough to have been his mother, — a woman who had seen the world and knew it well, and yet had not lost her faith or charitable kindness of heart. It was the lady whom Bertha had seen him attending when she had asked him what object he had in view, — the wife of the Secretary of State, whose first friendly feeling for him had become a most sincere and earnest regard, for which he was profoundly grateful.

"A man to whom such a woman is kind must be grateful," he had said, in speaking of her to Agnes Sylvestre. "A woman who is good and generous, who is keen, yet merciful, whose judgment is ripe, and whose heart is warm, who has the discernment of maturity and the gentleness of youth, — it is an honor to know her and be favored by her. One is better every time one is thrown with her, and leaves her presence with a stronger belief in all good things."

It had, perhaps, been this lady's affection for Professor Herrick which had, at the outset, directed her attention to his favorite; but, an acquaintance once established, there had been no need of any other impetus than she received from her own feminine kindliness, quickness of perception, and sympathy. The interest he awakened in most feminine minds he had at once awakened in her own.

"He looks," she said to herself, "as if he had a story, and hardly knew the depth of its meaning himself."

But, though she was dexterous enough at drawing deductions, and heard much of the small talk of society, she heard no story. He was at once soldier and scholar; he was kind, brave, and generous; men spoke well of him, and women liked him; his past and present entitled him to respect and admiration; but there was no story mentioned in any discussion of him. He seemed to have lived a life singularly uneventful, so far as emotional experiences were concerned.

"Nevertheless," she used to say, when she gave a few moments to sympathetic musing upon him, "nevertheless"—

She observed his good behavior, notwithstanding he did not enjoy himself greatly in society. He was attentive to his duties without being absorbed in them, and, when temporarily unoccupied, wore a rather weary and abstracted look.

"It is something like the look," she once remarked inwardly, "*something* like the look I have seen in the eyes of that bright and baffling little Mrs. Amory, who seems at times to be obliged to recall herself from somewhere."

She had not been the leader of this world of hers without seeing many things and learning many lessons; and, as she had stood giving her greeting to the passing multitude week after week, she had gained a wonderful amount of experience and knowledge of her kind. She had seen so many weary faces, so many eager ones, so many stamped with care and disappointment; bright eyes had passed before her which one season had saddened; she had heard gay voices change and soft ones grow hard; she had read of ambitions frustrated and hopes denied, and once or twice had seen with a pang that somewhere a heart had been broken.

Naturally, in thus looking on, she had given some attention to Bertha Amory, and had not been blind to the subtle changes through which she had passed. She thought she could date the period of these changes. She remembered the reception at which she had first noted that the girlish face had begun to assume a maturer look, and the girlish vivacity had altered its tones. This had happened the year after the marriage, and then Jack had been born, and when society saw the young mother again the change in her seemed almost startling. She looked worn and pale, and showed but little interest in the whirl about her. It was as if suddenly fatigue had overtaken her, and she had neither the energy nor the desire to rally from it. But, before the end of the season she had altered again, and had a touch of too brilliant color, and was gayer than ever.

"Rather persistently gay," said the older woman. "That is it, I think."

Lately there had been a greater change still and a more baffling one, and there had appeared upon the scene an element so new and strange as to set all ordinary conjecture at naught. The first breath of rumor which had wafted the story of Planefield's infatuation and the Westoria schemes had been met with generous displeasure and disbelief; but, as time went on, it had begun to be more difficult to make an effort against discussion which grew with each day and gathered material as it passed from one to another. The most trivial circumstance assumed the proportions of proof when viewed in the light of the general too vivacious interest. When Senator Planefield entered a room people instantly cast about in search of Mrs. Amory, and reposed entire confidence in the immediately popular theory that, but for the presence of the one, the absence of the other would have been a foregone conclusion. If they met each other with any degree of vivacity the fact was commented upon in significant asides; if Bertha's manner was cold or quiet it was supposed to form a portion of her deep-laid plan for the entire subjugation of her victim. It had, indeed, come to this at last, and Tredennis' friend looked on and listened bewildered to find herself shaken in her first disbelief by an aspect of affairs too serious to be regarded with indifference. By the time the season drew toward its close the rumor, which had at first been accepted only by rumor-lovers and epicures in scandal, had found its way into places where opinion had weight, and decision was a more serious matter. In one or two quiet establishments there was private debating of various rather troublesome questions, in which debates Mrs. Amory's name was frequently mentioned. Affairs as unfortunate as the one under discussion had been known to occur before, and it was not impossible that they might occur again; it was impossible to be blind to them; it was impossible to ignore or treat them lightly, and certainly something was due to society from those who held its reins in their hands for the time being.

"It is too great leniency which makes such things possible," some one remarked. "To a woman with a hitherto unspotted reputation and in an entirely respectable position they should be impossible."

It was on the very evening that this remark was made that Bertha expressed a rather curious opinion to Laurence Arbuthnot.

"It is dawning upon me," she said, "that I am not quite so popular as I used to be, and I am wondering why."

"What suggested the idea?" Laurence inquired.

"I scarcely know," she replied, a little languidly, "and I don't care so much as I ought. People don't talk to me in so animated a manner as they used to — or I fancy they don't. I am not very animated myself, perhaps. There is a great deal in that. I know I am deteriorating conversationally. What I say hasn't the right ring exactly, and I suppose people detect the false note, and don't like it. I don't wonder at it. Oh, there is no denying that I am not so much overpraised and noticed as I used to be!"

And then she sat silent for some time and appeared to be reflecting, and Laurence watched her with a dawning sense of anxiety he would have been reluctant to admit the existence of even to himself.

Chapter 27

A few days after this she told Richard that she wished to begin to make her arrangements for going away for the summer.

"What, so early!" he exclaimed, with an air of some slight discontent. "It has been quite cool so far."

"I remained too late last year," she answered; "and I want to make up for lost time."

They were at dinner, and he turned his wineglass about restlessly on the table-cloth.

"Are you getting tired of Washington?" he asked. "You seem to be."

"I am a little tired of everything just now," she said; "even"— with a ghost of a laugh —"of the Westoria lands and Senator Planefield."

He turned his wineglass about again.

"Oh," he said, his voice going beyond the borders of petulance, "it is plain enough to see that you have taken an unreasonable dislike to Planefield!"

"He is too large and florid, and absorbs too much of one's attention," she replied, coldly.

"He does not always seem to absorb a great deal of yours," Richard responded, knitting his delicate dark brows. "You treated him cavalierly enough last night, when he brought you the roses."

"I am tired of his roses!" she exclaimed, with sudden passion. "They are too big, and red, and heavy. They cost too much money. They fill all the air about me. They weight me down, and I never seem to be rid of them. I won't have any more! Let him give them to some one else!" And she threw her bunch of grapes on her plate, and dropped her forehead on her hands with a childish gesture of fatigue and despair.

Richard knit his brows again. He regarded her with a feeling very nearly approaching nervous dread. This would not do, it was plain.

"What is the matter with you?" he said. "What has happened? It isn't like *you* to be unreasonable, Bertha."

She made an effort to recover herself, and partly succeeded. She lifted her face and spoke quite gently and deprecatingly.

"No," she said. "I don't think it is; so you will be all the readier to overlook it, and allow it to me as a luxury. The fact is, Richard, I am not growing any stronger, and"—

"Do you know," he interrupted, "I don't understand that. You used to be strong enough."

"One has to be very strong to be strong *enough*" she replied, "and I seem to have fallen a little short of the mark."

"But it has been going on rather a long time, hasn't it?" he inquired. "Didn't it begin last winter?"

"Yes," she answered, in a low voice, "it *began* then."

"Well, you see, that is rather long for a thing of that sort to go on without any special reason."

"It has seemed so to me," she responded, without any change of tone.

"Haven't you a pretty good appetite?" he inquired.

She raised her eyes suddenly, and then dropped them again. He had not observed what a dozen other people had seen.

"No," she answered.

"Don't you sleep well?"

"No."

"Are you thinner? Well, yes," giving her a glance of inspection. "You are thinner. Oh! come, now, this won't do at all!"

"I am willing to offer any form of apology you like," she said.

"You must get. well," he answered; "that is all."

And he rose from his seat, went to the mantel for a cigarette, and returned to her side, patting her shoulder encouragingly. "You would not be tired of Planefield if you were well. You would like him well enough."

The change which settled on her face was one which had crossed it many a time without his taking note of it. Possibly the edge of susceptibilities so fine and keen as his is more easily dulled than that of sensitiveness less exquisite. She arose herself.

"That offers me an inducement to recover," she said. "I will begin immediately — to-day — this moment. Let me light your cigarette for you."

After it was done they sauntered into the library together and stood for a moment looking out of the window.

"Do you know," she said at length, laying her hand on his sleeve, "I think even you are not quite yourself. Are you an invalid, too?"

"I," he said. "Why do you think so?"

"For a very good reason," she answered. "For the best of reasons. Two or three times lately you have been a trifle out of humor. Are you aware of it? Such, you see, is the disadvantage of being habitually amiable. The slightest variation of your usually angelic demeanor lays you open to the suspicion of bodily ailment. Just now, for instance, at table, when I spoke to you about going away, you were a little — not to put too fine a point upon it — cross."

"Was I?"

Her touch upon his sleeve was Very soft and kind, and her face had a gentle, playful appeal on it.

"You really were," she returned. "Just a little — and so was I. It was more a matter of voice and manner, of course; but we didn't appear to our greatest advantage, I am afraid. And we have never done things like that, you know, and it would be rather bad to begin now, wouldn't it?"

"It certainly would," he replied. "And it is very nice in you to care about it."

"It would not be nice in me not to care," she said. "Just for a moment, you know, it actually sounded quite — quite married. It seemed as if we were on the verge of agreeing to differ about — Senator Planefield."

"We won't do it again," he said. "We will agree to make the best of him."

She hesitated a second.

"I will try not to make the worst," she returned. "There is always a best, I suppose. And so long as you are here to take care of me, I need not — need not be uncomfortable."

"About what?" he asked.

She hesitated again, and a shade of new color touched her cheek.

"I don't think I am over-fastidious," she said, "but he has a way I don't like. He is too fulsome. He admires me too much. He pays me too many compliments. I wish he would not do it."

"Oh! come, now," he said, gayly, "that is prejudice! It is worse than all the rest. I never heard you complain of your admirers before, or of their compliments."

She hesitated a moment again. It was not the first time she had encountered this light and graceful obstinacy, and found it more difficult to cope with than words apparently more serious.

"I have never had an admirer of exactly that quality before," she said.

"Oh," he said, airily, "don't argue from the ground that it is a bad quality!"

"Has it never struck you," she suggested, "that there is something of the same quality, whether it is good, bad, or indifferent, in all the persons who are connected with the Westoria lands? I have felt once or twice lately, when I have looked around the parlors, as if I must have suddenly emigrated, the atmosphere was so different. They have actually rather crowded out the rest — those men."

It was his turn to pause now, and he did so, looking out of the window, evidently ill at ease, and hesitant for the moment.

"My dear child," he said, at length, "there may be truth in what you say; but — I may as well be frank with you — the thing is necessary."

"Richard," she said, quickly, prompted to the question by a sudden, vague thought, "what have *you* to do with the Westoria lands? Why do you care so much about them?"

"I have everything to do with them — and nothing," he answered. "The legal business connected with them, and likely to result from the success of the scheme, will be the making of me, that is all. I haven't been an immense success so far, you know, and it will make me an immense success and a man of property. Upon my word, a nice little lobbyist *you* are, to look frightened at the mere shadow of a plot!"

"I am not a lobbyist," she exclaimed. "I never wanted to be one. That was only a part of the nonsense I have talked all my life. I have talked too much nonsense. I wish — I wish I had been different!"

"Don't allow your repentance to be too deep," he remarked, dryly. "You won't be able to get over it."

"It's too late for repentance; but I shall not be guilty of that particular kind of folly again. It was folly — and it was bad taste"—

"As I had not observed it, you might have been content to let it rest," he interrupted.

She checked herself in the reply she was about to make, clasping her hands helplessly.

"O Richard!" she said; "we are beginning again!"

"So we are," he responded, coolly; "we seem to have a tendency in that direction."

"And it always happens," she said, "when I speak of Senator Planefield, or of going away."

"You have fallen into the habit of wanting to go away lately," he answered. "You wanted to go to Europe"—

"I want to go still," she interposed, "very much."

"And I wish you to remain here," he returned, petulantly. "What's the use of a man's having a wife at the other side of the globe?"

She withdrew a pace and leaned against the side of the window, letting her eyes rest upon him with a little, bitter smile. For the moment she had less care of herself and of him than she had ever had before.

"Ah!" she said, "then you keep me here because you love me?"

"Bertha!" he exclaimed.

Even his equable triviality found a disturbing element in the situation.

"Richard," she said, "go and finish your cigarette out of doors. It will be better for both of us. This has gone far enough."

"It has gone too far," he answered, nervously. "It is deucedly uncomfortable, and it isn't our way to be uncomfortable. Can't we make it smooth again? Of course we can. It would not be like you to be implacable. I am afraid I was a trifle irritable. The fact is, I have had a great deal of business anxiety lately, — one or two investments have turned out poorly, — and it has weighed on my mind. If the money were mine, you know; but it is yours"—

"I have never wished you to feel the difference," she said.

"No," he replied. "Nothing could have been nicer than your way about it. You might have made me very uncomfortable, if you had been a hard, business-like creature; but, instead of that, you have been charming."

"I am glad of that," she said, and she smiled gently as he put his arm about her, and kissed her cheek.

"You have a right to your caprices," he said. "Go to your summer haunts of vice and fashion, if you wish to, and I will follow you as soon as I can; but we won't say any more about Europe, just at present, will we? Perhaps next year."

And he kissed her again.

"Perhaps next year or the year after," she repeated, with a queer little smile. "And — and we will take Senator Planefield with us."

"No," he answered, "we will leave him at home to invest the millions derived from the Westoria lands."

And he went out with a laugh on his lips.

A week later Colonel Tredennis heard from Richard that Bertha and the children were going away.

"When?" asked the colonel. "That seems rather sudden. I saw Janey two days ago, and did not understand that the time was set for their departure."

"It is rather sudden," said Richard. "The fact is, they leave Washington this morning. I should be with them now if it were not for a business engagement."

Chapter 28

The next few weeks were not agreeable ones to Richard Amory. There was too much feverish anxiety and uncertainty in them. He had not yet acquired the coolness and hardihood of experience, and he felt their lack in himself. He had a great deal at stake, more than at the outset it had seemed possible he could have under any circumstances. He began to realize, with no little discomfort, that he had run heavier risks than he had intended to allow himself to be led into running. When they rose before him in their full magnitude, as they did occasionally when affairs assumed an unencouraging aspect, he wished his enthusiasm had been less great. It could not be said that he had reached remorse for, or actual repentance of, his indiscretions; he had simply reached a point when discouragement led him to feel that he might be called upon to repent by misfortune. Up to this time it had been his habit to drive up to the Capitol in his *coupé*, to appear in the galleries, to saunter through the lobby, and to flit in and out of committee-rooms with something of the air of an amateur rather enjoying himself; he had made himself popular; his gayety, his magnetic manner, his readiness to be all things to all men had smoothed his pathway for him, while his unprofessional air had given him an appearance of harmlessness.

"He's a first-rate kind of fellow to have on the ground when a thing of this sort is going on," one of the smaller satellites once remarked. "Nobody's afraid of being seen with him. There's an immense deal in that. There are fellows who come here who can half ruin a man with position by recognizing him on the street. Regular old hands they are, working around here for years, making an honest living out of their native land. Every one knows them and what they are up to. Now, this one is different, and that wife of his" —

"What has she been doing?" flung in Planefield, who was present. "What has she got to do with it?"

He said it with savage uneasiness. He was full of restive jealousy and distrust in these days.

"I was only going to say that she is known in society," he remarked, "and she is the kind the most particular of those fellows don't object to calling on."

But, as matters took form and a more critical point was neared; as the newspapers began to express themselves on the subject of the Westoria lands scheme, and prophesy its failure or success; as it became the subject of editorials applauding the public-spiritedness of those most prominent in it, or of paragraphs denouncing the corrupt and self-seeking tendency of the times; as the mental temperature of certain individuals became a matter of vital importance, and the degree of cordiality of a greeting an affair of elation or despair, — Richard felt that his air of being an amateur was becoming a thing of the past. He was too anxious to keep it up well; he did not sleep at night, and began to look fagged, and it required an effort to appear at ease.

"Confound it!" he said to Planefield, "how can one be at ease with a man when his yes or no may be success or destruction to you? It makes him of too much consequence. A fellow finds himself trying to please, and it spoils his manner. I never knew what it was to feel a human being of any particular consequence before."

"You have been lucky," commented Planefield, not too tolerantly.

"I have been lucky," Richard answered; "but I'm not lucky now, and I shall be deucedly unlucky if that bill doesn't pass. The fact is, there are times when I half wish I hadn't meddled with it."

"The mistake *you* made," said Planefield, with stolid ill-humor, "was in letting Mrs. Amory go away. Now is the time you need her most. There's no denying that there are some things women can do better than men; and when a man has a wife as clever as yours, and as much of a social success, he's blundering when he doesn't call on her for assistance. One or two of her little dinners would be the very things just now for the final smoothing down of one or two rough ones who haven't opinions unless you provide them with them. She'd provide them with them fast enough. They'd only have one opinion when she'd done with them, if she was in one of the moods I've seen her in sometimes. Look how she carried Bowman and Pell off their feet the night she gave them the description of that row in the House. And Hargis, of North Carolina, swears by her; he's a simple, domesticated fellow, and was homesick the night I brought him here, and she found it out, — Heaven knows how, — and talked to him about his wife and children until he said he felt as if he'd seen them. He told me so with tears in his eyes. It is that kind of thing we want now."

"Well," said Richard, nervously, "it isn't at our disposal. I don't mind telling you that she was rather out of humor with the aspect of affairs before she went away, and I had one interview with her which showed me it would be the safest plan to let her go."

"Out of humor!" said Planefield. "She has been a good deal out of humor lately, it seems to me. Not that it's any business of mine; but it's rather a pity, considering circumstances."

Richard colored, walked a few steps, put his hands in his pockets, and took them out again. Among the chief sources of anxious trouble to him had been that of late he had found his companion rather difficult to get along with. He had been irritable, and even a trifle overbearing, and had at times exhibited an indifference to results truly embarrassing to contemplate, in view of the crisis at hand. When he intrenched himself behind a certain heavy stubbornness, in which he was specially strong, Richard felt himself helpless. The big body, the florid face, the doggedly unresponsive eye, were too much to combat against. When he was ill-humored Richard knew that he endeavored to conciliate him; but when this mood held possession he could only feel alarm and ask himself if it could be possible that, after all, the man might be brutal and false enough to fail him. There were times when he sat and looked at him unwillingly, fascinated by the likeness he found in him to the man who had sent poor Westor to his doom. Naturally, the old story had been revived of late, and he heard new versions of it and more minute descriptions of the chief actors, and it was not difficult for an overwrought imagination to discover in the two men some similarity of personal characteristics. Just at this moment there rose within him a memory of a point of resemblance between the pair which would have been extremely embarrassing to him if he had permitted it to assume the disagreeable form of an actual fact. It was the resemblance between the influences which had moved them. In both cases it had been a woman, — in this case it was his own wife, and if he had not been too greatly harassed he would have appreciated the indelicacy of the situation. He was not an unrefined person in theory, and his sensitiveness would have caused him to revolt at the grossness of such a position if he had not had so much at stake and been so overborne by his associates. His mistakes and vices were always the result of circumstance and enthusiasm, and he hurried past them with averted eyes, and refused to concede to them any substantiality. There is nothing more certain than that he had never allowed himself to believe that he had found Bertha of practical use in rendering Planefield docile and attracting less important luminaries. Bertha had been very charming and amiable, that was all; she was always so; it was her habit to please people, — her nature, in fact, — and she had only done what she always did. As a mental statement of the case, nothing could be more simple than this, and he was moved to private disgust by his companion's aggressive clumsiness, which seemed to complicate matters and confront him with more crude suggestions.

"I am afraid she would not enjoy your way of putting it," he said.

Planefield shut his teeth on his cigar and looked out of the window. That was his sole response, and was a form of bullying he enjoyed.

"We must remember that — that she does not realize everything," continued Richard, uneasily; "and she has not regarded the matter from any serious standpoint. It is my impression," he added, with a sudden sense of growing irritation, "that she wouldn't have anything to do with it if she thought it was a matter of gain or loss!"

Planefield made no movement. He was convinced that this was a lie, and his look out of the window was his reply to it.

Richard put his hands into his pockets again and turned about, irritated and helpless.

"You must have seen yourself how unpractical she is," he exclaimed. "She is a mere child in business matters. Any one could deceive her."

He stopped and flushed without any apparent reason. He found himself looking out of the window too, with a feeling of most unpleasant confusion. He was obliged to shake it off before he spoke again, and when he did so it was with an air of beginning with a fresh subject.

"After all," he said, "everything does not depend upon influence of that sort. There are other things to be considered. Have you seen Blundel?"

"You can't expect a man like Blundel," said Planefield, "to be easy to manage. Blundel is the possessor of a moral character, and when a man has capital like that — and Blundel's sharpness into the bargain — he is not going to trifle with it. He's going to hang on to it until it reaches its highest market value, and then decide which way he will invest it."

Richard dropped into a seat by the table. He felt his forehead growing damp.

"But if we are not sure of Blundel?" he exclaimed.

"Well, we are not sure of Blundel," was the answer. "What we have to hope is that he isn't sure of himself. The one thing you can't be sure of is a moral character. Impeccability is rare, and it is never easy for an outsider to hit on its exact value. It varies, and you have to run risks with it. Blundel's is expensive."

"There has been a great deal of money used," hesitated Richard; "a great deal."

Planefield resorted to the window again. It had not been his money that had been used. He had sufficient intellect to reap advantages where they were to be reaped, and to avoid indiscreet adventures.

"You had better go and see Blundel yourself," he said, after a pause. "I have had a talk with him, and made as alluring a statement of the case as I could, with the proper degree of caution, and he has had time to put the matter in the scales with his impeccability and see which weighs the heavier, and if they can't be made to balance. He will try to balance them, but if he can't — You must settle what is to be done between you. I have done my best."

"By Jove!" exclaimed Richard, virtuously, "what corruption!"

It was an ingenuous ejaculation, but he was not collected enough to appreciate the native candor of it himself at the moment. He felt that he was being hardly treated, and that the most sacred trusts of a great nation were in hands likely to betray them at far too high a figure. The remark amounted to an outburst of patriotism.

"Have they *all* their price?" he cried.

Planefield turned his head slowly and glanced at him over his shoulder.

"No," he said; "if they had, you'd find it easier. There's your difficulty. If they were all to be bought, or none of them were to be sold, you'd see your way."

It did not seem to Richard that his way was very clear at the present moment. At every step of late he had found new obstacles in his path and new burdens on his shoulders. People had so many interests and so many limitations, and the limitations were always related to the interests. He began to resolve that it was a very sordid and business-like world in which human lot was cast, and to realize that the tendency of humanity was to coarse prejudice in favor of itself.

"Then I had better see Blundel at once," he said, with feverish impatience.

"You haven't any time to lose," was Planefield's cool response. "And you will need all the wit you can carry with you. You are not going to offer *him* inducements, you know; you are only going to prove to him that his chance to do something for his country lies before him in the direction of the Westoria lands. After that" —

"After that," repeated Richard, anxiously.

"Do what you think safest and most practicable."

As the well-appointed equipage drew up under the archway before the lower entrance to the north wing of the Capitol, a group of men who stood near the door-way regarded it with interest. They did so because three of them were strangers and sight-seers, and the fourth, who was a well-seasoned Washingtonian, had called their attention to it.

"There," he said, with an experienced air, "there is one of them this moment. It is beginning to be regarded as a fact that he is mixed up with one of the biggest jobs the country has ever known. He is up to his ears in this Westoria business, it's believed, though he professes to be nothing more than a sort of interested looker-on and a friend of the prime movers. He's a gentleman, you see, with a position in society, and a pretty wife, who is a favorite, and the pretty wife entertains his friends; and when a man is in an uncertain frame of mind the husband invites him to dinner, and the pretty wife interests herself in him, — she knows how to do it, they say, — and he goes away a wiser and a better man, and more likely to see his way to making himself agreeable. Nothing professional about it, don't you see? All quite proper and natural. No lobbying about that, you know; but it helps a bill through wonderfully. I tell you there's no knowing what goes on in these tip-top parlors about here."

He said it with modest pride and exultation, and his companions were delighted. They represented the average American, with all his ingenuous eagerness for the dramatic exposure of crime in his fellow-man. They had existed joyously for years in the belief that Washington was the seat of corruption, bribery, and fraud; that it was populated chiefly with brilliant female lobbyists and depraved officials, who carried their privileges to market and bartered and sold them with a guileless candor, whose temerity was only to be equalled by its' brazen cheerfulness of spirit. They were, probably, not in the least aware of their mental attitude toward their nation's government; but they revelled in it none the less, and would have felt a keen pang of disappointment if they had been suddenly confronted with the fact that there was actually an element of most unpicturesque honesty in the House and a flavor of shameless impeccability in the Senate. They had heard delightful stories of "jobs" and "schemes," and had hoped to hear more. When they had been taken to the visitors' gallery, they had exhibited an earnest anxiety to be shown the members connected with the last investigation, and had received with private rapture all anecdotes connected with the ruling political scandal. They decided that the country was in a bad way, and felt a glow of honest pride in its standing up at all in its present condition of rottenness. Their ardor had been a little dampened by an incautious statement made by their friend and guide, to the effect that the subject of the investigation seemed likely to clear himself of the charges made against him, and the appearance of Richard Amory, with his personal attractions, his neat equipage, and his air of belonging to the great world, was something of a boon to them. They wished his wife had been with him; they had only seen one female lobbyist as yet, and she had been merely a cheap, flashy woman, with thin, rouged cheeks and sharp, eager eyes.

"Looks rather anxious, doesn't he?" one asked the other, as Amory went by. He certainly looked anxious as he passed them; but once inside the building he made an effort to assume something of his usual air of gay good cheer. It would not do to present himself with other than a fearless front. So he walked with a firm and buoyant tread through the great vaulted corridors and up the marble stairways, exchanging a salutation with one passer-by and a word of greeting with another.

He found Senator Blundel in his committee-room, sitting at the green-covered table, looking over some papers. He was a short, stout man, with a blunt-featured face, grayish hair, which had a tendency to stand on end, and small, shrewd eyes. When he had been in the House, his rising to his feet had generally been the signal for his fellow-members to bestir themselves and turn to listen, as it was his habit to display a sharp humor, of a rough-and-ready sort. Richard had always felt this humor coarse, and, having but little confidence in Blundel's possessing any other qualification for his position, regarded it as rather trying that circumstances should have combined to render his sentiments of such importance in the present crisis. Looking at the thick-set figure and ordinary face he felt that Planefield had been right, and that Bertha might have done much with him, principally because he presented himself as one of the obstacles whose opinions should be formed for them all the more on account of their obstinacy when once biassed in a wrong direction.

But there was no suggestion of these convictions in his manner when he spoke. It was very graceful and ready, and his strong points of good-breeding and mental agility stood him in good stead. The man before him, whose early social advantages had not been great, was not too dull to feel the influence of the first quality, and find himself placed at a secretly acknowledged disadvantage by it. After he had heard his name his small, sharp eyes fixed themselves on his visitor's handsome countenance, with an expression not easy to read.

"It is not necessary for me to make a new statement of our case," said Richard, easily. "I won't fatigue you and occupy your time by repeating what you have already heard stated in the clearest possible manner by Senator Planefield."

Blundel thrust his hands into his pockets and nodded.

"Yes," he responded. "I saw Planefield, and he said a good deal about it."

"Which, of course, you have reflected upon?" said Richard.

"Well, yes. I've thought it over — along with other things."

"I trust favorably," Richard suggested. Blundel stretched his legs a little and pushed his hands further down into his pockets.

"Now, what would you call favorably?" he inquired.

"Oh," replied Richard, with a self-possessed promptness, "favorably to the connecting branch."

It was rather a fine stroke, this airy candor, but he had studied it beforehand thoroughly and calculated its effect. It surprised Blundel into looking up at him quickly.

"You would, eh?" he said; "let us hear why."

"Because," Richard stated, "that would make it favorable to us."

Blundel was beguiled into a somewhat uneasy laugh.

"Well," he remarked, "you're frank enough."

Richard fixed upon him an open, appreciative glance.

"And why not?" he answered. "There is our strong point, — that we can afford to be frank. We have nothing to conceal. We have something to gain, of course — who has not?— but it is to be gained legitimately — so there is no necessity for our concealing that. The case is simplicity itself. Here are the two railroads. See," — and he laid two strips of paper side by side upon the table. "A connecting branch is needed. If it runs through this way," making a line with his finger, "it makes certain valuable lands immeasurably more valuable. There is no practical objection to its taking this direction instead of that, — in either case it runs through the government reservations, — the road will be built; somebody's property will be benefited, — why not that of my clients?"

Blundel looked at the strips of paper, and his little eyes twinkled mysteriously.

"By George!" he said, "that isn't the way such things are generally put. What you ought to do is to prove that nobody is to be benefited, and that you are working for the good of the government."

Richard laughed.

"Oh," he said, "I am an amateur, and I should be of no use whatever to my clients if they had anything to hide or any special reason to fear failure. We have opposition to contend with, of course. The southern line is naturally against us, as it wants the connecting branch to run in the opposite direction; but, if it has no stronger claim than we have, the struggle is equal. They are open to the objection of being benefited by the subsidies, too. It is scarcely ground enough for refusing your vote, that some one will be benefited by it. The people is the government in America, and the government the people, and the interest of both are too indissolubly connected to admit of being easily separated on public measures. As I said, I am an amateur, but I am a man of the world. My basis is a natural, human one. I desire to attain an object, and, though the government will be benefited, I am obliged to confess I am arguing for my object more than for the government."

This was said with more delightful, airy frankness than ever. But concealed beneath this genial openness was a desperate anxiety to discover what his companion was thinking of, and if the effect of his stroke was what he had hoped it would be. He knew that frankness so complete was a novelty, and he trusted that his bearing had placed him out of the list of ordinary applicants for favor. His private conviction, to which he did not choose to allow himself to refer mentally with any degree of openness, was that, if the man was honest, honesty so bold and simple must disarm him; and, if he was not, ingenuousness so reckless must offer him inducements. But it was not easy to arrive at once at any decision as to the tenor of Blunders thoughts. He had listened, and it being his habit to see the humor of things, he had grinned a little at the humor he saw in this situation, which was perhaps not a bad omen, though he showed no disposition to commit himself on the spot.

"Makes a good story," he said; "pretty big scheme, isn't it?"

"Not a small one," answered Richard, freely. "That is one of its merits."

"The subsidies won't have to be small ones," said Blundel. "That isn't one of its merits. Now, let us hear your inducements."

Richard checked himself on the very verge of a start, realizing instantaneously the folly of his first flashing thought.

"The inducements you can offer to the government," added Blundel. "You haven't gone into a thing of this sort without feeling you have some on hand."

Of course there were inducements, and Richard had them at his fingers' ends, and was very fluent and eloquent in his statement of them. In fact, when once fairly launched upon the subject, he was somewhat surprised to find how many powerful reasons there were for its being to the interest of the nation that the land grants should be made to the road which ran through the Westoria lands and opened up their resources. His argument became so brilliant, as he proceeded, that he was moved by their sincerity himself, and gained impetus through his confidence in them. He really felt that he was swayed by a generous desire to benefit his country, and enjoyed his conviction of his own honesty with a refinement which, for the moment, lost sight of all less agreeable features of the proceeding. All his fine points came out under the glow of his enthusiasm, — his grace of speech and manner; his picturesque habit of thought, which gave color and vividness to all he said, — his personal attractiveness itself.

Blundel bestirred himself to sit up and look at him with renewed interest. He liked a good talker; he was a good talker himself. His mind was of a practical business stamp, and he was good at a knock-down blow in argument, or at a joke or jibe which felled a man like a meat-axe; but he had nothing like this, and he felt something like envy of all this swiftness and readiness and polish.

When he finished, Richard felt that he must have impressed him; that it was impossible that it should be otherwise, even though there were no special external signs of Blundel being greatly affected. He had thrust his hands into his pockets as before, and his hair stood on end as obstinately.

"Well," he said, succinctly, "it is a good story, and it's a big scheme."

"And you?" — said Richard. "We are sure of your"—

Blundel took a hand out of his pocket and ran it over his upright hair, as if in a futile attempt at sweeping it down.

"I'll tell you what I'll do," he said. "I'll see you day after to-morrow."

"But" — exclaimed Richard, secretly aghast.

Blundel ran over his hair again and returned his hand to his pocket.

"Oh, yes," he answered. "I know all about that. You don't want to lose time, and you want to feel sure; but, you see, I want to feel sure, too. As I said, it's a big business; it's too big a business to assume the responsibility of all at once. *I'm* not going to run any risks. I don't say you want me to run any; but, you know, you are an amateur, and there may be risks you don't realize. I'll see you again."

In his character of amateur it was impossible for Richard to be importunate, but his temptations to commit the indiscretion were strong. A hundred things might happen in the course of two days; delay was more dangerous than anything else. The worst of it all was that he had really gained no reliable knowledge of the man himself and how it would be best to approach him. He had seen him throughout the interview just as he had seen him before it. Whether or not his sharpness was cunning and his bluntness a defence he had not been able to decide.

"At any rate, he is cautious," he thought. "*How* cautious it is for us to find out."

When he left him Richard was in a fever of disappointment and perplexity, which, to his ease and pleasure-loving nature, was torment.

"Confound it all!" he said. "Confound the thing from beginning to end! It will have to pay well to pay for this."

He had other work before him, other efforts to make, and after he had made them he returned to his carriage fatigued and overwrought. He had walked through the great corridors, from wing to wing, in pursuit of men who seemed to elude him like will-o'-the-wisps; he had been driven to standing among motley groups, who sent in cards which did not always intercede for them; he had had interviews with men who were outwardly suave and pliable, with men who were ill-mannered and impatient, with men who were obstinate and distrustful, and with men who were too much occupied with their own affairs to be other than openly indifferent; if he had met with a shade of encouragement at one point, he had found it amply balanced by discouragement at the next; he had seen himself regarded as an applicant for favor, and a person to be disposed of as speedily as possible, and, when his work was at an end, his physical condition was one of exhaustion, and his mental attitude marked chiefly by disgust and weariness of spirit.

This being the state of affairs he made a call upon Miss Varien, who always exhilarated and entertained him.

He found her in her bower, and was received with the unvarying tact which characterized her manner upon all occasions. He poured forth his woes, as far as they could be told, and was very picturesque about them as he reclined in the easiest of easy-chairs.

"It is my opinion that nothing can be done without money," he said, "which is disgraceful!"

"It is, indeed," acknowledged Miss Varien, with a gleam of beautiful little teeth.

She had lived in Washington with her exceptional father and entirely satisfactory mother from her earliest infancy, and had gained from observation — at which she was brilliant, as at all else — a fund of valuable information. She had seen many things, and had not seen them in vain. It may be even suspected that Richard, in his character of amateur, was aware of this. There was a suggestion of watchfulness in his glance at her.

"Things ought to be better or worse to simplify the system," she said.

"That is in effect what I heard said this morning," answered Richard.

"I am sorry it is not entirely new," she returned. "Was it suggested, also, that since we cannot have incorruptibility we might alter our moral standards and remove corruption by making all transactions mere matters of business? If there was no longer any penalty attached to the sale and barter of public privileges, such sale and barter would cease to be dishonor and crime. We should be better if we were infinitely worse. The theory may appear bold at first blush, — no, not at first blush, for blushes are to be done away with, — at first sight, I will say in preference; it may appear bold, but after much reflection I have decided that it is the only practicable one."

"It is undoubtedly brilliant," replied Richard; "but, as you say, it would simplify matters wonderfully. I should not be at such a loss to know what Senator Blundel will do, for instance, and my appetite for luncheon would be better."

"It might possibly be worse," suggested Miss Varien .

Richard glanced at her quickly.

"That is a remark which evidently has a foundation," he said. "I wish you would tell me what prompted it."

"I am not sure it was very discreet," was the reply. "My personal knowledge of Senator Blundel prompted it."

"You know him very well," said Richard, with some eagerness.

"I should not venture to say I knew any one very well," she said, in the captivating voice which gave to all her words such value and suggestiveness. "I know him as I know many other men like him. I was born a politician, and existence without my politics would be an arid desert to me. I have talked to him and read his speeches, and followed him in his career for some time. I have even asked questions about him, and, consequently, I know something of his methods. I *think* — you see, I only say I think — I know what he will do."

"In Heaven's name, what is it?" demanded Richard.

She unfurled her fan and smiled over it with the delightful gleam of little white teeth.

"He will take his time," she answered. "He is slow, and prides himself on being sure. Your bill will not be acted upon; it will be set aside to lie over until the next session of Congress."

Richard felt as if he changed color, but he bore himself with outward discretion.

"You have some ulterior motive," he said. "Having invited me to remain to luncheon, you seek to render me incapable of doing myself justice. You saw in my eye the wolfish hunger which is the result of interviews with the savage senator and the pitiless member of Congress. Now I see the value of your theory. If it were in practice, I could win Blundel over with gold. What is your opinion of his conscience as it stands?"

343

It was said with admirable lightness and answered in a like strain, but he had never been more anxiously on the alert than he was as he watched Miss Varien's vivacious and subtly expressive face.

"I have not reached it yet," she said. "And consciences are of such different make and material; I have not decided whether his is made of interest or honesty. He is a mixture of shrewdness and crudeness which is very baffling; just when you are arguing from the shrewdness the crudeness displays itself, and *vice versa*. But, as I said, I *think* your bill will not be acted upon."

And then they went into luncheon, and, as he ate his lobster-salad and made himself agreeable beyond measure, Richard wondered, with an inward tremor, if she could be right.

Chapter 29

Mrs. Sylvestre did not leave town early. The weather was reasonably cool, the house on Lafayette Square was comfortable, and Washington in spring is at its loveliest. She liked the lull after the season, and enjoyed it to its utmost, wisely refusing all invitations to fitful after-Lent gayeties. She held no more receptions, but saw her more intimate acquaintances in the evening, when they made their informal calls. With each week that passed, her home gave her greater pleasure and grew prettier.

"I never lose interest in it," she said to Arbuthnot. "It is a continued delight to me. I find that I think of it a great deal, and am fond of it almost as if it was a friend I had found. I think I must have been intended for a housewife."

Mrs. Merriam's liking for Laurence Arbuthnot having increased as their acquaintance progressed, his intimacy in the household became more and more an established fact.

"One should always number among one's acquaintance," the clever dowager remarked, "an agreeable, well-bred, and reliable man-friend, — a man one can ask to do things, if unforeseen occasions arise. He must be agreeable, since one must be intimate with him, and for the same reason he must be well-bred. Notwithstanding our large circle, we are a rather lonely pair, my dear."

Gradually Mrs. Sylvestre herself had found a slight change taking place in her manner toward Arbuthnot. She became conscious of liking him better, and of giving him more mental attention, as she saw him more familiarly. The idea dawned by slow degrees upon her that the triviality of which she accused him was of an unusual order; that it was accompanied by qualities and peculiarities which did not seem to belong to it. She had discovered that he could deny himself pleasures he desired; that he was secretly thoughtful for others; that he was — also secretly — determined, and that he had his serious moments, however persistently he endeavored to conceal them. Perhaps the professor had given her more information concerning him than she could have gained by observation in any comparatively short space of time. "This frivolous fellow," he said to her one night, laying an affectionate hand on Arbuthnot's arm, as they were on the point of leaving the house together, after having spent the evening there, —"this frivolous fellow is the friend of my old age. I wonder why."

"So do I," said Arbuthnot. "I assure you that you could not find a reason, professor."

"There is a kind of reason," returned the professor, "though it is scarcely worthy of the name. This frivolous fellow is not such a trifler as he seems, and it interests me to see his seriousness continually getting the better of him when he fancies he has got it under and trodden it under his feet."

Arbuthnot laughed again, — the full, careless laugh which was so excellent an answer to everything.

"He maligns me, this dissector of the emotions," he said. "He desires artfully to give you the impression that I am not serious by nature. I am, in fact, seriousness itself. It is the wicked world which gets the better of me."

Which statement Mrs. Sylvestre might have chosen to place some reliance in as being a plausible one, if she had not seen the professor at other times, when he spoke of this friendship of his. It was certainly a warm one, and then, feeling that there must be reason for it, she began to see these reasons for herself, and appreciate something of their significance and value.

The change which finally revealed itself in her manner was so subtle in its character that Arbuthnot himself could not be sure when he had first felt it; sometimes he fancied it had been at one time, and again at another, and even now it was not easy for him to explain to himself why he knew that they were better friends.

But there was an incident in their acquaintance which he always remembered as a landmark.

This incident occurred at the close of the season. One bright moonlight night, having a fancy for making a call upon Bertha, who was not well enough to go out for several days, Mrs. Sylvestre made the visit on foot, accompanied by her maid. The night was so pleasant that they were walking rather slowly under the trees near Lafayette Park, when their attention was attracted by the sound of suppressed sobbing, which came from one of two figures standing in the shadow, near the railings, a few yards ahead of them. The figures were those of a man and a young woman, and the instant she saw the man, who was well dressed, Agnes Sylvestre felt her heart leap in her side, for she recognized Laurence Arbuthnot. He stood quite near the woman, and seemed trying to console or control her, while she — less a woman than a girl, and revealing in her childish face and figure all that is most pathetic in youth and helplessness — wept and wrung her hands.

"You must be quiet and have more confidence in"— Agnes heard Arbuthnot say; and then, prompted by some desperate desire to hear no more, and to avoid being seen, she spoke to her maid.

"Marie," she said, "we will cross the street."

But when they had crossed the street some chill in the night air seemed to have struck her, and she began to shiver so that Marie looked at her in some affright.

"Madame is cold," she said. "Is it possible that madame has a chill?"

"I am afraid so," her mistress replied, turning about hurriedly. "I will not make the visit. I will return home."

A few minutes later, Mrs. Merriam, who had settled her small figure comfortably in a large arm-chair by the fire, and prepared to spend the rest of the evening with a new book, looked up from its first chapter in amazement, as her niece entered the room.

"Agnes!" she exclaimed. "What has happened? Are you ill? Why, child I you are as white as a lily."

It was true that Mrs. Sylvestre's fair face had lost all trace of its always delicate color, and that her hands trembled as she drew off her gloves.

"I began — suddenly — to feel so cold," she said, "that I thought it better to come back."

347

Mrs. Merriam rose anxiously. .

"I hope it is not malaria, after all," she said. "I shall begin to think the place is as bad as Rome. You must have some hot wine."

"Send it upstairs, if you please," said Agnes. "I am going to my room; there is a large fire there."

And she went out as suddenly as she had appeared.

"I really believe she does not wish me to follow her," said Mrs. Merriam to herself.

"*Is* this malaria?" And having pondered upon this question, while she gave orders that the wine should be heated, she returned to her book after doing it, with the decision, "No, it is not."

Agnes drank very little of the wine when it was brought. She sat by the fire in her room and did not regain her color. The cold which had struck her had struck very deep; she felt as if she could not soon get warm again. Her eyes had a stern look as they rested on the fire; her delicate mouth was set into a curve of hopeless, bitter scorn; the quiet which settled upon her was even a little terrible, in some mysterious way. She heard a ring at the door-bell, but did not move, though she knew a caller was allowed to go to Mrs. Merriam. She was not in a mood to see callers she could see nobody; she wished to be left alone; but, in about half an hour, a servant came into her room.

"Mr. Arbuthnot is downstairs, and Mrs. Merriam wishes to know if Mrs. Sylvestre is better."

Mrs. Sylvestre hesitated a second before she replied.

"Say to Mrs. Merriam that I am better, and will join her."

She was as white as ever when she rose, even a shade whiter, and she felt like marble, though she no longer trembled.

"I will go down," she said, mechanically. "Yes, I will go down."

What she meant to say or do when she entered the room below perhaps she had not clearly decided herself. As she came in, and Arbuthnot rose to receive her, he felt a startled thrill of apprehension and surprise.

"I am afraid you are not really better," he said. "Perhaps I should not have asked to be allowed to see you."

He had suddenly an absurd feeling that there was such distance between them — that something inexplicable had set them so far apart — that it might almost be necessary to raise his voice to make her hear him.

"Thank you," she replied. "I was not really ill," and passed the chair he offered her, as if not seeing it, taking another one which placed the table between them.

Arbuthnot gave her a steady glance and sat down himself. Resolving in a moment's time that something incomprehensible had happened, he gathered himself together with another resolve, which did equal credit to his intelligence and presence of mind. This resolution was that he would not permit himself to be overborne by the mystery until he understood what it was, and that he would understand what it was before he left the house, if such a thing were possible. He had the coolness and courage to refuse to be misunderstood.

"I should not have hoped to see you," he said, in a quiet, level tone, still watching her, "but Mrs. Merriam was so kind as to think you would be interested in something I came to tell her."

"Of course she will be interested," said Mrs. Merriam. "Such a story would interest any woman. Tell it to her at once."

"I wish you would do it for me," said Arbuthnot, with a rather reluctant accession of gravity. "It is really out of my line. You will make it touching — women see things so differently. I'll confess to you that I only see the miserable, sordid, forlorn side of it, and don't know what to do with the pathos. When that poor, little wretch cried at me and wrung her hands I had not the remotest idea what I ought to say to stop her — and Heaven knows I wanted her to stop. I could only make the mistaken remark that she must have confidence in me, and I would do my best for the childish, irresponsible pair of them, though why they should have confidence in me I can only say ' Heaven knows,' again."

After she had seated herself Agnes had lightly rested her head upon her hand, as if to shade her eyes somewhat. When Arbuthnot began to speak she had stirred, dropping her hand a moment later and leaning forward; at this juncture she rose from her chair, and came forward with a swift, unconscious-looking movement. She stood up before Arbuthnot, and spoke to him.

"I wish to hear the story very much," she said, with a thrill of appeal in her sweet voice. "I wish you to tell it to me. You will tell it as — as we should hear it."

Nothing but a prolonged and severe course of training could have enabled Arbuthnot to preserve at this moment his outward composure. Indeed, he was by no means sure that it was preserved intact; he was afraid that his blond countenance flushed a little, and that his eyes were not entirely steady. He felt it necessary to assume a lightness of demeanor entirely out of keeping with his mental condition.

"I appreciate your confidence in me," he answered, "all the more because I feel my entire inadequacy to the situation. The person who could tell it as you ought to hear it is the young woman who waylaid me with tears near Lafayette Park about half an hour ago. She is a very young woman, in fact, an infant, who is legally united in marriage to another infant, who has been in the employ of the government, in the building I adorn with my presence. Why they felt it incumbent upon themselves to marry on an income of seventy-five dollars a month they do not explain in any manner at all satisfactory to the worldly mind. They did so, however, and lived together for several months in what is described as a state of bliss. They had two small rooms, and the female infant wore calico gowns, and did her own ridiculous, sordid, inferior housework, and rejoiced in the society of the male infant when a grateful nation released him from his daily labors."

Agnes quietly slipped into the chair he had first placed for her. She did it with a gentle, yielding movement, to which he was so little blind that he paused a second and looked at the fire, and made a point of resuming his story with a lighter air than before.

"They could not have been either happy or content under such absurd circumstances," he said; "but they thought they were. I used to see the male infant beaming over his labors in a manner to infuriate you. His wife used to come down to bear him from the office to the two rooms in a sort of triumphal procession. She had round eyes and dimples in her cheeks, and a little, round head with curls. Her husband, whose tastes were simple, regarded her as a beauty, and was given to confiding his opinion of her to his fellow-clerks. There was no objection to him but his youth and innocence. I am told he worked with undue enthusiasm in the hope of keeping his position, or even getting a better one, and had guileless, frenzied dreams of being able, in the course of the ensuing century, to purchase a small house ' on time.' I don't ask you to believe me when I tell you that the pair actually had such a house in their imbecile young minds, and had saved out of their starvation income a few dollars toward making their first payment on it. I didn't believe the man who told me, and I assure you he is a far more reliable fellow than I am."

He paused a second more. Was it possible that he found himself obliged to do so?

"They said," he added, "they said they 'wanted a home.'"

He heard a soft, little sound at his side, — a soft, emotional little sound. It came from Mrs. Sylvestre. She sat with her slender hands clasped upon her knee, and, as the little sound broke from her lips, she clasped them more closely.

"Ah!" she said. "Ah! poor children!"

Arbuthnot went on.

"Ought I to blush to admit that I watched these two young candidates for Saint Elizabeth, and the poorhouse, with interest? They assisted me to beguile away some weary hours in speculation. I wondered when they would begin to be tired of each other; when they would find out their mistake, and loathe the paltriness of their surroundings; when the female infant would discover that her dimples might have been better invested, and that calico gowns were unworthy of her charms? I *do* blush to confess that I scraped an acquaintance with the male infant, with a view to drawing forth his views on matrimony and life as a whole. He had been wont to smoke inferior cigarettes in the days of his gay and untrammelled bachelorhood, but had given up the luxurious habit on engaging himself to the object of his affections. He remarked to me that 'a man ought to have principle enough to deny himself things when he had something to deny himself for, and when a man had a wife and a home he *had* something to deny himself for, and if he was a man he'd do it.' He was very ingenuous, and very fond of enlarging confidingly upon domestic topics and virtues and joys, and being encouraged could be relied upon so to enlarge — always innocently and with inoffensive, youthful enthusiasm — until deftly headed off by the soulless worldling. I gave him cigars, and an order of attention, which seemed to please him. He remarked to his fellow-clerks that I was a man who had 'principles' and 'feelings,' consequently I felt grateful to him. He had great confidence in 'principles.' The bold thought had presented itself to him that if we were more governed by 'principles,' as a nation, we should thrive better, and there would be less difficulty in steering the ship of state; but he advanced the opinion hesitantly, as fearing injustice to his country in the suggestion."

"You are making him very attractive," said Mrs. Merriam. "There is something touching about it all."

"He was attractive to me," returned Laurence, "and he was touching at times. He was crude, and by no means brilliant, but there wasn't an evil spot in him; and his beliefs were of a strength and magnitude to bring a blush to the cheek of the most hardened. He recalled the dreams of youth, and even in his most unintelligently ardent moments appealed to one. Taking all these things into consideration, you will probably see that it was likely to be something of a blow to him to find himself suddenly thrown out upon the world without any resource whatever."

"Ah!" exclaimed Mrs. Sylvestre, earnestly. "Surely you are not going to tell us"—

"That he has lost his office," said Laurence. "Yes. Thrown out. Reason — place wanted for some one else. I shouldn't call it a good reason myself. I find others who would not call it a good reason; but what are you going to do?"

"What did he do?" asked Agnes.

"He came into my room one day," answered Laurence, "'just as I was leaving it. He was white, and his lips trembled in a boyish way that struck me at the moment as being rather awful. He looked as if he had been knocked down. He said to me, 'Mr. Arbuthnot, I've lost my place,' and then, after staring at me a few seconds, he added, 'Mr. Arbuthnot, what would you do?'"

"It is very cruel," said Agnes. "It is very hard."

"It is as cruel as Death!" said Arbuthnot. "It is as hard as Life! That such a thing is possible — that the bread and home and hopes of any honest, human creature should be used as the small change of power above him, and trafficked with to sustain that power and fix it in its place to make the most of itself and its greed, is the burning shame and burden which is slung around our necks, and will keep us from standing with heads erect until we are lightened of it."

He discovered that he was in earnest, and recklessly allowed himself to continue in earnest until he had said his say. He knew the self-indulgence was indiscreet, and felt the indiscretion all the more when he ended and found himself confronted by Mrs. Sylvestre's eyes. They were fixed upon him, and wore an expression he had never had the pleasure of seeing in them before. It was an expression full of charming emotion, and the color was coming and going in her cheek.

"Go on," she said, rather tremulously, "if you please."

"I did not go on," he replied. "I regret to say I couldn't. I was unable to tell him what I should do."

"But you tried to comfort him?" said Agnes. "I am sure you did what you could."

"It was very little," said Laurence. "I let him talk, and led him on a little to — well, to talking about his wife. It seemed the only thing at the moment. I found it possible to recall to his mind one or two things he had told me of her, — probably doing it in a most inefficient manner, — but he appeared to appreciate the effort. The idea presented itself to me that it would be well to brace him up and give him a less deathly look before he went home to her, as she was not very well, and a childish creature at best. I probably encouraged him unduly; but I had an absurd sense of being somehow responsible for the preservation of the two rooms and the peace of mind of the female infant, and the truth is, I have felt it ever since, and so has she."

He was extremely conscious of Mrs. Sylvestre's soft and earnest eyes.

"That was the reason she called to see me to-night, and, finding I had just left the house, followed me. Tom is ill, — his name is Tom Bosworth. It is nearly two months since he lost his place, and he has walked himself to a shadow in making efforts to gain another. He has written letters and presented letters; he has stood outside doors until he was faint with hunger; he has interviewed members of Congress, senators, heads of departments, officials great and small. He has hoped and longed and waited, and taken buffetings meekly. He is not a strong fellow, and it has broken him up. He has had several chills, and is thin and nervous and excitable. Kitty — his wife's name is Kitty — is pale and thin too. „She has lost her dimples, and her eyes look like a sad little owl's, and always have tears in them, which she manages to keep from falling so long as Tom is within sight. To-night she wanted to ask me if I knew any ladies who would give her sewing. She thinks she might sew until Tom gets a place again."

"I will give her sewing," exclaimed Agnes. "I can do something for them if they will let me. Oh, I am very glad that I can!"

"I felt sure you would be," said Arbuthnot. "I thought of you at once, and wished you could see her as I saw her."

She answered him a little hurriedly, and he wondered why her voice faltered.

"I will see her to-morrow," she said, "if you will give me the address."

"I have naturally wondered if it was possible that anything could be done for the husband," he said. "If you could use your influence in any way, — you see how inevitably we come to that; it always becomes a question of influence; our very charities are of the nature of schemes; it is in the air we breathe."

"I will do what I can," she replied. "I will do anything — anything you think would be best."

Mrs. Merriam checked herself on the very verge of looking up, but though by an effort she confined herself to apparently giving all her attention to her knitting-needles for a few moments, she lost the effect of neither words nor voice. "No," she made mental comment, "it was *not* malaria."

Arbuthnot had never passed such an evening in the house as this one proved to be, and he had spent many agreeable evenings there. To-night there was a difference. Some barrier had melted or suddenly broken down. Mrs. Sylvestre was more beautiful than he had ever seen her. It thrilled his very soul to hear her speak to him and to look at her. While still entirely ignorant of the cause of her displeasure against him he knew that it was removed; that in some mysterious way she had recognized the injustice of it, and was impelled by a sweet, generous penitence to endeavor to make atonement. There was something almost like the humility of appeal in her voice and eyes. She did not leave him to Mrs. Merriam, but talked to him herself. When he went away, after he had left her at the parlor door, she lingered a moment upon the threshold, then crossed it, and followed him into the hall. They had been speaking of the Bosworths, and he fancied she was going to ask some last question. But she did not; she simply paused a short distance from where he stood and looked at him. He had often observed it in her, that she possessed the inestimable gift of being able to stand still and remain silent with perfect grace, in such a manner that speech and movement seemed unnecessary; but he felt that she had something to say now and scarcely knew how best to say it, and it occurred to him that he might, perhaps, help her.

"You are very much better than you were when I came in," he said.

She put out her hand with a gentle, almost grateful gesture.

"Yes, I am much better," she said. "I was not well — or happy. I thought that I had met with a misfortune; but it was a mistake."

"I am glad it was a mistake," he answered. "I hope such things will always prove so."

And, a quick flush rising to his face, he bent and touched with his lips the slim, white fingers lying upon his palm.

The flush had not died away when he found himself in the street; he felt its glow with a sense of anger and impatience.

"I might have known better than to do such a thing," he said. "I *did* know better. I am a fool yet, it seems — a fool!"

But, notwithstanding this, the evening was a landmark. From that time forward Mrs. Merriam looked upon the intimacy with renewed interest. She found Agnes very attractive in the new attitude she assumed toward their acquaintance. She indulged no longer in her old habit of depreciating him delicately when she spoke of him, which was rarely; her tone suggested to her relative that she was desirous of atoning to herself for her past coldness and injustice. There was a delicious hint of this in her manner toward him, quiet as it was; once or twice Mrs. Merriam had seen her defer to him, and display a disposition to adapt herself to his opinions, which caused a smile to flicker across her discreet countenance. Their mutual interest in their *protégés* was a tie between them, and developed a degree of intimacy which had never before existed. The day after hearing their story Agnes had paid the young people a visit. The two rooms in the third story of a boarding-house presented their modest household goods to her very touchingly. The very bridal newness of the cheap furniture struck her as being pathetic, and the unsophisticated adornments in the form of chromos and bright tidies — the last, Kitty's own handiwork — expressed to her mind their innocent sentiment. Kitty looked new herself, as she sat sewing, in a little rocking-chair, drawn near to the sofa on which Tom lay, flushed and bright-eyed after his chill; but there were premonitory signs of wear on her pretty, childish face. She rose, evidently terribly nervous and very much frightened at the prospect of receiving her visitor, when Mrs. Sylvestre entered, and, though reassured somewhat by the mention of Arbuthnot's name, glanced timorously at Tom in appeal for assistance from him. Tom gave it. His ingenuous mind knew very little fear. He tried to stagger to his feet, smiling, but was so dizzy that he made an ignominious failure, and sat down again at Agnes' earnest request.

"Thank you," he said. "I will, if you don't mind. It's one of my bad days, and the fever makes my head go round. Don't look so down-hearted, Kitty. Mrs. Sylvestre knows chills don't count for much. You see," he said to Agnes, with an effort at buoyancy of manner, "they knock a man over a little, and it frightens her."

Agnes took a seat beside the little rocking-chair, and there was something in the very gentleness of her movements which somewhat calmed Kitty's tremor.

"It is very natural that she should feel anxious, even when there is only slight cause," Mrs. Sylvestre said, in her low, sweet voice. "Of course, the cause is slight in your case. It is only necessary that you should be a little careful."

"That's all," responded Tom. "A man with a wife and home can't be too careful. He's got others to think of besides himself."

But, notwithstanding his cheerfulness and his bright eyes, he was plainly weaker than he realized, and was rather glad to lie down again, though he did it apologetically.

"Mr. Arbuthnot came in this morning and told us you were coming," he said. "You know him pretty well, I suppose."

"I see him rather frequently," answered Agnes; "but perhaps I do not know him very well."

"Ah!" said Tom. "You've got to know him very well to find out what sort of fellow he is; you've got to know him as *I* know him — as *we* know him. Eh! Kitty?"

"Yes," responded Kitty, a little startled by finding herself referred to; "only you know him best, Tom. You see, you're a man"—

"Yes," said Tom, with innocent complacency, "of course it's easier for men to understand each other. You see" — to Agnes, though with a fond glance at Kitty — "Kitty was a little afraid of him. She's shy, and hasn't seen much of the world, and he's such a swell, in a quiet way, and when she used to come to the office for me, and caught a glimpse of him, she thought he was always making fun of everything."

"I thought he *looked* as if he was," put in Kitty. "And his voice sounded that way when he spoke to you, Tom. I even used to think, sometimes, that he was laughing a little at *you* — and I didn't like it."

"Bless you!" responded Tom, "he wasn't thinking of such a thing. He's got too much principle to make friends with a fellow, and then laugh at him. What I've always liked in him was his principle."

"I think there are a great many things to like in him," said Mrs. Silvestre.

"There's everything to like in him," said Tom, "though, you see, I didn't find that out at first. The truth is, I thought he was rather too much of a swell for his means. I've told him so since we've been more intimate, and he said that I was not mistaken; that he was too much of a swell for his means, but that was the fault of his means, and the government ought to attend to it as a sacred duty. You see the trouble is he hasn't a family. And what a fellow he would be to take care of a woman! I told him that, too, once, and he threw back his head and laughed; but he didn't laugh long. It seemed to me that it set him off thinking, he was so still after it."

"He'd be very good to his wife," said Kitty, timidly. "He's very kind to me."

"Yes," Tom went on, rejoicing in himself, "he sees things that men don't see, generally. Think of his noticing that you weren't wrapped up enough that cold day we met him, and going into his place to get a shawl from his landlady, and making me put it on !"

"And don't you remember," said Kitty, "the day he made me so ashamed, because he said my basket was too heavy, and would carry it all the way home for me?"

Tom laughed triumphantly.

"He would have carried a stove-pipe just the same way," he said, "and have looked just as cool about it. You'd no need to be ashamed; *he* wasn't. And it's not only that: see how he asks me about you, and cheers me up, and helps me along by talking to me about you when I'm knocked over, and says that you mustn't be troubled, and I must bear up, because I've got you to take care of, and that when two people are as fond of each other as we are, they've got something to hold on to that will help them to let the world go by and endure anything that don't part them."

"He said that to me, too, Tom," said Kitty, the ready tears starting to her eyes. "He said it last night when I met him on the street and couldn't help crying because you were ill. He said I must bear up for you — and he was so nice that I forgot to be afraid of him at all. When I began to cry it frightened me, because I thought he wouldn't like it, and that made it so much worse that I couldn't stop, and he just put my hand on his arm and took me into Lafayette Park, where there was a seat in a dark corner under the trees. And he made me sit down and said, ' Don't be afraid to cry. It will do you good, and you had better do it before me than before Tom. Cry as much as you like. I will walk away a few steps until you are better.' And he did, and I cried until I was quiet, and then he came back to me and told me about Mrs. Sylvestre."

"He's got feelings ," said Tom, a trifle brokenly, —"he's got feelings and — and principles. It makes a man think better of the world, even when he's discouraged, and it's dealt hard with him."

Mrs. Sylvestre looked out of the nearest window; there was a very feminine tremor in her throat, and something seemed to be melting before her eyes; she was full of the pain of regret and repentance;

there rose in her mind a picture of herself as she had sat before the fire in her silent room; she could not endure the memory of her own bitter contempt and scorn; she wished she might do something to make up for that half hour; she wished that it were possible that she might drive down to the Treasury and present herself at a certain door, and appeal for pardon with downcast eyes and broken voice. She was glad to remember the light touch upon her hand, even though it had been so very light, and he had left her after it so hurriedly.

"I am glad he spoke to you of me," she said. "I — I am grateful to him. I think I can help you. I hope you will let me. I know a great many people, and I might ask for their influence. I will do anything — anything Mr. Arbuthnot thinks best."

Tom gave her a warmly grateful glance, his susceptible heart greatly moved by the sweetness and tremor of her voice. She was just the woman, it seemed to him, to be the friend of such a man as his hero; only a woman as beautiful, as sympathetic, and having that delicate, undefinable air of belonging to the great enchanted world, in which he confidingly believed Arbuthnot figured with unrivalled effect, could be worthy of him. It was characteristic of his simple nature that he should admire immensely his friend's social popularity and acquirements, and dwell upon their unbounded splendor with affectionate reverence.

"He's a society fellow," he had said to Kitty, in his first description of him. "A regular society fellow! Always dressed just so, you know — sort of quiet style, but exactly up to the mark. He knows everybody and gets invited everywhere, though he makes believe he only gets taken in because he can dance and wait in the supper-room. He's out somewhere every night, bless you, and spends half his salary on kid gloves and flowers. He says people ought to supply them to fellows like him, as they supply gloves and hat-bands at English funerals. He doesn't save anything; you know, he can't, and he knows it's a mistake, but you see when a fellow is what he is, it's not easy to break off with everything. These society people want such fellows, and they *will* have them."

It had been this liberal description of his exalted position and elegant habits which had caused Kitty to stand greatly in awe of him, at the outset, and to feel that her bearing would never stand the test of criticism by so proficient an expert, and she had trembled before him accordingly and felt herself unworthy of his condescending notice, until having, on one or two occasions, seen something in his manner which did not exactly coincide with her conception of him as a luxurious and haughty worldling, she had gained a little courage. She had been greatly alarmed at the sight of Mrs. Sylvestre, feeling vaguely that she, also, was a part of these mysterious splendors; but after she heard the soft break in the tone in which she said, with such gentle simplicity, "I will do anything — anything — Mr. Arbuthnot thinks best," she felt timorous no more, and allowed herself to be led into telling her little story, with a girlish pathos which would have melted Agnes Sylvestre's heart, if it had not been melted already. It might, perhaps, better have been called Tom's story than her own, as it was all about Tom, — Tom's struggles, Tom's disappointments, Tom's hopes, which all seemed prostrated; the little house Tom had been thinking of buying and making nice for her; the member of Congress who had snubbed Tom; the senator who had been rough with him; the cold he had taken; the chills and fevers which had resulted; the pain in his side. "We have used all our money," she ended, with a touching little catch of her breath, —"if it had not been for Mr. Arbuthnot — Mr. Arbuthnot"—

"Yes," said Tom, wofully, "he'll have to go without a pair or so of gloves this month and smoke fewer cigars; and I couldn't have believed that there was a man living I could have borne to take money from, but, somehow, he made it seem almost as if he owed it to me."

When Mrs. Sylvestre went away she left hope and comfort behind her. Kitty followed her into the passage with new light in her eyes.

"If I have the sewing," she said, clasping her hands, "it will be *such* a load off Tom's mind to know that we have a little money, that he will get better. And he knows I like sewing; so, perhaps, he will not mind it so much. I am so thankful to you! If Tom will only get well," she exclaimed, in a broken whisper, —"if Tom will only get well!" And, suddenly, in response to some look on Agnes' face, and a quick, caressing gesture, she leaned forward, and was folded in her arms.

It is very natural to most women to resort to the simple feminine device of tears, but it was not often Mrs. Sylvestre so indulged herself, and there were tears in her eyes and in her voice, too, as she held the gentle, childish creature to her breast. She had felt a great deal during the last twenty-four hours, and the momentary display of emotion was a relief to her. "He will get better," she said, with almost maternal tenderness, "and you must help him by taking care of yourself, and giving him no cause for anxiety. You must let me help to take care of you. We will do all we can," — and there was something akin to fresh relief to her in the mere use of the little word "we."

Chapter 30

Mrs. Merriam saw faint traces of tears in Mrs. Sylvestre's eyes when she returned from her call on the Bosworths, and speculated, with some wonder, as to what her exact mental condition was, but asked very few questions, feeling that, upon the whole, she would prefer to hear the version of the story given to Mr. Arbuthnot when he called. He did so the following evening, and, having seen the Bosworths in the interval, had comments of his own to make.

"It was very good in you to call so soon," he said to Agnes.

"I wished very much to call," she replied. "I could not have waited longer."

"You left a transcendent impression," said Arbuthnot. "Tom was very enthusiastic, and Kitty feels that all their troubles are things of the past."

"They talked to me a great deal of you," said Agnes. "I felt after hearing them that I had not known you very well — and wished that I had known you better."

She said it with a sweet gravity which he found strangely disturbing; but his reply did not commit him to any special feeling.

"They will prove fatal to me, I see," he said. "Don't allow them to prejudice you against me in that manner."

"I wish," she said, "that my friends might be prejudiced against me in the same way."

Then he revealed a touch of earnestness in spite of himself. They had both been standing upon the hearth, and he took a step toward her.

"For pity's sake," he said, "don't overrate me! Women are always too generous. Don't you see, you will find me out, and then it will be worse for me than before."

She stood in one of her perfect, motionless attitudes, and looked down at the rug.

"I wish to find you out," she said, slowly. "I have done you injustice."

And then she turned away and walked across the room to a table where there were some books, and when she returned she brought one of them with her and began to speak of it. He always felt afterward that the memory of this "injustice," as she called it, was constantly before her, and he would have been more than human if he had not frequently wondered what it was. He could not help feeling that it had taken a definite form, and that she had been betrayed into it on the evening he had first spoken to her of the Bosworths, and that somehow his story had saved him in her eyes. But he naturally forbore to ask questions or even touch upon the subject, and thanked the gods for the good which befell him as a result of the evil he had escaped. And yet, as the time passed by, and he went oftener to the house, and found keener pleasure in each visit, he had his seasons of fearing that it was not all going to be gain for him; when he faced the truth, indeed, he knew that it was not all gain, and yet he was not stoic enough to turn his back and fly.

"It will cost!" he said to himself. "It will cost! But" —

And then he would set his lips together and be silent for an hour or so, and those of his acquaintance who demanded constant vivacity from him began to wonder among themselves if he was quite the fellow he had been. If the friendship was pleasant during the season, it was pleasanter when the gayeties ceased and the spring set in, with warmer air and sunshine, and leaves and blossoms in the parks. There was a softness in the atmosphere not conducive! to sternness of purpose and self-denial. As he walked to and from his office he found his thoughts wandering in paths he felt were dangerous, and once, unexpectedly meeting Mrs. Sylvestre when so indulging himself, he started and gained such sudden color that she flushed also, and, having stopped to speak to him, forgot what she had intended to say, and was a little angry, both with herself and him, when a confusing pause followed their greeting.

Their interest in the Bosworths was a tie between them which gave them much in common. Agnes went to see them often, and took charge of Kitty, watching over and caring for her in a tender, half-maternal fashion. Arbuthnot took private pleasure in contemplating. He liked to hear Kitty talk about her, and, indeed, had on more than one occasion led her with some dexterity into doing so. It was through Kitty, at last, that his mystery was solved for him.

This happened in the spring. There had been several warm days, one so unusually warm, at last, that in the evening Mrs. Sylvestre accepted his invitation to spend an hour or so on the river with him. On their way there they stopped to leave a basket of fruit for Tom, whose condition was far from being what they had hoped for, and while making their call Kitty made a remark which caused Arbuthnot's pulse to accelerate its pace somewhat.

"When you saw me crying on the street that night," she began, addressing Agnes. Arbuthnot turned upon her quickly.

"What night?" he asked.

"The night you took me into Lafayette Square," said Kitty; "Mrs. Sylvestre saw me, though I did not know it until yesterday. She was going to call on Mrs. Amory, and"—

Arbuthnot looked at Agnes; he could not have for borne, whatever the look had cost him. The color came into her cheek and died out.

"Did you?" he demanded.

"Yes," she answered, and rose and walked to the window, and stood there perfectly still.

Arbuthnot did not hear the remainder of Kitty's remarks. He replied to them blindly, and as soon as possible left his chair and went to the window himself.

"If you are ready, perhaps we had better go," he said.

They went out of the room and down the stairs in silence. He wanted to give himself time to collect his thoughts, and get the upper hand of a frantic feeling of passionate anger which had taken possession of him. If he had spoken he might have said something savage, which he would have repented afterward in sackcloth and ashes. His sense of the injustice he had suffered, however momentary, at the hands of this woman whose opinion he cared for, was natural, masculine, and fierce. He saw everything in a flash, and for a moment or so forgot all else in his bitterness of spirit. But his usual coolness came to the rescue when this moment was past, and he began to treat himself scornfully, as was his custom. There was no reason why she should not think ill of him, circumstances evidently having been against him, he said to himself; she knew nothing specially good of him; she had all grounds for regarding him as a creature with neither soul nor purpose nor particularly fixed principles, and with no other object in life than the gratification of his fancies; why should she believe in him against a rather black array in the form of facts? It was not agreeable, but why blame her? He would not blame her or indulge in any such personal folly. Then he glanced at her and saw that the color had not come back to her face. When he roused himself to utter a civil, commonplace remark or so, there was the sound of fatigue in her voice when she answered him, and it was very low. She did not seem inclined to talk, and he had the consideration to leave her to herself as much as possible until they reached the boat-house. He arranged her cushions and wraps in the boat with care and dexterity, and, when he took the oars, felt that he had himself pretty well in hand. The river was very quiet, and the last glow of sunset red was slowly changing to twilight purple on the water; a sickle-shaped moon hung in the sky, and somewhere farther up the shore a night bird was uttering brief, plaintive cries. Agnes sat at the end of the boat, with her face a little turned away, as if she were listening to the sound. Arbuthnot wondered if she was, and thought again that she looked tired and a little pathetic. If he had known all her thoughts he would have felt the pathos in her eyes a thousand times more keenly.

She had a white hyacinth in her hand, whose odor seemed to reach him more powerfully at each stroke of the oars, and at last she turned and spoke, looking down at the flower.

"The saddest things that are left to one of a bitter experience," she said, in a low voice, "are the knowledge and distrust that come of it."

"They are very natural results," he replied, briefly.

"Oh, they are very hard!" she exclaimed. "They are very hard. They leave a stain on all one's life, and — and it can never be wiped away.

Sometimes I think it is impossible to be generous — to be kind — to trust at all"—

Her voice broke; she put her hands up before her face, and he saw her tremble.

"One may have been innocent," she said, "and have believed — and thought no evil — but after one has been so stained"—

He stopped rowing.

"There is no stain," he said. "Don't call it one."

"It must be one," she said, "when one sees evil, and is suspicious, and on the alert to discover wrong. But it brings suffering, as if it were a punishment. I have suffered."

He paused a second and answered, looking backward over his shoulder.

"So did I — for a moment," he said. "But it is over now. Don't think of me."

"I must think of you," she said. "How could I help it?"

She turned a little more toward him and leaned forward, the most exquisite appeal in her delicate face, the most exquisite pathos in her unsteady voice.

"If I ask you to forgive me," she said, "you will only say that I was forgiven before I asked. I know that. I wish I could say something else. I wish — I wish I knew what to do."

He looked up the river and down, and then suddenly at her. The set, miserable expression of his face startled her, and caused her to make an involuntary movement.

"Don't do anything — don't say anything!" he said. "I can bear it better."

And he bent himself to his oars and rowed furiously.

She drew back, and turned her face aside. Abrupt as the words were, there was no rebuff in them; but there was something else which silenced her effectually. She was glad of the faint light, and her heart quickened, which last demonstration did not please her. She had been calm too long to enjoy any new feeling of excitement; she had liked the calmness, and had desired beyond all things that it should remain undisturbed.

"There is one prayer I pray every morning," she had once said to

366

Bertha, earnestly. "It is that the day may bring nothing to change the tone of my life."

She had felt a little ripple in the current ever since the eventful night, and had regretted it sorely, and now, just for the moment, it was something stronger. So she was very still as she sat with averted face, and the hour spent upon the water was a singularly silent one.

When they returned home they found Colonel Tredennis with Mrs. Merriam, but just on the point of leaving her.

"I am going to see Amory," he said. "I have heard some news he will consider bad. The Westoria affair has been laid aside, and will not be acted upon this session, if at all. It is said that Blundel heard something he did not like, and interfered."

"And you think Mr. Amory will be very much disappointed?" said Agnes.

"I am afraid so," answered Tredennis.

"And yet," said Agnes, "it isn't easy to see why it should be of so much importance to him."

"He has become interested in it," said Mrs. Merriam. "That is the expression, isn't it? It is my opinion that it would be better for him if he were less so. I have seen that kind of thing before. It is like being bitten by a tarantula."

She was not favorably inclined toward Richard. His sparkling moods did not exhilarate her, and she had her private theories concerning his character. Tredennis she was very fond of; few of his moods escaped her bright eyes; few of the changes in him were lost upon her. When he went away this evening she spoke of him to Agnes and Arbuthnot.

"If that splendid fellow does not improve," she said, ' he will begin to grow old in his prime. He is lean and gaunt; his eyes are dreary; he is beginning to have lines on his forehead and about his mouth. He is enduring something. I should be glad to be told what it is."

"Whatever he endured," said Agnes, "he would not tell people. But I think 'enduring' is a very good word."

"How long have you known him?" Mrs. Merriam asked of Arbuthnot.

"Since the evening after his arrival in Washington on his return from the West," was the reply.

"Was he like this then?" rather sharply.

Arbuthnot reflected.

"I met him at a reception," he said, "and he was not Washingtonian in his manner. My impression was that he would not enjoy our society, and that he would finally despise us; but he looked less fagged then than he does now. Perhaps he begins to long for his daily Pi-ute. There *are* chasms which an effete civilization does not fill."

"You guess more than you choose to tell," was Mrs. Merriam's inward thought. Aloud she said:

"He is the finest human being it has been my pleasure to meet. He is the natural man. If I were a girl again I think I should make a hero of him, and be unhappy for his sake."

"It would be easy to make a hero of him," said Agnes.

"Very!" responded Arbuthnot. "Unavoidable, in fact." And he laid upon the table the bit of hyacinth he had picked up in the boat and brought home with him. "If I carry it away," was his private thought, "I shall fall into the habit of sitting and weakening my mind over it. It is weak enough already." But he knew, at the same time, that Colonel Tredennis had done something toward assisting him to form the resolution. "A trivial masculine vanity," he thought, "not unfrequently strengthens one's position."

In the meantime Tredennis went to Amory. He found him in the room which was, in its every part, so strong a reminder of Bertha. It wore a desolate look, and Amory had evidently been walking up and down it, pushing chairs and footstools aside carelessly, when he found them in his way. He had thrown himself, at last, into Bertha's own special easy-chair, and leaned back in it, with his hands thrown out over its padded arms. He had plainly not slept well the night before, and his dress had a careless and dishevelled look, very marked in its contrast with the customary artistic finish of his attire.

He sprang up when he saw Tredennis, and began to speak at once.

"I say!" he exclaimed, "this is terrible!"

"You have been disappointed," said Tredennis.

"I have been rui" — he checked himself; "disappointed isn't the word," he ended. "The whole thing has been laid aside — *laid aside* — think of it! as if it were a mere nothing; an application for a

368

two-penny half-penny pension! Great God! what do the fellows think they are dealing with?"

"Who do you think is to blame?" said the colonel, stolidly.

"Blundel, by Jove! — Blundel, that fool and clown!" and he flung himself about the room, mumbling his rage and irritation.

"It is not the first time such a thing has happened," said Tredennis, "and it won't be the last. If you continue to interest yourself in such matters you will find that out, as others have done before you. Take my advice, and give it up from this hour."

Amory wheeled round upon him.

"Give it up!" he cried, "I can't give it up, man! It is only laid aside for the time being. Heaven and earth shall be moved next year — Heaven and earth! The thing won't fail — it *can't* fail — a thing like that; a thing I have risked my very soul on!"

He dashed his hand through his tumbled hair and threw himself into the chair again, quite out of breath.

"Ah, confound it!" he exclaimed, "I am too excitable! I am losing my hold on myself."

Tredennis rose from his seat, feeling some movement necessary. He stood and looked down at the floor. As he gazed up at him Amory entered a fretful mental protest against his size and his air of being able to control himself. He was plainly deep in thought even when he spoke, for his eyes did not leave the' floor.

"I suppose," he said, "this is really no business of mine. I wish it was."

"What do you mean?" said Amory.

Tredennis looked up.

"If it were my business I would know more about it," he said, — "I would know what *you* mean, and how deep you have gone into this — this accursed scheme."

The last two words had a sudden ring of intensity in their sound, which affected Amory tremendously. He sprang up again and began to pace the floor.

"Nothing ever promised so well," he said, "and it will turn out all right in the end — it must! It is the delay that drives one wild. It will be all right next season — when Bertha is here."

369

"What has she to do with it?" demanded Tredennis.

"Nothing very much," said Amory, restively; "but she is effective."

"Do you mean that you are going to set her to lobbying?"

"Why should you call it that? I am not going to set her at anything. She has a good effect, that is all. Planefield swears that if she had stayed at home and taken Blundel in hand he would not have failed us."

Tredennis looked at him stupefied. He could get no grasp upon him. He wondered if a heavy mental blow would affect him. He tried it in despair.

"Do you know," he said, slowly, "what people are beginning to say about Planefield?"

"They are always saying something of Planefield. He is the kind of man who is always spoken of."

"Then," said Tredennis, "there is all the more reason why his name should not be connected with that of an innocent woman."

"What woman has been mentioned in connection with him?"

"It has been said more than once that he is in love with — your wife, and that his infatuation is used to advance your interests."

Richard stopped on his walk.

"Then it is a confoundedly stupid business," he said, angrily. "If she hears it she will never speak to him again. Perhaps she has heard it; perhaps that was why she insisted on going away. I thought there was something wrong at the time."

"May I ask," said Tredennis, "how it strikes *you*?"

"Me!" exclaimed Richard. "As the most awkward piece of business in the world, and as likely to do me more harm than anything else could."

He made a graceful, rapid gesture of impatience.

"Everything goes against me!" he said. "She never liked him from the first, and if she has heard this she will never be civil to him again, or to any of the rest of them. And, of course, she is an influence, in a measure; what clever woman is not? And why should she not use her influence in one way as well as another? If she were a clergyman's wife she would work hard enough to gain favors. It is only a trifle that she should make an effort to be agreeable to men who will be pleased by her civility. She would do it if there were nothing to be gained. Where are you going? What is the matter?" for Tredennis had walked to the table and taken his hat.

"I am going into the air," he answered; "I am afraid I cannot be of any use to you to-night. My mind is not very clear just now. I must have time to think."

"You look pale," said Amory, staring at him. "You look ghastly. You have not been up to the mark for months. I have seen that. Washington does not agree with you."

"That is it," was Tredennis' response. "Washington does not agree with me."

And he carried his hat and his pale and haggard countenance out into the night, and left Richard gazing after him, feverish, fretted, thwarted in his desire to pour forth his grievances and defend himself, and also filled with baffled amazement at his sudden departure.

Chapter 31

Mrs. Amory did not receive on New Year's day. The season had well set in before she arrived in Washington. One morning in January Mrs. Sylvestre, sitting alone, reading, caught sight of the little *coupé* as it drew up before the carriage-step, and, laying aside her book, reached the parlor door in time to meet Bertha as she entered it. She took both her hands and drew her toward the fire, still holding them.

"Why did I not know you had returned?" she said. "When did you arrive?"

"Last night," Bertha answered. "You see I come to you early."

It was a cold day and she was muffled in velvet and furs. She sat down, loosened her wrap and let it slip backward, and as its sumptuous fulness left her figure it revealed it slender to fragility, and showed that the outline of her cheek had lost all its roundness. She smiled faintly, meeting Agnes' anxious eyes.

"Don't look at me," she said. "I am not pretty. I have been ill. You heard I was not well in Newport? It was a sort of low fever, and I am not entirely well yet. Malaria, you know, is always troublesome. But you are very well?"

"Yes, I am well," Agnes replied.

"And you begin to like Washington again?"

"I began last winter."

"How did you enjoy the spring? You were here until the end of June."

"It was lovely."

"And now you are here once more, and how pretty everything about you is!" Bertha said, glancing around the room. "And you are ready to be happy all winter until June again. Do you know, you look

372

happy. Not excitably happy, but gently, calmly happy, as if the present were enough for you."

"It is," said Agnes, "I don't think I want any future."

"It would be as well to abolish it if one could," Bertha answered; "but it comes — *it comes*!"

She sat and looked at the fire a few seconds under the soft shadow of her lashes, and then spoke again.

"As for me," she said, "I am going to give dinner-parties to Senator Planefield's friends."

"Bertha!" exclaimed Agnes.

"Yes," said Bertha, nodding gently. "It appears somehow that Richard belongs to Senator Planefield, and, as I belong to Richard, why, you see"—

She ended with a dramatic little gesture, and looked at Agnes once more.

"It took me some time to understand it," she said. "I am not quite sure that I understand it quite thoroughly even now. It is a little puzzling, or, perhaps, I am dull of comprehension. At all events, Richard has talked to me a great deal. It is plainly my duty to be agreeable and hospitable to the people he wishes to please and bring in contact with each other."

"And those people?" asked Agnes.

"They are political men: they are members of committees, members of the House, members of the Senate; and their only claim to existence in our eyes is that they are either in favor of or opposed to a certain bill not indirectly connected with the welfare of the owners of Westoria lands."

"Bertha," said Agnes, quickly, "you are not yourself."

"Thank you," was the response, "that is always satisfactory, but the compliment would be more definite if you told me who I happened to be. But I can tell you that I am that glittering being, the female lobbyist. I used to wonder last winter if I was not on the verge of it; but now I know. I wonder if they all begin as innocently as I did, and find the descent — isn't it a descent? — as easy and natural. I feel queer, but not exactly disreputable. It is merely a matter of being a dutiful wife and smiling upon one set of men instead of another.

Still, I am slightly uncertain as to just how disreputable I am. I was beginning to be quite reconciled to my atmosphere until I saw Colonel Tredennis, and I confess he unsettled my mind and embarrassed me a little in my decision."

"You have seen him already?"

"Accidentally, yes. He did not know I had returned, and came to see Richard. He is quite intimate with Richard now. He entered the parlor and found me there. I do not think he was glad to see me. I left him very soon."

She drew off her glove, and smoothed it out upon her knee, with a thin and fragile little hand upon which the rings hung loosely. Agnes bent forward and involuntarily laid her own hand upon it.

"Dear," she said.

Bertha hurriedly lifted her eyes.

"What I wish to say," she said, "was that the week after next we give a little dinner to Senator Blundel, and I wanted to be sure I might count on you. If you are there — and Colonel Tredennis — you will give it an unprofessional aspect, which is what we want. But perhaps you will refuse to come?"

"Bertha," said Mrs. Sylvestre, "I will be with you at any time — at all times — you wish for or need me."

"Yes," said Bertha, reflecting upon her a moment, "I think you would."

She got up and kissed her lightly and without effusion, and then Agnes rose, too, and they stood together.

"You were always good," Bertha said. "I think life has made you better instead of worse. It is not so always. Things are so different — everything seems to depend upon circumstances. What is good in me would be far enough from your standards to be called wickedness."

She paused abruptly, and Agnes felt that she did so to place a check upon herself; she had seen her do it before. When she spoke again it was in an entirely different tone, and the remaining half-hour of her visit was spent in the discussion of every-day subjects. Agnes listened, and replied to her with a sense of actual anguish. She could have borne better to have seen her less self-controlled; or she fancied so, at least. The summer had made an alteration in her, which it was almost impossible to describe. Every moment revealed some new, sad change in her, and yet she sat and talked commonplaces, and was bright, and witty, and epigrammatic until the last.

"When we get our bill through," she said, with a little smile, just before her departure, "I am to go abroad for a year, — for two, for three, if I wish. I think that is the bribe which has been offered me. One must always be bribed, you know."

As she stood at the window watching the carriage drive away, Agnes was conscious of a depression which was very hard to bear. The brightness of her own atmosphere seemed to have become heavy, — the sun hid itself behind the drifting, wintry clouds, — she glanced around her room with a sense of dreariness. Something carried her back to the memories which were the one burden of her present life.

"Such grief cannot enter a room and not leave its shadow behind it," she said. And she put her hand against the window-side, and leaned her brow upon it sadly. It was curious, she thought, the moment after, that the mere sight of a familiar figure should bring such a sense of comfort with it as did the sight of the one she saw approaching. It was that of Laurence Arbuthnot, who came with a business communication for Mrs. Merriam, having been enabled, by chance, to leave his work for an hour. He held a roll of music in one hand and a bunch of violets in the other, and when he entered the room was accompanied by the fresh fragrance of the latter offering.

Agnes made a swift involuntary movement toward him.

"Ah!" she said, "I could scarcely believe that it was you."

He detected the emotion in her manner and tone at once.

"Something has disturbed you," he said. "What is it?"

"I have seen Bertha," she answered, and the words had a sound of appeal in them, which she herself no more realized or understood than she comprehended the impulse which impelled her to speak.

"She has been here! She looks so ill — so worn. Everything is so sad! I"—

She stopped and stood looking at him.

"Must I go away?" he said, quietly. "Perhaps you would prefer to be alone. I understand what you mean, I think."

"Oh, no!" she said, impulsively, putting out her hand. "Don't go. I am unhappy. It was — it was a relief to see you."

And when she sank on the sofa, he took a seat near her and laid the violets on her lap, and there was a faint flush on his face.

The little dinner, which was the first occasion of Senator Blundel's introduction to the Amory establishment, was a decided success.

"We will make it a success," Bertha had said. "It *must* be one." And there was a ring in her voice which was a great relief to her husband.

"It will be one," he said. "There is no fear of *your* failing when you begin in this way." And his spirits rose to such an extent that he became genial and fascinating once more, and almost forgot his late trials and uncertainties. He had always felt great confidence in Bertha.

On the afternoon of the eventful day Bertha did not go out. She spent the hours between luncheon and the time for dressing with her children. Once, as he passed the open door of the nursery, Richard saw her sitting upon the carpet, building a house of cards, while Jack, and Janey, and Meg sat about her enchanted. A braid of her hair had become loosened and hung over her shoulder; her cheeks were flushed by the fire; she looked almost like a child herself, with her air of serious absorbed interest in the frail structure growing beneath her hands.

"Won't that tire you?" Richard asked.

She glanced up with a smile.

"No," she said, "it will rest me."

He heard her singing to them afterward, and later, when she went to her dressing-room, he heard the pretty lullaby die away gradually as she moved through the corridor.

When she appeared again she was dressed for dinner, and came in buttoning her glove, and at the sight of her he uttered an exclamation of pleasure.

"What a perfect dress!" he said. "What is the idea? There must be one."

She paused and turned slowly round so that he might obtain the full effect.

"You should detect it," she replied. "It is meant to convey one."

"It has a kind of dove-like look," he said.

She faced him again.

"That is it," she said, serenely. "In the true artist spirit, I have attired myself with a view to expressing the perfect candor and simplicity of my nature. Should you find it possible to fear or suspect me of ulterior motives — if you were a senator, for instance?"

"Ah, come now!" said Richard, not quite so easily, "that is nonsense! You have no ulterior motives."

She opened her plumy, dove-colored fan and came nearer him.

"There is nothing meretricious about me," she said.

"I am softly clad in dove color; a few clusters of pansies adorn me; I am covered from throat to wrists; I have not a jewel about me. Could the effect be better?"

"No, it could not," he replied, but suddenly he felt a trifle uncomfortable again, and wondered what was hidden behind the inscrutable little gaze she afterwards fixed upon the fire.

But when Blundel appeared, which he did rather early, he felt relieved again. Nothing could have been prettier than her greeting of him, or more perfect in its attainment of the object of setting him at his ease. It must be confessed that he was not entirely at his ease when he entered, his experience not having been of a nature to develop in him any latent love for general society. He had fought too hard a fight to leave him much time to know women well, and his superficial knowledge of them made him a trifle awkward, as it occasionally renders other men astonishingly bold. In a party of men all his gifts displayed themselves"; in the presence of women he was afraid that less substantial fellows had the advantage of him, — men who could not tell half so good a story or make half so exhilarating a joke. As to this special dinner he had not been particularly anxious to count himself among the guests, and was not very certain as to how Planefield had beguiled him into accepting the invitation.

But ten minutes after he had entered the room he began to feel mollified. Outside the night was wet and unpleasant, and not calculated to improve a man's temper; the parlors glowing with fire-light and twinkling wax candles were a vivid and agreeable contrast to the sloppy rawness. The slender, dove-colored figure, with its soft, trailing draperies, assumed more definitely pleasant proportions, and in his vague, inexperienced, middle-aged fashion he felt the effect of it. She had a nice way, this little woman, he decided; no nonsense or airs and graces about her; an easy manner, a gay little laugh. He did not remember exactly afterward what it was she said which first wakened him up, but he found himself laughing and greatly amused, and when he made a witticism he felt he had reason to be proud of, the gay little peal of laughter which broke forth in response had the most amazingly exhilarating effect upon him, and set him upon his feet for the evening. Women seldom got all the flavor of his jokes. He had an idea that some of them were a little afraid of them and of him, too. The genuine mirth in Bertha's unstudied laughter was like wine to him, and was better than the guffaws of a dozen men, because it had a finer and a novel flavor. After the joke and the laugh the ice was melted, and he knew that he was in the humor to distinguish himself.

Planefield discovered this the moment he saw him, and glanced at Richard, who was brilliant with good spirits.

"She's begun well," he said, when he had an opportunity to speak to him. "I never saw him in a better humor. She's pleased him somehow. Women don't touch him usually."

"She will end better," said Richard. "He pleases her."

He did not displease her, at all events. She saw the force and humor of his stalwart jokes, and was impressed by the shrewd, business-like good-nature which betrayed nothing. When he began to enjoy himself she liked the genuineness of his enjoyment all the more because it was a personal matter with him, and he seemed to revel in it.

"He enjoys *himself*," was her mental comment, "really *himself*, not exactly the rest of us, except as we stimulate him, and make him say good things."

Among the chief of her gifts had always been counted the power of stimulating people, and making them say their best things, and she made the most of this power now. She listened with her brightest look, she uttered her little exclamations of pleasure and interest at exactly the right moment, and the gay ring of her spontaneous sounding laugh was perfection. Miss Varien, who was one of her guests, sat and regarded her with untempered admiration.

"Your wife," she said to Amory, in an undertone, "is simply incomparable. It is not necessary to tell you that, of course; but it strikes me with fresh force this evening. She really seems to enjoy things. That air of gay, candid delight is irresistible. It makes her seem to that man like a charming little girl — a harmless, bright, sympathetic little girl. How he likes her!"

When she went in to dinner with him, and he sat by her side, he liked her still more. He had never been in better spirits in his life; he had never said so many things worth remembering; he had never heard such sparkling and vivacious talk as went on round this particular table. It never paused or lagged. There was Amory, all alight and stirred by every conversational ripple which passed him; there was Miss Varien, scintillating and casting off showers of sparks in the prettiest and most careless fashion; there was Laurence Arbuthnot, doing his share without any apparent effort, and appreciating his neighbors to the full; there was Mrs. Sylvestre, her beautiful eyes making speech almost superfluous, and Mrs. Merriam, occasionally casting into the pool some neatly weighted pebble, which sent its circles to the shore; and in the midst of the coruscations Blundel found himself, somehow, doing quite his portion of the illumination. Really these people and their dinner-party pleased him wonderfully well, and he was far from sorry that he had come, and far from sure that he should not come again if he were asked. He was shrewd enough, too, to see how much the success of everything depended upon his own little companion at the head of the table, and, respecting success beyond all things, after the manner of his kind, he liked her all the better for it. There was something about her which, as Miss Varien had said, made him feel that she was like a bright, sympathetic little girl, and engendered a feeling of fatherly patronage which was entirely comfortable. But, though she rather led others to talk than talked herself, he noticed that she said a sharp thing now and then; and he liked that, too, and was greatly amused by it. He liked women to be sharp, if they were not keen enough to interfere with masculine prerogatives. There was only one person in the company he did not find exhilarating, and that was a large, brown-faced fellow, who sat next to Mrs. Merriam, and said less than might have been expected of him, though, when he spoke, his remarks were well enough in their way. Blundel mentioned him afterward to Bertha when they returned to the parlor.

"That colonel, who is he?" he asked her. "I didn't catch his name exactly. Handsome fellow; but he'd be handsomer if" —

"It is the part of wisdom to stop you," said Bertha, "and tell you that he is a sort of cousin of mine, and his perfections are such as I regard with awe. His name is Colonel Tredennis, and you have read of him in the newspapers."

"What!" he exclaimed, turning his sharp little eyes upon Tredennis, — "the Indian man? I'm glad you told me that. I want to talk to him." And, an opportunity being given him, he proceeded to do so with much animation, ruffling his stiff hair up at intervals in his interest, his little eyes twinkling like those of some alert animal.

He left the house late and in the best of humors. He had forgotten for the time being all questions of bills and subsidies. Nothing had occurred to remind him of such subjects. Their very existence seemed a trifle problematical, or, rather, perhaps it seemed desirable that it should be so.

"I feel," he said to Planefield, as he was shrugging himself into his overcoat, "as if I had rather missed it by not coming here before."

"You were asked," answered Planefield.

"So I was," he replied, attacking the top button of the overcoat. "Well, the next time I am asked I suppose I shall come."

Then he gave his attention to the rest of the buttons.

"A man in public life ought to see all sides of his public," he said, having disposed of the last one." Said some good things, didn't they? The little woman isn't without a mind of her own, either. When is it she receives?"

"Thursdays," said Planefield.

"Ah, Thursdays."

And they went out in company. Her guests having all departed, Bertha remained for a few minutes in the parlor. Arbuthnot and

Tredennis went out last, and as the door closed upon them she looked at Richard.

"Well?" she said.

"Well!" exclaimed Richard. "It could not have been better!"

"Couldn't it?" she said, looking down a little meditatively.

"No," he responded, with excellent good cheer, "and you see how simple it was, and — and how unnecessary it is to exaggerate it and call it by unpleasant names. What we want is merely to come in contact with these people, and show them bow perfectly harmless we are, and that when the time comes they may favor us without injury to themselves or any one else. That's it in a nutshell."

"We always say 'us,' don't we?" said Bertha, —"as if we were part-proprietors of the Westoria lands ourselves. It is a little confusing, don't you think so?"

She paused and looked up with one of her sudden smiles.

"Still I don't feel exactly sure that I have been — but no, I am not to call it lobbying, am I? What must I call it? It really ought to have a name."

"Don't call it anything," said Richard, faintly conscious of his dubiousness again.

"Why, what a good idea!" she answered. "What a good way of getting round a difficulty — not to give it a name! It almost obliterates it, doesn't it? It is an actual inspiration. We won't call it anything. There is so much in a name — too much, on the whole, really. But — without giving it a name — I have behaved pretty well and advanced our — your — whose interests?"

"Every body's," he replied, with an effort at lightness. "Mine particularly. I own that my view of the matter is a purely selfish one. There is a career before me, you know, if all goes well."

He detected at once the expression of gentleness which softened her eyes as she watched him.

"You always wanted a career, didn't you?" she said.

"It isn't pleasant," he said, "for a man to know that he is not a success."

"If I can give you your career," she said, "you shall have it, Richard. It is a simpler thing than I thought, after all." And she went upstairs to her room, stopping on the way to spend a few minutes in the nursery.

Chapter 32

The professor sat in his favorite chair by his library fire, an open volume on his knee, and his after-dinner glass of wine, still unfinished, on the table near him. He had dined a couple of hours ago with Mr. Arbuthnot, who had entertained him very agreeably and had not long since left him to present himself upon some social scene.

It was of his departed guest that he was thinking as he pondered, and of certain plans he had on hand for his ultimate welfare, and his thoughts so deeply occupied him that he did not hear the sound of the doorbell, which rang as he sat, nor notice any other sound until the door of the room opened and some one entered. He raised his head and looked around then, uttering a slight ejaculation of surprise.

"Why, Bertha!" he said. "My dear! This is unexpected."

He paused and gave her one of his gently curious looks. She had thrown her cloak off as she came near him, and something in her appearance attracted his attention.

"My dear," he said, slowly, "you look to-night as you did years ago. I am reminded of the time when Philip first came to us. I wonder why?"

There was a low seat near his side, and she came and took it.

"It is the dress," she said. "I was looking over some things I had laid aside, and found it. I put it on for old acquaintance' sake. I have never worn it since then. Perhaps I hoped it would make me feel like a girl again."

Her tone was very quiet, her whole manner was quiet; the dress was simplicity itself. A little lace kerchief was knotted about her throat.

"That is a very feminine idea," remarked the professor, seeming to give it careful attention. "Peculiarly feminine, I should say. And — does it, my dear?"

"Not quite," she answered. "A little. When I first put it on and stood before the glass I forgot a good many things for a few moments, and then, suddenly, I heard the children's voices in the nursery, and Richard came in, and Bertha Herrick was gone. You know I was Bertha Herrick when I wore this — Bertha Herrick, thinking of her first party."

"Yes, my dear," he responded, "I — I remember."

There were a few moments of silence, in which he looked abstractedly thoughtful, but presently he bestirred himself.

"By the by," he said, "that reminds me. Didn't I understand that there was a great party somewhere to-night? Mr. Arbuthnot left me to go to it, I think. I thought there was a reason for my surprise at seeing you. That was it. Surely you should have been at the great party instead of here."

"Well," she replied, "I suppose I should, but for some curious accident or other — I don't know what the accident is or how it happened — I should have had an invitation — of course if it had chanced to reach me; but something has occurred to prevent it doing so, I suppose. Such things happen, you know. To all intents and purposes I have not been invited, so I could not go. And I am very glad. I would rather be here."

"I would rather have you here," he returned, "if such seclusion pleases you. But I can hardly imagine, my dear, how the party" —

She put her hand on his caressingly.

"It cannot be an entire success," she said. "It won't, in my absence; but misfortunes befall even the magnificent and prosperous, and the party must console itself. I like to be here — I like very much to be here."

He glanced at her gray dress again.

"Bertha Herrick would have preferred the party," he remarked.

"Bertha Amory is wiser," she said. "We will be quiet together — and happy."

They were very quiet. The thought occurred to the professor several times during the evening. She kept her seat near him, and talked to

384

him, speaking, he noticed, principally of her children and of the past; the time she had spent at home before her marriage seemed to be present in her mind.

"I wonder," she said once, thoughtfully, "what sort of girl I was? I can only remember that I was such a happy girl! Do *you* remember that I was a specially self-indulgent or frivolous one? But I am afraid you would not tell me, if you did."

"My dear," he said, in response, "you were a natural, simple, joyous creature, and a great pleasure to us."

She gave his hand a little pressure.

"I can remember that you were always good to me," she said. "I used to think you were a little curious about me, and wondered what I would do in the future. Now it is my turn to wonder if I am at all what you thought I would be?"

He did not reply at once, and then spoke slowly.

"There seemed so many possibilities," he said. "Yes; I thought it possible that you might be — what you are."

It was as he said this that there returned to his mind the thought which had occupied it before her entrance. He had been thinking then of something he wished to tell her, before she heard it from other quarters, and which he felt he could tell her at no more fitting time than when they were alone. It was something relating to Laurence Arbuthnot, and, curiously enough, she paved the way for it by mentioning him herself.

"Did you say Laurence was here to-night?" she asked.

"Yes," he replied, "he was so good as to dine with me."

"He would say that you were so good as to invite him," she said. "He is very fond of coming here."

"I should miss him very much," he returned, "if he should go away."

She looked up quickly, attracted by his manner.

"But there is no likelihood of his going away," she said.

"I think," he answered, "that there maybe, and I wished to speak to you about it."

He refrained from looking at her; he even delicately withdrew his hand, so that if hers should lose its steadiness he might be unconscious of it.

"Go away!" she exclaimed, — "from Washington? Laurence! Why should you think so? I cannot imagine such a thing."

"He does not imagine it himself yet," he replied, "I am going to suggest it to him."

Her hand was still upon his knee, and he felt her start.

"You are!" she said; "why and how? Do you think he will go? I do not believe he will."

"I am not sure that he will," he answered, "but I hope so; and what I mean is that I think it may be possible to send him abroad."

She withdrew her hand from his knee.

"He won't go," she said; "I am sure of it."

He went on to explain himself, still not looking at her.

"He is wasting his abilities," he said; "he is wasting his youth; the position he is in is absurdly insignificant; it occurred to me that if I used, with right effect, the little influence I possess, there might finally be obtained for him some position abroad, which would be at least something better, and might possibly open a way for him in the future. I spoke to the Secretary of State about it, and he was very kind, and appeared interested. It seems very possible, even probable, that my hopes will be realized."

For a few seconds she sat still; then she said, abstractedly:

"It would be very strange to be obliged to live our lives without Laurence; they would not be the same lives at all. Still, I suppose it would be best for him; but it would be hard to live without Laurence. I don't like to think of it."

In spite of his intention not to do so, he found himself turning to look at her. There had been surprise in her voice, and now there was sadness, but there was no agitation, no uncontrollable emotion.

"Can it be," he thought, "that she is getting over it? What does it mean?"

She turned and met his eyes.

"But, whether it is for the best or not," she said, "I don't believe he will go."

"My dear," he said, "you speak as if there was a reason."

"I think there is a reason," she answered, "and it is a strong one."

"What is it?" he asked.

"There is some one he is beginning to be fond of," she replied; "*that* is the reason."

He kept his eyes fixed upon her.

"Some one he is *beginning* to be fond of?" he repeated.

"I don't know how it will end," she said. "I am sometimes afraid it can only end sadly, but there is some one he would find it hard to leave, I am sure."

The professor gradually rose in his chair until he was sitting upright."

"I wish," he said, "that you would tell me who it is."

"I do not think he would mind your knowing," she answered. "It seems strange you have not seen. It is Agnes Sylvestre."

The professor sank back in his chair, and looked at the bed of coals in the grate.

"Agnes *Sylvestre*!" he exclaimed; "*Agnes* Sylvestre!"

"Yes," she said; "and in one sense it is very hard on him that it should be Agnes Sylvestre. After all these years, when he has steadily kept himself free from all love affairs, and been so sure that nothing could tempt him, it cannot be easy for him to know that he loves some one who has everything he has not — all the things he feels he never will have. He is very proud and very unrelenting in his statement of his own circumstances, and he won't try to glaze them over when he compares them with hers. He is too poor, she is too rich — even if she loved him."

"Even!" said the professor. "Is it your opinion that she does not?"

"I do not know," she answered. "It has seemed to me more probable that — that she liked Colonel Tredennis."

"I thought so," said the professor. "I must confess that I thought so; though, perhaps, that may have been because my feeling for him is so strong, and I have seen that he"—

"That he was fond of her?" Bertha put in as he paused to reflect.

"I thought so," he said again. "I thought I was sure of it. He sees her often; he thinks of her frequently, it is plain; he speaks of her to me; he sees every charm and grace in her. I have never heard him speak of any other woman so."

"It would be a very suitable marriage," said Bertha; "I have felt that from the first. There is no one more beautiful than Agnes — no one sweeter — no one more fit" —

She pushed her seat back from the hearth and rose from it.

"The fire is too warm," she said. "I have been sitting before it too long."

There was some ice-water upon a side table and she went to it and poured out a glass, and drank it slowly. Then she took a seat by the centre-table and spoke again, as she idly turned over the leaves of a magazine without looking at it.

"When first Agnes came here," she said, "I thought of it. I remember that when I presented Philip to her I watched to see if she impressed him as she does most people."

"She did," said the professor. "I remember his speaking of it afterward, and saying what a charm hers was, and that her beauty must touch a man's best nature."

"That was very good," said Bertha, faintly smiling. "And it was very like him. And since then," she added, "you say he has spoken of her often in the same way and as he speaks of no one else?"

"Again and again," answered the professor. "The truth is, my dear, I am fond of speaking of her myself, and have occasionally led him in that direction. I have wished for him what you have wished."

"And we have both of us," she said, half sadly, "been unkind to poor Laurence."

She closed the magazine.

"Perhaps he will go, after all," she said. "He may see that it is best. He may be glad to go before the year is ended."

She left her book and her chair.

"I think I must go now," she said, "I am a little tired."

He thought that she looked so, and the shadow which for a moment had half lifted itself fell again.

"No," he thought, "she has not outlived it, and this is more bitter for her than the rest. It is only natural that it should be more bitter."

When he got up to bid her good-night she put a hand upon either of his shoulders and kissed him.

"I am glad I was not invited to the grand party, dear," she said, "I have liked this better. It has been far better for me."

There were only a few yards of space between her father's house and her own, and in a few seconds she had ascended the steps and entered the door. As she did so she heard Richard in the parlor, speaking rapidly and vehemently, and, entering, found that he was talking to Colonel Tredennis. The colonel was standing at one end of the' room, as if he had turned around with an abrupt movement; Richard was lying full length upon a sofa, looking uneasy and excited, his cushions tumbled about him. They ceased speaking the moment they saw her, and there was an odd pause, noticing which she came forward and spoke with an effort at appearing at ease.

"Do you know that this seems like contention?" she said. "Are you quarrelling with Richard, Colonel Tredennis, or is he quarrelling with you? And why are you not at the reception?"

"We are quarrelling with each other violently," said Richard, with a half laugh. "You arrived barely in time to prevent our coming to blows. And why are you not at the reception?"

Bertha turned to Tredennis, who for a moment seemed to have been struck dumb by the sight of her. The memories the slender gray figure had brought to the professor rushed back upon him with a force that staggered him. It was as if the ghost of something dead had suddenly appeared before him and he was compelled to hold himself as if he did not see it. The little gray gown, the carelessly knotted kerchief, — it seemed so terrible to see them and to be forced to realize through them how changed she was. He had never seen her look so ill and fragile as she did when she turned to him and spoke in her quiet, unemotional voice.

"This is the result of political machination," she said. "He has forgotten that we were not invited. Being 'absorbed in affairs of state he no longer keeps an account of the doings of the giddy throng."

Then he recovered himself.

"You were not invited," he said. "Isn't there some mistake about that? I thought"—

"Your impression naturally was that we were the foundation-stone of all social occasions," she responded; "but this time they have dispensed with us. We were not invited."

"Say that you did not receive your invitation," put in Richard, restlessly. "The other way of stating it is nonsense."

She paused an instant, as if his manner suggested a new thought to her.

"I wonder," she said, slowly, "if there *could* be a reason; but no, I think that is impossible. It must have been an accident. But you," she added to Tredennis, "have not told me why you are not with the rest of the world."

"I came away early," he answered. "I was there for an hour."

He was glad that she did not sit down; he wished that she would go away; it would be better if she would go away and leave them to themselves again.

"It was very gay, I suppose," she said. "And you saw Agnes?"

"I have just left her," he replied.

"You ought to have stayed," she said, turning away with a smile. "It would have been better than quarrelling with Richard."

And she went out of the room and left them together, as he had told himself it would be best she should.

He did not look at her as she ascended the staircase; he stood with his back to the open door, and did not speak until he heard her go into the room above them. Then he addressed Richard.

"Do you understand me now?" he said, sternly. "This is the beginning!"

"The beginning!" exclaimed Richard, with a half-frantic gesture. "If this is the beginning — and things go wrong — imagine what the end will be!"

The room Bertha had entered was the nursery. In the room opening out of it Jack and Janey slept in their small beds. Upon the hearth-rug lay a broken toy. She bent to pick it up, and afterward stood a moment holding it in her hand without seeing it; she still held it as she sank into a chair which was near her.

"I will stay here a while," she said. "This is the best place for me."

For a few minutes she sat quite still; something like a stupor had settled upon her; she was thinking in a blind, disconnected way of Agnes Sylvestre. Everything would be right at last. Agnes would be happy. This was what she had wished — what she had intended from the first — when she had brought them together. It was she who had brought them together. And this was the plan she had had in her mind when she had done it; and she had known what it would cost her even then. And then there came back to her the memory of the moment when she had turned away from them to pour out Laurence's coffee with hands she could not hold still, and whose tremor he saw and understood. Poor Laurence! he must suffer too! Poor Laurence!

She looked down suddenly at the broken toy in her hand.

"I will stay here more," she said. "It is better here. There is nothing else! And if I were a good woman I should want nothing else. If I had only not spoken to Agnes, — that was the mistake; if she will only forget it! *Some* one should be happy — *some* one! It will be Agnes."

She got up and went into the children's room, and knelt down by Janey's bed, laying the toy on the coverlet. She put her arms around the child and spoke her name.

"Janey!" she said. "Janey!"

The child stirred, opened her eyes, and put an arm sleepily about her neck.

"I said my prayers," she murmured. "God bless mamma and papa — and everybody! God bless Uncle Philip!"

Bertha laid her face near her upon the pillow.

"Yes," she said, brokenly. "You belong to me and I belong to you. I will stay here, Janey — with you."

Chapter 33

Sometimes during the winter, when she glanced around her parlor on the evenings of her receptions, Bertha felt as if she was in a waking dream, — so many people of whom she seemed to know nothing were gathered about her; she saw strange faces on every side; a new element had appeared, which was gradually crowding out the old, and she herself felt that she was almost a stranger in it. Day by day, and by almost imperceptible degrees at first, various mysterious duties had devolved upon her. She had found herself calling at one house because the head of it was a member of a committee, at another because its mistress was a person whose influence over her husband it would be well to consider; she had issued an invitation here because the recipients must be pleased, another there because somebody was to be biassed in the right direction. The persons thus to be pleased and biassed were by no means invariably interesting. There was a stalwart Westerner or so, who made themselves almost too readily at home; an occasional rigid New Englander, who suspected a lack of purpose in the atmosphere; and a stray Southerner, who exhibited a tendency towards a large and rather exhaustive gallantry. As a rule, too, Bertha was obliged to admit that she found the men more easily entertained than the women, who were most of them new to their surroundings, and privately determined to do themselves credit and not be imposed upon by appearances; and when this was not the case were either timorously overpowered by a sense of their inadequacy to the situation, or calmly intrenched behind a shield of impassive composure, more discouraging than all else. It was not always easy to enliven such material: to be always ready with the right thing to say and do; to understand, as by inspiration, the intricacies of every occasion and the requirements of every mental condition, and while Bertha spared no effort, and used her every gift to the best of her ability, the result, even when comparatively successful, was rather productive of exhaustion, mental and physical.

"They don't care about me," she said to Arbuthnot one night, with a rueful laugh, as she looked around her. "And I am always afraid of their privately suspecting that I don't care about them. Sometimes when I look at them I cannot help being overpowered by a sense of there being a kind of ludicrousness in it all. Do you know, nearly every one of them has a reason for being here, and it is never by any chance connected with my reason for inviting them. I could give you some of the reasons. Shall I? Some of them are feminine reasons, and some of them are masculine. That woman at the end of the sofa — the thin, eager-looking one — comes because she wishes to accustom herself to society. Her husband is a "rising man," and she is in love with him, and has a hungry desire to keep pace with him. The woman she is talking to has a husband who wants something Senator Planefield may be induced to give him — and Senator Planefield is on his native heath here; that showy little Southern widow has a large claim against the government, and comes because she sees people she thinks it best to know. She is wanted because she has a favorite cousin who is given patriotically to opposing all measures not designed to benefit the South. It is rather fantastic when you reflect upon it, isn't it?"

"You know what I think about it without asking," answered Arbuthnot.

"Yes, you have told me," was her response; "but it will be all over before long, and then — Ah! there is Senator Blundel! Do you know, it is always a relief to me when he comes; "and she went toward him with a brighter look than Arbuthnot had seen her wear at any time during the entire evening.

It had taken her some time herself to decide why it was that she liked Blundel and felt at ease with him; in fact, up to the present period she had scarcely done more than decide that she did like him. She had not found his manner become more polished as their acquaintance progressed; he was neither gallant nor accomplished; he was always rather full of himself, in a genuine, masculine way. He was blunt, and by no means tactful; but she had never objected to him from the first, and after a while she had become conscious of feeling relief, as she had put it to Arbuthnot, when his strong, rather aggressive, personality presented itself upon the scene. He was not difficult to entertain, at least. Finding in her the best of listeners he entertained himself by talking to her, and by making sharp jokes, at which they both laughed with equal appreciation. He knew what to talk about too, and what subjects to joke on; and, however apparently communicative his mood might be, his opinions were always kept thriftily in hand.

"He seems to talk a good deal," Richard said, testily; "but, after all, you don't find out much of what he really thinks."

Bertha had discovered this early in their acquaintance. If the object in making the house attractive to him was that he might be led to commit himself in any way during his visits, that object was scarcely attained. When at last it appeared feasible to discuss the Westoria lands project in his presence, he showed no unwillingness to listen or to ask questions; but, the discussion being at an end, if notes had been compared no one could have said that he had taken either side of the question.

"He's balancing things," Planefield said. "I told you he would do it. You may trust him not to speak until he has made up his mind which side of the scale the weight is on."

When these discussions were being carried on Bertha had a fancy that he was more interested than he appeared outwardly. Several times she had observed that he asked her questions afterward which proved that no word had dropped on his ear unheeded, and that he had, for some reason best known to himself, reflected upon all he had heard. But their acquaintance had a side entirely untouched by worldly machinations, and it was this aspect of it which Bertha liked. There was something homely and genuine about it. He paid her no compliments; he even occasionally found fault with her habits, and what he regarded as the unnecessary conventionality of some of her surroundings; but his good-natured egotism never offended her. A widower without family, and immersed in political business, he knew little of the comforts of home life. He lived in two or three rooms, full of papers, books, and pigeon-holes, and took his meals at a hotel.

He found this convenient, if not luxurious, and more than convenience it had never yet occurred to him to expect or demand. But he was not too dull to appreciate the good which fell in his way; and after spending an hour with the Amorys on two or three occasions, when he had left the scene of his political labors fagged and out of humor, he began to find pleasure and relief in his unceremonious visits, and looked forward to them. There came an evening when Bertha, in looking over some music, came upon a primitive ballad, which proved to be among the recollections of his youth, and she aroused him to enthusiasm by singing it. His musical taste was not remarkable for its cultivation; he was strongly in favor of pronounced melody, and was disposed to regard a song as incomplete without a chorus; but he enjoyed himself when his prejudices were pandered to, and Bertha rather respected his courageous, if benighted, frankness, and his obstinate faith in his obsolete favorites. So she sang "Ben Bolt" to him, and "The Harp that once through Tara's Halls," and others far less classical and more florid, and while she sang he sat ungracefully, but comfortably, by the fire, his eyes twinkling less watchfully, the rugged lines of his blunt-featured face almost settling into repose, and sometimes when she ended he roused himself with something like a sigh.

"Do you like it?" she would say. "Does it make you forget 'the gentleman from Indiana' and the 'senator from Connecticut'?"

"I don't want to forget them," he would reply with dogged good-humor. "They are not the kind of fellows it is safe to forget, but it makes my recollections of them more agreeable."

But after a while there were times when he was not in the best of humors, and when Bertha had a fancy that he was not entirely at ease or pleased with herself. At such times his visits were brief and unsatisfactory, and she frequently discovered that he regarded her with a restless and perturbed expression, as if he was not quite certain of his own opinions of her.

"He looks at me," she said to Richard, "as if he had moments of suspecting me of something."

"Nonsense!" said Richard. "What could he suspect you of?"

"Of nothing," she answered. "I think that was what we agreed to call it."

But she never failed to shrink when the twinkling; eyes rested upon her with the disturbed questioning in their glance, and the consciousness of this shrinking was very bitter to her in secret.

When her guest approached her on the evening before referred to, she detected at once that he was not in a condition of mind altogether unruffled. The glances he cast on those about him were not encouraging, and the few nods of recognition he bestowed were far from cordial; his hair stood on end a trifle more aggressively than usual, and his short, stout body expressed a degree of general dissatisfaction which it was next to impossible to ignore.

Bertha did not attempt to ignore it.

"I will tell you something before you speak to me," she said. "Something has put you out of humor."

He gave her a sharp glance, and then looked away over the heads of the crowd.

"There is always enough to put a man out of humor," he said. "What a lot of people you have here to-night! What do they come for?"

"I have just been telling Mr. Arbuthnot some of the reasons," she answered. "They are very few of them good ones. You came hoping to recover your spirits."

"I came to look at you," he said.

He was frequently blunt, but there was a bluntness about this speech which surprised her. She answered him with a laugh, however.

"I am always worth looking at," she said. "And now you have seen me"—

He was looking at her by this time, and even more sharply than before. It seemed as if he was bent upon reading in her face the answer to the question he had asked of it before, but he evidently did not find it.

"There's something wrong with you," he said. "I don't know what it is. I don't know what to make of you."

"If you could make anything of me but Bertha Amory," she replied, "you might do a service to society; but that is out of the question, and as to there being something wrong with me, there is something wrong with all of us. There is something wrong with Mr. Arbuthnot, he is not enjoying himself; there is something wrong with Senator Planefield, who has been gloomy all the evening."

"Planefield," he said. "Ah! yes, there he is! Here pretty often, isn't he?"

"He is a great friend of Richard's," she replied, with discretion.

"So I have heard," he returned. And then he gave his attention to Planefield for a few minutes, as if he found him also an object of deep interest. After this inspection he turned to Bertha again.

"Well," he said, "I suppose you enjoy all this, or you wouldn't do it?"

"You are not enjoying it," she replied. "It does not exhilarate you as I hoped it would."

"I am out of humor," was his answer. "I told you so. I have just heard something I don't like. I dropped in here to stay five minutes, and take a look at you and see it" —

He checked himself and rubbed his upright hair impatiently, almost angrily.

"I am not sure that you mightn't be enjoying yourself better," he said, "and I should like to know something more of you than I do."

"If any information I can give you" — she began.

"Come," he said, with a sudden effort at better humor, "that is the way you talk to Planefield. We are too good friends for that."

His shrewd eyes fixed themselves on her as if asking the unanswered question again.

"Come!" he said. "I'm a blunt, old-fashioned fogy, but we are good, honest friends, — and always have been."

She glanced across the room at Richard, who was talking to a stubborn opposer of the great measure, and making himself delightful beyond description. She wished for the moment that he was not quite so picturesque and animated; then she gathered herself together.

"I think we have been," she said. "I hope you will believe so."

"Well," he answered, "I shouldn't like to believe anything else."

She thought that perhaps he had said more than he originally intended; he changed the subject abruptly, made a few comments upon people near them, asked a few questions, and finally went away, having scarcely spoken to any one but herself.

"Why did he not remain longer?" Richard asked afterward, when the guests were gone and they were talking the evening over.

"He was not in the mood to meet people," Bertha replied. "He said he had heard something he did not like, and it had put him out of humor. I think it was something about me."

"About you!" Richard exclaimed. "Why, in Heaven's name, about you?"

"His manner made me think so," she answered, coldly. "And it would not be at all unnatural. I think we may begin to expect such things."

"Upon my word," said Richard, starting up, "I think that is going rather far. Don't you see"— with righteous indignation —"what an imputation you are casting on me? Do you suppose I would allow you to do anything that — that"—

She raised her eyes and met his with an unwavering glance.

"Certainly not," she said, quickly. And his sentence remained unfinished, not because he felt that his point had been admitted, but because, for some mysterious reason, it suddenly became impossible for him to say more.

More than some of late, when he had launched into one of his spasmodic defences of himself, he had found himself checked by this intangible power in her uplifted eyes, and he certainly did not feel his grievances the less for the experiences.

Until during the last few months he had always counted it as one of his wife's chief charms that there was nothing complicated about her, that her methods were as simple and direct as a child's. It had never seemed necessary to explain her. But he had not found this so of late. He had even begun to feel that, though there was no outward breach in the tenor of their lives, an almost inpalpable barrier had risen between them. He expressed no wish she did not endeavor to gratify; her manner toward himself, with the exception of the fleeting moments when he had felt the check, was entirely unchanged; the spirit of her gayety ruled the house, as it had always done; and yet he was not always sure of the exact significance of her jests and laughter. The jests were clever, the laugh had a light ring; but there was a difference which puzzled him, and which, because he recognized in it some vague connection with himself, he tried in his moments of leisure to explain. He had even spoken of it to Colonel Tredennis on occasions when his mood was confidential.

"She used to be as frank as a child," he said, "and have the lightest way in the world; and I liked it. I am a rather feather-headed fellow myself, perhaps, and it suited me. But it is all gone now. When she laughs I don't feel sure of her, and when she is silent I begin to wonder what she is thinking of."

The thing she thought, the words she said to herself oftenest were: "It will not last very long." She said them over to herself at moments she could not have sustained herself under but for the consolation she found in them. Beyond this time, when what she faced from day to day would be over, she had not yet looked.

"It is a curious thing," she said to Arbuthnot, "but I seem to have ceased even to think of the future. I wonder sometimes if very old people do not feel so — as if there was nothing more to happen."

There was another person who found the events of the present sufficient to exclude for the time being almost all thought of the future. This person was Colonel Tredennis, who had found his responsibilities increase upon him also, — not the least of these responsibilities being, it must be confessed, that intimacy with Mr. Richard Amory of which Bertha had spoken.

"He is very intimate with Richard," she had said, and she had every reason for making the comment.

At first it had been the colonel who had made the advances, for reasons of his own, but later it had not been necessary for him to make advances. Having found relief in making his first reluctant half-confidences, Richard had gradually fallen into making others. When he had been overpowered by secret anxiety and nervous distrust of everything, finding himself alone with the colonel, and admiring and respecting above all things the self-control he saw in him, — a self-control which meant safety and silence under all temptations to betray the faintest shadow of a trust reposed in him, — it had been impossible for him to resist the impulse to speak of the trials which beset him; and, having once spoken of them, it was again impossible not to go a little farther, and say more than he had at first intended. So he had gone on from one step to another until there had come a day when the colonel himself had checked him for an instant, feeling it only the part of honor in the man who was the cooler of the two, and who had nothing to risk or repent.

"Wait a moment," he said. "Remember that, though I have not asked questions so far, I am ready to hear anything you choose to say, but don't tell me what you might wish you had kept back to-morrow."

"The devil take it all," cried Richard, dashing his fist on the table. "I must tell some one, or I shall go mad." But the misery which impelled him notwithstanding, he always told his story in his own way, and gave it a complexion more delicate than a less graceful historian might have been generous enough to bestow. He "had been too sanguine and enthusiastic; he had made mistakes; he had been led by the duplicity of a wily world into follies; he had been unfortunate; those more experienced than himself had betrayed the confidence it had been only natural he should repose in them. And throughout the labyrinth of the relation he wound his way, — a graceful, agile, supple figure, lightly avoiding an obstacle here, dexterously overstepping a barrier there, and untouched by any shadow but that of misfortune.

At first he spoke chiefly of the complications which bore heavily upon him; and these complications, arising entirely from the actions of others, committed him to so little that the colonel listened with apprehension more grave than the open confession of greater blunders would have awakened in him. "He would tell more," he thought, "if there were less to tell."

The grim fancy came to him sometimes as he listened, that it was as if he watched a man circling about the edge of a volcano, drawing nearer and nearer, until at last, in spite of himself, and impelled by some dread necessity, he must plunge headlong in. And so Richard circled about his crater: sometimes drawn nearer by the emotion and excitement of the moment, sometimes withdrawing a trifle through a caution as momentary, but in each of his circlings revealing a little more of the truth. The revelations were principally connected with the Westoria lands scheme, and were such in many instances as the colonel was not wholly unprepared to hear. He had not looked on during the last year for nothing, and often, when Richard had been in gay good spirits, and had imagined himself telling nothing, his silent companion had heard his pleasantries with forebodings which he could not control. He was not deceived by any appearance of entire frankness, and knew that he had not been told all until one dark and stormy night, as he sat in his room, Richard was announced, and came in pallid, haggard, beaten by the rain, and at the lowest ebb of depression. He had had a hard and bitter day of it, and it had followed several others quite as hard and bitter; he had been fagging about the Capitol, going the old rounds, using the old arguments, trying new ones, overcoming one obstacle only to find himself confronted with another, feeling that he was losing ground where it was a matter of life and death that he should gain it; spirits and courage deserting him just when he needed them most; and all this being over, he dropped into his office to find awaiting him there letters containing news which gave the final blow.

He sat down by the table and began his outpourings, graceful, attractive, injured. The colonel thought him so, as he watched him and listened, recognizing meanwhile the incompleteness of his recital, and making up his mind that the time had come when it was safer that the whole truth should be told. In the hours in which he had pondered upon the subject he gradually decided that such an occasion would arrive; and here it was.

So at a certain fitting juncture, just as Richard was lightly skirting a delicate point, Tredennis leaned forward and laid his open hand on the table with a curious simplicity of gesture.

"I think," he said, "you had better tell me the whole story. You have never done it yet. What do you say?"

The boarder on the floor below, who had heard him walking to and fro on the first New Year's night he had spent in Washington, and on many a night since, heard his firm, regular tread again during the half hour in which Richard told, in fitful outbursts, what he had not found himself equal to telling before. It was not easy to tell it in a very clear and connected matter; it was necessary to interlard it with many explanations and extenuations, and even when these were supplied there was a baldness about the facts, as they gradually grouped themselves together, which it was not agreeable to contemplate; and Richard felt this himself gallingly.

"I know how it appears to you," he said; "I know how it sounds! That is the maddening side of it, — it looks so much worse than it really is! There is not a man living who would accuse me of intentional wrong. Confound it! I seem to have been forced into doing the very things it was least natural to me to do! Bertha herself would say it, — she would understand it. She is always just and generous!"

"Yes," said the colonel; "I should say she had been generous."

"You mean that I have betrayed her generosity!" cried Richard. "That, of course! I expected it."

"You will find," said the colonel, "that others will say the same thing."

He had heard even more than his worst misgivings had suggested to him, and the shock of it had destroyed something of his self-control. For the time being he was in no lenient mood.

"I know what people will say!" Richard exclaimed. "Do you suppose I have not thought of it a thousand times? I know what I should say if I did not know the circumstances. It is the circumstances that make the difference."

"The fact that they are your circumstances, and not another man's," began Tredennis; but there he checked himself. "I beg your pardon," he said, coldly. "I have no right to meet your confidence with blame. It will do no good. If I can give you no help, I might better be silent. There were circumstances which appeared extenuating to you, I suppose."

He was angered by his own anger, as he had often been before. He told himself that he was making the matter a personal cause, as usual; but how could he hear that her very generosity and simplicity had been used against her by the man who should have guarded her interests as his first duty, without burning with sharp and fierce indignation.

"If I understand you," he said, "your only hope of recovering what you have lost lies in the success of the Westoria scheme?"

"Yes," answered Amory, with his forehead on his hands, "that is the diabolical truth!"

"And you have lost?"

"Once I was driven into saying to you that if the thing should fail it would mean ruin to me. That was the truth, too."

The colonel stood still.

"Ruin to you!" he said. "Ruin to your wife —ruin to your children — serious loss to the old man who" —

"Who trusted me!" Richard finished, gnawing his white lips. "I see it in exactly the same light myself, and it does not make it easier to bear. That is the way a thing looks when it fails. Suppose it had succeeded. It may succeed yet. They trusted me, and, I tell you, I trusted myself."

It was easy to see just what despair would seize him if the worst came to the worst, and how powerless he would be in its clutches. He was like a reed beaten by the wind, even now. A sudden paroxysm of fear fell upon him.

"Great God!" he cried. "It can't fail! What could I say to them — how could I explain it?"

A thousand wild thoughts surged through Tredennis' brain as he heard him. The old sense of helplessness was strong upon him. To his upright strength there seemed no way of judging fairly of, or dealing practically with, such dishonor and weakness. What standard could be applied to a man who lied agreeably in his very thoughts of himself and his actions? He had scarcely made a statement during the last hour which had not contained some airy falsehood. Of whom was it he thought in his momentary anguish? Not of Bertha — not of her children — not of the gentle old scholar, who had always been lenient with his faults. It was of himself he was thinking — of Richard Amory, robbed of his refined picturesqueness by mere circumstance and placed by bad luck at a baleful disadvantage!

For a few minutes there was a silence. Richard sat with his brow upon his hands, his elbows on the table before him. Tredennis paced to and fro, looking downward. At length Richard raised his head. He did so because Tredennis had stopped his walk.

"What is it?" he asked.

Tredennis walked over to him and sat down. He was pale, and wore a set and rigid look, the chief characteristic of which was that it expressed absolutely nothing. His voice was just as hard and expressed as little when he spoke.

"I have a proposition to make to you," he said, "and I will preface it by the statement that, as a business man, I am perfectly well aware that it is almost madness to make it. I say 'almost.' Let it rest there. I will assume the risks you have run in the Westoria scheme. Invest the money you have charge of in something safer. You say there are chances of success. I will take those chances."

"*What!*" cried Richard. "*What!*"

He sat upright, staring. He did not believe the evidence of his senses; but Tredennis went on, without the quiver of a muscle, speaking steadily, almost monotonously.

"I have money," he said. "More than you know, perhaps. I have had recently a legacy which would of itself make me a comparatively rich man. That I was not dependent upon my pay you knew before. I have no family. I shall not marry. I am fond of your children, of Janey particularly. I should have provided for her future in any case. You have made a bad investment in these lands; transfer them to me and invest in something safer."

"And if the bill fails to pass!" exclaimed Richard.

"If it fails to pass I shall have the land on my hands; if it passes I shall have made something by a venture, and Janey will be the richer; but, as it stands, the venture had better be mine than yours. You have lost enough."

Richard gave his hair an excited toss backward, and stared at him as he had done before; a slight, cold moisture broke out on his forehead.

"You mean"— he began, breathlessly.

"Do you remember," said Tredennis, "what I told you of the comments people were beginning to make? They have assumed the form I told you they would. It is best for — for your children that they should be put an end to. If I assume these risks there will be no farther need for you to use — to exert yourself." He began to look white about the mouth, and through his iron stolidity there was

404

something revealed before which Richard felt himself quail. "The night that Blundel came in to your wife's reception, and remained so short a time, he had heard a remark upon the influence she was exerting over him, and it had had a bad effect. The remark was made publicly at one of the hotels." He turned a little whiter, and the something all the strength in him had held down at the outset leaped to the surface. "I have no wife to — to use," he said; "if I had, by Heavens, I would have spared her!"

He had held himself in hand and been silent a long time, but he could not do it now.

"She is the mother of your children," he cried, clenching his great hand. "And women are beginning to avoid her, and men to bandy her name to and fro. You have deceived her; you have thrown away her fortune; you have used her as an instrument in your schemes, I, who am only an outsider, with no right to defend her — I defend her for her father's sake, for her child's, for her own! You are on the verge of ruin and disgrace. I offer you the chance to retrieve yourself — to retrieve her! Take it, if you are a man!"

Richard had fallen back in his chair breathless and ashen. In all his imaginings of what the future might hold he had never thought of such a possibility as this, — that it should be this man who would turn upon him and place an interpretation so fiercely unsparing upon what he had done! Under all his admiration and respect for the colonel there had been hidden, it must be admitted, an almost unconscious touch of contempt for him, as a rather heavy and unsophisticated personage, scarcely versatile or agile enough, and formed in a mould somewhat obsolete and quixotic, — a safe person to confide in, and one to invite confidence passively by his belief in what was presented to him; a man to make a good listener and to encourage one to believe in one's own statements, certainly not a man to embarrass and discourage a historian by asking difficult questions or translating too literally what was said. He had not asked questions until to-night, and his face had said very little for him on any occasion. Among other things Richard had secretly — though leniently — felt him to be a trifle stolid, and had amiably forgiven him for it. It was this very thing which made the sudden change appear so keen an injustice and injury; it amounted to a breach of confidence, that he should have formed a deliberate and obstinate opinion of his own, entirely unbiassed by the presentation of the case offered to him. He had spoken more than once, it was true, in a manner which had suggested prejudice; but it had been the prejudice of the primeval mind, unable to adjust itself to modern conditions and easily disregarded by more experienced. But now! — he was stolid no longer. His first words had startled Richard beyond expression. His face said more for him than his words; it burned white with the fire it had hidden so long; his great frame quivered with the passion of the moment; when he had clenched his hand it had been in the vain effort to hold it still; and yet the man who saw it recognized in it only the wrath and scorn which had reference to himself. Perhaps it was best that it should have been so, — best that his triviality was so complete that he could see nothing which was not in some way connected with his own personality.

"Tredennis," he gasped out, "you are terribly harsh! I did not think you"—

"Even if I could lie and palter to you," said Tredennis, his clenched hand still on the table, "this is not the time for it. I have tried before to make you face the truth, but you have refused to do it. Perhaps you had made yourself believe what you told me, — that no harm was meant or done. *I* know what harm has been done. I have heard the talk of the hotel corridors and clubs!" His hand clenched itself harder and he drew in a sharp breath.

"It is time that you should give this thing up," he continued, with deadly determination. "And I am willing to shoulder it. Who else would do the same thing?"

"No one else," said Richard, bitterly. "And it is not for my sake you do it either; it is for the sake of some of your ideal fancies that are too fine for us worldlings to understand, I swear!" And he felt it specially hard that it was so.

"Yes," replied the colonel, "I suppose you might call it that. It is not for your sake, as you say. It has been one of my fancies that a man might even deny himself for the sake of an — an idea, and I am not denying myself. I am only giving to your child, in one way, what

I meant to give to her in another. She would be willing to share it with her mother, I think."

And then, somehow, Richard began to feel that this offer was a demand, and that, even if his sanguine mood should come upon him again, he would not find it exactly easy to avoid it. It seemed actually as if there was something in this man — some principle of strength, of feeling, of conviction — which almost constituted a right by which he might contend for what he asked; and before it, in his temporary abasement and anguish of mind, Richard Amory faltered. He said a great deal, it is true, and argued his case as he had argued it before, being betrayed in the course of the argument by the exigencies of the case to add facts as well as fancies. He endeavored to adorn his position as much as possible, and, naturally, his failure, was not entire. There were hopes of the passage of the bill, sometimes strong hopes, it seemed; if the money he had invested had been his own; if it had not been for the failure of his speculations in other quarters; if so much had not depended upon failure and success, — he would have run all risks willingly. There were, indeed, moments when it almost appeared that his companion was on the point of making a capital investment, and being much favored thereby.

"It is really not half so bad as it seems," he said, gaining cheerfulness as he talked. "But, after such a day as I have had, a man loses courage and cannot look at things collectedly. I have been up and down in the scale a score of times in the last eight hours. That is where the wear and tear comes in. A great deal depends on Blundel; and I had a talk with him which carried us farther than we have ever been before."

"Farther," said Tredennis. "In what direction?"

Richard flushed slightly.

"I think I sounded him pretty well," he said. "There is no use mincing matters; it has to be done. We have never been able to get at his views of things exactly, and I won't say he went very far this afternoon; but I was in a desperate mood, and — well, I think I reached bottom. He half promised to call at the house this evening. I dare say he is with Bertha now."

Something in his flush, which had a slightly excited and triumphant air, something in his look and tone, caused Tredennis to start in his chair.

"What is he there for?" he said. "What do you mean?"

Richard thrust his hands in his pockets. For a moment he seemed to have lost all his grace and refinement of charm, — for the moment he was a distinctly coarse and undraped human being.

"He has gone to make an evening call," he said. "And if she manages him as well as she has managed him before, — as well as she can manage any man she chooses to take in hand, and yet not give him more than a smile or so, — your investment, if you make it, may not turn out such a bad one."

Chapter 34

Bertha had spent the greater part of the day with her children, as she had spent part of many days lately. She had gone up to the nursery after breakfast to see Jack and Janey at their lessons, and had remained with them and given herself up to their entertainment. She was not well; the weather was bad; she might give herself a holiday, and she would spend it in her own way, in the one refuge which never failed her.

"It is always quiet here," she said to herself. "If I could give up all the rest — all of it — and spend all my days here, and think of nothing else, I might be better. There are women who live so. I think they must be better in every way than I am — and happier. I am sure I should have been happier if I had begun so long ago."

And as she sat, with Janey at her side, in the large chair which held them both, her arm thrown round the child's waist, there came to her a vague thought of what the unknown future might form itself into when she "began again." It would be beginning again when the sea was between the new life and the old; everything would be left behind — but the children. She would live as she had lived in Virginia, always with the children — always with the children. "It is the only safe thing," she thought, clasping Janey closer. "Nothing else is safe for a woman who is unhappy. If one is happy one may be gay, and look on at the world with the rest; but there are some who must not look on — who dare not."

"Mamma," said Janey, "you are holding me a little too close, and your face looks — it looks — as if you were thinking."

Bertha laughed to reassure her. They were used to this gay, soft laugh of hers, as the rest of the world was. If she was silent, if the room was not bright with the merriment she had always filled it with, they felt themselves a trifle injured, and demanded their natural rights with juvenile imperiousness. "Mamma always laughs," Jack had once announced to a roomful of company. "She plays new games with us and laughs, and we laugh too. Maria and Susan are not funny. Mamma is funny, and like a little girl grown up. We always have fun when she comes into the nursery."

"It is something the same way in the parlor," Planefield had said, showing his teeth amiably, and Bertha, who was standing near Colonel Tredennis, had laughed in a manner to support her reputation, but had said nothing. So she laughed now, not very vivaciously, perhaps.

"That was very improper, Janey," she said, "to look as if I was thinking. It is bad enough to be thinking. It must not occur again."

"But if you were thinking of a story to tell us," suggested Jack, graciously, "it wouldn't matter, you see. You might go on thinking."

"But the story was not a new one," she answered. "It was sad. I did not like it myself."

"We should like it," said Janey.

"If it's a story," remarked Jack, twisting the string round his top, "it's all right. There was a story Uncle Philip told us."

"Suppose you tell it to me," said Bertha.

"It was about a knight," said Janey, "who went to a great battle. It was very sorrowful. He was strong, and happy, and bold, and the king gave him a sword and armor that glittered and was beautiful. And his hair waved in the breeze. And he was young and brave. And his horse arched its neck. And the knight longed to go and fight in the battle, and was glad and not afraid; and the people looked on and praised him, because they thought he would fight so well. But just as the battle began, before he had even drawn his sword, a stray shot came, and he fell. And while the battle went on he lay there dying, with his hand on his breast. And at night, when the battle was over, and the stars came out, he lay and looked up at them, and at the dark-blue sky, and wondered why he had been given his sword and armor, and why he had been allowed to feel so strong, and glad, and eager, — only for that. But he did not know. There was no one to tell him. And he died. And the stars shone down on his bright armor and his dead face."

"I didn't like it myself," commented Jack. "It wasn't much of a story. I told him so."

"He was sorry he told it," said Janey, "because I cried. I don't think he meant to tell such a sad story."

"He wasn't funny, that day," observed Jack. "Sometimes he isn't funny at all, and he sits and thinks about things; and then, if we make him tell us a story, he doesn't tell a good one. He used to be nicer than he is now."

"I love him," said Janey, faithfully; "I think he is nice all the time."

"It wasn't much of a story, that is true," said Bertha. "There was not enough of it."

"He died too soon," said Jack.

"Yes," said Bertha; "he died too soon, that was it, — too soon." And the laugh she ended with had a sound which made her shudder.

She got up from her rocking-chair quickly.

"We won't tell stories," she said. "We will play. We will play ball and blind-man's bluff — and run about and get warm. That will be better."

And she took out her handkerchief and tied it over her eyes with unsteady hands, laughing again, — laughing while the children laughed, too.

They played until the room rang with their merriment. They had not been so gay together for many a day, and when the game was at an end they tried another and another, until they were tired and ready for their nursery dinner. Bertha did not leave them even then. She did not expect Richard home until their own dinner-hour in the evening, so she sat at the children's table and helped them herself, in the nurse's place; and they were in high spirits, and loquacious and confidential.

When the meal was over they sat by the nursery fire, and Meg fell asleep in her mother's arms; and after she had laid her on her bed Bertha came back to Jack and Janey, and read and talked to them until dusk began to close in about them. It was as they sat so together that a sealed package was brought to her by a servant, who said it had been left at the door by a messenger. It contained two letters, —

one addressed to Senator Blundel, and one to herself, — and both were in Richard's hand.

"I suppose something has detained him, and I am not to wait dinner," she thought, as she opened the envelope bearing her own name.

The same thing had occurred once or twice before, so it made but little impression upon her. There were the usual perfectly natural excuses. He had been very hard at work and would be obliged to remain out until some time past their dinner-hour. He had an engagement at one of the hotels, and could dine there; he was not quite sure that he should be home until late. Then he added, just before closing:

"Blundel said something about calling this evening. He had been having a hard day of it and said he wanted a change. I had a very satisfactory talk with him, and I think he begins to see the rights of our case. Entertain him as charmingly as possible, and if he is not too tired, and is in a good humor, hand him the enclosed letter. It contains testimony which ought to be a strong argument, and I think it will be."

Bertha looked at the letter. It was not at all imposing, and seemed to contain nothing more than a slip of paper. She put it down on the mantel and sighed faintly.

"If he knew what a service he would do me by seeing the rights of the case," she said to herself, "I think he would listen to their arguments. I think he likes me well" enough to do it. I believe he would enjoy being kind to me. If this should be the end of it all, it would be worth the trouble of being amusing and amiable one evening."

But she did not look forward with any great pleasure to the prospect of what was before her. Perhaps her day in the nursery had been a little too much for her; she was tired, and would have been glad to be left alone. But this was not to be. She must attire herself, in all her bravery, and sing, and laugh, and be gay a little longer. How often had she done the same thing before? How often would she do it again?

"There are some people who are born to play comedy," she said afterward, as she stood before her mirror, dressing. "They can do nothing else. I am one of them. Very little is expected of me, only that I shall always laugh and make jokes. If I were to try tragedy, that would be a better jest than all the rest. If I were to be serious, what a joke that would be!"

She thought, as she had done a thousand times, of a portrait of herself which had been painted three years before. It had been her Christmas gift to Richard, and had been considered a great success. It was a wonderfully spirited likeness, and the artist had been fortunate in catching her brightest look.

"It is the expression that is so marvellous," Richard had often said. "When I look at it I always expect to hear you laugh."

"Are they never tired of it?" she said; "never tired of hearing me laugh? If I were to stop some day and say, 'See, I am tired of it myself. I have tears as well as the rest of you. Let me'" — She checked herself; her hands had begun to tremble — her voice; she knew too well what was coming upon her. She looked at herself in the glass.

"I must dress myself carefully," she said, "if I am to look vivacious. One's attire is called upon to do a great deal for one when one has a face like that."

Outwardly her attire had done a great deal for her when, after she had dined alone, she sat awaiting her guest. The fire burned brightly; the old songs lay upon the piano; a low stand, with a pretty coffee service upon it, was drawn near her; a gay little work-basket, containing some trifle of graceful work, was on her knee. Outside, the night was decidedly unpleasant. "So unpleasant," she said to herself, "that it will surprise me if he comes." But though by eight o'clock the rain was coming down steadily, at half-past eight she heard the familiar heavy tread upon the door-step, and her visitor presented himself.

What sort of humor he was in when he made his entry Bertha felt that it was not easy to decide; but it struck her that it was not a usual humor, and that the fatigues of the day had left their mark upon him. He looked by no means fresh, and by the time he had seated himself felt that something had disturbed him, and that it was true that he needed distraction.

It had always been very simple distraction she offered him; he had never demanded subtleties from her or any very great intellectual effort; his ideas upon the subject of the feminine mind were, perhaps, not so advanced as they might have been, and belonged rather to the days and surroundings of his excellent, hard-worked mother and practical, unimaginative sisters than to a more brilliant world. Given a comfortable seat in the pretty room, the society of this pretty and smiling little person, who poured out his coffee for him, enjoyed his jokes, and prattled gayly of things pleasant and amusing, he was perfectly satisfied. What he felt the need of was rest and light recreation, cheerfulness, and appreciation, a sense of relief from the turmoil and complications of the struggling, manoeuvring, overreaching, ambitious world he lived in.

Knowing this, Bertha had given him what he enjoyed, and she offered him no other entertainment this evenings She gave him his cup of coffee, and talked to him as he drank it, telling him an amusing story or so of the children or of people he knew.

"I have been in the nursery all day," she said. "I have been playing blind-man's buff and telling stories. You have never been in the nursery, have you? You are not like Colonel Tredennis, who thinks the society there is better than that we have in the parlor."

"Perhaps he's not so far wrong," said her guest, bluntly, "though I have never been in the nursery myself. I have a nursery of my own up at the Capitol, and I don't always find it easy to manage."

"The children fight, I have heard," said Bertha, "and sometimes call each other names; and it is even reported that they snatch at each other's toys and break those they cannot appropriate. I am afraid the discipline is not good!"

"It isn't," he answered, "or there isn't enough of it."

He set his coffee-cup down and watched her as she leaned back in her chair and occupied herself with the contents of her work-basket.

"Do you go into the nursery often," he asked, "or is it out of the fashion?"

"It is out of the fashion," she answered, "but"— She stopped and let her work rest on her knee as she held it. "Will you tell me why you ask me that?" she said, and her face changed as she spoke.

"I asked you because I didn't know," he answered. "It seemed to me you couldn't have much time for things of that sort. You generally seem to be pretty busy with one thing and another. I don't know much about fashionable life and fashionable women. The women I knew when I was a boy — my own mother and her sisters — spent the most of their time with their children; and it wasn't such a bad way either. They were pretty good women."

"Perhaps it was the best way," said Bertha, "and I dare say they were better for it. I dare say we compare very unfavorably with them."

"You don't compare at all," he returned. "I should not compare you. I don't know how it would work with you. They got old pretty soon, and lost their good looks; but they were safe, kind-hearted creatures, who tried to do their duty and make the best of things. I don't say they were altogether right in their views of life; they were narrow, I suppose, and ran into extremes, but they had ways a man likes to think of, and did very little mischief."

"I could scarcely estimate the amount of mischief I do," said Bertha, applying herself to her work cheerfully; "but I do not think my children are neglected. Colonel Tredennis would probably give a certificate to that effect. They are clothed quite warmly, and are occasionally allowed a meal, and I make a practice of recognizing them when I meet them on the street."

She was wondering if it would not be better to reserve the letter until some more auspicious occasion. It struck her that in the course of his day's fatigues he had encountered some problem of which he found it difficult to rid himself. There were signs of it in his manner. He wore a perturbed, preoccupied expression, and looked graver than she had ever seen him. He sat with his hands in his pockets, his hair on end, his bluff countenance a rather deeper color than usual, and his eyes resting upon her.

"This isn't an easy world," he said, "and I suppose it is no easier for women than for men. I shouldn't like to be a woman myself, and have to follow my loader, and live in one groove from beginning to end. It is natural that some should feel the temptation to try to get out of it, and use their power as men use theirs; but it does not pay — it can't. Women were meant to be good — to be good and honest and true, and — and innocent."

It was an amazingly ingenuous creed, and he presented it with a rough simplicity and awkwardness which might have been laughable but for their heavy sincerity. Bertha felt this seriousness instantaneously, and, looking up, saw in his sharp little eyes a suggestion of feeling which startled her.

"Wondering what I'm thinking of?" he said. "Well, I am thinking of you. I've thought of you pretty often lately, and to-night I've a reason for having you in .my mind."

"What is the reason?" she asked, more startled than before.

He thrust his hands deeper into his pockets; there was no mistaking the evidences of strong emotion in his face.

"I am a friend of yours," he said. "You know that; you've known it some time. My opinion of you is that you are a good little woman, — the right sort of a little woman, — and I have a great deal of confidence in you."

"I hope so," said Bertha.

She felt that as he gained warmth and color she lost them; she thought of the letter which lay on the mantelpiece within a few feet of him, and wished that it was not so near. There had been evil spoken of her, and he had heard it. She realized that, and knew that she was upon her defence, even while she had no knowledge of what she was to defend herself against.

"I hope so," she said again, tremulously. "I hope so, indeed; "and her eyes met his with a helplessness more touching than any appeal she could have made.

It so moved him that he could remain quiet no longer, but sprang to his feet and drew his hand from his pocket and rubbed it excitedly over his upright hair.

"Damn it!" he broke forth, "let them say what they will, — let what will happen, I'll believe in you! Don't look at me like that; you are a good little woman, but you are in the wrong place. There are lies and intrigues going on about you, and you are too — too bright and pretty to be judged fairly by outsiders. You don't know what you are mixed up in; how should you? Who is to tell you? These fellows who dangle about and make fine speeches are too smooth-tongued, even when they know enough. I'll tell you. I never paid you compliments or made love to you, did I? I'm no good at that; but I'll tell you the truth, and give you a bit of good advice. People are beginning to talk, you see, and tell lies. They have brought their lies to me; I don't believe them, but others will. There are men and women who come to your house who will do you no good, and are more than likely to do you harm. They are a lot of intriguers and lobbyists. You don't want that set here. You want honest friends, and an innocent, respectable home for your children, and a name they won't be ashamed of. Send the whole set packing, and cut yourself loose from them."

Bertha stood up also. She had forgotten the little work-basket, and still held it in her hands, suspended before her.

"Will you tell me," she said, "what the lies were, — the lies you heard?"

Perhaps she thought, with a hopeless pang, they were not lies at all; perhaps he had only heard what was the truth, that she had been told to try to please him, that his good-will might be gained to serve an end. Looked at from Richard's stand-point that had been a very innocent thing; looked at from his stand-point it might seem just what it had seemed to herself, even in the reckless, desperate moment when she had given way.

He paused a moment, barely a moment, and then answered her.

"Yes," he said, "I will tell you if you want to know. There has been a big scheme on hand for some time, — there are men who must be influenced; I am one of them, and people say that the greater part of the work is carried on in your parlors here, and that you were set on me because you were a clever little manoeuverer, and knew your business better than"! should be likely to suspect. That is what they say, and that is what I must believe, because"—

He stopped short. He had drawn nearer the mantelpiece, and as he spoke some object lying upon it caught his eye. It was the letter directed to himself, lying with the address upward, and he took it in his hand.

"What is this?" he demanded. "Who left it here?"

Bertha stood perfectly motionless. Richard's words came back to her: "Give it to him if he is in a good humor. It contains arguments which I think will convince him." Then she looked at Blundel's face. If there could be any moment more unfit than another for the presentation of arguments it was this particular one. And never before had she liked him so well or valued his good opinion so highly as she did now, when he turned his common, angry, honest face upon her.

"What is it?" he said again. "Tell me."

She thought of Richard once more, and then of the children sleeping upstairs, and of the quiet, innocent day she had spent with them. They did not know that she was an intriguing woman, whom people talked of; she had never realized it herself to the full until this moment. They had delicately forborne giving any name to the thing she had done; but this man, who judged matters in a straightforward fashion, would find a name for it. But there was only one answer for her to make.

"It is a letter I was to give you," she said.

"And it is from your husband?"

"I have not read it," she replied.

He stopped short a moment and looked at her — with a sudden suggestion of doubt and bewilderment that was as bad as a blow.

"Look here!" he said. "You were going to give it to me, — you intended to do it."

"Yes."

He gave her another look, — amazement, anger, disbelief, struggling with each other in it, — and then thrust his obstinate fists into his pockets again and planted himself before her like a rock.

"By the Lord I" he said. "I won't believe it!"

The hard common-sense which had been his stronghold and the stand-by of his constituents for many a year came to his rescue. He might not know much of women; but he had seen intrigue, and trickery, and detected guilt, and it struck him if these things were here, they were before him in a new form.

"Now," he said, "tell me who gave it to you."

"You will know that," she answered, "when you read it."

"Tell me," he demanded, "if you know what is in it."

"I know something," she replied, "of what is in it."

"By Jove!" he exclaimed, "I'd give a great deal to know how much."

Only Richard could have told him how much or how little, and he was not there.

418

"Come," he said, as she made no reply, "they might easily deceive you. Tell me what you know, and I will believe you, — and there are very few women in your place I would say as much to."

"I do not think," she answered, "that they have deceived me."

"Then," he returned, his face hardening, "*you* have deceived *me!*"

"Yes," she answered, turning white, "I suppose I have."

There was a moment of dead silence, in which his shrewd eyes' did their work as well as they had done it at any time during his fifty years of life. Then he spoke to her again.

"They wanted me here because they wanted to make use of me," he said. "You knew that."

"They did not put it in that way," she answered. "I dare say you know that."

"You were to befool me as far as you could, and make the place agreeable to me, — you knew that?"

She turned paler.

"I — I have liked you very sincerely I" she broke forth, piteously. "I have liked you! Out of all the rest, that one thing was true! Don't — ah, don't think it was not."

His expression for a moment was a curiously undecided one; he was obliged to rally himself with a sharp rub at his hair.

"I'll tell you what I think of that when you have answered me another question," he said. "There is a person who has done a great deal of work in this matter, and has been very anxious about it, probably because he has invested in it more money than he can spare, — buying lands and doing one thing and another. That person is your husband, Mr. Richard Amory. Tell me if you knew that."

The blood rushed to her face and then left it again.

"Richard!" she exclaimed. "Richard!" and she caught at the mantel and held to it.

His eyes did not leave her for an instant. He nodded his head with a significance whose meaning was best known to himself.

"Sit down," he said. "I see you did not know that."

She did as he told her. It was as if such a flash of light had struck across her mental vision as half blinded her.

"Not Richard!" she cried out; and even as she said it a thousand proofs rushed back upon her and spoke the whole shameful truth for themselves.

Blundel came nearer to her, his homely, angry face, in spite of its anger, expressing honest good feeling as strongly as any much handsomer one might have done.

"I knew there had been deep work somewhere," he said. "I saw it from the first. As for you, you have been treated pretty badly. I supposed they persuaded you that you might as well amuse one man as another, — and I was the man. I dare say there is more behind than I can see. You had nothing to gain as far as you knew, that's plain enough to me."

"No," she exclaimed, "it was not I who was to gain! They did not think of — of me!"

"No," he went on, "they lost sight of you rather often when they had a use for you. It's apt to be the way. It's time some one should think of you, and I mean to do it. I am not going to say anything more against those who — made the mistake" (with a resentful shuffle of his shoulders as he put it thus mildly) ,"than I can help, but I am going to tell you the truth. I have heard ugly stories for some time, and I've had my suspicions of the truth of them; but I meant to wait for proof, and it was given me this afternoon. More was said to me than it was safe to say to an honest man, and I let the person who talked go as far as he would, and he was too desperate to be cautious. I knew a bold move was to be made, and I guessed it would be made to-night."

He took the envelope from his pocket where he had tucked it unopened. His face grew redder and hotter.

"If it were not for you," he said; "if I didn't have faith in your being the honest little woman I took you for; if I didn't believe you spoke the truth when you said you liked me as honestly as I liked you, — though the Lord knows there is no proof except that I do believe you in spite of everything, — I'd have the thing spread the length and breadth of the land by to-morrow morning, and there would be such an uproar as the country has not seen for a year or so."

"Wait!" said Bertha, half-starting from her seat. "I did not understand before. This is too much shame. I thought it was — only a letter. I did not know" —

He went to the fire.

"I believe that, too," he said, grimly; "but it is not a little thing I'm doing. I'm denying myself a great deal. I'd give five years of my life" — He straightened out his short, stout arm and closed hand with a robust gesture, and then checked himself. "You don't know what is in it. I don't know. I have not looked at it. There it goes." And he tossed it into the fire.

"The biggest fool of all," he said, "is the fool who takes every man for a knave. Do they think a country like this has been run for a century by liars and thieves? There have been liars and thieves enough, but not enough to bring it to a stand-still, and that seems to argue that there has been an honest man or so to keep a hand on their throats. When there are none left — well, it won't be as safe to belong to the nation as it is to-day, in spite of all that's bad in it."

The envelope had flamed up, and then died down into tindery blackness. He pointed to it.

"You can say it is there," he said, "and that I didn't open it, and they may thank you for it. Now I am going."

Bertha rose. She put her hand on the mantel again.

"If I do not thank you as I ought," she said, brokenly, "you must forgive me. I see all that you have spared me, but — I have had a heavy blow." He paused to look at her, rubbing his upright hair for the last time, his little eyes twinkling with a suspicious brightness, which had its softness too. He came back and took her hand, and held it in an awkward, kindly clasp.

"You are a good little woman," he said. "I'll say it to you again. You were not cut out to be made anything else of. You won't be anything else. You are young to be disappointed and unhappy. I know all that, and there doesn't seem much to say. Advice wouldn't amount to much, and I don't know that there is any to give."

They moved slowly toward the door together. When they stood upon the threshold he dropped her hand as awkwardly as he had taken it, and made a gesture toward the stairway, the suspicious brightness of his eyes more manifest than ever.

"Your children are up there asleep," he said, unsteadily. "Go to them."

And turning away, shrugged himself into his overcoat at the hat-stand, opened the door for himself, and went out of the house without another word.

Chapter 35

The last words of his half-reluctant, half-exultant confession had scarcely left Richard Amory's lips when Tredennis rose from his chair. "If you can," he said, "tell me the literal truth. Blundel is at your house with your wife. There is something she is to do. What is it?"

"She is to hand him an envelope containing a slip of paper," said Richard, doggedly. "That is what she is to do."

Tredennis crossed the room, and took his hat from its place.

"Will you come with me," he said, "or shall I go alone?"

"Where?" asked Richard.

Tredennis glanced at his watch.

"He would not call until late, perhaps," he said, "and she would not give it to him at once. It is ten now. We may reach there in time to spare her that, at least."

Richard bit his lip.

"There seems to be a good deal of talk of sparing her," he said. "Nobody spares me. Every folly I have been guilty of is exaggerated into a crime. Do you suppose that fellow isn't used to that sort of thing? Do you suppose I should have run the risk if he had not shown his hand this afternoon? She knows nothing of what she is to give him. There is no harm done to her."

"How is he to know she is not in the plot?" said Tredennis. "How is he to guess that she is not — what she has been made to seem to be? What insult is he not at liberty to offer her if he chooses?"

"She will take care of herself," said Richard. "Let her alone for that."

"By Heaven!" said Tredennis. "She has been let alone long enough. Has she ever been anything else but alone? Has there been one human creature among all she knew to help or defend or guide her? Who has given her a thought so long as she amused them and laughed with the rest? Who"—

Richard got up, a dawning curiosity in his face.

"What is the matter with *you?*" he said. "Have you been" —

The words died away. The colonel's gleaming eye stopped him.

"We will go at once, if you please," said Tredennis, and strode out of the room before him.

When they reached the house Bertha was still standing where her guest had left her a few moments before, and but one glance at her face was needed to show both of them that something unusual had occurred.

"You have had Blundel here?" Richard asked, with an attempt at his usual manner, which ill-covered his excitement. "We thought we saw him crossing the street."

"Yes," she answered. "He has just left me."

She turned suddenly and walked back to the hearth.

"He left a message for you," she said. "That is it," — and she pointed to the last bit of tinder flickering on the coals.

"The — letter!" exclaimed Richard.

"Yes," she answered. "Do you want Colonel Tredennis to hear about the letter, Richard, or does he know already?"

"He knows everything," answered Richard, "as every one else will to-morrow or the day after."

For a moment his despair made him so reckless that he did not make an effort at defence. He flung himself into a chair and gave up to the misery of the hour.

"You knew," said Bertha, looking toward Tredennis, "and did not tell me. Yes, I forgot," — with a bitter little smile, —"there was something you warned me of once and I would not listen, and perhaps you thought I would not listen now. If you know, will you tell me what was in the letter? I do not know yet, and I want to hear it put into words. It was money — or an offer of money? Tell me, if you please."

"It was money," said Richard, defiantly. "And there are others who have taken the same thing peacefully enough."

"And I was to give it to him because — because he was a little more difficult, and seemed to be my friend. Do all female lobbyists do such things, Richard, or was I honored with a special service?"

"It is not the first time it has been done," he answered, "and it won't be the last."

"It is the first time I have done it," she returned, "and it will be the last. The — risk is too great."

Her voice shook a little, but it was perfectly cold; and, though her eyes were dilated, such fire as might have been in them was quenched by some light to which it would have been hard to give a name.

"I do not mean the risk to myself," she said to Richard. "That I do not count. I meant risk to you. When he burned the letter he said, 'Tell them I did it for your sake, and that it is safer for them that I did it.'"

"What else did he say?" asked Richard, desperately. "He has evidently changed his mind since this afternoon."

"He told me you had a reason for your interest in the scheme, which was not the one you gave me. He told me you had invested largely in it, and could not afford to lose."

Richard started up, and turned helplessly toward Tredennis. He had not expected this, just yet at least.

"I — I"— he faltered.

The colonel spoke without lifting his eyes from the floor.

"Will you let me explain that?" he asked. "I think it would be better."

There was a moment's silence, in which Bertha looked from one to the other.

"You?" she said.

Richard's lids fell. He took a paper-knife from the table he leaned against, and began to play with it nervously. He had become a haggard, coarsened, weakened copy of himself; his hair hung in damp elf-locks over his forehead; his lips were pale and dry; he bit them to moisten them.

"The money," said Tredennis, "was mine. It was a foolish investment, perhaps; but the money — was mine."

"Yours!" said Bertha. "You invested in the Westoria lands!"

She put her hand in its old place on the mantel, and a strange laugh fell from her lips.

"Then I have been lobbying for you, too," she said. "I — wish I had been more successful."

Richard put his hand up, and pushed back the damp, falling locks of hair from his forehead restlessly.

"*I* made the investment," he said, "and I am the person to blame, as usual; but you would have believed in it yourself."

"Yes," she answered; "I should have believed in it, I dare say. It has been easy to make me believe, but I think I should also have believed in a few other things, — in the possibility of their being honor and good faith"—

She paused an instant, and then began again.

"You told me once that you had never regarded me seriously. I think that has been the difficulty — and perhaps it was my fault. It will not be necessary to use me any more, and I dare say you will let me go away for a while after a week or so. I think it would be better."

She left her place to cross the room to the door. On her way there she paused before Colonel Tredennis.

"I beg your pardon," she said, and went on.

At the door she stopped again one moment, fronting them both, her head held erect, her eyes large and bright.

"When Senator Blundel left me," she said, "he told me to go to my children. If you will excuse me, I will go."

And she made a stately little bow, and left them.

Chapter 36

The great social event of the following week was to be the ball given yearly for the benefit of a certain popular and fashionable charity. There was no charity so fashionable, and consequently no ball so well attended; everybody was more or less interested; everybody of importance appeared at it, showing themselves for a few moments at least. Even Mrs. Merriam, who counted among the privileges earned by a long and unswervingly faithful social career, the one of immunity from all ordinary society duties, found herself drawn into the maelstrom, and enrolled on the list of patronesses.

"You may do all the work, my dear," she said to Mrs. Sylvestre, "and I will appropriate the credit."

But she was not so entirely idle as she professed to be, and indeed spent several mornings briskly driving from place to place in her comfortable carriage, and distinguished herself by exhibiting an executive ability, a promptness and decision in difficulty, which were regarded with secret awe and admiration by her younger and less experienced colleagues. She had been out doing such work on the afternoon of the day before the ball, and returned home at her usual hour; but not in her usual equable frame of mind. This was evident when she entered the room where Mrs. Sylvestre sat talking to Colonel Tredennis, who had called. There were indeed such signs of mental disturbance in her manner that Mrs. Sylvestre, rising to greet her, observed them at once.

"I am afraid you have had an exciting morning," she said, "and have done too much work."

"My dear," was the reply, "nothing could be more true than that I have had an exciting morning."

"I am sorry for that," said Agnes.

"I am sorry for it," said Mrs. Merriam; "more sorry than I can say." Then turning to Tredennis, "I am glad to find you here. I have been hearing some most extraordinary stories; perhaps you can tell me what they mean."

"Whom do they concern?" asked Agnes. "We are entertained by many stories."

"They will disturb you as much as they have disturbed me," Mrs. Merriam answered. "They have disturbed me very much. They concern our little friend, Mrs. Amory."

"Bertha!" exclaimed Agnes.

Her tender heart beat quickly, and a faint flush showed itself on her cheek; she looked up at Colonel Tredennis with quick, questioning eyes. Perhaps she was not as unprepared for the statement as she might have been. She had seen much during the last few weeks which had startled and alarmed her. Mrs. Merriam looked at Tredennis also.

"You may be able to guess something of what the rumors form themselves upon," she said. "Heaven knows there has been enough foundation for anything in that miserable Westoria land scheme."

"You have heard something of it this morning?" said Tredennis.

"I have heard nothing else," was the answer. "The Westoria land scheme has come to an untimely end, with a flavor of scandal about it, which may yet terminate in an investigation. The whole city is full of it, and stories of Mrs. Amory and her husband are the entertainment offered you on all sides. I say 'Mrs. Amory and her husband,' because it is Mrs. Amory who is the favorite topic. She has been making the most desperate efforts to influence people; her parlors have been filled with politicians and lobbyists all the season; the husband was deeply involved in the matter; bribes have been offered and taken; there are endless anecdotes of Senator Planefield and his infatuation, and the way in which it has been used. She would have accomplished wonders if it had not been for Senator Blundel, who suspected her and led her into betraying herself. It is Senator Blundel who is credited with having been the means of exploding the whole affair. He has been privately investigating the matter for months, and had an interview with Mrs. Amory the other night, in which he accused her of the most terrible things, and threatened her with exposure. That is the way the stories run."

"Oh, this is very cruel," said Agnes. "We must do something. We must try; we cannot let such things be said without making an effort against them."

"Whatever is done must be done at once," replied Mrs. Merriam. "The conclusion of the matter is that there seems actually to be a sort of cabal formed against her."

"You mean" — began Agnes, anxiously.

"I mean," said Mrs. Merriam, "that my impression is that if she appears at the ball there are those who will be so rude to her that she will be unable to remain."

"Aunt Mildred!" exclaimed Agnes, in deep agitation. "Surely such a thing is impossible."

"It is not only not impossible," returned Mrs. Merriam, "but it is extremely probable. I heard remarks which assured me of that."

"She must not go!" said Agnes. "We must manage to keep her at home. Colonel Tredennis"—

"The remedy must go deeper than that," he answered. "The fact that she did not appear would only postpone the end. The slights she avoided one night would be stored up for the future, we may be sure."

He endeavored to speak calmly, but it was not easy, and he knew too well that such a change had come upon his face as the two women could not but see. Though he had feared this climax so long, though he had even seen day by day the signs of its approach, it fell upon him as a blow at last, and seemed even worse than in his most anxious hour he had thought it might be.

"She has friends," he said; "her friends have friends. I think there are those — besides ourselves — who will defend her."

"They must be strong," remarked Mrs. Merriam.

"There are some of them," he answered, "who are strong. I think I know a lady whose opinion will not go for nothing, who is generous enough to use her influence in the right direction."

"And that direction?" said Mrs. Merriam.

"If the opposing party finds itself met by a party more powerful than itself," he said, "its tone will change; and as for the story of

Senator Blundel I think I can arrange that he will attend to that himself."

"Mere denial would not go very far, I am afraid," said Mrs. Merriam. "He cannot deny it to two or three score of people."

"He can deny it to the entire community," he answered, "by showing that their intimacy remains unbroken."

"Ah!" cried Agnes, "if he would only go to the ball, and let people see him talking to her as he used to; but I am sure he never went to a ball in his life!"

"My dear," said Mrs. Merriam, "that is really a very clever idea, if he could be induced to go."

"He is an honest man," said Tredennis, flushing. "And he is her friend. I believe that sincerely; and I believe he would prove it by going anywhere to serve her."

"If that is true," said Mrs. Merriam, "a great deal will be accomplished, though it is a little difficult to figure to one's self how he would enjoy a ball."

"I think we shall have the pleasure of seeing," replied the colonel. "I myself" — He paused a moment, and then added: "I chance to have a rather intimate acquaintance with him; he has interested himself in some work of mine lately, and has shown himself very friendly to me. It would perhaps be easier for me to speak to him than for any other friend of Mrs. Amory."

"I think you would do it better than any other friend," Mrs. Merriam said, with a kindly look at him.

The truth was that, since his first introduction to Colonel Tredennis, Blundel had taken care that the acquaintance should not drop. He had found the modest warrior at once useful and entertaining. He had been able to gather from him information which it was his interest to count among his stores, and, having obtained it, was not ungrateful, and, indeed, was led by his appreciation of certain good qualities he recognized in him into something bordering on an attachment for his new friend.

"I like that fellow," he used to say, energetically.

And realizing something of this friendliness, and more of the honor and worth of his acquaintance, the colonel felt that he might hope to reach his heart by telling his story simply and with dignity, leaving the rest to him. As for the lady of whom be had spoken, he had but little doubt that that kind and generous heart might be reached; he had seen evidences of its truth and charity too often to distrust them. It was, of course, the wife of the Secretary of State he was thinking of, — that good and graceful gentlewoman, whose just and clear judgment he knew he could rely upon, and whose friendship would grant him any favor.

"She is very generous and sympathetic," he said, "and I have heard her speak most kindly of Mrs. Amory. Her action in the matter must have weight, and I have confidence that she will show her feeling in a manner which will make a deep impression. She has always been fond of Professor Herrick."

"That is as clever an idea as the other," said Mrs. Merriam. "She has drawn her lines so delicately heretofore that she has an influence even greater than was wielded by most of those who have occupied her position. And she is a decided and dignified person, capable of social subtleties."

"Oh!" exclaimed Mrs. Sylvestre, "it seems very hard that it should be Bertha who should need such defence."

"It is miserable," said Mrs. Merriam, impatiently. "It is disgraceful when one considers who is the person to blame. It is very delicate of us not to use names, I suppose; but there has been enough delicacy — and indelicacy — and I should like to use them as freely as other people do. I think you remember that I have not been very fond of Mr. Richard Amory."

When Colonel Tredennis left them he turned his steps at once toward the house of the woman who was his friend, and upon whose assistance so much depended. To gain her sympathy seemed the first thing to be done, and one thought repeated itself again and again in his mind, "How shall I say it best?"

But fortune favored him, and helped him to speak as he had not anticipated that it would.

The lady sat alone in her favorite chair in her favorite room, when he was ushered into her presence, as he had frequently happened to be before somewhere about the same hour. A book lay open upon her lap, but she was not reading it, and, he fancied, had not been doing so for some time. He also fancied that when she saw him her greeting glance had a shade of relief in it, and her first words seemed to certify that he was not mistaken.

"I am more than usually glad to see you," she said. "I think that if you had not appeared so opportunely I should have decided in about half an hour that I must send for you."

"I am very fortunate to have come," he answered, and he held her kind hand a moment, and there came into his face a look so anxious that, being in the habit of observing him, she saw it.

"Are you very well?" she asked, gently. "I am afraid not. You are rather pale. Sit down by my chair and let me look at you.""

"Am I pale?" said the colonel. "You are very good to notice it, though I am not ill. I am only — only" —

She looked at him with grave interest.

"Have you," she said, — "have you heard ill news of some friend? Is that it? I am afraid it is!"

"Yes," he answered, "that is it; and I am afraid you have heard of it, too."

"I am afraid I have," she returned. "Such things travel quickly. I have heard something which has distressed me very much. It is something I have heard faint rumors of before, but now it has taken on a definite form. This morning I was out, and this afternoon I have had some callers who were not averse to speaking plainly. I have heard a great many things said which have given me pain, and which embarrass me seriously. That was the reason I was wishing to see you. I felt that you would at least tell me a story without prejudice. There is a great deal of prejudice shown, of course. We need expect nothing else. I am sure Professor Herrick can know nothing of this. Will you tell me what you yourself know?"

"That is what I came to do," said the colonel, still paler, perhaps. "There is a great deal to tell — more than the world will ever know. It is only to such as you that it could be told."

There was more emotion in his voice and face than he had meant to reveal; perhaps something in the kind anxiousness of his companion's eyes moved him; he found that he could not sit still and speak as if

432

his interest was only the common one of an outsider, so he rose and stood before her.

"I cannot even tell you how it is that I know what I do to be true," he said. "I have only my word, but I *know* you will believe me."

"You may be sure of that," she answered.

"I *am* sure of it," he returned, "or I should not be here, for I have no other proof to offer. I came to make an appeal to you in behalf of a person who has been wronged."

"In behalf of Mrs. Amory?" she said.

"Yes," he replied, "though she does not know I am here, and will never know it. It scarcely seems my business, perhaps; she should have others to defend her; but there are no others who, having the interest of relationship, might not be accused of self-interest too. There is a slight tie of kinship between us, but it is only a slight one, and we have not always been very good friends, perhaps, though it must have been my own fault. I think I never pleased her very well, even when I saw her oftenest. She was used to brighter companionship. But her father liked me; we were friends, warm and close. I have felt almost as if I was his son, and have tried to spare him the knowledge of what would have hurt him. During the last few weeks I think he has had suspicions which have disturbed him, but they have not been suspicions of trouble to his child."

"I felt sure of that," the lady remarked.

"*She* has no suspicions of the true aspect of affairs," he continued, "though she has lately gained knowledge of the wrong done her. It has been a great wrong. She has not been spared. Her inexperience made her a child in the hands of those who used her as their tool. She understands now that it is too late — and it is very bitter to her."

"You knew her when she was a girl," his companion said, with her kind eyes on his sad, stern face.

"Yes," he answered, "when she was a girl and happy, and with all of life before her, and — she did not fear it."

"I knew her, too," she replied. "She has greatly changed since then."

"I saw that when I returned here," he said. And he turned his head aside and began to take up and set down a trifle on the mantel. "At first I did not understand it," he added. "Now I do. She has not changed without reason. If she has seemed light, there are women, I suppose, who hide many a pain in that way. She has loved her children, and made them happy — I know that, at least — and — and she has been a kind wife and an innocent woman. It is her friends who must defend her."

"She needs their defence," said his hearer. "I felt that when I was out this morning, and when my callers were with me, an hour ago." She held out her hand with sympathetic frankness. "I am her friend," she said, "and her father's — and yours. I think you have some plan; there is something you wish me to do. Tell me what it is."

"Yes," he answered, "there is something I wish you to do. No one else can do it so well. There are people who intend to testify to their belief in the stories they have heard by offering her open slights. It is likely that the attempt will be made to-morrow night at the ball. If you testify to your disbelief and disapproval by giving her your protection, the popular theory will be shaken, and there will be a reaction in her favor."

"It is not to be denied," she said, "that it is only women who can aid her. It is women who say these things, as a rule, and who can unsay them. The actions of men in such matters are of less weight than they should be, though it is true there is one man who might do her a service" —

"You are thinking of Senator Blundel," he said. "I — we have thought of that. We think — hope that he will come to the ball."

"If he does, and shows himself friendly toward her," she returned, "nothing more can be said which could be of much importance. He is the hero of the story, as I dare say you have heard. If he remains her friend, that proves that he did not accuse her of plotting against him, and that he has no cause for offence. If the story of the grand scene between them is untrue, the foundation-stone is taken away, and, having the countenance of a few people who show their confidence with tact and discretion, she is safe. I will go to the ball, my friend, and I will use what influence I possess to insure that she is not badly treated."

"I knew you would be kind to her," Tredennis said, with kindling

434

eyes. "I have seen you kind before to those who needed kindness, even to those who did not deserve it — and she does!"

"Yes, yes, I am sure she does!" she answered. "Poor child! Poor child!"

And she gave him her hand again, and, as he wrung it in his, her eyes were fuller of sympathy than ever.

He reached Senator Blunders rooms an hour later, and found him in the midst of his papers and pigeonholes, — letters and pamphlets to right of him, to left of him, before and behind him.

"Well," he said, by way of greeting, "our Westoria friends are out of humor this morning."

"So I have heard," Tredennis answered.

"And they may well be — they may well be," he said, nodding sharply. "And there are some fine stories told, of course."

"I have come to tell you one myself, sir," said Tredennis.

"What!" cried Blundel, turning on his chair, —"you have a story?"

"Yes," returned the colonel, "not a pleasant one, and as it concerns you I will waste as few words as possible."

He wasted no words at all. The story was a brief one, but as forcible as simple words could make it. There was no effort to give it effectiveness, and yet there were touches here and there which appealed to the man who heard it as he had been rarely appealed to before.

They brought before him things which had found a lodging in corners of his practical political mind, and had haunted him rather pathetically since the night he had shrugged himself into his overcoat, and left the slight, desolate-looking figure behind him. He had enjoyed his friendship too much not to regret it now that he felt it was a thing of the past; he had felt the loss more than once of the new element it had introduced into his life, and had cast about in his mind in vain for a place where he could spend a spare hour or so as pleasantly as he had often spent such hours in a bright parlor he knew of. Before Tredennis had half finished his relation he was moving restlessly in his chair, and uttering occasional gruff ejaculations, and when it came to an end he sprang up, looking not a trifle heated.

"That's it, is it?" he exclaimed. "They have been inventing something new about her, have they, and dragged me into it into the bargain?

And they are making up plots against her, — poor little woman! — as if she hadn't been treated badly enough. A lot of gossips, I'll wager!"

"Some of them are good enough," said the colonel. "They only mean to signify their disapproval of what they would have the right to condemn if it were a truth instead of a lie."

"Well, they shall not do it at my expense, that's all," was the answer. "It is a lie from beginning to end, and I will do something toward proving it to them. I don't disapprove of her, — they shall see that. She's a genuine good little thing. She's a lady. Any fool can see that. She won *me* over, by George! when everything was against her. And she accused nobody when she might have said some pretty hard true things, and nine women out of ten would have raised the very deuce. She's got courage, and — yes, and dignity, and a spirit of her own that has helped her to bear many a bitter thing without losing her hold on herself, I'd be willing to swear. Look here," he added, turning suddenly and facing Tredennis, "how much do you know of her troubles? Something, I know, or you wouldn't be here."

"Yes," answered the colonel, "I know something."

"Well," he continued, in an outburst of feeling, "I don't ask how much. It's enough, I dare say, to make it safe for me to speak my mind, — I mean safe for her, not for myself. There's a fellow within a hundred miles of here I should like to thrash within an inch of his life; and an elegant, charming, amiable fellow he is too, who, possibly, persuaded himself that he was doing her very little injury."

"The injury has been done nevertheless," said Tredennis, gravely. "And it is her friends who must right it."

"I'm willing to do my share," said Blundel. "And let that fellow keep out of my way. As to this ball — I never went to a ball in my life, but I will appear at this one, and show my colors. Wait a minute!" As if an idea had suddenly struck him. "Go to the ball? — I'll *take* her there myself."

The spirit of combat was aroused within him; the idea presented itself to him with such force that he quite enjoyed it. Here, arraigned on one side, were these society scandal-mongers and fine ladies; here, on the other, was himself, Samuel Blundel, rough and blunt, but determined enough to scatter them and their lies to the four winds.

He rather revelled in the thought of the struggle, if struggle there was to be. He had taken active part in many a row in the House in which the odds had been against him, and where his obstinate strength had outlived the subtle readiness of a dozen apparently better equipped men. And his heart was in this deed of valor too; it glowed within him as he thought how much really depended upon him. Now, this pretty, bright creature must turn to him for protection and support. He almost felt as if he held her gloved hand resting upon his burly arm already with a clinging touch.

"I'll take her myself," he repeated. "I'll go and see her myself, and explain the necessity of it — if she does not know all."

"She does not know all yet," said Tredennis, "and I think she was scarcely inclined to go to the ball; but I am sure it will be better that she should go."

"She will go," said Blundel, abruptly. "I'll make her. She knows *me*. She will go if I tell her she must. That is what comes of being an old fellow, you see, and not a lady's man."

He had not any doubt of his success with her, and, to tell the truth, neither had Colonel Tredennis. He saw that his blunt honesty and unceremonious, half-paternal domineering would prove to her that he was in the right, even if she were at first reluctant; and this being settled, and the matter left in Blunders hands, the colonel went away. Only before going he said a few words, rather awkwardly.

"There would be nothing to be gained by mentioning my name," he said. "It is mere accident that — that I chance to know what I have spoken of. She does not know that I know it. I should prefer that she should not."

"What!" said Blundel, — "she is not to know how you have been standing by her?"

"She knows that I would stand by her if she needed me. She does not need me; she needs you. I have nothing to do with the matter. I don't wish to be mentioned."

When he was gone Blundel rubbed his hair backward and then forward by way of variety.

"Queer fellow!" he said, meditatively. "Not quite sure I've exactly

437

got at him yet. Brave as a lion and shy as a" boy. Absolutely afraid of women."

Chapter 37

In less than an hour his card was brought to Bertha as she sat with her children. She read it with a beating heart, and, having done so, put down Meg and her picture-book.

"I will go down at once," she said to the servant.

In two minutes she was standing in the middle of the parlor, and her guest was holding her hand in his, and looking at her earnestly and curiously.

"You didn't expect to see me here, did you?" he said.

"No," she answered; "but you are kind to come."

"I didn't expect to be here myself," he said. "Where is your husband? Somebody told me he had gone away."

"He is in New York," she replied.

He gave her one of his sharp glances and drew her toward a chair.

"Sit down by me," he said. "You are in no condition to be kept standing. I want to talk to you. You mustn't look like that," he said. "It won't do. You are worn out, but you mustn't give up. I have come to order you to do something."

"I will do anything you tell me," she answered.

"You will? Well, that's good! I thought you would, too. I want you to take me to this ball that is to be given to-morrow night."

She started in amazement.

"To the ball!" she exclaimed.

"Surprises you, doesn't it? I supposed it would; it surprises me a little, but I want to go nevertheless, and I have a reason."

"I am sure it is a good one," she said.

"It is," he answered. "None but the best would take me there. I never went to a ball in my life. *You* are the reason. I am going to take care of *you*."

A faint, sad smile touched her lips.

"Some one has said something more against me," she said, "and you want to defend me. Don't take the trouble. It is not worth while."

"The place is full of lies about you," he answered, suddenly and fiercely. "And I *am* going to defend you. No one else can. They are lies that concern me as well as you."

"Will you tell me what they are?" she asked.

He saw there was no room for hesitation, and told her what the facts were. As he spoke he felt that they did not improve in the relation, and he saw the blood rise to her cheeks, and a light grow in her eyes. When he had finished the light was a brilliant spark of fire.

"It is a charming story," she said.

"*We* will show them what sort of a story it is," he answered, "to-morrow night 1"

"You are very good to me," she said.

Suddenly she put her hand to her side.

"Ah!" she exclaimed, "it seems very strange that they should be saying these things of Bertha Amory."

She looked at him with a hopeless appeal in her eyes.

"Do they all believe them?" she said. "Ah, how can they? They know I was not — like that! I have not done anything! I have been unhappy, but — but I" —

She stopped a moment — or was stopped by her breaking voice.

"This has been too much for you," he said. "You are ill, child!"

"I have been ill for some time," she answered. "And the last few days have been very hard."

She made an effort to recover herself.

"I will go to the ball," she said, "if you think it best."

"It *is* best," he replied. "And you need not be afraid"—

"I am not afraid," she interposed, quickly, and the spark of fire showed itself in her eyes again. "I might allow myself to be beaten, if it were not for my children; but, as it is, you will see that I will not be beaten. I will be well for to-morrow night at least. I will not look like a victim. They will see that I am not afraid."

"It is they who will be beaten," said Blundel, "if anything depends on me! Confound it! I shall *like* to do it."

Chapter 38

He went home quite eager for the fray, and his eagerness was not allowed to flag. The favorite story came to his ears again and again. Men met him in the streets, and stopped to speak of it; others dropped into his rooms to hear the truth from himself, when he went to his hotel to dine; talkers standing in groups in the lobbies turned to look at him, and when he had passed them returned to their conversation with renewed interest. To the first man who referred to the matter he listened until he had said his say. Then he answered him.

"You want to hear the truth about that," he said, "don't you?"

"That, of course," was the reply.

"And you want to be able to *tell* the truth about it when you are asked questions?"

"Most certainly."

"Well, then, the truth is that there isn't a word of truth in it from beginning to end; and if you want to *tell* the truth, say it's a lie, and add that I said so, and I am prepared to say so to every man who wants to interview me; and, what is more, every man who tells another that it is a lie does me a favor that gives him a claim on me."

He repeated the same thing in effect each time an opportunity presented itself, and as these opportunities were frequent and each time he gained something of heat and lost something of temper and patience, he was somewhat tired and by no means in the best of humors when he sat down to his dinner, in the big, glaring, crowded hotel dining-room, amid the rattle of knives, forks, and crockery, the rushing to and fro of excited waiters, and the incoming and outgoing of hungry people. His calmness was not added to by observing that the diners at the tables near him discovered him as with one accord almost as soon as he entered, and cast glances of interest at him between the courses.

"Perfectly dreadful scene, they say," he heard one lady remark, with an unconscious candor born of her confidence that the clatter of dishes would drown all sound. "Went down on her knees to him and wrung her bands, imploring him to have mercy on her. Husband disappeared next day. Quite society people too. She has been a great deal admired."

What further particulars the speaker might have entered into there is no knowing, as she was a communicative person and plainly enjoyed her subject; but just at this juncture the lady to whom she was confiding her knowledge of the topics of the hour uttered an uneasy exclamation.

"Gracious! Maria!" she said. "He has heard you! I am sure he has! He has turned quite red — redder than he was — and he is looking at us! O Maria!" in accents sepulchral with fright, "he is getting up! He is coming to speak to us! O — Mari!"—

He was upon them at that very moment. He was accustomed to public speaking, and his experience led him to the point at once. He held his newspaper half folded in his hand, and, as had been said, he was a trifle redder than usual; but his manner was too direct to be entirely devoid of dignity.

"I beg your pardon," he said, "but my name is Blundel."

The most hopelessly terrified of the ladies found herself saying that he "was very kind," and the one who had told the story gasped faintly, but with an evident desire to propitiate, that she "had heard so."

"I take the liberty of mentioning it," he added, "because I have been sitting quite near to you and chanced to overhear what you were saying, and as you are evidently laboring under an impression I am interested in correcting, I felt obliged to intrude on you with a view to correcting it. I have been denying that story all day. It isn't true. Not a word of it. I never said an unkind word to the lady you mention, and I never had an unkind thought of her. No one has any right to speak ill of her. I am her friend. You will excuse my interrupting you. Here is my card." And he laid the card on the table, made a bow not so remarkable for grace, perhaps, as for perfect respectfulness, and marched back to his table.

There were few people in the room who did not turn to look at him as he sat down again, and nine out of ten began to indulge in highly colored speculations as to why he had addressed the women and who they were. There had never been a more popular scandal than the Westoria land scheme; the magnitude of it, the element of romance connecting itself with it, the social position of the principal schemers, all endeared it to the public heart. Blundel himself had become a hero, and had the rumors regarding his irreproachable and dramatic conduct only been rife at a time of election they would have assured him an overwhelming majority. Perhaps as he approached the strangers' table there had been a fond, flickering hope cherished that these two apparently harmless women were lobbyists themselves, and that their disguise was to be rent from them, and their iniquities to be proclaimed upon the spot. But the brief episode ended with apparent tameness, and the general temperature was much lowered, the two ladies sinking greatly in public opinion, and the interest in Blundel himself flagging a little. There was one person, however, who did not lose interest in him. This was a little, eager, birdlike woman who sat at some distance from him, at a small table, alone. She had seen his every movement since his entrance, and her bright, dark eyes followed him with an almost wistful interest. It was Miss Jessup; and Miss Jessup was full to the brim, and pressed down and running over, with anecdotes of the great scandal, and her delicate little frame almost trembled with anxious excitement as she gazed upon him and thought of what might be done in an interview.

He had nearly finished his dinner before he caught sight of her, but as he was taking his coffee he glanced down the room, saw and recognized her.

"The very woman!" he exclaimed, under his breath. "Why didn't I think of that before?" And in five minutes Miss Jessup's heart was thrilled within her, for he had approached her, greeted her, and taken the seat she offered him.

"I have come," he said, "to ask a favor of you."

"Of me!" said Miss Jessup. "That does not sound exactly natural. I have generally asked favors of you. I have just been looking at you and making up my mind to ask one."

"Wanted to interview me," he asked, — "didn't you?"

She nodded her head, and her bright eyes brightened.

"Well," sturdily, "I *want* you to interview me. Go ahead and do it."

"You *want* to be interviewed!" she exclaimed, positively radiant with innocent joy. "No! Really?"

"I am here for that purpose," he answered.

She left her seat instantly.

"Come into the parlor," she said. "It is quiet there at this time. We can sit where we shall not be disturbed at all."

They went into the parlor and found at the far end of it the quiet corner they needed, and two chairs. Miss Jessup took one and Blundel the other, which enabled him to present his broad back to all who entered. Almost before he was seated Miss Jessup had produced her neat notebook and a pencil.

"Now," she said, "I am ready for anything; but I must say I don't see how I am favoring *you*."

"You are going to favor me by saving me the trouble of contradicting a certain story every half-hour," he said.

"Ah!" ejaculated Miss Jessup, her countenance falling a little; "it is not true?"

"Not a word of it."

Humane little creature as she was, as she glanced down at her note-book, Miss Jessup felt that some one had been a trifle defrauded.

"And there was no scene?"

"No."

"And you did not threaten to expose her?"

"No."

"And you wish me to tell people that?"

"Yes, as pointedly as possible, in as few words as possible, and without mentioning names if possible."

"Oh, it would not be necessary to mention names; everybody would understand the slightest reference."

"Well, when you have done that," said Blundel, "you have granted me my favor."

"And you want it to be brief?" said Miss Jessup.

"See here," said Blundel; "you are a woman. I want you to speak the truth for another woman as plainly, and — as delicately as a woman can. A man would say too much or too little; that is why I come to you."

She touched her book with her pencil, and evidently warmed at once.

"I always liked her," she said, with genuine good feeling, "and I could not help hoping that the story was not true, after all. As it was public property, it was my business to find out all about it if I could; but I couldn't help being sorry. I believe I can say the right thing, and I will do my best. At any rate, it will be altogether different from the other versions."

"There won't be any other versions if I can prevent it," returned Blundel. "I shall have some interviews with newspaper men to-night, which will accomplish that end, I hope."

"Ah!" exclaimed Miss Jessup, "then mine will be the only statement."

"I hope so," he answered. "It will be if I have any influence."

"Oh, then," she said, "you have done me a favor, after all."

"It won't balance the favor you will have done me," he replied, "if you do your best in this matter. You see, I know what your best is, and I depend on it."

"Well," she said, "it is very kind of you to say so, and I will try to prove myself worth depending on, but"— And she scribbled a little in her notebook. "I don't mind telling you that the reason that is strongest in my mind is quite an unprofessional one. It is the one you spoke of just now. It is because I am a woman, too."

"Then she is safe," he returned. "Nothing could make her safer. And I am grateful to you beforehand, and I hope you will let me say so."

And they shook hands and parted the best of friends, notwithstanding that the interview had dwindled down into proportions quite likely to be regarded by the public as entirely insignificant.

Chapter 39

It had certainly been expected by the public that the morning papers would contain some interesting reading matter, and in some respects these expectations were realized. The ignominious failure of the Westoria land scheme was discussed with freedom and vigor, light being cast upon it from all sides, but upon the subject which had promised most there was a marked silence. Only in one paper there appeared a paragraph — scarcely more — written with much clearness and with a combined reserve and directness which could not fail to carry weight. It was very well done, and said so much in little, and with such unmistakable faith in its own statements and such suggestions of a foundation for that faith, that it was something of a shock to those who had delighted in the most elaborate ornamentation of the original story. In effect it was a denial not only of the ornamentation, but of the story itself, and left the liberal commentator not a fact to stand upon, so that he became temporarily the prey of discouragement and spiritual gloom, which was not a little added to by the events of the day.

There was, however, no sense of discouragement in the mind of Senator Blundel as he attired himself for the fray when night arrived. His mood was a fine combination of aggressiveness, generous kindliness, hot temper, and chivalric good feeling. He thought all day of the prospect before him, and in the afternoon went to the length of calling at a florist's and ordering a bouquet to be sent to Mrs. Amory, choosing it himself and feeling some pride in the good taste of his selection. He was so eager, indeed, that the day seemed quite long to him, and he dressed so early after dinner that he had two or three hours to wait before his carriage arrived.

But it did arrive at last, and he went down to it, drawing on with some difficulty an exceedingly tight pair of gloves, the obduracy of whose objections to being buttoned gave him something to combat with and suited his frame of mind to a nicety.

He was not called upon to wait very long after his entrance into the parlor. A few moments after his arrival Bertha came down. She was superbly dressed in white; she carried his roses and violets, and there burned upon her cheeks a color at once so delicate and brilliant that he was surprised by it. He had, indeed, rather expected to see her paler.

"Upon my soul," he said, "you don't look much frightened!"

"I am not frightened at all," she answered.

"That is a good thing," he returned. "We shall get on all the better for it. I never saw you with a brighter color."

She touched her cheek with her gloved finger.

"It is not rouge," she said. "I have been thinking of other parties I have attended — and of how these ladies will look at me to-night — and of what they possibly said of me yesterday — and it has been good for me."

"It was not so good for them, however," he suggested, regarding her with new interest. Her spirit pleased him; he liked it that she was not ready to allow herself to be beaten down, that she held her head erect and confronted her enemies with resolute eyes; he had a suspicion that there were women enough who would have been timorous and pathetic.

"I could not hurt them," she replied. "It would matter very little what I thought or said of them; it is only they who can harm me."

"They shall none of them harm you," he said, stoutly.

"I will see to that; but I'm glad you are looking your best."

But she could not help seeing that he was a trifle anxious about her. His concern manifested itself in occasional touches of half-paternal kindliness which were not lost upon her. He assisted her to put on her wrap, asked her if it was warm enough, ordered her to draw it closely about her, and tucked her under his arm as he led her out to the carriage with an air of determined protection not to be mistaken.

Perhaps his own views as to what form of oppression and opposition they were to encounter were rather vague. He was sufficiently accustomed to the opposition of men, but not to that of women; but, whatever aspect it assumed upon this occasion, he was valiantly determined not to be moved by it.

"I can't dance with you," he said, "that's true — I wish I could; but I will see that you have plenty of partners."

"I don't think the difficulty will be in the partners," Bertha replied, with a faint smile. "The men will not be unkind to me, you will see."

"They won't believe it, eh?" said Blundel. Her eyes met his, and the faint smile had a touch of bitterness.

"Some of them will not believe it," she answered; "and some will not care."

There was not the slightest shade of any distrust of herself or her surroundings, either in her face or manner, when, on reaching their destination, she made her way into the cloak-room. The place was already crowded — so crowded that a new-comer was scarcely noticeable. But, though she seemed to see nothing, glancing to neither right nor left, and occupying herself with the removal of her wraps, and with a few calm last touches bestowed upon her toilet before a mirror, scarcely a trifle escaped her. She heard greetings, laughter, gay comments on the brilliancy and promise of the ball; she knew where stood a woman who would be likely to appear as an enemy, where stood another who might be neutral, and another who it was even possible might be a friend. But she meant to run no risks, and her long training in self-control stood her in good stead; there was neither consciousness nor too much unconsciousness in her face; when the woman whom she had fancied might lean toward friendliness saw and bowed to her, she returned the greeting with her pretty, inscrutable smile, the entire composure of which so impressed the matron who was disposed to neutrality that she bowed also, and so did some one near her. But there were others who did not bow, and there were those who, discovering the familiar, graceful figure, drew together in groups, and made an amiable comment or so. But she did not seem to see them. When, taking up her flowers and her white ostrich-feather fan, she passed down the little lane, they expressed their disapproval by making way for her as she turned toward the door. She was looking at two ladies who were entering, and, general attention being directed toward them, they were discovered to be Mrs. Sylvestre and Mrs. Merriam.

"Now," it was asked, "what will *they* do?"

What they did was very simple in itself, but very remarkable in the eyes of the lookers-on. They paused and spoke to the delinquent in quite their usual manner.

"We would ask you to wait for us," Mrs. Merriam was heard to say, finally, "but there are so many people here to be attended to, and we saw Senator Blundel waiting for you at the door. May I tell you how pretty your dress is, and how brilliant you are looking?"

"Senator Blundel!" was repeated by the nearest groups. "It could not be Senator Blundel who is with her."

But those who were near enough to the door were subjected to the mental shock of seeing that it was Senator Blundel himself. He appeared in festal array, rubicund, and obstinately elate, and, stepping forward, took his charge's hand, and drew it within his portly arm.

"What!" he said, "you are not pale yet — and yet there were plenty of them in there. What did they do?"

"Three of them were good enough to bow to me," she answered, "and the rest drew away and discussed me in undertones. The general impression was, I think, that I was impudent. I did not feel impudent, and I don't think I looked so."

"Poor little woman!" he said. "Poor little woman!"

"No! no!" she exclaimed, looking straight before her, with dangerously bright eyes; "don't say that to me. Don't pity me, please — just yet — it isn't good for me. I need — I need"—

There was a second or so of dead silence. She did not tell him what she needed.

When they entered the ball-room a waltz was being played, and the floor was thronged with dancers; the ladies who formed the committee of reception stood near the door; a party of guests had just received the usual greetings and retired. The commandress-in-chief turned to meet the newcomers. She was a stately and severe dowager, with no intention of flinching from her duty; but her sudden recognition of the approaching senatorial figure was productive of a bewilderment almost too great for her experience to cope with. She looked, caught her breath, lost it and her composure at one and the same time, cast a despairing glance at her aides, and fell a victim to circumstances. Here was the subject under ban calmly making the most graceful and self-possessed obeisance before her, and her escort was the man of whom it had been said that a few days ago he had exposed her infamous plotting. This was more than even the most experienced matron could be prepared for. It must be admitted that her presence of mind deserted her, and that her greetings were not marked by the ready tact which usually characterized them.

"My first ball, madam," remarked the senator, scenting difficulty in the breeze, and confronting it boldly. "But for my friend, Mrs. Amory, I am afraid I should not be here. I begin to feel indebted to her already."

"It promises very well," said Bertha. "I never saw the room gayer. How pretty the decorations are!"

They passed on to make room for others, leaving the estimable ladies behind them pale with excitement, and more demoralized than they would have been willing to admit.

"What does it mean?" they asked one another. "They appear to be the best of friends! What are we to understand?"

There was one kindly matron at the end of the line who looked after the pair with an expression of sympathy which was rather at variance with the severity of the role she had been called upon to enact.

"It appears," she said, "as if the whole story might be a fabrication, and the senator determined to prove it so. I hope with all my heart he will."

By the time they reached their seats the news of their arrival had made the circle of the room. Bertha herself, while she had listened with a smile to her escort's remarks, had seen amazement and recognition flash out upon a score of faces; but she had preserved her smile intact, and still wore it when she took her chair. She spoke to Blundel, waving her fan with a soft, even motion.

"We have run the gauntlet," she said, "and we have chosen a good position. Almost everybody in the room has seen us; almost every one in the room is looking at us."

"Let them look!" he answered. "I have no objection to it."

"Ah, they will look!" she returned. "And we came to be — to be looked at. And it is very good of you to have no objections. Do I seem perfectly at ease? I hope so — though I am entirely well aware that at least a hundred people are discussing me. Is the expression of my eyes good — careless enough?"

"Yes, child, yes," he answered, a little uneasily. There was an undertone in her voice which troubled him, much as he admired her spirit and self-control.

"Thank you," she said. "Here is a bold man coming to ask me to dance. I told you the men would not be afraid of me. I think, if you approve of it, I will dance with him."

"Go and dance," he answered.

When her partner bore her away he took charge of her flowers and wrap in the most valiant manner, and carried them with him when he went to pay his respects to the matrons of his acquaintance who sat against the wall discussing with each other the most exciting topic of the hour, and who, when he addressed them, questioned him as closely as good-breeding would permit, upon all subjects likely to cast light upon this topic.

"Never was at a ball in my life before," he admitted. "Asked Mrs. Amory to bring me. Wanted to see how I should like it."

"With Mrs. Amory?" remarked matron No. 1. "She is dancing, I believe."

"Yes," he said, good-naturedly. "She will be dancing all night, I suppose, and I shall be carrying her flowers; but I don't mind it — in fact, I rather like it. I dare say there are two or three young fellows who would be glad enough to be in my place."

"I have no doubt," was the reply. "She has been very popular — and very gay."

"She is very popular with me," said the senator, "though I am an old fogy, and don't count. We are great friends, and I am very proud to be her escort to-night. I feel I am making my *début* under favorable circumstances."

There could be no doubt of his sentiments after that.

He was her friend. He admired her. He even made a point of saying so. What became of the story of the scandal? It seemed to have ended in nothing and worse than nothing; there was something a little ridiculous about such a tame termination to such an excitement. One or two of the ladies who had found it most absorbing looked aimlessly into space, and an embarrassed silence fell upon them.

Bertha ended her dance and returned to her seat. Her color was even brighter than before, and her smile was more brilliant. For a few moments a little group surrounded her, and her programme was half full. Blundel came back to his post like a sentinel. If she had been looked at before, she was regarded now with a double eagerness. Those who were not dancing watched her every movement; even those who danced asked each other questions. The group about her chair was added to and became gayer, but there were no women numbered in the circle. The general wonder was as to what would be done in the end. So far, round dances only had been danced. The next dance was a quadrille. The music struck up, and the dancers began to take their places. As they did so a party entered the room and made its way toward the end where the group stood about the chair. Bertha did not see it; she was just rising to take her station in the set nearest to her. The matron of the party, who was a figure so familiar in social circles as to be recognized at once by all who saw her, was accompanied by her daughter and an escort. It was the wife of the Secretary of State, and her cavalier was Colonel Tredennis.

"There is Mrs. Amory," she said to him as they approached. "She is taking her place in the quadrille. One moment, if you please."

Experience had taught her all that might be feared, and a quick eye showed her that something was wrong. Bertha advanced to her place, laughing a little at some jest of her partner's. She had not seen who the dancers were. The jest and the laugh ended, and she looked, up at her *vis-à-vis*. The lady at his side was not smiling; she was gazing steadily at Bertha herself. It seemed as if she had been waiting to catch her eye. It was the "great lady," and, having carried the figurative pebble until this fitting moment, she threw it. She spoke two or three words to her partner, took his arm, turned her back, and walked away.

Bertha turned rather pale. She felt the blood ebb out of her face. There was no mistaking the significance of the action, and it had not escaped an eye. This was more than she had thought of. She made a movement, with what intention she herself was too much shaken to know, and, in making it, her eyes fell upon a face whose expression brought to her an actual shock of relief. It was the face of the kind and generous gentlewoman who had just entered, and who, at this moment, spoke to her daughter.

"My dear," she said, "I think you promised Colonel Tredennis the first quadrille. Go and take that vacant place, and when you speak to Mrs. Amory ask her to come and talk to me a little as soon as the dance is over."

There was a tone of gentle decision in her voice and a light in her eye which were not lost upon the bystanders. She gave Bertha a bow and smile, and sat down. The most fastidious woman in Washington — the woman who drew her lines so delicately that she had even been called almost too rigorous; the woman whose well-known good taste and good feeling had given her a power mere social position was powerless to bestow — had taken the subject of the hour's scandal under her protection, and plainly believed nothing to her discredit.

In five minutes the whole room was aware of it. She had greeted Mrs. Amory cordially, she had openly checkmated an antagonist, she had sent her own daughter to fill the place left vacant in the dance.

"She would not have done that if she had not had the best of reasons," it was said.

"And Senator Blundel would scarcely be here if the story had been true."

"He has told several of his friends that he is here to prove that it is *not* true!"

"He denied it again and again yesterday."

"It was denied in one of the morning papers, and they say he kept it out of the rest because he was determined she should not be more publicly discussed."

"She is not one of the women who have been in the habit of giving rise to discussion."

"She is a pretty, feminine-looking little creature."

"Poor girl! It must have been bitter enough for her."

"Rather fine of old Blundel to stand by her in this way."

"He would not do it if there was not something rather fine in her. He is not a ladies' man, old Sam Blundel. Look at him! How he looms up behind his bouquet!"

The tide of public opinion had taken a turn. Before the dance had ended two or three practical matrons, who were intimately known to Colonel Tredennis' friendly supporter, had made their way to her and asked her opinion and intentions frankly, and had received information calculated to set every doubt at rest.

"It is scarcely necessary for me to speak of my opinion of the matter," the lady said, "when we have the evidence of Senator Blundel's presence here with Mrs. Amory to-night. I should feel myself unpardonably in the wrong if I did not take the most open measures in the defence of the daughter of my old friend, who has been treated most unjustly. And I cannot help hoping that she will have other defenders than myself."

Several of the matrons so addressed were seated within speaking range when Bertha came to her friend at the close of the dance, and she recognized at once on approaching them that she need fear them no longer. But she could not say much in response to their greetings; she answered them briefly, bowed slightly, and sat down in the chair near the woman who had protected her. She could even say but little to her; the color had died out of her face at last; the strain she had borne so long had reached its highest tension to-night, and the shock of the moment, received through an envious woman's trivial spite, slight as it might have been in itself, represented too much to her. As he had passed her in the dance and touched her hand, Tredennis had felt it as cold as ice, and the look of her quiet, white face had been almost more than he could bear to see."

"Bertha," he had said to her once, "for God's sake, take courage!"

But she had not answered him. A few months ago she would have

455

given him a light, flippant reply, if her very soul had been wrung within her, but now she was past that.

As she sat, afterwards, by the wife of the Secretary of State, her hand shook as she held her fan.

"You were very kind to me just now," she said, in a low voice. "I cannot express my thanks as I wish."

"My dear," was the reply, "do not speak of it. I came to take care of you. I think you will have no more trouble. But I am afraid this has been too much for you. You are shivering a little."

"I am cold," Bertha answered. "I — feel as if — something strange had happened to me. It was not so before. I seem — to have lost courage."

"But you must not lose courage yet," she said, with a manner at once soft and firm. "A great many people are looking at you. They will be very curious to know how you feel. It is best that you should not let them see."

She spoke rather rapidly, but in a low voice. No one near could hear. She was smiling, as if the subject of the conversation was the least important in the world.

"Listen to me," she said, in the same manner, "and try to look as if we were speaking of ordinary topics. I dare say you feel as if you would prefer to go away, but I think you must remain. Everybody here must understand that you have friends who entirely disbelieve all that has been said against you, and also that they wish to make their confidence in you public. I should advise you to appear to enjoy yourself moderately well. I think I wish you to dance several times again. I think there will be no difficulty in arranging the next square dance. When the presidential party arrives, the President will, I have no doubt, be pleased to talk to you a little. It would be republican to say that it is absurd to consider that such a thing can be of consequence; but there are people with whom it will have weight. As soon as possible, I shall send you down to the supper-room with Senator Blundel. A glass of wine will do you good. Here is Senator Blundel now. Do you think you can talk to him in your usual manner?"

"I will try," said Bertha. "And, if I do not, I think he will understand."

He did understand. The little incident had been no more lost upon him than upon others. He was glowing with repressed wrath, and sympathy, and the desire to do something which should express his feeling. He saw at once the change which had come upon her, and realized to the full all that it denoted. When he bore her off to the supper-room he fairly bristled with defiance of the lookers-on who made way for them.

"Confound the woman!" he said. "If it had only been a man!"

He found her the most desirable corner in the supper-room, and devoted himself to her service with an assiduity which touched her to the heart.

"You have lost your color," he said. "That won't do. We must bring it back."

"I am afraid it will not come back," she answered.

And it did not, even though the tide had turned, and that it had done so became more manifest every moment. They were joined shortly by Colonel Tredennis and his party, and by Mrs. Merriam and hers. It was plain that Mrs. Amory was to be alone no more; people who had been unconscious of her existence in the ball-room suddenly recognized it as she sat surrounded by her friends; the revulsion of feeling which had taken place in her favor expressed itself in a hundred trifles. But her color was gone, and returned no more, though she bore herself with outward calmness. It was Colonel Tredennis who was her first partner when they returned to the ball-room. He had taken a seat near her at the supper-table, and spoken a few words to her.

"Will you give me a place on your card, Bertha?" he had said, and she had handed it to him in silence.

He was not fond of dancing, and they had rarely danced together, but he wished to be near her until she had had time to recover herself. Better he than another man who might not understand so well; he knew how to be silent, at least.

So they went through their dance together, exchanging but few words, and interested spectators looked on, and one or two remarked to each other that, upon the whole, it appeared that Mrs. Amory was rather well supported, and that there had evidently been a mistake somewhere.

And then the colonel took her back to her seat, and there were new partners; and between the dances one matron after another found the way to her, and, influenced by the general revulsion of feeling, exhibited a cordiality and interest in marked contrast with the general bearing at the outset of the evening. Perhaps there were those who were rather glad to be relieved of the responsibility laid upon them. When the presidential party arrived it was observed that the President himself was very cordial when he joined the group at the end of the room, the centre figure of which was the wife of his friend and favorite cabinet officer. It was evident that he, at least, had not been affected by the gossip of the hour. His greeting of Mrs. Amory was marked in its kindness, and before he went away it was whispered about that he also had felt an interest in the matter when it had reached his ears, and was not sorry to have an opportunity of indirectly expressing his opinion.

The great lady took her departure in bitterness of spirit; the dances went on, Bertha went through one after another, and between her waltzes held her small court, and was glanced at askance no more. Any slight opposition which might have remained would have been overpowered by the mere force of changed circumstances. Before the evening was at an end it had become plain that the attempt to repress and overwhelm little Mrs. Amory had been a complete failure, and had left her better defended than it had found her.

"But she has lost something," Senator Blundel said to himself, as he watched her dancing. "Confound it! — I can see it — she is not what she was three months ago; she is not what she was when she came into the room."

Tredennis also recognized the change which had come upon her, and before long knew also that she had seen his recognition of it, and that she made no effort to conceal it from him. He felt that he could almost have better borne to see her old, careless gayety, which he had been wont to resent in secret bitterness of heart.

Once, when they chanced to stand alone together for a moment, she spoke to him quickly.

"Is it late?" she asked. "We seem to have been here so long! I have danced so much. Will it not soon be time to go home?"

"Do you want to go home?" he asked.

"Yes," she answered, almost breathlessly; "the music seems so loud it bewilders me a little. How gay it is! How the people dance! The sound and motion make me blind and dizzy. Philip!"

The tone in which she uttered his name was so low and tense that he was startled by it.

"What is it?" he asked.

"If there are many more dances, I am afraid — I cannot go through them — I think — I am breaking down, and I must not — I must not! Tell me what to do!"

He made a movement so that he stood directly before her and shielded her from the observation of those near them. He realized the danger of the moment.

"Look up at me!" he said. "Try to fix your eyes on me steadily. This feeling will pass away directly. You will go soon and you must not break down. Do not let yourself be afraid that you will."

She obeyed him like a child, trying to look at him steadily.

"Tell me one more dance will be enough," she said, "and say you will dance it with me if you can."

"I will," he answered, "and you need not speak a word."

When the senator found himself alone in the carriage with her his sense of the triumph achieved found its expression in words.

"Well," he said, "I think we have put an end to *that* story."

"Yes," Bertha answered, "they will not say anything more about me. You have saved me from that."

She leaned forward and looked out of the window. Carriages blocked the street, and were driving up and driving away; policemen were opening and shutting doors and calling names loudly; a few street-Arabs stood on the pavement and looked with envious eyes at the bright dresses and luxurious wraps of the party passing under the awning; the glare of gas-light fell upon a pretty face upturned to its companions, and a girl's laugh rang out on the night air. Bertha turned away. She looked at Senator Blundel. Her own face had no color.

"I think," she said, — "I think I have been to my last ball."

"No — no," he answered. "That's nonsense. You will dance at many a one."

"I think," she said, — "I think this is the last."

Senator Blundel did not accompany her into the house when they reached it. He left her at the door, almost wringing her small cold hand in his stout warm one.

"Come!" he said. "You are tired now, and no wonder, but to-morrow you will be better. You want sleep and you must have it. Go in, child, and go to bed. Good-night. God bless you! You will — be better to-morrow."

She went through the hall slowly, intending to go to her room, but when she reached the parlor she saw that it was lighted. She had given orders that the servants should not sit up for her, and the house was silent with the stillness of sleep. She turned at the parlor door and looked in. A fire still burned in the grate, her own chair was drawn up before it, and in the chair sat a figure, the sight of which caused her to start forward with an exclamation, — a tall, slender, old figure, his gray head bowed upon his hand.

"Papa!" she cried. "Can it be you, papa? What has happened?"

He rose rather slowly, and looked at her; it was evident that he had been plunged in deep thought; his eyes were heavy, and he looked aged and worn. He put out his hand, took hers, and drew her to him.

"My dear," he said. "My dear child!"

She stood quite still for a moment, looking up at him.

"You have come to tell me something," she said, at length, in a low, almost monotonous voice. "And it is something about Richard. It is something — something wretched."

A slight flush mounted to his cheek, — a flush of shame.

"Yes," he answered, "it is something wretched."

She began to shake like a leaf, but it was not from fear.

"Then do not be afraid," she said; "there is no need! Richard — has not spared me!"

It was the first time through all she had borne and hidden, through all the years holding, for her, suffering and bitterness and disenchantment which had blighted all her youth, — it was the first time she had permitted her husband's name to escape her lips when she could not compel herself to utter it gently, and that, at last, he himself had forced such speech from her was the bitterest indignity of all.

And if she felt this, the professor felt it keenly, too. He had marked her silence and self-control at many a time when he had felt that the fire that burned in her must make her speak; but she had never spoken, and the dignity of her reserve had touched him often.

"What is it that Richard has done now, papa?" she said.

He put a tremulous hand into his pocket, and drew forth a letter.

"Richard," he said, —"Richard has gone abroad."

She had felt that she was to receive some blow, but she had scarcely been prepared for this. She repeated his words in bewilderment.

"Richard has gone abroad"

The professor put his hand on her shoulder.

"Sit down, my dear," he said. "You must sit down."

There was a chair near her; it stood by the table on which the professor had been wont to take his cup of tea; she turned and sat down in this chair, and resting her elbows on the table, dropped her forehead upon her hands. The professor drew near to her side; his gentle, refined old face flushed and paled alternately; his hands were tremulous; he spoke in a low, agitated voice.

"My dear," he said, "I find it very hard to tell you all — all I have discovered. It is very bitter to stand here upon your husband's hearth, and tell you — my child and his wife — that the shadow of dishonor and disgrace rests upon him. He has not been truthful; we have — been deceived."

She did not utter a word.

"For some time I have been anxious," he went on; "but I blame myself that I was not anxious sooner. I am not a business man; I have not been practical in my methods of dealing with him; the fault was in a great measure mine. His nature was not a strong one, — it was almost impossible for him to resist temptation; I knew that, and should have remembered it. I have been very blind. I did not realize what was going on before my eyes. I thought his interest in the Westoria scheme was only one of his many whims. I was greatly to blame."

"No," said Bertha; "it was not you who were to blame. I was more blind than you — I knew him better than — than any one else."

"A short time ago," said the professor, "I received a letter from an old friend who knows a great deal of my business affairs. He is a business man, and I have been glad to entrust him with the management of various investments. In this manner he knew something of the investment of the money which was yours. He knew more of Richard's methods than Richard was aware of. He had heard rumors of the Westoria land scheme, and had accidentally, in the transaction of his business, made some discoveries. He asked me if I knew the extent to which your fortune had been speculated with. Knowing a few facts, he was able to guess at others"—

Bertha lifted her face from her hands.

"My money!" she exclaimed. "My fortune!"

"He had speculated with it at various times, sometimes gaining, sometimes losing; the Westoria affair seems to have dazzled him — and he invested largely"—

Bertha rose from her chair.

"It was Philip Tredennis' money he invested," she said. "Philip Tredennis"—

"It was not Philip's money," the professor answered; "that I have discovered. But it was Philip's generosity which would have made it appear so. In this letter — written just before he sailed — Richard has admitted the truth to me — finding what proof I had against him."

Bertha lifted her hands and let them fall at her sides.

"Papa," she said, "I do not understand this — I do not understand. Philip Tredennis! He gave money to Richard! Richard accepted money from him — to shield himself, to — This is too much for me!"

"Philip had intended the money for Janey," said the professor, "and when he understood how Richard had involved himself, and how his difficulties would affect you and your future he made a most remarkable offer: he offered to assume the responsibility of Richard's losses. He did not intend that you should know what he had done. Such a thing would only have been possible for Philip Tredennis, and it was because I knew him so well, that, when I heard that it was his money that had been risked in the Westoria lands, I felt that something was wrong. He was very reticent, and that added to my suspicions. Then I made the discoveries through my friend, and my accusations of Richard forced him to admit the truth."

"The truth!" said Bertha, —"that *I* was to live upon Philip Tredennis' money; that, having been ruined by my husband, I was to be supported by Philip Tredennis' bounty!"

"Richard was in despair," said the professor, "and in his extremity he forgot"—

"He forgot *me*!" said Bertha. "Yes, he forgot — a great many things."

"It has seemed always to be Philip who has remembered," said the professor, sadly. "Philip has been generous and thoughtful for us from first to last."

Bertha's hand closed itself.

"Yes," she cried; "always Philip — always Philip!"

"What could have been finer and more delicate than his care and planning for you in this trouble of the last few days, to which I have been so blind!" said the professor.

"*His* care and planning!" echoed Bertha, turning slowly toward him. "His! Did you not hear that Senator Blundel"—

"It was he who went to Senator Blundel," the professor answered. "It was he who spoke to the wife of the Secretary of State. I learned it from Mrs. Merriam. Out of all the pain we have borne, or may have to bear, the memory of Philip's faithful affection for us"—

He did not finish his sentence. Bertha stopped him. Her clenched hand had risen to her side, and was pressed against it.

"It was Philip who came to me in my trouble in Virginia," she said. "It was Philip who saw my danger and warned me of it when I would not hear him; but I could not know that I owed him such a debt as this!"

"We should never have known it from him," the professor replied. "He would have kept silent to the end."

Bertha looked at the clock upon the mantel.

"It is too late to send for him now," she said; "it is too late, and a whole night must pass before"—

"Before you say to him — what?" asked the professor.

"Before I tell him that Richard made a mistake," she answered, with white and trembling lips; "that he must take his money back — that I will not have it."

She caught her father's arm and clung to it, looking into his troubled face.

"Papa," she said, "will you take me home again? I think you must, if you will. There seems to be no place for me. If you will let me stay with you until I have time to think."

The professor laid his hand upon hers and held it closely.

"My dear," he said, "my home is yours. It has never seemed so much mine since you left it; but this may not be so bad as you think. I do not know how much we may rely upon Richard's hopes, — they are not always to be relied upon, — but it appears that he has hopes of retrieving some of his losses through a certain speculation he seems to have regarded as a failure, but which suddenly promises to prove a success."

"I have never thought of being poor," said Bertha; "I do not think I should know how to be poor. But, somehow, it is not the money I am thinking of; that will come later, I suppose. I scarcely seem to realize yet"—

Her voice and her hand shook, and she clung to him more closely.

"Everything has gone wrong," she said, wildly; "everything must be altered. No one is left to care for me but you. No one must do it but you. Now that Richard has gone, it is not Philip who must be kind to me — not Philip — Philip last of all!"

"Not Philip?" he echoed. "*Not* Philip?"

And, as he said it, they both heard feet ascending the steps at the front door.

"My child," said the professor, "that is Philip now. He spoke of calling in on me on his way home. Perhaps he has been anxious at finding me out so late. I do not understand you — but must I go and send him away?"

"No," she answered, shuddering a little, as if with cold, "it is for me to send him away. But I must tell him first about the money. I am glad he has come. I am glad another night will not pass without his knowing. I think I want to speak to him alone — if you will send him here, and wait for a little while in the library."

She did not see her father's face as he went away from her; he did not see hers; she turned and stood upon the hearth with her back toward the door.

She stood so when, a few minutes afterward, Philip Tredennis came in; she stood so until he was within a few feet of her. Then she moved a little and looked up.

What she saw in him arrested for the moment her power to speak, and for that moment both were silent. Often as she had recognized the change which had taken place in him, often as the realization of it had wrung her heart, and wrung it all the more that she had understood so little, she had never before seen it as she saw it then. All the weariness, the anxious pain, the hopeless sadness of his past, seemed to have come to the surface; he could endure no more; he had borne the strain too long, and he knew too well that the end had come. No need for words to tell him that he must lose even the poor and bitter comfort he had clung to; he had made up his mind to that when he had defended her against the man who himself should have been her defence.

So he stood silent and his deep eyes looked out from his strong, worn, haggard face, holding no reproach, full only of pity for her.

There was enough to pity in her. If she saw anguish in his eyes, what he saw in hers as she uplifted them he could scarcely have expressed in any words he knew; surely there were no words into which he could have put the pang their look gave him, telling him as it did that she had reached the point where she could stand on guard no more.

"Richard," she said at length, "has gone away."

"That I knew," he answered.

"When?" she asked.

"I had a letter from him this morning," he said.

"You did not wish to tell me?" she returned.

"I thought," he began, "that perhaps"— and stopped.

"You thought that he would write to me too," she said. "He — did not."

He did not speak, and she went on.

"When I returned to-night," she said, "papa was waiting for me.

He had received a letter, too, and it told him — something he suspected before — something I had not suspected — something I could not know"—

Her voice broke, and when she began again there was a ring of desperate appeal to it.

"When I was a girl," she said, "when you knew me long ago, what was there of good in me that you should have remembered it through all that you have known of me since then? — there must have been something — something good or touching — something more than the goodness in yourself — that made you pitiful of me, and generous to me, and anxious for my sake. Tell me what it was."

"It was," he said, and his own voice was low and broken too, and his deep and sad eyes wore a look she had never seen before, — the look that, in the eyes of a woman, would have spoken of welling tears, — "it was — yourself."

"Myself!" she cried. "Oh, if it was myself, and there were goodness and truth, and what was worth remembering in me, why did it not save me from what I have been — and from what I am to-day? I do not think I meant to live my life so badly then; I was only careless and happy in a girlish way. I had so much faith and hope, and believed so much in all good things; and yet my life has all been wrong, and I seem to believe no more, and everything is lost to me; and since the days when I looked forward there is a gulf that I can never, never pass again."

She came nearer to him, and a sob broke from her.

"What am I to say to you," she said, "now that I know all that you have done for me while I — while I — Why should you have cared to protect me? I was not kind to you — I was not careful of your feelings"—

"No," he answered. "You — were not."

"I used to think that you despised me," she went on; "once I told you so. I even tried to give you the reason. I showed my worst self to you; I was unjust and bitter; I hurt you many a time."

He seemed to labor for his words, and yet he labored rather to control and check than to utter them.

"I am going away," he said. "When I made the arrangement with

Richard, of which you know, I meant to go away. I gathered, from what your father said, that you mean to render useless my poor effort to be of use to you."

"I cannot" — she began, but she could go no farther.

"When I leave you — as I must," he said, "let me at least carry away with me the memory that you were generous to me at the last."

"At the last," she repeated after him, "the last!"

She uttered a strange, little inarticulate cry. He saw her lift up one of her arms, look blindly at the bracelet on her wrist, drop it at her side, and then stand looking up at him.

There was a moment of dead silence.

"Janey shall take the money," she said; "I cannot."

What the change was that he saw come over her white face and swaying figure he only felt, as he might have felt a blow in the dark from an unknown hand. What the great shocks was that came upon him he only felt in the same way.

She sank upon the sofa, clinging to the cushion with one shaking hand. Suddenly she broke into helpless sobbing, like a child's, tears streaming down her cheeks as she lifted her face in appeal.

"You have been good to me," she said. "You have been kind. Be good to me — be kind to me — once more. You must go away — and I cannot take from you what you want to give me; but I am not so bad as I have seemed — or so hard! What you have wished me to be I will try to be! I will live for my children. I will be — as good — as I can. I will do anything you tell me to do — before you leave me! I will live all my life afterward — as Bertha Herrick might have lived it! Only do not ask me to take the money!"

For a few seconds all the room was still. When he answered her she could barely hear his voice.

"I will ask of you nothing," he said.

He lifted her hand and bowed his head over it. Then he laid it back upon the cushion. It lay there as if it had been carved from stone.

"Good-by," he said. "Good-by."

He saw her lips part, but no sound came from them.

So he went away. He scarcely felt the floor beneath his feet. He saw nothing of the room about him. It seemed as if there was an endless journey between himself and the door through which he was to pass. The extremity of his mortal agony was like drunkenness.

When he was gone, she fell with a shudder, and lay still with her cheek against the crimson cushion.

The professor was sitting at her bedside when she opened her eyes again. Her first recognition was of his figure, sitting, the head bowed upon the hand, as she had seen it when she came first into the house.

"Papa!" she said, "you are with me?"

"Yes, my dear," he answered.

"And — there is no one else?"

"No, my dear."

She put out her hand and laid it upon his arm. He thought, with a bitter pang, that she did it as she had often done it in her girlhood, and that, in spite of the change in her, she wore a look which seemed to belong to those days too.

"You will stay with me," she said. "I have come back to you."

Chapter 40

Miss Jessup was very eloquent in the paragraph which she devoted to the announcement of the departure of Colonel Tredennis, "the well-known hero of the plains, whose fine, bronzed face and soldierly figure have become so familiar to us during the past three seasons." She could scarcely express the regret felt by the many friends he had made, on losing him, and, indeed, there ran throughout the flowers of speech a suggestion of kindly, admiring sympathy and womanly good-feeling which quite went to the colonel's heart, and made him wonder at his own good fortune when he read the paragraph in question. He was far away from Washington when the paper reached him. He had become tired of life at the Capital, it was said, and had been glad to exchange with a man who found its gayeties better suited to him.

"It is true," he said to himself when he heard of this report, "that they were not suited to me, nor I to them."

How he lived through the weeks, performing the ordinary routine of his duty, and bearing with him hour by hour, night and day, the load of grief and well-nigh intolerable anguish which he knew was never to be lighter, he did not know. The days came and went. It was morning, noon, or night, and he did not feel the hours either long or short. There were nights when, his work being done, he returned to his quarters and staggered to his seat, falling upon it blind and sick with the heavy horror of the day.

"This," he would say, again and again, "*this* is unnatural. To bear such torture and live through it seems scarcely human."

Sometimes he was so wrought upon by it physically that he thought he should not live through it; but he bore so much that at last he gained a hopeless faith in his own endurance. He was not alone. It was as he had told her it would be. From the hour that he looked his last upon her, it seemed that her face had never faded from before his aching eyes. He had all the past to live over again, all its bitter mysteries to read in a new light and to learn to understand.

There was time enough now for him to think it all over slowly, to recall to his mind every look and change and tone; her caprices, her coldness, the wounds she had given him, he bore them all again, and each time he came back with a pang more terrible to that last moment — to that last look, to her last, broken words.

"O God!" he cried, "does *she* bear this too?"

He knew nothing of her save what he gained at rare intervals from Miss Jessup's society column, which he read deliberately from beginning to end as each paper reached him. The friends of Mrs. Amory, Miss Jessup's first statement announced, would regret to learn that the health of that charming young wife and mother was so far from being what was to be desired, that it necessitated a temporary absence from those social circles of which she was so bright and graceful an ornament. For a while her name was missing from the lists of those who appeared at the various entertainments, and then he began occasionally to see it again, and found a little sad comfort in the thought that she must be stronger. His kind, brown face changed greatly in these days; it grew lean and haggard and hopeless, and here and there a gray thread showed itself in his close, soldier-cropped hair. He planned out heavy work for himself, and kept close in his quarters, and those of his friends who had known him before his stay in Washington began to ask each other what had so broken Philip Tredennis.

The first time that Mrs. Amory appeared in society, after her indisposition, was at the house of her friend, Mrs. Sylvestre. During her temporary seclusion she had seen Mrs. Sylvestre frequently. There had been few days when Agnes had not spent some hours with her. When she had been denied to every one else Agnes was admitted.

"It is only fatigue, this," Bertha had said; "but other people tire me so! You never tire me."

She was not confined to her bed. She had changed her room, taking possession of the pretty pink and blue chamber, and lay upon the sofa through the days, sometimes looking at the fire, often with her eyes closed.

The two conversed but little; frequently there was silence between them for some time; but Agnes knew that she was doing as Bertha wished when she came and sat with her.

At the end of a week Mrs. Sylvestre came in one morning and found Bertha dressed and sitting in a chair.

"I am going downstairs," she said.

"Do you think you are strong enough?" Agnes asked. She did not look so.

"I must begin to try to do something," was the indirect reply. "One must always begin. I want to lie still and not speak or move; but I must not do that. I will go downstairs, and I think I should like to see Laurence."

As she went down the staircase she moved very slowly, and Agnes saw that she clung to the balustrade for support. When she reached the parlor door she paused for a moment, then crossed the threshold a little hurriedly, and went to the sofa and sat down. She was tremulous, and tears had risen to her eyes from very weakness.

"I thought I was stronger," she said. But she said nothing more until, a few moments later, she began to speak of Tom and Kitty, in whom she had been much interested. It had been at her suggestion that, after diverse fruitless efforts, the struggle to obtain Tom a "place" had been abandoned, and finally there had been procured for him a position, likely to prove permanent, in a house of business, where principles might be of value. Tom's lungs were still a trifle delicate, but he was rapturously happy in the small home, to purchase which Mrs. Sylvestre had advanced the means, and his simple bliss was greatly added to by the advent of Kitty's baby.

So they talked of Tom and Kitty and the baby, and of Arbuthnot, and his friendship for them, and the oddities of it, and his way of making his efforts and kindness seem more than half a jest.

"No one can be kinder than Laurence," Bertha said. "No one could be a truer friend."

"I think so now," Agnes answered, quietly.

"He is not so light, after all," said Bertha. "Perhaps few of us are quite as light as we seem."

"I did him injustice at first," Agnes replied. "I understand him better now."

"If he should go away you would miss him a little," said Bertha. "He is a person one misses when he is absent."

"Does he"— Agnes began. "I have not heard him speak of going away."

"There is just a likelihood of it," Bertha returned. "Papa has been making an effort for him with the Secretary of State. He might be sent abroad."

"I have not heard him refer to the possibility," said Agnes. Her manner was still quiet, but she had made a slight involuntary movement, which closed the book she held.

"I do not think papa has spoken to him for some time," Bertha replied. "And when he first referred to his plan Laurence thought it out of the question, and did not appear to regard it seriously."

For a few moments Mrs. Sylvestre did not speak. Then she said:

"Certainly it would be much better for him than to remain here."

"If he should go," said Bertha, "no one will miss him as I shall. We used to be so gay together, and now" —

She did not end her sentence, and for a while neither of them spoke again, and she lay quite still. Agnes remained to dine with her, and in the evening Arbuthnot came in.

When he entered the bright, familiar room he found himself glancing round it, trying to understand exactly what mysterious change had come upon it. There was no change in its belongings, — the touches of color, the scattered trifles, the pictures and draperies wore their old-time look of having been arranged by one deft hand; but it did not seem to be the room he had known so long, — the room he had been so fond of, and had counted the prettiest and most inspiring place he knew.

Bertha had not left the sofa; she was talking to Agnes, who stood near her. She had a brilliant flush on her cheeks, her eyes were bright when she raised them to greet him, and her hand, as he took it, was hot and tremulous.

"Naturally," she said, "you will begin to vaunt yourself. You told me I should break down if I did not take care of myself, and I have broken down — a little. I am reduced to lying on sofas. Don't you know how I always derided women who lie on sofas? This is retribution; but don't meet it with too haughty and vainglorious a spirit; before Lent I shall be as gay as ever."

"I don't doubt it," he answered. "But in the meantime allow me to congratulate you on the fact that the sofa is not entirely unbecoming."

"Thank you," she said. "Will you sit down now and tell me — tell me what people are saying?"

"Of" — he began.

She smiled.

"Of me," she answered. "They were saying a great deal of me a week ago; tell me what they say now. You must hear in going your giddy rounds."

"*You* are very well treated," he replied. "There is a certain great lady who is most uncomfortably commented upon. I can scarcely imagine that she enjoys it."

Her smile ended in a fatigued sigh.

"The tide turned very quickly," she said. "It is well for me that it did. I should not have had much mercy if I had stood alone. Ah! it was a good thing for me that you were all so brave. You might have deserted me, too — it would have been very simple — and then — then the gates of paradise would have been shut against me."

"That figure of speech meaning —?" suggested Arbuthnot.

"That I should have been invited to no more dinner-parties and receptions; that nobody would have come up to my Thursday Evenings; that Miss Jessup would never again have mentioned me in the *Wabash Gazette*."

"That would have been very bitter," he answered.

"Yes," she returned, "it would have been bitter, indeed."

"Do you know," he said next, "that I have come to-night partly for the reason that I have something to tell you?"

"I rather suspected it," she replied, "though I could scarcely explain why."

"Am I to hear it, too?" inquired Agnes.

473

"If you are kind enough to be interested," he answered. "It will seem a slight enough affair to the world at large, but it seems rather tremendous to me. I feel a trifle overpowered and nervous. Through the kind efforts of Professor Herrick I have been honored with the offer of a place abroad."

Bertha held out her hand.

"Minister to the Court of St. James!" she said. "How they will congratulate themselves in London!"

"They would," he replied, "if an ill-adjusted and singularly unappreciative government had not particularized a modest corner of Germany as standing in greater need of my special abilities." But he took her offered hand.

When he glanced at Mrs. Sylvestre — truth to say he had taken some precautions against seeing her at all as he made his announcement — he found her bestowing upon him one of the calmest of her soft, reflective looks.

"I used to like some of those quiet places in Germany," she said; "but you will find it a change from Washington."

"I think," he answered, "that I should like a change from Washington; "and as soon as he had spoken he detected the touch of acrid feeling in his words.

"I should fancy myself," she said, her soft look entirely undisturbed, "that it might be agreeable after one had been here some time."

He had always admired beyond expression that touch of half-forgetful, pensive calmness in her voice and eyes, but he did not enjoy it just now.

"It is a matter of temperament, I suppose," was his thought; "but, after all, we have been friends."

Neither could it be said that he enjoyed the pretty and picturesque stories of German life she told afterward. They were told so well that they brought very near the life he might expect to lead, and he was not exactly in the mood to care to stand face to face with it. Bui he controlled himself sufficiently to make an excellent audience, and never had been outwardly in better spirits than he was after the stories were told. He was cool mid vivacious; he told a story or two himself; he was in good voice when he went to the piano and sang. They were all laughing when Agnes left the room to put on her wraps to return home.

When she was gone the laugh died down with odd suddenness.

"Larry," said Bertha, "do you really want to go?"

"No," he answered, turning sharply, "I don't want to go. I loathe and abhor the thought of it."

"You want," she said, "to stay here?"

"Yes, I do," was his reply, "and that decides me."

"To go?" she asked, watching his pale, disturbed face.

"Yes, to go! There is nothing to stay here for. I need the change. I have been here long enough — too long!"

"Yes," she returned, "I think you have been here too long. You had better go away — if you think there is nothing to stay for."

"When a man has nothing to offer"— he broke off and flushed up hotly. "If I had a shadow of a right to a reason for staying," he exclaimed, "do you suppose I should not hold on to it, and fight for it, and demand what belonged to me? There might be a struggle — there would be; but no other man should have one jot or tittle that persistence and effort might win in time for me! A man who gives up is a fool! I have nothing to give up. I haven't even the right to surrender! I hadn't the right to enter the field and take my wounds like a man! It is pleasant to reflect that it is my own — fault. I trifled with my life; now I want it, and I can't get it back."

"Ah!" she said, "that is an old story!"

And then Agnes returned, and he took her home.

On their way there they talked principally of Tom and Kitty.

"They will miss you greatly," Agnes said.

"They will be very kind to do it," was his reply.

"We shall all miss you," she added.

"That will be kinder still," he answered. "Might I be permitted to quote the ancient anecdote of the colored warrior, who, on running away in battle, was reproached and told that a single life counted as nothing on such great occasions, and that if he had fallen he would not have been missed, — his reply to this heroic statement of the case being, that he should have been likely to miss himself. I shall miss myself, and already a gentle melancholy begins to steal over me. I am not the gleesome creature I was before good luck befell me."

But, despite this lightness of tone, their walk was not a very cheerful one; indeed, after this speech they were rather quiet, and they parted with few words at the door, Arbuthnot declining to go into the house.

When Agnes entered alone Mrs. Merriam looked up from her novel in some surprise.

"I thought I heard Mr. Arbuthnot," she said.

"He left me at the door," Mrs. Sylvestre answered.

"What!" said Mrs. Merriam, "without coming to say good-night to me! I wanted to tell him what a dissipated evening I have been spending with my new book."

"He has been telling us good news," said Agnes, standing before the fire and loosening her furs. "He has been offered a consulship."

Mrs. Merriam closed her book and laid it on the table.

"Will he accept it?" she asked.

"He could scarcely refuse it," Agnes replied. "It is a decided advance; he likes the life abroad, and it might even lead to something better in the future; at least one rather fancies such things are an opening."

"It is true," reflected Mrs. Merriam, "that he seems to have no particular ties to hold him in one place rather than another."

"None," said Agnes. "I don't know whether that is his fortune or his misfortune."

"His fortune," said Mrs. Merriam. "He is of the nature to know how to value them. Perhaps, after all, he may form them if he goes abroad. It is not too late."

"Perhaps so," said Agnes. "That would be another reason why it would be better for him to go."

"Still," remarked Mrs. Merriam, "for my own part, I don't call it good news that he is going,"

"I meant," said Agnes, "good news for him."

"It is bad news for us," Mrs. Merriam replied. "He will leave a gap. I have grown inconveniently fond of him myself."

But Agnes made no response, and soon afterward went to her room in silence. She was rather silent the next day when she made her visit to Bertha. Mrs. Merriam observed that she was rather silent at home;

but, having seen her retire within herself before, she was too just to assign a definite reason for her quiet mood. Still she watched her with great interest, which had a fashion of deepening when Laurence Arbuthnot appeared upon the scene. But there was no change in her manner toward Arbuthnot. She was glad to see him; she was interested in his plans. Her gentle pleasure in his society seemed neither greater nor less than usual; her gentle regret at his approaching absence from their circle said absolutely nothing. In the gayeties of the closing season they saw even more of each other than usual.

"It will be generous of you to allow me a few additional privileges," Arbuthnot said; "an extra dance or so, for instance, on occasion; a few more calls that I am entitled to. Will you kindly, if you please, regard me in the light of a condemned criminal, and be lenient with me in my last moments?"

She did not refuse to be lenient with him. Much as he had been in the habit of enjoying the evenings spent in her parlor, he had never spent evenings such as fell to him in these last days. Somehow it happened that he found her alone more frequently. Mrs. Merriam had letters to write, or was otherwise occupied; so it chanced that he saw her as it had not been his fortune to see her very often.

But it was decided that he was to spend no more winters in Washington, for some time, at least; and, though he spent his evenings thus agreeably, he was making daily preparation for his departure, and it cannot be said that he enjoyed the task. There had been a time, it is true, when he would have greeted with pleasure the prospect of the change before him; but that time was past.

"I am having my bad quarter of an hour," he said, "and it serves me right."

But as the days slipped by he found it even a worse quarter of an hour than he had fancied it would be. It cost him an effort to bear himself as it was only discretion that he should. His one resource lay in allowing himself no leisure. When he was not otherwise occupied, he spent his time with his friends. He was oftenest with the professor and Bertha. He had some quiet hours in the professor's study, and in the parlor, where Bertha sat or lay upon the sofa before the fire. She did not allow herself to lie upon the sofa often, and refused to be regarded as an invalid; but Arbuthnot never found himself alone with her without an over- powering realization of the change which had taken place in her. But she rarely spoke of herself.

"There is nothing more," she said, once, "to say about *me*."

She was willing enough to speak of him, however, and of his future, and her gentleness often moved him deeply.

"We have been such good friends," she would say, —"such good friends. It is not often that a man is as true a friend to a woman as you have been to me. I wish — oh, I wish you might be happy!"

"It is too late," he would reply, "but I shall not waste time in complaining. I will even try not to waste it in regretting."

But he knew that he did waste it so, and that each passing day left a sharper pang behind it, and marked a greater struggle.

There is a great deal of trouble in this world," the professor said to him, simply, after watching him a few minutes one day. "I should like to know what *you* are carrying with you to Germany."

"I am carrying nothing," Arbuthnot answered. "That is my share."

They were smoking their cigars together, and through the blue haze floating about him the professor looked out with a sad face.

"Do you," he said, — "do you leave anything behind you?"

"Everything," said Arbuthnot. The professor made a disturbed movement.

"Perhaps," he said, "this was a mistake. Perhaps it would be better if you remained. It is not yet too late" —

"Yes, it is," Arbuthnot interposed, with a faint laugh. "And nothing would induce me to remain."

It was on the occasion of a reception given by Mrs. Sylvestre that he was to make his last appearance in the social world before his departure. He had laid his plans in such a manner that, having made his adieus at the end of the evening, half an hour after retiring from the parlors he would be speeding away from Washington on his way to New York.

"It will be a good exit," he said. "And the eye of the unfeeling world being upon me, I shall be obliged to conceal my emotions, and you will be spared the spectacle of my anguish."

There were no particular traces of anguish" upon his countenance when he presented himself, the evening in question having arrived. He appeared, in fact, to be in reasonably good spirits. Nothing could have been more perfect than the evening was from first to last: the picturesque and charming home was at its best; Mrs. Sylvestre the most lovely central figure in its picturesqueness; Mrs. Merriam even more gracious and amusing than usual. The gay world was represented by its gayest and brightest; the majority of those who had appeared on the night of the ball appeared again. Rather late in the evening Blundel came in, fresh from an exciting debate in the Senate, and somewhat flushed and elated by it. He made his way almost immediately to Bertha. Those who stood about her made way for him as he came. She was not sitting alone to-night; there seemed no likelihood of her being called upon to sit alone again. She had not only regained her old place, but something more. The professor had accompanied her, and at no time was far away from her. He hovered gently about in her neighborhood, and rarely lost sight of her. He had never left her for any great length of time since the night Tredennis had gone away. He had asked her no questions, but they had grown very near to each other, and any mystery he might feel that he confronted only made him more tender of her.

When Senator Blundel found himself standing before her he gave her a sharp glance of scrutiny.

"Well," he said, "you are rested and better, and all the rest of it. Your pink gown is very nice, and it gives you a color and brightens you up."

"I chose the shade carefully," she answered, smiling. "If it had been deeper it might have taken some color away from me. I am glad you like it."

"But you are well?" he said, a little persistently. He was not so sure of her, after all. He was shrewd enough to wish she had not found it necessary to choose her shade with such discretion.

She smiled up at him again.

"Yes, I am well," she said. "And I am very glad to see you again."

But for several seconds he did not answer her; standing, he looked at her in silence as she remembered his doing in the clays when she had felt as if he was asking himself and her a question. But she knew it was not the same question he was asking himself now, but another one, and after he had asked it he did not seem to discover the answer to it, and looked baffled and uncertain, and even disturbed and anxious. And yet her pretty smile did not change in the least at any moment while he regarded her. It only deserted her entirely once during the evening. This was when she said her last words to Arbuthnot. He had spent the previous evening with her in her own parlor. Now, before she went away, — which she did rather early, — they had a few minutes together in the deserted music-room, where he took her while supper was in progress.

Neither of them had any smiles when they went in together and took their seats in a far corner.

Bertha caught no reflected color from her carefully chosen pink. Suddenly she looked cold and worn.

"Laurence!" she said, "in a few hours"— and stopped.

He ended for her.

"In a few hours I shall be on my way to New York."

She looked down at her flowers and then up at him.

"Oh!" she said, "a great deal will go with you. There is no one now who could take from me what you will. But that is not what I wanted to say to you. "Will you let me say to you what I have been thinking of for several days, and wanting to say?"

"You may say anything," he answered.

"Perhaps," she went on, hurriedly, "it will not make any difference when it is said; I don't know." She put out her hand and touched his arm with it; her eyes looked large and bright in their earnest appeal.

"Don't be angry with me, Larry," she said; "we have been such good friends, — the best, *best* friends. I am going home soon. I shall not stay until the evening is over. You must, I think, until every one is gone away. You might — you might have a few last words to say to Agnes'."

"There is nothing," he replied, "that I could say to her."

"There might be,' she said tremulously, "there might be — a few last words Agnes might wish to say to you."

He put his head down upon his hand and answered in a low tone:

"It is impossible that there should be."

480

"Larry," she said, "only you can find out whether that is true or not, and — don't go away before you are quite sure. Oh! do you remember what I told you once? — there is only one thing in all the world when all the rest are tried and done with. So many miss it, and then everything is wrong. Don't be too proud, Larry; don't reason too much. If people are true to each other, and content, what does the rest matter? I want to know that some one is happy like that. I wish it might be you. If I have said too much, forgive me; but you may be angry with me. I will let you — if you will not run the risk of throwing anything away."

There was a silence.

"Promise me," she said, "promise me."

"I cannot promise you," he answered.

He left his seat.

"I will tell you," he said. "I am driven to-night — driven! I never thought it could be so, but it is — even though I fancied I had taught myself better. I am bearing a good deal. I don't know how far I may trust myself. I have not an idea about it. It is scarcely safe for me to go near her. I have not been near her often to-night. I am *driven*. I don't know that I shall get out of the house safely. I don't know how far I can go, if I *do* get out of it, without coming back and making some kind of an outcry to her. One can't bear everything indefinitely. It seems to me now that the only decent end to this would be for me to go as quickly as possible, and not look back; but there never was a' more impotent creature than I know I am to-night.] The sight of her is too much for me. She looks like a tall, white flower. She is a little pale to-night — and the look in her eyes — I wish she were pale for sorrow — for me. I wish she was suffering; but she is not."

"She could not tell you if she were," said Bertha.

"That is very true," he answered.

"Don't go away," she said, "until you have said good-by to her alone."

"Don't you see," he replied, desperately, "that I am in the condition to be unable to go until I am actually forced? Oh," he added, bitterly, "rest assured I shall hang about long enough!" But when he returned to the supper-room, and gave his attention to his usual duties, he was entirely himself again, so far as his outward bearing went. He bore about ices and salads, and endeared himself beyond measure to dowagers, with appetites, who lay in wait. He received their expressions of grief at his approaching departure with decorum not too grave and sufficiently grateful. He made himself as useful and agreeable as usual.

"He is always ready and amiable, that Mr. Arbuthnot," remarked a well-seasoned, elderly matron, who recognized useful material when she saw it.

And Agnes, who had chanced to see him just as his civilities won him this encomium, reflected upon him for a moment with a soft gaze, and then turned away with a secret thought her face did not betray.

At last the rooms began to thin out. One party after another took its departure, disappearing up the stairs and reappearing afterward, descending and passing through the hall to the carriages, which rolled up, one after another, as they were called. Agnes stood near the doorway with Mrs. Merriam, speaking the last words to her guests as they left her. She was still a little pale, but the fatigues of the evening might easily have left her more so. Arbuthnot found himself lingering with an agonizing sense of disgust at his folly. Several times he thought he would go with the rest, and then discovered that the step would cost him a struggle to which he was not equal. Agnes did not look at him; Mrs. Merriam did.

"You must not leave us just yet," she said. "We want your last moments. It would be absurd to bid you good-night as if we were to see you to-morrow. Talk to me until Agnes has done with these people."

He could have embraced her. He was perfectly aware that, mentally, he had lost all his dignity, but he could do nothing more than recognize the fact with unsparing clearness, and gird at himself for his weakness.

"If I were a boy of sixteen," he said inwardly, "I should comport myself in something the same manner. I could grovel at this kind old creature's feet because she has taken a little notice of me."

But at length the last guest had departed, the last carriage had been called and had rolled away. Agnes turned from the doorway and walked slowly to the fire-place.

"How empty the rooms look!" she said.

"You should have a glass of wine," Mrs. Merriam suggested. "You are certainly more tired than you should be. You are not as strong as I was at your age."

Arbuthnot went for the glass of wine into the adjoining room. He was glad to absent himself for a moment.

"In ten minutes I shall be out of the house," he said; "perhaps in five."

When he returned to the parlor Mrs. Merriam had disappeared. Agnes stood upon the hearth, looking down. She lifted her eyes with a gentle smile.

"Aunt Mildred is going to ask you to execute a little commission for her," she said. "She will be down soon, I think."

For the moment he was sufficiently abandoned and ungrateful to have lost all interest in Mrs. Merriam. It seemed incredible that he had only ten minutes before him and yet could retain composure enough to reply with perfect steadiness.

"Perhaps," he thought, desperately, "I am not going to do it so villanously, after all."

He kept his eyes fixed very steadily upon her. The soft calm of her manner seemed to give him a sort of strength. Nothing could have been sweeter or more unmoved than her voice.

"I was a little afraid you would go away early," she said, "and that we could not bid you good-by quietly."

"Don't bid me good-by too quietly," he answered. "You will excuse *my* emotion, I am sure?"

"You have been in Washington," she said, "long enough to feel sorry to leave it."

He glanced at the clock.

"I have spent ten years here," he said; "one grows fond of a place, naturally."

"Yes," she replied.

Then she added:

"Your steamer sails" —

"On Wednesday," was his answer.

It was true that he was driven. He was so hard driven at this moment that he glanced furtively at the mirror, half fearing to find his face ashen.

"My train leaves in an hour," he said; "I will bid you" —

He held out his hand without ending his sentence. She gave him her slender, cold fingers passively.

"Good-by!" she said.

Mrs. Merriam was not mentioned. She was forgotten. Arbuthnot had not thought once of the possibility of her return.

He dropped Agnes' hand, and simply turned round and went out of the room.

His ten minutes were over; it was all over. This was his thought as he went up the staircase. He went into the deserted upper room where he had left his overcoat. It was quite empty, the servant in charge having congratulated himself that his duties for the night were over, and joined his fellows downstairs. One overcoat, he had probably fancied, might take care of itself, especially an overcoat sufficiently familiar with the establishment to outstay all the rest. The garment in question hung over the back of a chair. Arbuthnot took it up and put it on with unnecessary haste; then he took his hat; then he stopped. He sank into the chair and dropped his brow upon his hand; he was actually breathless. He passed through a desperate moment as he sat there; when it was over he rose, deliberately freed himself from his coat again, and went downstairs. "When he reentered the parlor Agnes rose hurriedly from the sofa, leaving her handkerchief on the side-cushion, on which there was a little indented spot. She made a rapid step toward him, her head held erect, her eyes at once telling their own story, and commanding him to disbelieve it; her face so inexpressibly sweet in its sadness that his heart leaped in his side.

"You have left something?" she said.

"Yes," he answered, "I left — you."

She sat down upon the sofa without a word. He saw the large tears well up into her eyes, and they helped him to go on as nothing else would have done.

"I couldn't go away," he said. "There was no use trying. I could not leave you in that cold way, as if our parting were only an ordinary, conventional one. There is nothing conventional about my side of it.

I am helpless with misery. I have lost my last shred of self-respect. I had to come back and ask you to be a little kinder to me. I don't think you know how cold you were. It was like death to drop your hand and turn away like that. Such a thing must be unendurable to a man who loves a woman."

He came nearer.

"Beggars should be humble," he said. "I am humble enough. I only ask you to say good-by a little more kindly."

Her eyes were full and more beautiful than ever. She put out her hand and touched the sofa at her side.

"Will you sit here?" she said. ,

"What!" he cried, — "I?"

"Yes," she answered, scarcely above her breath, "no one else." He took the place and her slender hand.

"I have no right to this," he said. "No one knowst that so well as I. I am doing a terrible, daring thing."

"It is a daring thing for us both," she said. "I have always been afraid; but it cost me too much when you went out of the door."

"Did it?" he said, and folded her hand close against his breast. "Oh!" he whispered, "I will be very tender to you."

She lifted her soft eyes.

"I think," she said, "that is what I need."

Chapter 41

The next six months Laurence Arbuthnot spent in his quiet corner of Germany, devoting all his leisure moments to the study of certain legal terms to which he had given some attention at a previous time, when, partly as a whim, partly as the result of a spasm of prudence, he had woven himself a strand of thread to cling to in the vague future by taking a course of law. His plan now was to strengthen this thread until it might be depended upon, and he spared no determined and persistent effort which might assist him to the attainment of this object.

"I find myself an astonishingly resolute person," he wrote to Agnes. "l am also industrious. Resolution and industry never before struck me as being qualities I might lay claim to with any degree of justice. Dr. Watts himself, with his entirely objectionable bee, could not ' improve each shining hour ' with more vigor than I do, but — I have an object, and the hours are shining. Once there seemed no reason for them. It is not so now. I will confess that I used to hate these things. Do you repose sufficient confidence in me yet to believe me when I tell you that I actually feel a dawning interest in Blackstone, and do not shudder at the thought of the lectures I shall attend in Paris? Perhaps I do not reflect upon them with due deliberation and coolness — I cannot help remembering that you will be with me."

When he resigned his position and went to Paris she was with him. He had made a brief visit to Washington and taken her away, leaving Mrs. Merriam to adorn the house in Lafayette Square, and keep its hearth warm until such time as they should return. It was when they were in Paris that they had the pleasure of meeting Mr. Richard Amory, who was very well known and exceedingly popular in the American colony. He was in the most delightful, buoyant spirits: he had been very fortunate; a certain investment of his had just turned out very well, and brought him large returns. He was quite willing to talk about it and himself, and was enraptured at seeing his friends. The news of their marriage delighted him; he was enchanting in his warm interest in their happiness. He seemed, however, to have only pleasantly vague views on the subject of the time of his probable return to America.

"There is no actual necessity for it," he said, " and I find the life here delightful. Bertha and the children will probably join me in the spring, and we may ramble about for a year or so." And he evidently felt he had no reason to doubt the truth of this latter statement. Bertha had been present at her friend's marriage. She had been with her almost constantly during the last days preceding it. She found great pleasure in Agnes' happiness. There had been no change in her own mode of life. Janey and Jack went out with her often, and when she was at home spent the greater part of the time with her. She helped them with their lessons, played with them, and made a hundred plans for them. They found her more entertaining than ever. Others found her no less entertaining. The old bright circle closed about her as before, and was even added to. Mr. Amory had been called abroad by business, and might return at any moment. The professor was rarely absent from his daughter's parlors when she had her guests about her. The people who had been interested in the Westoria scheme disappeared or became interested in something else. Senator Planefield had made one call after Richard's departure, and then had called no more. Bertha had seen him alone for a short time, and before he took his leave, looking a trifle more florid than usual, he had thrown into the grate a bouquet of hothouse roses.

"Damn all this!" he cried, savagely. "What a failure it has been!"

"Yes," said Bertha; "it has been a great failure."

Senator Blundel did not disappear. He began to like the house again, and to miss his occasional evening there if anything deprived him of it. He used to come and talk politics with the professor, and hear Bertha sing his favorite ballads of sentiment. During the excitement preceding the presidential election the professor found him absorbingly interesting. The contest was a close and heated one, and the usual national disasters were prophesied as the inevitable results of the final election of either candidate. Bertha read her way industriously through the campaign, and joined in their arguments with a spirit which gave Blundel keen delight. She read a great deal to her father, and made herself his companion, finding that she was able to help him with his work.

"I find great comfort in you, my child," he said gently to her once, when she had been reading.

"Do you, dearest?" she answered, and she went to him, and, standing near him, touched his gray hair with her cheek. "I find great comfort in you," she said, in a low voice. "We seem to belong to each other as if — a little as if we had been left together on a desert island."

When she went away for the summer with her children the professor went with her. He had never wondered at and pondered over her as he did in these days. Her incomings and outgoings were as they had always been. She shared the summer gayeties and went her way with her world, but it was but a short time before the kind old eyes looking on detected in her the lack of all that had made her what she had been in the past. They returned to Washington the day after the election of the new President. Their first evening at home was spent in reading the newspapers and discussing the termination of the campaign.

When Bertha rose to go to her room she stood a moment looking at the fire, and there was something in her face which attracted the professor's attention.

"My dear," he said, "tell me what you are thinking of."

She lifted her eyes and made an effort to smile, but the smile died out and left her face blank and cold.

"I am thinking of the last inaugural ball," she said, "and of Larry — and Richard — and of how I danced and laughed — and laughed — and that I shall never laugh so again."

"Bertha," he said, "my child!"

"No," she said, "never, never, — and I did not mean to speak of it — only just for a moment it all came back; "and she went quickly away without finishing.

After the election there came the usual temporary lull, and the

488

country settled itself down to the peaceful avocation of reading stories of the new President's childhood, and accounts of his daily receptions of interested friends and advisers. The only reports of excitement came from the Indian country, where little disturbances were occurring which caused anxiety among agents and frontiersmen. Certain tribes were dissatisfied with the arrangements made for them by the government, quarrels had taken place, and it had become necessary to keep a strict watch upon the movements of turbulent tribes. This state of affairs continued throughout the winter; the threatened outbreak was an inestimable boon to the newspapers, but, in spite of the continued threatenings, the winter was tided over without any actual catastrophies.

"But we shall have it," Colonel Tredennis said to his fellow-officers; "I think we cannot escape it."

He had been anxious for some time, and his anxiety increased as the weeks went by. It was two days before the inaugural ceremonies that the blow fell. The colonel had gone to his quarters rather early. A batch of newspapers had come in with the eastern mail, and he intended to spend his evening in reading them. Among these there were Washington papers, which contained descriptions of the preparations made for the ceremonies, — of the triumphal arches and processions, of the stands erected on the avenue, of the seats before the public buildings, of the arrangements for the ball. He remembered the belated flags and pennants of four years before, the strollers in the streets, his own feelings as he had driven past the decorations, and at last his words:

"I came in with the Administration; I wonder if I shall go out with it, and what will have happened between now and then."

He laid his paper down with a heavy sigh, even though he had caught a glimpse of Miss Jessup's letter on the first sheet. He could not read any more; he had had enough. The bitter loneliness of the moment overpowered him, and he bowed his face upon his arms, leaning upon the pile of papers and letters on the table. He had made, even mentally, no complaint in the last month. His hair had grown grizzled and his youth had left him; only happiness could have brought it back, and happiness was not for him. Every hour of his life was filled with yearning sadness for the suffering another than himself might be bearing; sometimes it became intolerable anguish; it was so to-night.

"I have no part to play," he thought; "every one is used to my grim face; but she — poor child! — poor child! — they will not let her rest. She has worn her smile too well."

Once, during the first winter of his stay in Washington, he had found among a number of others a little picture of herself, and had asked her for it. It was a poor little thing, evidently lightly valued; but he had often recalled her look and words as she gave it to him.

"Nobody ever wanted it before," she bad said. "They say it is too sad to be like me. I do not mind that so much, I think. I had rather a fancy for it. Yes, you may have it, if you wish. I have been gay so long — let me be sad for a little while, if it is only in a picture."

He had carried it with him ever since. He had no other relic of her. He took it from his breast-pocket now, and looked at it with aching eyes.

"So long!" he said. "So long!" And then again, "Poor child! poor child!"

The next instant he sprang to his feet. There was a sound of hurried feet, a loud knocking at his door, which was thrown open violently. One of his fellow-officers stood before him, pale with excitement.

"Tredennis," he said, "the Indians have attacked the next settlement. The devils have gone mad. You are wanted"—

Tredennis did not speak. He gave one glance round the room, with its blazing fire and lonely, soldierly look; then he put the little picture into his pocket and went out into the night.

Chapter 42

In all her honest, hard-worked little life Miss Jessup had never done more honest, hard work than she was called upon to do on the day of the inauguration. She had written into the small hours the night before; she had described bunting and arches, evergreens and grand stands, the visiting regiments, club uniforms, bands, banners, torch-lights and speeches, and on the eventful day she was up with the dawn, arranging in the most practicable manner her plans for the day. With letters containing a full and dramatic description of the ceremonies to be written to four western papers, and with extra work upon the Washington weekly and daily, there was no time to be lost. Miss Jessup lost none. Each hour of the clay was portioned off — each minute, almost. Now she was to take a glance at the procession from the steps of the Treasury; now she wits to spend a few moments in a balcony overlooking another point; she was to see the oath administered, hear the President's address and form an estimate of his appreciation of the solemnity of the moment; she was to take his temperature during the afternoon, and be ready to greet him at the ball, and describe dresses, uniforms, decorations, flags, and evergreens again. Even as she took her hasty breakfast she was jotting down appropriate items, and had already begun an article, opening with the sentence, "Rarely has Washington witnessed a more brilliant spectacle," etc.

It could scarcely be said that she missed anything when she went her rounds later. No familiar face escaped her; she recognized people at windows, in carriages, on platforms. Among others she caught a glimpse of Mrs. Amory, who drove by on her way to the Capitol with her father and Jack and Janey.

"She looks a little tired about the eyes," thought Miss Jessup. "She has looked a little that way all the season, though she keeps going steadily enough. They work as hard as the rest of us, in their way, these society women. She will be at the ball to-night, I dare say."

Bertha herself had wondered if she would find herself there. Even as she drove past Miss Jessup, she was thinking that it seemed almost impossible; but she had thought things impossible often during the winter which had gone by, and had found them come to pass and leave her almost as before. Gradually, however, people had begun to miss something in her. There was no denying, they said, that she had lost some of her vivacity and spirit; some tone had gone from her voice; something of color from her manner. Perhaps she would get over it. Amory had not behaved well in the Westoria land affair, and she naturally felt his absence and the shadow under which he rested.

"Very gradually," she said to the professor once, "I think I am retiring from the world. I never was really very clever or pretty. I don't hide it so well as I used to, and people are finding me out. Often I am a little dull, and it is not likely they will forgive me that."

But she was not dull at home, or the professor never thought so. She was not dull now, as she pointed out objects of interest to Jack and Janey.

"I wish Uncle Philip were here!" cried Jack. "He would have his sword on and be in uniform, and he would look taller than all the rest, — taller than the President."

The day was very brilliant to the children; they were as indefatigable as Miss Jessup, and missed as little as if they had been in search of items. The blare of brazen instruments, the tramp of soldiers, the rattle of arms, the rushing crowds, the noise and color and excitement, filled them with rapture. When they finally reached home they were worn out with their delights. Bertha was not less fatigued; but, after the nursery was quiet and the children were asleep, she came down to dine with the professor.

"And we will go to the ball for an hour," she said. "We cannot submit to having it described to us for the next two weeks by people who were there."

The truth was that she could not sit at home and listen to the carriages rolling by, and watch the dragging hours with such memories as must fill them.

So at half-past ten she stood in her room, putting the last touches to her toilet, and shortly afterward she was driving with the professor toward the scene of the night's gayeties. She had seen the same scene on each like occasion since her eighteenth year. There was nothing new about it to-night; there was some change in dances and music, but the same types of people crowded against each other, looking on at the dancing, pointing out the President, asking the old questions, and making the old comments; young people whirled together in the centre of the ballroom, and older ones watched them, with some slight wonder at the interest they evinced in the exercise. Bertha danced only a few quadrilles. As she went through them she felt again what she had felt on each such occasion since the night of the ball of the last year, — the music seemed too loud, the people too vivacious, the gayety about her too tumultuous; though, judged by ordinary standards, there could have been no complaint against it.

But, notwithstanding this feeling, she lingered longer than she had intended, trying to hide from herself her dread of returning home. No one but herself knew — even the professor did not suspect — how empty the house seemed to her, and how its loneliness grew and grew until sometimes it overpowered her and became a sort of deadly presence. Richard's empty rooms were a terror to her; she never passed their closed doors without a shock.

At half-past twelve, however, she decided to go home. She had just ended a dance with a young *attaché* of one of the legations; he was a brilliantly hued and graceful young butterfly, and danced and talked well. There had been a time when she had liked to hear his sharp, slightly satirical nonsense, and had enjoyed a dance with him. She had listened to-night, and had used her pretty smile at opportune moments; but she was glad to sit down again.

"Now," she said to him, "will you be so good as to find my father for me, and tell him I will go home?"

"I will, if I must," he answered. "But otherwise"—

"You will if you are amiable," she said. "I blush to own that I am tired. I have assisted in the inaugural ceremonies without flinching from their first step until their last, and I begin to feel that His Excellency is safe and I may retire."

He found her a quiet corner and went to do her bidding. She was partly shielded by some tall plants, and was glad of the retreat they afforded her. She sat and let her eyes rest upon the moving crowd promenading the room between the dances; the music had ceased, and she could catch snatches of conversation as people passed her. Among the rest were a pretty, sparkling-eyed girl and a young army officer who attracted her. She watched them on their way round the circle twice, and they were just nearing her for the second time when her attention was drawn from them by the sound of voices near her.

"Indian outbreak," she heard. "Tredennis! News just came in."

She rose from her seat. The speakers were on the other side of the plants. One of them was little Miss Jessup, the other a stranger, and Miss Jessup was pale with agitation and professional interest, and her notebook trembled in her little, bird-like hand.

"Colonel Tredennis!" she said. "Oh! I knew him. I liked him — every one did — every one! What are the particulars? Are they really authenticated? Oh, what a terrible thing!"

"We know very few particulars," was the answer; "but those we know are only too well authenticated. We shall hear more later. The Indians attacked a small settlement, and a party went from the fort to the rescue. Colonel Tredennis commanded it. The Indians were apparently beaten off, but returned. A little child had been left in the house, through some misunderstanding, and Tredennis heard it crying as the Indians made their second attack, and went after it. He was shot as he brought it out in his arms."

Little Miss Jessup burst into tears and dropped her notebook.

"Oh!" she cried. "He was a good, brave man! He was a good man!"

The band struck up a waltz. The promenading stopped; a score or two of couples took their place upon the floor, and began to whirl swiftly past the spot where Bertha stood; the music seemed to grow faster and faster, and louder, and still more loud.

Bertha stood still.

She had not moved when the professor came to her. He himself wore a sad, grief-stricken face; he had heard the news too; it had not taken it long to travel around the room.

"Take me home," she said to him. "Philip is dead! Philip has been killed!"

He took her away as quickly as he could through the whirling crowd of dancers, past the people who crowded, and laughed, and listened to the music of the band.

"Keep close to me!" she said. "Do not let them see my face!"

When they were shut up in the carriage together she sat shuddering for a moment, he shuddering, also, at the sight of the face he had hidden; then she trembled into his arms, clung to his shoulder, cowered down and hid herself upon his knee, slipped down kneeling upon the floor of the carriage, and clung to him with both her arms.

"I never told you that I was a wicked woman," she said. "I will tell you now; always — always I have tried to hide that it was Philip — Philip!"—

"Poor child!" he said. "Poor, unhappy — most unhappy child!" All the strength of her body seemed to have gone into the wild clasp of her slender arms.

"I have suffered," she said. "I have been broken; I have been crushed. I knew that I should never see him again, but he was alive. Do you think that I shall some day have been punished enough?"

He clasped her close to his breast, and laid his gray head upon her brown one, shedding bitter tears.

"We do not know that this is punishment," he said.

"No," she answered. "We do not know. Take me home to my little children. Let me stay with them. I will try to be a good mother — I will try" —

She lay in his arms until the carriage stopped. Then they got out and went into the house. When they closed the door behind them, and stood in the hall together, the deadly silence smote them both. They did not speak to each other. The professor supported her with his arm as they went slowly up the stairs. He had extinguished the light below before they came up. All the house seemed dark but for a glow of fire-light coming through an open door on the first landing. It was the door Philip Tredennis had seen open the first night when

495

he had looked in and had seen Bertha sitting in her nursery-chair with her child on her breast. There they both stopped. Before the professor's eyes there rose, with strange and terrible clearness, the vision of a girl's bright face looking backward at him from the night, the light streaming upon it as it smiled above a cluster of white roses. And it was this that remained before him when, a moment afterward, Bertha went into the room and closed the door.

THE END.

www.ingramcontent.com/pod-product-compliance
Ingram Content Group UK Ltd.
Pitfield, Milton Keynes, MK11 3LW, UK
UKHW040642280225
455688UK00003B/81